P9-DBT-548

TOUCHING KATHRYN

"I mean you," he breathed against her neck.

"So sweet and fresh. So infinitely innocent. And yet here"—he reached between their bodies to run a hand down her breastbone and on to her belly—"deep inside your soul you crave the darkest of passions."

Adrian slid a hand down her backside, and drew her pelvis tightly to his with a confident yank.

He ignored her squeak of protest and covered her mouth with his . . .

Books by Jacquelyn Frank

The Nightwalkers
Jacob
Gideon
Elijah
Damien
Noah

The Shadowdwellers
Ecstasy
Rapture
Pleasure

The Gatherers
Hunting Julian
Stealing Kathryn

Published by Kensington Publishing Corporation

STEALING KATHRYN

THE GATHERERS

JACQUELYN FRANK

ZEBRA BOOKS
KENSINGTON PUBLISHING CORP.
http://www.kensingtonbooks.com

ZEBRA BOOKS are published by

Kensington Publishing Corp.
119 West 40th Street
New York, NY 10018

All Kensington titles, imprints, and distributed lines are available at special quantity discounts for bulk purchases for sales promotion, premiums, fund-raising, educational, or institutional use.

Special book excerpts or customized printings can also be created to fit specific needs. For details, write or phone the office of the Kensington Special Sales Manager: Attn.: Special Sales Department. Kensington Publishing Corp., 119 West 40th Street, New York, NY 10018. Phone: 1-800-221-2647.

Zebra and the Z logo Reg. U.S. Pat. & TM Off.

ISBN-13: 978-1-4201-0984-9
ISBN-10: 1-4201-0984-7

First Printing: May 2010

10 9 8 7 6 5 4 3 2 1

Printed in the United States of America

Prologue

"Light. Now."

The stifling blackness was cut almost rudely by the sound of a striking match. The torch made of rag and kerosene caught the puny flame, held it, and exploded in a flare of fire.

The light chased the darkness back into tighter packs of shadow, where it hesitated at the borders of its ragged, imperfectly constructed circle of illumination. It wavered wanly at its edges, as if it knew it was nowhere near powerful enough to obliterate the darkness and dared not push its limits.

"Light, Master," the torch holder announced needlessly. His eyes were gobbling up the sight of the magnificent twisting flames. His pupils had dwindled to tiny, brackish pinpoints at the sudden brightness. His eyes hurt, but still he stared at the delicious fire as it licked and devoured its fuel. He continued to gaze at it in utter fascination even after his eyes had burned dry from the near heat and his neglect in remembering to blink.

"Closer, Cronos."

Cronos finally blinked, wincing at the painfully sudden lubrication. Then he obediently shuffled forward, his spindly legs working hard not to trip over themselves. The Master, he knew, would have no patience for his usual clumsiness this eve.

Something told him that this night was special, different from all the others. He could almost hear the complex, ominous machinations of the Master's thoughts.

He moved forward, the light progressing with him and creeping slowly along the floor before it began to hesitatingly encircle the Master, as if afraid of the darkness it battled back from around the enormous cloaked figure.

"Stand."

Cronos froze midstep.

Gingerly, without moving himself or the torch a millimeter closer, he put his raised foot down. He released an anxious, shaky breath as quietly as he could. Then, willing himself not to be entranced by the torch flames again, he looked with curious expectancy to the Master.

The Master's back was to him, so all he could really see was the expanse of the coal-black cloak stretching across his broad, bulky shoulders. From there it cascaded in massive, flowing folds to the bare stone floor, where it swept the dust-laden gray slab. Upward, the Master's head was covered, hidden completely within a deep-hooded cowl.

Cronos was glad of this. It was always easier to watch when he could not see the Master's chilling features. Yet he knew the Master was well aware that he was watching. Cronos kept his simple thoughts carefully neutral.

There was no movement for many heartbeats.

Then slowly, the Master extended a pale, long-fingered hand from the ebony abyss of himself. A large onyx ring glittered from the third finger of this hand, flames catching the facets until it looked as if the ring was burning as well. To Cronos it was a most fascinating effect. Almost too fascinating for his easily distracted mind.

The hand reached farther.

To the mirror.

The mirror was a breathtakingly eerie thing and it, too, never failed to earn Cronos's attention. It was the shape of an inverted triangle that spanned the entire height of the wall, nearly two feet taller than the Master's towering figure. The glass gleamed with dark foreboding, a wicked midnight blue and perfectly unflawed. There was an iron framework bordering its three edges. This brown-black ornate edge curled forward toward the glass in arching fingers of twisted metal, looking rather like the Venus flytrap plants up in the Master's study.

The Master's hand continued heading for the blue glass mirror, every inch of motion a proclamation of respectful reverence.

Cronos always held his breath at this point, waiting, wondering, almost hoping that this trap, too, would spring, closing upon the Master and gobbling him up like insignificant fly meat.

Fearfully, Cronos checked his thoughts, though the Master likely was not listening to them presently. It was safer not to take any chances, however. And no matter how anxious he was for his own safety, Cronos still could not look away.

There was no reflection of light where there should be in the inky, watery glass.

Only a ghostly reproduction of a pale hand reaching. . .

The Master's fingertips touched the glass gently, stroking downward in an almost loving caress. His hand turned palm side up, slowly, so slowly, as a lover might do when carefully cupping a woman's soft, full breast.

Then with precision and intensity, the fingertips trailed patiently upward.

The Master's head turned, just enough so that Cronos could see beyond the borders of the cowl.

Eyes of malachite and black widened slightly as they fixed on the progress of his own hand against the mirror. They were large, haunted eyes with pupils that flickered with swift-moving phantoms of death, suffering wraiths, and impending misfortunate fate. Set into deeply shadowed sockets, the eyes seemed to fairly glow with their wicked splendor.

This eerie illumination was fringed with lush, spiky lashes that curled upward in abundance. These lashes were deceptive, mockingly emulating those of an innocent, wide-eyed child whose lashes seemed to go on forever. These were not innocent. They were reaching.

Reaching. Reaching toward thick black brows. Brows that seemed to curl down in their centers, as if attracted toward the lashes. Both were waiting.

Waiting for the tiniest morsel of a fly.

Cronos's stomach turned sour and he shuddered as he looked quickly to the floor. He could never look long upon those eyes, even when they weren't trained piercingly upon him. Even when they weren't boring into him and sucking . . . sucking at his frantic, twisted soul.

Little fly that he was.

But he quickly drew his faint courage back around himself and looked eagerly back to the mirror and the thing he knew was about to happen.

Gently, without a ripple or a single smudge of a fingerprint, the Master's hand slipped into the blue waters of the glass.

The Master drew in an audible breath. It was almost a sound of pleasure, echoing in the vast room before disappearing in the refuge of the smothering shadows. He leaned forward slightly until his wrist had become enveloped by the mirror as well. An oppressive feeling of power began to bleed forbiddingly into the room. The torchlight quavered and dimmed, beaten back by this new, overwhelming darkness.

Suddenly, an electric blue and white finger of energy, like a small bolt of lightning, jumped from one of the curling tendrils of the mirror's iron frame. Cutting a quick, jagged path to the Master's wrist, it touched and ricocheted off. It rebounded in a precise V, heading directly to the framework on the opposite side of the mirror.

This one spark was the first of a cascade of similar bolts of static energy, each starting from and ending at a new claw of the reaching frame.

A charge built in the room, causing Cronos's hair to stand on end in long gray spikes. The mirror was alive with lightning now. The Master's eyes reflected the blue-white glow with unearthly intensity and a hunger for its power.

Then the mirror went abruptly dark and forbidding again. Yet the hot, nerve-tingling charge of power continued to fill the room until it created a whining hum.

The Master yanked back his hand, suddenly alive with movement as he shoved the cowl back from his head. A contorted growl erupted from him as he tore the entire cloak from himself, revealing his ghostly white, naked flesh.

He stepped up to the glass in such a way that one step might take him entirely through, his muscles flexing and twitching with potency and expectation.

The step was taken.

Cronos blinked once as the Master disappeared.

The torch guttered once before dying.

Chapter 1

He entered her sleeping mind with an unexpected thrust of force. But he should not have been surprised by her resistance. She always resisted sleeping, it seemed, as if she didn't have time for it and wished she could do away with the restful state completely.

Not that it was going to be restful now that he was there.

At the moment there was no cohesion to the visions in her mind, the things surrounding him merely remnants of the electrical impulses and memories of things from the boring waking world in which she lived. He didn't understand why anyone would want to wake up. The worlds of the mind were so vast and creative and could keep a person entertained forever.

Of course, they could also torment them endlessly, he conceded with a private little smile to himself. The emotion-evoking land of nightmares could range from simple guilt and self-induced fears to the roaring dramatics of beasts and the running from or falling to certain death.

The latter was a somewhat lazy method, he felt. It took the finesse of a true artist to work an environment and the mind of his subject in such a way as to turn every part of her own psyche into an antenna of fear, emitting the emotion in powerful, satiating waves of energy. Energy he needed. Energy he craved.

He found her at the very center of her mind, the exhausted need for sleep having forced her under, and her uncooperative imagination was simply tossing up flickering images of a sick girl in bed or her father's robust laugh.

"No, no, this will not do at all," he murmured.

He painted their surroundings in perfect pitch of night, the sparkle of stars above and below them as if they were flying among them. She was, as yet, unaware of him, but she responded to the change in her surroundings with awe and wonderment. Her heart raced at being unsure of her footing. Physics and reality were suspended, but her mind had a hard time accepting that.

When a subject first began to dream, the person was only a black shape of himself or herself. Like a person in a head-to-toe body stocking, the subject had no color, no hair, no skin or bone. Just the semiformed black mannequin the subject's perspective allowed for at first. But depending on the nature of the dream, that would quickly change. The heavy and encumbered could become thin and spry, the ugly could become beautiful, and the beautiful could become plain; all according to the subconscious needs of the dreamer at hand.

But what he liked about this particular woman was that she never once altered her base appearance. The moment she began to dream with him, the blackness would melt away, giving shape to her tall frame with its wickedly long legs and the wide expanse of hips that filled out every outfit she wore with such a nicely pronounced curvature that led to an equally delectable backside. She was busty as well, every movement making her curve in one way or another. Her face was something else, though, aristocratic and elegantly planed, the look of a stern but beautiful schoolteacher. Perhaps it was the tight and strict ponytail she kept the incredible length of her chestnut hair in or it was her gray eyes that made her seem so severe at first, but then she would smile or cry and it would all change. Or she would become gloriously angry and her beauty would truly explode.

He was convinced that this was the way she looked in the waking world. There was never any variation and, in his opinion, there was hardly any need for it. The changes in her appearance came later, by his hand, when it suited his mood, and it was rarely anything more dramatic than the nature of her clothing.

Tonight she was flying and her usual jeans and T-shirt were unacceptable. With a thought he dropped a long white gown over her head, the simple silk flowing from shoulders to toes, outlining the curved perfection of her body, clinging to the beauty of her breasts and their outthrust nipples.

She liked the gift, the pleasure clear on her lovely face, and he couldn't help but stare at her just a few moments longer. They had so little time together, and . . .

. . . and there were rules he must follow.

Shapeless and dark, he thrust himself up against her from behind, his arm ringing her shoulders and his brute's body like a solid wall of muscle and masculinity against her. She startled, her hands immediately going to the arm that held her so tightly. She didn't call out a name, telling him that she didn't have any notable men in her life whom she felt would come up on her like this. Why the idea should please him, he didn't know. Nor did he care.

He wrapped his hand around her neck, the delicate length of her throat so unexpectedly narrow compared to the rest of her voluptuous body that he had a moment of fear that he had grabbed her too hard. Then he laughed at himself because it was only a dream, and grabbing her too hard was a part of the nightmare to come.

He could see into her mind, all her thoughts and emotions, all the trials of her life . . . and most of all, every fear she had ever had. It impressed him that she did not have very many things that scared her. She was as tough as she was beautiful. But everyone had fears no matter how tough a person was, and she was no exception. He merely enjoyed the challenge for what it was. She began to struggle against him in earnest, her feet and legs flailing as she tried to kick him. But she couldn't hurt him here in this place. Not really.

Enjoying how she fought him, he threw her down on the bed that suddenly appeared. He followed over her, a dark hulking figure she could not make out or fight off no matter how hard she tried. She gritted her teeth in frustration, and he simply held her there, trapped and immobile.

"Who are you? What do you want?" she wanted to know. Then he paid great attention to the details of her trapped body. How soft she felt. How incredibly perfect she seemed. As far as jobs went, this wasn't the worst one to have.

"You tell me first," he taunted her, his voice like gravel and sand. "Obey me or you will not like the consequences."

She thought about it, the stubborn set of her lips telling him she'd rather get her teeth pulled than tell him anything, but in the end her psychological make-up was going to defeat her.

"Kathryn," she spat out.

Kathryn. Oh, how he loved to hear her name. He asked her for it every time, just to hear that defiant burst of passionate declaration. In the first three or four dreams he hadn't asked for her name, not wanting to attach himself to her too personally, perhaps knowing on some level that there was a danger of it with this creature that was not present in others. Now he knew, and he could not take back the knowing. And he didn't want to. He liked her name. Liked her. It was as bold and glorious as she was. She was, he thought heatedly, a one-of-a-kind and most perfect thing.

He rose over her, relieving her of the burden of his weight as he hovered above her. She might not be able to make his features out, but her mind would interpret his menacing and covetous expression as he ran his eyes over her stretched-out body. He reached to hold her hands above her head in one of his, then raked a hard hand and curved fingers down over her face, throat, and chest.

"You always fight," he growled, and his harsh hand yanked up the gown and exposed her legs all the way to her thighs. The movement was such a hard one that she shimmied in all of her softest places, emphasizing just how much of a woman she really was. "But I know what you really want," he told her as his hand scorched up over her thigh and his palm briefly cupped her bare sex. Kathryn gasped and lifted a leg as if to kick him, only succeeding in opening herself to him.

After all, as far as struggles went, this one was quite mild. Perhaps she was beginning to remember the game. Perhaps she was becoming too complacent.

"So, you have no desire to fight?" he asked her hotly, his breath coming quick even though she was being too easy. Just being this close to her stirred him to distraction. "Where is your fear?"

As he said it everything around the room exploded into flames. The only thing left untouched was the bed, but the heat felt all too real and dangerous. Kathryn cried out, struggling harder now to get out from under him, to get away from the thing she feared the most. He could feel her heart racing; she was panting hard for her breath. He tore at the top of her gown, exposing her to the waist, pulling her breast out to meet his mouth.

When she screamed it was with a splendid combination of terror and arousal. She was filled with confusion as to why she would react in such a way. But he knew her mind far better than she did, and knew that the excitement of a forcible seduction was one of her darkest fantasies, one she would only ever indulge in here, where it was safe. The fear of the fire only heightened the adrenaline coursing through her. The more intense the danger, the more excited she became.

But still the key element was in her resistance to herself. She felt how she responded and thought it was wrong. She felt shame and guilt, like something was defective within her because she grew wet as he gnawed and devoured her nipple over and over again. He wished then that he could truly taste her skin, truly smell the scent of her. He wanted her in real dimensions, not these imaginary ones. He shifted up to crush his mouth upon hers, the full perfection of her mouth calling to him incessantly, day and night, with no quiet to be had. Frustration wormed through him as he kissed her with great passion but could experience none of the depth and flavor of her. He knew she could feel his passionate intentions, but he was just outside of truth of definition to her as well.

With a roar of fury he burst away from the bed and the object of his dissatisfaction. Ever since he had stumbled upon her the first time, he had been utterly obsessed. He'd tried time and again to stop, to carry on his work elsewhere, to fill his time with better sources of fear and focus.

But always she lured him back, with her infuriating perfection and needful body. She craved so many dark and wonderful things; she had the deepest of fears and yet faced them with such unbelievable courage. She was utterly fascinating.

And he wanted her.

Not just in this realm he was limited to, but beyond it. In the real. He would take her—*yes!* Yes, he could keep her then, keep her for his very own, and no one could stop him. No one would dare to stop him.

He reached out for her, pulling her to her feet and into the fire. Her dress immediately caught flame at the hem and she screamed, struggling to brush away the flames.

"Tell me where you live and I'll make it all stop," he promised her.

"Stop it! Please!"

"Tell me," he coaxed her as the flames leapt higher against her.

Drowning in terror and flame, she did.

Ripping out of the horrifying nightmare with a gasp, Kathryn instantly tried to beat out flames that no longer existed. Her sudden movement nearly toppled her out of the plain wooden chair she'd pulled up to her sister's bedside. It took her a moment to shake off her disorientation, to realize she had fallen asleep while watching over Jillian. She hurriedly left her chair to lean over her sister's bed. Jillian was shivering weakly, her breath rasping in a sickening staccato rhythm.

"Hush, now. Rest, love," she crooned gently to the sick girl.

Kathryn rubbed the grit of weariness from her eyes as she turned to the bedside table. It took her a moment to focus on the paraphernalia there. There were bottles of medicine, a thermometer, and a large china basin with rags soaking in water and melting ice. The bottle labels were a confusion to her for a moment as she tried to get a grasp on her weary concentration. Then she found what she was looking for. She tumbled two small aspirin from one bottle into her palm, hoping to keep Jillian's fever down. Then Kathryn grabbed a glass of cool water and turned back to Jillian, maneuvering herself behind the frail ten-year-old's head and lifting it until she could manage to wrangle the medicine down the child's throat.

Jillian accepted the pills well enough for someone who had occasionally been too weak to swallow, and it gave Kathryn a glimmer of hope. What she wouldn't give for the simplicity of children's liquid medicine right then. But in the bush of Australia you had to make do with what was in your supplies, and the colorful syrup had run out a while back.

"There now, what a good girl you are," she praised Jillian softly, stubbornly believing that the child could somehow hear her. She spent a moment stroking her sister's thin, pale red hair. Then she slid gingerly from the bed.

Kathryn waited anxiously for several minutes until she was certain the child had quieted again and was resting as peacefully as she could. Then she straightened stiffly, her hands pressing into the aching curve of her lower back. She looked at her watch, trying to determine what day it was as well as the time. She had called for help almost twenty-four hours ago, but things took time out in the bush. But it should be soon. Hopefully very soon.

Kathryn felt her exhaustion with sudden acuteness. Dizziness washed through her and she touched fingertips to her forehead in an attempt to steady herself and her swaying vision.

"Father," she prayed fiercely, "give me strength." She gritted her teeth as a harsher wave of vertigo spilled over her.

Kathryn . . .

Kathryn gasped softly when the low, thick whisper reached her ears. She whirled around drunkenly, taking in the madly tilting room to see who had spoken her name.

A macabre chill rushed her flesh.

"Papa?" she asked breathlessly, widening her eyes in an attempt to focus.

But no one was there but her and Jillian.

Kathryn reached to grasp one of the spiraling bedposts, clinging to it as she searched herself for a store of strength she might not yet have tapped.

There was none.

Kathryn fought back tears.

She must *find* the strength!

Somehow.

She was the only one left for her desperately ill family to depend on.

She waited, breathing deeply, for the room to stop pitching and rolling around her. She dared not close her eyes. She would surely succumb to the persistent, lurking need to sleep that had harried her every step these last days. She simply did not have the time or the luxury for sleep. And anyway, whenever she did fall asleep, there was nothing there for her but terrible and disturbing dreams. Sometimes, like before, all-out nightmares.

Slowly the room righted itself, becoming once again the firm, solidly built expanse of sturdy antique furnishings it had always been.

Taking another deep breath, Kathryn took a moment to tuck a straggling tendril of hair back behind her ear. She slipped a palm against her slightly rounded stomach, wishing it would settle as the room had. She couldn't remember the last time she'd eaten anything, but it seemed very unimportant when the lives of her family were at risk.

Then she took the firmest steps she could manage to the door. She was halfway along the hallway when her vision blurred again and the floor fell away with sickening speed. She collapsed to her knees and hands, jarring her joints as she realized the floor was still very much where it was supposed to be, it was merely her head and her vision leaving much to be desired.

"Get up, Kathryn Louise Macdonough," she commanded herself fiercely. "You're the daughter of Connor Macdonough, the granddaughter of Fiona Macdonough. You shame the Macdonough name if you quit now!"

Somehow, after this empowering speech, she managed to drag herself back up to her feet, using the wall as her main support. She slid herself along it so that she could tell right from left and up from down while using it for the stability her betraying eyes would not provide. She finally reached her father's door.

"Kathryn."

The whisper was louder this time. Nearer.

She convinced herself that it had been her father after all, even though it sounded nothing like him. But the sickness could very easily have put that rough, mournful lilt into his words . . . couldn't it?

Kathryn shrugged off another foreboding chill. She had been living in a stranger's body for well over a week now, exhaustion robbing her of all that had felt normal. A new, strange feeling seeping into her bones was not all that new *or* strange an occurrence to her anymore.

She pushed herself into Connor Macdonough's room and moved to the bed, steeling herself for the weakened image of her father. The preparation did not work. As she bent to change the cloth on his forehead, now heated through with his fever, her eyes misted with tears.

Her father had been a large, robust man. He filled rooms with his very presence and had made stone walls vibrate with a mere laugh. But now her poor papa was but a shadow of himself. In just a week he'd lost a noticeable amount of weight from this wretched flu. His hands, which until now had still been able to toss her around despite her twenty-two years of age and full-grown womanhood, were now knobbed joints and thin, translucent skin. His merry cheeks had lost their natural color, only the occasional spike of fever making them blush.

Kathryn cursed the pilot of the supply plane that had come out to them a little less than two weeks ago. He had brought this vile sickness with him, his simple sneezes and sniffles dooming her father and sister to suffer. The nearest medical help was much too far to drive to by conventional means, and all that rough country and dust while strapped in a car would do her family no good. No, the best thing was to wait for an airlift. Which should be soon. Hopefully very soon.

Kathryn laid the fresh cloth on her father's forehead, biting her lip brutally hard. She wouldn't let herself think about the worst. Help was coming. She would go downstairs and call once again, pestering the authorities with all she had to make them come for her family.

The only other option would be to give up . . . and to bury them next to her sweet, unfortunate mother. The hard life out in this wild country had claimed her mother's life three years earlier.

Pain of that too-recent loss flooded her, but again she fought back the despairing thoughts. Now was not the time for mourning. Right now, she had to keep her already foggy head as clear as she could if she was to complete her rounds and make her call to civilization.

Then, maybe, she could rest.

For a small while.

"Kathryn!"

"Yes, Papa, Kathryn's here," she murmured automatically. She looked down at her father's face.

He was as still as death. There was barely breath enough in him to sustain his life—never mind to speak her name in that strong, growling whisper.

"Who is here?" she demanded in sudden panic, clutching her father's bed linens to steady herself as she looked around the room wildly. "Who is here?"

Fear tightened her throat and her heart began to pound. It made her overtaxed body work harder than it should, making her weak again as vertigo struck with a vengeance.

The air became thick around her suddenly and her nostrils flared as she tried to suck in a breath. She smelled something tart and tangy, like nutmeg. Nutmeg and a rich, dank, musty odor like a room long overdue for an airing. Her skin prickled and the hairs on the back of her arms and neck rose as a tingling sensation of stinging heat crept over her.

"Kathryn."

The voice was upon her now. Behind her. Coming into her ear with warmth and nearness as if the speaker was just at her back.

She spun around, terror clutching at her.

There was no one.

But she could feel heat! The heat and warmth of a person. The electric aura of a powerful, unexplained presence.

"Oh my God, I'm going out of my mind!" Kathryn tried her damnedest to get a grip on herself, telling herself it was just exhaustion toying with her mind, fearing she was finally succumbing to the same illness as her family.

Then heat and a suffocating thickness washed over her. Her vision went black, with spots of green floating before her. Then the spots went a luminescent yellow, like cat's eyes did when caught between shadows and candlelight.

A scream caught in her mouth, barricaded at her lips by something that felt like a chilled, smothering hand.

"Kathryn, my beauty."

There were disembodied fingers at her throat, soft and warm—

No! Cold now! So cold!

The ghostly caress stroked her. She trembled helplessly as that chill touch drifted over her everywhere, her neck and throat, her breast, belly, and hip, touching against her flesh as though she did not wear any clothes at all. Kathryn tried again and again to scream, to struggle, but she was paralyzed everywhere but her mind. Who was doing this to her? Why could she not see? Had she somehow fallen asleep without realizing it and now suffered another cruel nightmare?

No! It was all too real. Too sickeningly real.

"Perfect." The cloying, hoarse vocalization rang with undertones of demented pleasure. Then those fingers were at her throat again, gently palpating the wildly rushing pulse they discovered there.

"Sleep," the voice commanded, as rough as sand, then as smooth as glass, "sleep!"

Kathryn crumpled lifelessly into the waiting demon's embrace.

"Light. Now."

Cronos nearly jumped out of his clammy skin when the command came out of the darkness.

He had not even heard the Master return.

The torch flared brightly, revealing the bulk of the Master, the fact that he was once again cloaked, and that he held a great object within the cloak's folds.

Cronos had to stay the urge to run forward and get a better look at the Master's new treasure.

"What is it, Master?" Cronos crowed, his gleeful face turned respectfully to the floor in hopes that his properly respectful subservience would win a response. "Is it a pretty treasure?"

"It is my prettiest treasure yet, Cronos," the Master said, his voice rolling around the room in such a way that the shadows seemed to shift eagerly to absorb it. The Master rarely deigned to speak to him, never mind use so many words in this place.

In this way, Cronos knew the Master was pleased with that night's plunder.

"To the treasure tower, my lord?" Cronos asked eagerly. He dared not move without permission and there was no telling if the routine would be the usual one if this was so special a spoil.

"Lead."

Cronos almost fell on his face as he scurried to obey. He felt the Master's dark presence behind him, overwhelming and just shy of treading over him.

It wouldn't be the first time.

Cronos's toothpick legs had to coordinate their steps three times faster to stay ahead of the Master's ground-devouring stride. One misstep on Cronos's part and he would be a loud crunch beneath his employer's heavy foot.

But he did not mind. There would still be new treasure to see! Joy! What joy it was to see the Master's new treasures. Sometimes Cronos was more ecstatic than even the Master was about his acquisitions.

They traveled swiftly up out of the depths of the

dungeons, Cronos lighting the way as they took spiraling stairs up and up and up.

Cronos's pallor was nearly blue-gray from lack of oxygen by the time they reached the treasure tower's main floor.

He doused the torch. Here there were large sconces embedded in the smooth marble walls, and nearly a hundred candles in stands between the mid-chamber's massive marble columns.

Now no longer dependent on Cronos to light the way, the Master strode past him, his cloak whipping the little toady hard in his wake.

Cronos caught the flailing fabric hard in the side of his head and his valiant efforts to remain upright failed. He received a face full of marble floor, loosening several already damaged teeth.

The Master was oblivious.

He took to another flight of stairs, his steps a ringing clang against the ornate black iron.

When he reached the uppermost level, he traversed the long hall to a set of colossal double doors. So huge were they that it seemed it might take five strong men on either side to push them open.

But all it took was a momentary glitter of intent from malachite eyes. The doors swung soundlessly, easily open and the Master was not even forced to break his stride as he entered. The room beyond the intricately carved doors gleamed gaudily back at him, the bright resplendence of it making him narrow his eyes.

There was ornate paneling upon the massive, curving walls, constructed of the purest gold and crafted by a brilliant artist who had incorporated into the design his adoration for the four seasons of the years. Golden suns and filigreed autumn leaves in multicolored gold glistened all around him.

The entire circular floor, enormous in diameter, was carpeted with a single hand-woven rug. It was a tapestry of silken threads that had taken a madwoman all 101 years of her life to design and create. Every god and goddess known to any man, woman, or child in her world had been depicted within its weavings. Every beast of superstition and legend, every imaginary creature from all manner of folklore. The Master even saw several representations of himself crafted amusingly into the loom.

Then there was the ceiling. It was streamed in multihued satin bunting. The dye master who had colored each magnificent bolt had been a genius out of his time. He had managed to create a palate of colors that might never again be rediscovered or even named.

The Master strode past mounted things, things encased in protective glass, crystal, and amber. Each a treasure with remarkable history.

But they were old curiosities to him now, and presently not attractive enough to gain his attention.

In the center of the unique museum was a bed. It was roughly three times the size of most large beds, with feather-stuffed ticks full of the softest quills from the most unique and rarest birds. But its true value came from the fact that none of the birds had been harmed or killed because of its creation. Each feather had molted out naturally and been painstakingly collected.

The bedspread was knitted lace made of delicate, strong webbings of silk, in a style used this once and never again.

The Master laid his latest and by far greatest treasure upon the very center of this bed.

Kathryn.

She slept. He had commanded it to be so. Enchanting her into a repose like those of Aurora, Snow White, and countless other sleeping princesses of fairy tales and lore. She was a beauty beyond all their combined beauty—if a bit wan and bedraggled from her exhaustion. But all this would be remedied soon enough and she would far surpass the radiance of anything else on display in the room. He could tell just by looking at her. He was satisfied to see she was exactly as she had portrayed herself in her dreams. Her honesty was just one more sparkling detail to add to her perfection.

"Kathryn."

The name rumbled from deep in his chest like an ensemble of bass range instruments brought together to serenade a waiting heart.

Her rich, earthen brown hair would be long and naturally coiled, he knew, when not crammed into the vicious twisted tail hanging askew at the top of her head. Her face was long and strong, yet somehow delicately boned with its femininity. The eyes, when opened, would be fathomless and dove gray. She bore the lips of a seductress, able to create a luring smile or a heartbreaking pout, and when parted invitingly they could boil blood. Any and all of these would come naturally without malice, intention, or cunning. Altogether she was the ultimate jewel, made to far outshine the thousands adorning her compatriot treasures in the room.

The Master's blood churned with awakened intensity, his nostrils flaring as he drew in the true scent of her with greed and unmitigated delight. She smelled of sweetness and salt, a combination of artifice and naturalness. She used some sort of perfume, a combination of differing scents in different areas of her body. In her hair, under her arms, and between her breasts. There he lingered, smelling how sultry sweet she was and feeling the warmth of her radiating against him. He hulked over his treasure as dark, bestial things stirred to wicked life within him.

He suddenly backed off, throwing himself in violent retreat from the temptation of her. A low, animal-like sound, somewhere between a purr, a growl, and a bark, rolled from him as he tried to regain control over the dark urges and twisting images feeding through his mind. His powers had allowed him to taste the desires of hundreds of thousands of women, but with her it had been different. With her there had been so little control. He was afraid that he might lose control and harm her.

He had to remove himself from her now, or he might spoil his new treasure.

It bothered him that he had slipped in his self-control. It was an event that must never be allowed to happen. He was a creature made up of hellish, unruly internal demons. He must always retain perfect order of himself or risk chaos; risk disapproval and censure, perhaps a violent punishment. Or worse, he would cause himself to suffer. When chaos reigned, he was his own worst enemy and it was his treasures that were the first to suffer. It was all things of beauty he would methodically begin to destroy.

Above all else, these treasures—this particular treasure most of all—must be kept safe.

Especially from himself.

Chapter 2

"Adrian?"

Adrian's malachite eyes darted up to meet his sister's troubled gaze across the expanse of the table. Candlelight flickered across her exquisite features, licking at her in contrary shadow and light.

"Adrian, why will you not let me see this latest treasure of yours?"

She was suspicious and more than a little upset, he could tell.

"It is not ready," he said with quiet simplicity.

"But why will you not even tell me what it is? You have always delighted in giving me the histories that make each of your acquisitions so unique."

Adrian narrowed his eyes on his twin sister. Aerlyn. Known the worlds over as Maya, Epona, Mari, and more, but ever to him she was Aerlyn, his steady, his guide back from the night. It was her wisdom and goodness that tempered his evil and carefully cultured chaos. She was also the frustrating force that held him ever in check, forced him to keep from giving in to the desire to run amok through the minds of the worlds.

For he was Adrian. Angus, Sandman, Morpheus, Bogeyman, all these, but ever Adrian to her. Hers was the mirror of light and healing and dreams. His was of dark fantasies, oppressive guilt, and nightmares.

She, the only one ever destined to love him . . . and she the only one he might once have felt that alien emotion for. That is, if he could stop hating her for her interference with his desires.

"Aerlyn, the treasure is mine." His tone brooked no argument. It was his way of warning her to back off.

"Brother." She quieted a moment to remove the reprimand from her tone. She must tread carefully with him. His was a delicate balance of control, one so easily set asunder. "Adrian. You have never known me to interfere with any of your baubles in the past. I am concerned that *you* are concerned I might. You have not done something of which I might be forced to disapprove, have you?"

"Your approval is irrelevant." His voice dropped an octave with a threatening hint of patience being lost.

But he was on the defensive for a reason, Aerlyn mused. She narrowed silver eyes on him, her soft countenance drawing into an image of piercing discernment as she tried to measure her sibling's motives.

"There are rules, Adrian. Rules we both must

obey. And rules we must both guard each other from breaking. You know very well my approval is unavoidably relevant." She leaned a little closer, trying to probe his thoughts, but he was shoving up a black, guarding wall against her. "That little toad you keep to assist you, the one you call Companion, has been mooning about the fortress in perpetual orgasm for the entire day now. Whatever it is you have brought has obviously made a singular impression on him."

"Cronos is but a fool, and too easily impressed." Adrian's dark lips thinned and parted to reveal a gleaming row of ivory teeth, two of which were long, sleek fangs.

It was Adrian's version of a smile.

Aerlyn was not so easily swayed.

"That is true." She nodded curtly. "But I am not. Something is amiss in this house. Did you think I would not be able to feel it? There is a new energy here. A peculiar one." She leaned forward, candlelight enhancing the silver starlike patterns in the ebony curtain of her hair. "What have you done, Adrian?"

Adrian lurched suddenly from his chair, the last vestiges of his tenuous control of himself gone in an instant. He roared in outrage as his fists crashed violently upon the table. Aerlyn sat back calmly as he shoved the table clear across the room with one powerfully enraged sweep of his arm.

Dishes, candles, and splintered wood struck the distant wall and floor in a din of discordant crashes. Adrian loomed threateningly over his sister, casting ominous shadows over her cream white skin and gown.

"Do not presume to censure me this time, Aerlyn!" he spat, his eyes like maddened emerald fire and his features mottling and twisting in anger.

"And if I do not, who will?" She cocked a silver-black brow. "The Ampliphi put me in charge of keeping you under control, Adrian, and I will not fail them. It is one thing that I must allow you to torment the dreams of innocents without rhyme or reason, but it is you who presume too much if you think I will let you take your spoils in manic measure!" She rose up slowly, her personal energy giving him pause as it enveloped his, making him flinch angrily. "You will show me what you have pilfered, my brother. If it is an acceptable bit of fluff, you are certainly welcome to keep it with the rest of your silly baubles. I even encourage it. You know it pleases me to see you take such avid interest in things of beauty. It makes me feel you may yet prove to have a heart in that monstrously black chest of yours." She paused for a breath. "But there is some beauty to which you know full well you do not have rights!"

"I have taken nothing not within my rights!" Adrian's menacing eyes bored down into her stubborn ones. "And you have no rights in judging my collection!"

Aerlyn sighed softly at her brother's stubborn nature. She could not, of course, allow him to have his way. The strange energy he had brought to their house did not belong there. She already suspected what the source might be. She was filled with suspicious dread at the idea that her brother might have done the inconceivable.

That he might have brought an intelligent, living creature there.

Such folly could mean their very destruction. She could not allow this madness to continue.

"We shall see about that."

She turned, the gossamer train of her dress flaring out behind her as she drifted swiftly from the room.

"Aerlyn!"

Adrian was consumed with raging, defiling blackness. It spilled from his heart, feeding the vile, chaotic monster that always dwelled just within reach of him.

He caught up to his sister in three massive strides and drew back an enormous arm. There was a brief flash of clarity that warned him he was flirting with unknown disaster, but his madness went on unimpeded. Malevolent energy gleamed briefly off the claws growing from his thickened fingertips.

His eyes glared blackly as they fixed on a target at the back of her vulnerable neck. For that brief, tremulous moment, he could see right through her flesh to the delicate structure of her spine.

It took but one blow to strike his hatefully beloved sister down.

Kathryn bolted upright in bed, a terrified scream ripping from her throat. But although she was wide awake now, the terrible nightmare was still with her.

A vicious dark beast with terrible claws rending my body in two.

Her throbbing heart ached with its rapid flight within her breast, her neck and back cramped with tortuous pain. A quick hand flew to her throat, her fingers nervously feeling her jugular as if to seek damage.

The touch made her recall with an almost avid fascination the eerie feeling of cool, deathly fingers fondling her pulse.

She shuddered and tried to shake the feeling off. It was all just a series of memories from an endlessly twisting nightmare, she told herself. But she had to admit to herself that she had never had such a dream in all her life, and it was hard to fight her feelings of hysteria. "Easy," she spoke calmingly to herself, "it's just anxiety from a combination of bad dreams and I'm just wiped out from caring for my family."

She slowly focused on her surroundings.

She realized instantly she was not familiar with the bed she was in. Completely surrounded by the intricate brocade of luxurious bed curtains, she was closed into the confines of the bed. Feeling disoriented and suddenly anxious, she moved her hand to her throat, her fingertips stumbling onto the unfamiliar heaviness she realized was lying against her collarbone. It was cold, metal. She looked down and saw a cascade of thin gold wire weaving around large, breathtaking purple stones that looked like amethysts. The jeweled necklace fell from the base of her neck all the way to the tops of her breasts.

That was when she realized she was not in familiar clothing either. She had never owned anything as girly as this dress, which left her shoulders and cleavage almost completely exposed. It was made of a fine fabric like silk, soft and clingy. She was beginning to feel a very real sense of fearful unease as she scrambled to her knees and pulled the sheer violet fabric of her skirt up for inspection. She could practically see through the material, making it far more like lingerie than an actual dress, and that understanding sent a feeling of sinking dread into the pit of her stomach. And then there were the stones, the glittering glasslike stones that looked like diamonds that had been dusted abundantly onto the dress.

They looked so real.

They couldn't be real diamonds! She had not thought there could be so many so small and so perfectly identical to one another, not to mention that they should be wasted on a nightgown!

And whatever was this creation doing on *her* body?

Who had dressed her in this gown?

Where was she?

She fought back the wave of nauseating fear this question drove into her throat, crawling madly over the bed to the bed curtains. She tore through the brocade, falling clumsily to the floor as she did.

She struggled to her feet, staggering as a dizzy spell threatened her equilibrium. "Oh no, not this again," she whispered in dismay as she clung to a curtain to steady herself. She felt strange, as if she were reviving from a drug-induced stupor.

It was that moment that the full impact of the room struck her crazed senses.

"Sweet Father save me," she uttered. Her voice

echoed back to her from the cathedral ceilings
and the far distant walls. The size of it! She had
never seen such an enormous room! She looked
around wildly, her eyes burning with the sight of
all the things she could not hope to comprehend.
It looked like a vast hoard of treasure, as if it had
been gathered together by a mighty dragon or was
perhaps awaiting Aladdin to come and find it. It
was a display of the finest of metals and most precious of stones, all gleaming gaudily at once.
There were other things, huge paintings, peculiar
tapestries, and amazing sculptures. And almost
every single item was on display in some way, be it
in a case or a frame, hanging up or in a box or . . .

On her neck.

With desperate, clawing hands, Kathryn grabbed
the jeweled necklace and tore it from her neck.
She cut herself in the process, but hardly noticed as
she cast the cloyingly lovely thing as far from herself
as she could manage. There was a bracelet as well,
and rings, each of which followed the necklace in
their fates.

What was this place?

How had she come to be here?

Her heart was beating so fast with confused terror that her entire chest hurt. Panic washed over
her until she could barely breathe. There were
hundreds, thousands of things on display. Things
whose purpose or name she couldn't even guess.
Some dreadful instinct told her she was not meant
to see these things.

This unreal, malignant splendor loomed up
around her like demon phantoms of beauty from
places and times unknown to her.

Kathryn was drawing heavily for breath as she realized things were much more disturbing than they appeared.

"Dad!" She tore her fingers through her loose coiling hair, which had, unknown to her, been arranged just so. "Jillian!"

She started to run in a single direction. The walls were so far away, and she couldn't even make out the doors. Everything looked the same, covered in an intricate gold inlay that went fully around the room. Then her legs seemed to go suddenly weak, the strength wobbling out from under her. She tripped over her own feet and smacked into the carpeted floor. But in spite of the painstakingly made rug, she cracked her head hard as she fell, the stone beneath the carpeting so very unforgiving. Finally, overloaded with shock and fear, seeing brilliant stars in her vision, she collapsed. The last thing she saw was those stars.

Stars.

And a curtain of soft, midnight black.

"Fool!"

Cronos braced himself for the blow that would likely kill him. It came hard and fast, hurling him an incredible distance before he crumpled to the floor.

Adrian whirled around, threw back his head, and clenched his fists as he released a howl of insane wrath. It expelled a great deal of his frustration, and so he was calmer when he fell to one knee beside his damaged keepsake.

He rolled her over with great care and tenderness. His harsh breath caught when her head lolled to the side, revealing the torn flesh at her throat and the bleeding cut across her forehead where she had struck it.

"No." The word quavered with unendurable pain as he touched the wounds.

Ruined.

She had been ruined by his foolish neglect. She shouldn't have been able to regain consciousness, but when he had lost his control earlier, he had lost his power over her sleep.

Never, never once, had any of his precious possessions been damaged while in his care.

Perhaps, though, this damage could be repaired.

But he knew nothing of healing.

Adrian cradled his treasure close to his chest, holding her and yet afraid to hold her. He had not meant for any harm to come to her, but harm had come regardless. All of the darkness he toyed with while captaining the nightmares of people—he knew what evil was and the deep, ugly places those people could go. He had simply wanted to remove her from that ugly world, to take her from all the pain she had been suffering. He had done so against every rule, he knew, had even attacked his sister, whom he truly loved, only to have it come to this?

The remorse that filled him then was sudden and bracing. The energy of it was intense and powerful. He drew in a breath of surprise at the feel of it. It was not a dark emotion, like the ones he was used to wallowing in, but neither was it a bright one. It was a peculiar shade of gray, and yet . . . so strong. Yes . . . he had felt it before. In certain dreams, there was guilt and sadness. Sometimes so strong it would overwhelm him, just as it was doing in that moment.

Confused and having struck down the two people who always helped him when he needed it, Adrian was lost as to what to do or feel. He gathered up his Kathryn and hurried her back over to the bed. As he had done before, he carefully arranged her limbs, smoothed her nightgown down until it was perfectly straight, and then painstakingly arranged every single curl of her glorious hair.

But as hard as he tried, the perfection of it was flawed and ruined by those terrible marks on her body. Frustrated, he roared out angrily, trying to shake off the waves of pain riding through him with such inexplicable potency. He tried leaving the room, barely making it off the bed before he collapsed to the floor. He lay there panting for a long minute, trying to make himself get up and not understanding why he couldn't. And then, finally, his psyche shorted out and Adrian lost consciousness.

Something was pulling Kathryn, drawing her.

She had been floating in a benign gray void of nothingness. Somehow she knew that she had been there for quite some time.

But something was now beckoning her away from it.

Slowly, with a soft sigh, she came around. She

opened her eyes with a hesitant flutter of her lashes.

Then she heard again what it had been that had called her back to consciousness.

A moan.

It was a low, tortured sound. The sound of someone in unbearable pain.

And whoever that someone was, he was very close by.

She sat up slowly, blinking once. She was aware of feeling stronger. Of feeling more well rested than she had been in a very long time. She did not even feel afraid this time as she quickly looked around the strange room. Of course, she wasn't quite brave enough to look at any one thing for any length of time, either.

Then the moan came again, drawing her full attention quickly to the floor beside her.

She gasped softly.

Whoever he was, he had to be the most massive man she had ever laid eyes on. Well, maybe with the exception of the color plates of giants in her childhood fairy-tale books. Still, the difference between seeing a drawing of a mythical giant and finding yourself sitting and staring at a real one was quite vast. Why, the width of his shoulders might be nearly twice the length of one of her arms from fingertips to shoulder! Of course, she was a little small, according to some people.

She bit her lip and leaned closer with irresistible curiosity so she could get a better look at him.

He was on his forearms and knees, his face bur-

rowed into his hands. He was dressed entirely in
black. The clothing, what she could see of it, was
alien to her in its fashion. Even the fabrics looked
strangely coarse. It was nothing she had ever
worked her needle through, and she prided herself on being a remarkably fair seamstress.

She could see the back of his large head. His
features were further hidden by an outrageously
thick and long tumble of silken black hair that
sprouted from his scalp, tumbling forward over his
neck and face. She followed the line of that neck,
picking out the distinction of his bold spine
through his shirt fabric and the spread of the back
of an immense rib cage. His waist was narrower,
though probably still as wide as her thigh was long.
His hips were less wide, but in a similar proportion
to the rest of his physique. The legs, tucked in a
rather fetal manner beneath himself, were the size
of good-sized and very sturdy tree trunks.

Sweet Father, he was twice the size of any man
anywhere! She suspected he would dwarf her own
husky father.

Another tormented groan rose from the object
of her fascination, snapping Kathryn's attention
back to the huge man's obvious distress, as well as
her present situation. She warned herself to exercise caution. She might be a scrapper, but there
was nothing she could expect to do against someone so much bigger than she was. It was likely, she
told herself, that this was the person who had all
the answers to what was going on.

Well, that meant she needed him to talk. And he
wasn't likely to do much of that if he was hurting.

And besides, he sounded almost sad as he made those painful little sounds.

She scuttled off the bed. Approaching him slowly and carefully lowering herself to her knees beside him, she leaned over him and laid her hands on his shoulders as comfortingly as she could.

"Can I help you?" When she received no immediate response, she moved forward a little farther and sought to gain his attention by placing her hand in his hair at the back of his head. "Here now, let me help you. Please."

Kathryn gave a yelp of shocked surprise when he suddenly lurched away from her touch, stumbling and crashing heavily to the floor, trying to crawl away from her. He barely progressed another foot before collapsing face-first into the carpeting. He whined piercingly, like an animal in raw, anguished agony, making the hair on the back of her neck raise up as if someone had just trod across her grave.

Kathryn's heart stuttered and her eyes widened. She had never heard such a horribly inhuman sound before. It was terrifying. But as he whimpered softly again, she knew it was the most pitiful thing she'd ever heard and there was no way she could even pretend to ignore him. Bolstering her courage, hesitating with each movement, she slid cautiously back to his side.

"Please," she begged softly, "let me help you."

She touched him again and he reacted as if she had burned him. He recoiled, an agonized roar splitting her ears as it tore from the huddled black mass before her.

"Leave me alone!"

She fell back away from the booming power of his voice rattling the treasures around them in their casings. *It must be the acoustics and the vastness of the room that made it amplify in such an ominous way.*

She felt icy cold fingers of dread stroking at her throat.

There's something familiar about that voice.

Her nightmare! He was the one who had been in her—

But no! Then that would mean it—all of this—either all of this was still the same dream or—

Or it was all real? If so, then he was the one who had touched her time and again in unwelcome ways. It didn't seem possible, but why else would she know his voice if it hadn't somehow been real? And it was this monstrous man who had somehow spirited her away from her home and had subjected her to all this awful terror and fear. Trapped her there like one of these shiny baubles to be gaped at and toyed with.

Bastard! she thought with unaccustomed vileness. *Soulless bastard!* Her family had been dying and he had violated them and her by stealing her away! Kidnapping her!

"Bastard!" she screeched, the thought of her abandoned and helpless family riling her up like a madwoman. "You bloody bastard of hell!"

She was no longer sympathetic to his pain as she flew into him, pummeling him with her relatively small fists. Somewhere in her enraged mind, a quiet voice told her she was probably doing him little or no harm. He was so much bigger than she, and Kathryn could now feel the thick masses of

muscles beneath her battering hands. But regardless, it made her feel better to fight back. Then
she, who had never wished harm on the slightest of
creatures, felt joy that he was in pain. Utter, mind-
numbing joy.

She was completely unaware of the ripple of re-
newed strength that was shuddering through her victim. She was oblivious to the fact that his agonized
moans were replaced with a soft sigh of something
slightly but distantly akin to pleasure.

The next thing she was aware of was a bone-
chilling, wickedly rolling laugh. Then he surged up
before her like a monolith of black rage.

She froze, her entire body locking. No breath.
No blink. Not a glimmer of movement as her
shocked eyes tried to absorb the impact of the face
looming above hers.

He was hideous!

She had never seen such a grotesque compila-
tion of features and was paralyzed with panic that
she was seeing it now. The entire face was bloated
over warped, distended bones. His forehead and
jaw jutted out in a way that would give his profile a
crescent shape. Cheekbones, fat with flesh, pro-
truded starkly before falling into the contrasting
concave cheeks themselves. His eyes were enormous, though sunken, the lids above and under
colored in brown shadow in severe contrast to the
pristine white of the rest of his complexion. The
eyes themselves she had seen before. They were a
brackish, swamplike black and green. The blackness in them twisted into horrifying shapes and
mysteries her mind could not bear.

But the worst of it, the utmost horror of him,

was his mouth. The upper lip was abnormally larger than the lower one. And as he released a malevolent laugh, she saw the wicked gleam of two fangs.

Vicious, monstrous fangs.

Kathryn screamed.

Awful! Terrible! She had never seen anything—

He seized suddenly, twisting slightly as a look of pain—pleasure?—coursed through him. Then his dreadful eyes were upon hers, sending frenzied fright bolting into her.

But before she could move, his hands came out and seized her by her upper arms. He dragged her hard up against his chest, cold and hot sensations bleeding into her wherever he contacted her flesh.

"Kathryn," that dreadful voice hissed in exultant evil, "you are mine, Kathryn. Forever! I thought your purity would be the greatest treasure." He threw back his head and laughed with terrible glee. "Wrong! So wrong! Your corruption . . . the corruption of all your innocence will be my glory! Look at me! There was pain, horrible pain, but all it took was your rage, your sweet rage to make me pulse with power again!" His malignant eyes bored into hers and she felt as though her very soul were being coerced from her. "Mine! Forever!"

"No!" She shook her head madly, struggling to be free, to get away from his sulfurous breath and damning words. "I will do nothing to please you!"

"Oh, but you already have." He seemed to become incredibly calmer then as his eyes roamed intimately over every part of her. He reached out as if in a trance and stroked her fine hair. She recoiled, her stomach turning madly as she shuddered in revulsion. "You are so beautiful. Such a treasure. I have never had such a treasure as you. I was wrong to think you would be most beautiful in an enchanted repose. I like you much better awake, Kathryn." She felt long, clawlike nails scrape down the length of her throat; then they seemed to retract a little, leaving his fingertips flush against her. "I can feel your life's blood here. It is hot. Sweet. So vital and pure. Precious cargo in an even more invaluable container." He pulled back a little, shaking his head as if there were intense thoughts warring within him. His eyes flashed a hundred shades of green in a matter of seconds.

"Don't touch me!" She struggled in vain within his grasp. "You can't do this to me! I am a . . . a free human being! Please. You can't just keep me here!"

Kathryn felt hot tears slipping down her face. He was marveling over her like a thing, like a valuable piece of art or an antique . . . like just another one of the dumbly exquisite treasures she had seen around her. Was that what this was, then? A treasure room, and she the latest curiosity?

"Free, eh? Trapped on that ranch in the Australian wilderness with your father, playing mother to your sister because you know he cannot take care of her for himself? When, in your heart, you want to run to the city and experience a fully different sort of life. So what difference is it from being your father's captive, when you can just as easily be mine? Accept your fate, Kathryn. Be thankful. There could be worse fates."

"None that I can imagine could be worse than being a pet to a monster like you!" she cried, wrenching herself madly now in order to be free.

Her words angered him and she felt the claws in his fingers extending as if in response to the emotion roaring through his eyes and growling from his chest.

"You dare much!" he hissed. "I hold your fate in my hands, little creature! How easy it would be to corrupt you! How delightful. It could be my greatest pleasure if I wish it!"

"No!" Rage washed through her and she lunged, reaching up blindly, striking for his face with her own nails.

But something made her catch herself mid-action. Like a tossed coin, she flipped from tails to heads and the world rushed in a mad whirl around her.

Kathryn, this is not you, a quiet inner voice seemed to whisper.

She looked up into his eyes in stunned confusion. She was further troubled by the shock registering in his midnight green pupils. He had expected her to hit him, she realized on a quick, calm level of her brain. He hadn't expected her to be able to stay the urge that . . . *that he had been feeding into her!* It was him! He was making her feel these things, and probably enjoying it! Corrupting her would give him pleasure, he had said. Well, she would not give in to his evil influence. She would not!

Kathryn suddenly had a mad idea.

He had pulled away in agony when she had touched him with kind, gentle hands. It occurred to her that this might be the only means of escape she would find.

It was insane. There was no reason for it to have

any foundation in truth. But hadn't there been endless stories, some stranger than this, where the antithesis of good or of evil could harm each other? If he could hurt her . . .

Softly, slowly, she quieted her thoughts. She relaxed in his grip and searched her mind for a pleasant memory or thought. One that would not lead her to anger or fear.

She ignored him when his eyes narrowed on her.

"What are you doing?" he asked, his voice ominous and threatening.

What if, like any wild beast, he was unable to help what he was? she considered. Kathryn reached out and stroked the creature's chest with all the sympathy in her heart, her thoughts making it easier to touch him with honest caring.

His howl was so sharp, so sudden, that she almost lost her tenuous hold on her concentration. To her surprise, relief and bewilderment, her idea was working. He was in pain once again.

But she refused to take joy in that; it was not in her true nature to take joy in that. It was his presence that had caused those earlier feelings. But now that she was aware of them, blocking them from herself intentionally, she was free to feel honest pity for the thing that he was.

Her thoughts seemed to wrench into him like a hot poker spearing his heart. He jerked his hold from her as if she burned him. Kathryn screamed out in surprised pain as his claws scored the delicate skin on her arms. But she found a mind-clearing strength in her pain. She advanced on him even as he reeled backward.

"Let me help you." She intoned the words gently, carefully. "You cannot help what you are. I can see that now. But you cannot be all evil. I have always been taught, have always believed that there is some good in everything. Even if just a little." She did believe that. There must be something in him that was good. It was his fight against it that was probably causing him such agony.

Somehow, she knew this to be the truth of it.

"Sleep!" he screamed suddenly, his voice at a peculiar high pitch as he cast a desperate hand sweeping in her direction. "You will sleep!"

Kathryn staggered suddenly as a stunning wave of exhaustion rushed her. *What the hell is this?* she wondered, gasping for breath as she tried to balance on her own feet. It was some kind of a spell! She looked at him through hazy vision and saw the utter shock and disbelief in his eyes that his spell had not worked properly. It gave her confidence, and some of her strength began to bleed back into her. She stepped forward again.

"I will not sleep. I will stay awake. I will stay with you forever, remember? You will either have to fight me forever, or give in to what is right! Don't worry," she murmured soothingly, "I will care for you." Just as she had cared for her sick family. Just as she had cared for any living thing in pain or in need all of her twenty-two years on Earth. Because the universe had created her to love all things.

He fell to the floor with a crash, writhing like a tormented demon from the darkest pit in hell.

But Kathryn didn't know how long it would last. She didn't know what to do next. She felt honest remorse fill her heart at his plight and his agony.

Suddenly, she wanted to leave. If what he was was all he could be, she did not wish to be the cause of his pain for another moment. She wanted to get away so he could be at peace.

The compassionate thought just about killed him.

Then, out of nowhere, a gnomelike little man leapt out at Kathryn, backhanding her fiercely across her face.

Kathryn was flung backward, landing hard on her back so all the air rushed from her body. She was shaking her dizzy head and tasting her own blood as she watched the new intruder. He seemed to back off from her in sudden terror, clutching his hand as if in regret of what he had done and alternatively pulling his gray hair out with anxiety. He cast beady dung-colored eyes between her and the monster lying prone on the floor.

"Oh, Cronos. Oh, Cronos. Oh, Cronos," he repeated in dismay over and over again.

Kathryn tried to get up, but he screamed like a harpy and ran at her, raising his hand threateningly over her. He laughed in relief when she reflexively cowered from another painful blow.

"You stay! You stay! Bad treasure! Bad, bad treasure! To hurt the Master is *bad!* Cronos hurt treasure, damaged treasure, but the Master will not mind this time. He damaged you too. Yes, I see. Yes, I do." He seemed ecstatic with his own thought processes, pacing madly to and fro between the two bodies in the room. One he feared, yet he had found power over her. The other he feared even more, but wanted to help out of mindless devotion.

"Master! Get up! Get away! Flee from the bad treasure! Shall I kill it? Shall I throw it away? It will never hurt you then!"

The Master was suddenly lurching to his feet, still staggered with blinding pain, but strong enough to grab Cronos by the scruff of his neck and lift him up to look into his eyes.

"Do . . . not . . . touch!" the Master gasped in agonized stammers. "Do you . . . hear me? Never touch . . . her again!"

Then he cast the gray little man aside and staggered unseeingly to a set of doors Kathryn hadn't even had a chance to notice.

"No!" she screamed. "I won't let you leave me here!" She was up and running, determined not to lose her last chance at escape. The creature was too weak to fight her and the little man had been ordered not to harm her.

But she made the mistake of letting the rage he influenced in her come through. When he turned, shifting back his massive shoulders to glare coldly in her eyes, his pain was obviously ebbing. She gasped, skidding on the carpet to stop the forward motion that would carry her right into him. She stopped, but one massive arm swung out to her, black claws rending the skirt of her gown as he seized hold of it and used it to drag her forward.

"Mine," he growled. "Forever."

Then he shoved her back, allowing himself and the awful little man to exit unimpeded out of the door. It was slamming shut as she flung herself against it.

She screamed, and screamed, and screamed.

* * *

Adrian staggered down the grand hallway, the effects of her attack not so easily shaken off this time. He needed his mirror. He needed to lose himself in the comfort of its darkness. There he would hide until Aerlyn could recover. It was she who had kept him from feeling these agonies, he knew that now. She was such an eager receptacle for good that it had never had a chance to touch him before.

So this was what happened when it did, eh? It was horrible! He had never thought such a fate could be his. But it served as justified penance for the sin he had committed against his sister.

Another wave of pain crashed into him suddenly, more painful than anything the little conniving creature in his treasure room had given him.

What *she* had given him was secondhand. His present feelings of remorse and repentance were his own, and the fact that such good could be born so suddenly in one so black made it a powerful thing.

He was at the head of the stairs when it hit and he lurched forward and over, tumbling helter-skelter down the curving staircase.

Hours later—or was it days?—Kathryn sobbed in exhausted despair, her cheek pressed to the smooth wooden door as if it could bring her closer to the other side. She was crumpled upon the floor, leaning heavily against the sickeningly lovely portal of her prison.

"Please!" she cried hoarsely, her voice rasping weakly from overuse. "Let me out. Please!"

She had used a hundred, a thousand, similar pleas. She had begged and cajoled with insane single-mindedness for her freedom, exhausting every resource of appeal or possible influence she could come up with.

Why was this happening to her? What had she done to deserve this particular unbearable hell?

Had she somehow sinned? Had she been some-how complacent in her gift of freedom that she must now have it so brutally torn away from her? She had never kept a pet; she had even shied from catching fireflies as a child when other children seized and kept the poor things bouncing madly in mason jar jails.

"Why are you doing this to me?" she screamed suddenly, rising to her knees and pounding her fists on the massive wooden gateway before her. She wailed in frustrated misery, pummeling the doors with the same hazed mania she had used against the monster's body earlier. She continued until her bruised skin began to split and bleed. "Let me out! Let me out! You don't own me! I won't let you own me! I will die first!" She was screeching at the top of her vocal cords, but that had come to be a sound barely above a rasping ex-halation due to the abuse they had suffered. "Do you hear me? I will die first!"

She collapsed to the floor then, her body too weak with exhaustion and despair to maintain her battle. She wept piteously, her face pressed into the delicate woven textures of the rug. Her head ached, throbbing from inflamed sinuses and the sounds of all her screams still echoing in her ears.

She had never known such despondency. She could not find her usual fortitude, which had always seen her through all kinds of difficult situations in her life. The unknown but well-imagined path of her fate had robbed her of her will to be strong. The fight bled out of her, her spirit ailing and falling away into murky grayness.

She would never be free again, she thought over and over again. She had seen kidnappings on crime shows and they never ended well, especially the longer they went on. And with her family ill, there was no one to even report her missing. They would never find her.

She was doomed to live out her life trapped in this gilded cage. She would die and decay until her polished bones were all that would be left. Then, even in death, her skeleton would be hung amongst these other treasures to be mused and mulled over like any museum piece with a fascinating tidbit of history or gossip connected to it.

Lost.

Forever lost.

She would never see her father or sister again, and this, above all, pierced her heart. For all she knew they had likely died alone and uncared for in their beds because she, their last hope for life, had been spirited away to this monstrous place, wherever it was.

Any distance that took her from her family's bedsides was too far away.

Slowly Kathryn drifted even farther away into the gray void of her thoughts.

She would never have a husband, would never be wife to a man she loved more than life itself.

She felt her dreams of romance drift into dust. She would never know the answers to those secrets of love between a man and a woman. There would not be holding or being touched with infinite caring and tenderness by the hand of a strong male who loved her. Where was the wondrous kinship of sharing her life with a husband and family? Dying. All these dreams were no longer hers to have. This also meant she would not be a mother, would not feel a new generation of Macdonough blood quicken in her body, and would not labor to bring that life into the world.

Kathryn finally was slipping into sleep again as exhaustion robbed away even her ability to think.

Tears slipped from her eyes when a distant, subconscious thought realized that there would not even be dreams in this sleep to allow her escape.

Chapter 3

Aerlyn's eyes fluttered open to darkness.

She sighed in consternation. Truly, she thought, her damned fool of a brother had ventured much too far this time!

She sat up quickly, glided off the bed and onto her bare feet as if she had never been injured at all. She paused to take a mental inventory and was perturbed to realize she had been unconscious for three days and nights.

Three days and nights where her brother had most likely run amok without her to censure or balance his damages. The impact of the imbalance would be phenomenal, no doubt. There would likely be a great deal of repair work to be done on her part if she was to set this disruption to rights.

She was halfway down the hall when an eerie sensation crept into her.

Something was amiss.

"Adrian?" she called warily, her resonant voice

echoing like music into every corner and cubby of the entire fortress. "Adrian! I am awake and truly in a rare fit at you. Adrian! Answer me!"

Aerlyn felt a sudden sense of foreboding creep over her, twisting around her like ivy that smothered the very life out of an unfortunate tree.

. . . Aerlyn . . .

The voice that came to her mind was accompanied by a sheet of falling blackness. She was in his mind, or maybe just the place between their minds, she couldn't be positive.

"Adrian." The relief in her voice was enormous, if short-lived.

. . . I think I am dying, Aerlyn. There is so much pain. . . .

Aerlyn caught her breath. The idea of someone of her brother's strength and power dying was ludicrous, but for him to think so could only mean that he was in inconceivable agony. Adrian was not supposed to feel pain like she did. He was a master of pain and fear; therefore, they never touched him. Adrian felt at home in his normal darknesses: his rages, his hate, and other similar emotions. These were natural things, comfortable things to him.

Whatever in the universe would cause him pain? She should be the only source that could theoretically cause such a phenomenon. But she had been in blank repose for three days and nights, healing from his attack on her.

"Where are you?" she asked anxiously.

. . . The treasure tower. In the atrium . . .

His thoughts seemed to dim around her. He was weakening.

"I am coming."

She sped to his side as fast as her feet would take her, uncaring of the energy she was burning or the aches that still remained in her body because he had been cruel and abusive to her. It didn't matter. Adrian could not help what he had become for the sake of so many. Part of it was her fault for not handling the situation better. He needed more and more careful handling and understanding as the nights wore on into years of toil and darkness. She was there to watch over him, to help keep him sane and grounded, and now she feared she had failed him.

She ran into the atrium and found him lying on the floor, the fluorescent pink of his blood pooled around his head. She knelt beside him, gently touching his misshapen head. He lifted it to her, his whole body shaking in pain and outright fear.

"What's happening to me?" he asked hoarsely.

Aerlyn gasped in utter shock, a hand flying to her mouth as she stared into her brother's changing face. The sharper points that had twisted his features over time were smoother now, and as she looked she could swear she could see the pieces of the face she had once loved on her brother. But years of endless poison had turned him into this rough beast and she had faced the loss of his looks long ago, just as he had done. But she didn't understand any more than he did why he was so contorted and changed. Even the hands he held out to her seemed less rough, with the somewhat less vicious claws he used when in a fit of raging temper.

Whatever was happening to him, it was a painful

thing. She could read it all over his expression and in the tension of his body language. She reached to press a hand to his head, where blood was still seeping from a deep gash, and she used her free hand to check him for any other obvious injuries.

"Adrian, you have to tell me what is going on. I know you've done something. Tell me what it is so I can help to fix it."

"No!" he wrenched out stubbornly.

"You don't have a choice!" she shouted at him, her voice bouncing up off the glass ceiling.

He snarled at her, showing the tip of a fang in the process. Aerlyn was unimpressed and the direct glare of her eyes let him know that. She refused to give him quarter. Something was very wrong, and whatever it was needed to be dealt with. It was bad enough he had to live his life in a perpetual state of wrongness. She didn't want him in physical agony along with it.

"The treasure," he growled through his teeth, his reluctance clear. "You'll know when you see it."

Aerlyn looked up the winding staircase to the huge doors that housed Adrian's precious treasure room. It was his and his alone. She was never allowed beyond the doors without his strict escort. She had always abided by that because she had always felt he deserved something all his own, something no one could touch but him. Something beautiful to help balance out the dreadfulness of what he had to do every night. She had seen the exquisite collection on and off over the past two years since he had started collecting, when Adrian had been feeling magnanimous or especially proud of an acquisition. It was hard for him to share, though. The darkness inside him was so covetous of his bright and beautiful things that even letting someone look at them was sometimes too much to ask.

Aerlyn wanted to help her brother, but she wanted to know what could possibly be in that room that could hurt him so badly. What kind of creature was it? And she knew it was a living thing because she could feel it even stronger now that she was closer. She slowly rose to her full height, leaving Adrian at her feet, where he huffed angrily because he didn't have the strength to stop her or go with her or do whatever it was his instincts were crying out for him to do in order to protect what he felt was his. She made no mistake that this was what motivated him. He was not thinking of her safety in the least. Or perhaps he didn't think she would be in any danger.

She took to the stairs rapidly, her feet flying up with incredible speed. She reached the landing and ran to the hulking doors that protected the room beyond. She threw the bolt, wondering why he would bother to lock the doors from the outside. She used both hands and pushed with all her strength.

The doors opened and there, right on the floor beside the opening, was Adrian's treasure.

Oh no! What has he done?

Aerlyn rushed to kneel by the poor girl's side, shock numbing her hands and face as she dared to touch her. The other woman was wounded in several ways, including her fists being bruised from what had no doubt been a most violent banging on her prison door.

Aerlyn sat back on her heels and dashed away tears of anger and frustration. How was she going to fix this? Why would Adrian do such a thing? Maybe he was much further gone than she had thought. Maybe the insanity of his work had really and truly driven him over the edge of all reason. She could bear losing pieces of her brother bit by bit for the sake of the greater good, but was he now irretrievable? Was this why he was suffering so much agony? Because he had crossed a line and now would never come back?

No. She had to pray that wasn't the case. She had to consult with the Ampliphi about what to do. This girl was human, and she had been exposed to who knew what. Most likely to Adrian himself. Surely she could deduce what he had brought her there for. Or perhaps she was thinking he had more nefarious purposes. Regardless, if she had seen Adrian, she knew she wasn't being held by a deranged human. The deformity of her brother's body and features made him look anything but human.

Yet his heart and soul were still there, somewhere, trying to stay intact. Aerlyn knew this as she looked down onto the beautiful face of the treasure he'd chosen above all others. Why, she wondered, had he picked this particular woman? She was very pretty, and she had lovely skin, but Aerlyn had seen far more exquisite creatures among the humans. So why had Adrian chosen *her*?

It was one of many questions Adrian needed to answer. But first Aerlyn had to make sure the other woman would be safe and comfortable. She took her back to the bed in the treasure room for now, just a place to keep her safe while she tried to figure this all out. Then she walked across the room and lightly smacked Cronos's face until he was conscious. When he saw Aerlyn in the treasure room, it was clear by his meek and cowering expression that he realized the jig was up.

"Yes, you'd best be afraid of me," she breathed on a hiss of air. "You are his Companion. It is your duty to see to his care and his needs. I depend on you to tell me when he steps over the line of what is permissible. And then when he does, you *help* him?"

"He would hurt me if I told!"

"Not half as much as I will if I catch you in my sight again! The Ampliphi will hear of this, and once and for all I'll have your useless carcass removed from duty!"

The sniveling Cronos suddenly disappeared and a sly, wicked little thing came out to play. "If you tell about me, then you will tell about Adrian. They will punish him for stealing the girl. They will see how far gone he truly is and they will destroy him."

Aerlyn felt her stomach fill with lead, the weight of it slamming down hard inside her. Cronos was right. If the Ampliphi found out about what Adrian had done, they might very well have him executed. It didn't matter to them that it was unfair to ask such a harsh, corrupting duty of him; they would say he should have retired before it had gone too far.

But when Adrian had accepted his post those

many years ago, he had told Aerlyn that he would take it for as long as he could and then take it some more. Anything to keep another from suffering the way he was now suffering. He had been strong in such amazing ways then. Now he was strong in frightening ones.

They had to fix this problem without the Ampliphi knowing about it. They somehow had to give the girl back to the Earth plane and not risk exposure at the same time. Then, once the girl had been safely returned to her life, Aerlyn would force Adrian to retire from his post. He had done enough. More than enough. As it was, she knew she would never know her brother as the man he had once been. His corruption was too deep.

But for the moment, she had to deal with Cronos.

"Very well," she said through tight lips, "you shall have a reprieve . . . for now." Aerlyn didn't like the smug look that crossed his features, but there wasn't much she could do about it. As Adrian's Companion, Cronos was exposed to a great deal of the energies Adrian managed. The backwash of it had poisoned him just like it had her brother, although not nearly on the same scale. Also, Aerlyn wasn't certain she'd ever really liked Cronos to begin with. A relatively simpleminded creature, Cronos was very dedicated to his work, and to Adrian, but his motives had never been clear to her. Adrian at least had dedication to his people to compel him.

But Cronos . . .

"Your Master is at the foot of the stairs, injured and bleeding. See to him immediately."

Cronos jumped at the command, a look of despair entering his eyes for a moment. Whatever his motivations were from moment to moment, Cronos was devoted to his Master.

Aerlyn gave the woman in the bed one last look, then left the room and bolted the doors.

Chapter 4

Kathryn moaned softly, stirring in her sleep.

As she felt consciousness coming on herself, she felt piercing soreness in her throat, the heated, burned feeling of her face, and stiffness throughout her hands and her entire body.

She opened her eyes, dreading what she would see.

She saw a very normal-looking wood-beamed ceiling.

Her eyes widened in shock. What had happened to the colored streamers? She sat up swiftly, twisting around . . .

. . . and fell out of the bed.

She landed on a wooden floor with a crash. Pressing her torso up on trembling arms, she stared in dizzy confusion at the pretty, but rather ordinary, Turkish-style rug beneath her. She looked rapidly around herself, turning her head like an owl's as she tried to make sense of where she was. It was a large room, yes, but no bigger than her father's bedroom. In fact, the four-poster bed, the polished wooden floor, and the stone walls were all very similar to the ones in her own home.

But not quite. This room was somewhat newer, better kept, and of a more modern design. The ranch she had grown up on had been in her family for generations and the wear and tear of the years certainly showed, no matter how much she had tried to keep it up.

Kathryn shook her head to clear it, wondering if she was dreaming. Truly, this was simply a figment of wishful thinking. She was probably still sleeping in that awful room on the floor before those horrid, entrapping doors.

She looked down at her hands suddenly. They were black and blue and cut, as if she had been pounding on a door in desperate need to escape. Then she noticed her gown. It was plain white cotton, reaching neck to ankles, with ruffles at the borders of her wrists, hem, and throat. So simple and conservative. The fabric so wonderfully plain. But before she let herself get excited about any of what she was seeing, she narrowed her eyes and went about making a closer inspection of her surroundings.

"What trick is this now?" she wondered aloud.

Just then, the doors to the room swung open swiftly, startling a cry from her.

Kathryn's shocked eyes ran the entire course of the tall, stunningly beautiful woman who had entered. She had never fathomed that a woman could be so tall! Surely she must be almost six feet in height, only an inch or so shorter than Kathryn's own father. Her entire carriage made her seem taller still, as she held herself in an erect and statuesque manner. Her figure was divine. Round and full at the hips and breasts, flat across the ribs, and almost absurdly thin at her waist.

She was wearing a gorgeous dress made of ice blue linen, its tailored perfection and the elegance with which she wore it speaking volumes for her wealth and sophistication right off the bat. She had sleek black hair, peppered with shiny silver strands, that was swept into a high catch, only to let loose a cascade of coils and waves down the back of her head and neck.

The woman's eyes widened suddenly as they fell on Kathryn's stunned, upturned face. Kathryn watched in fascination as the peculiar sterling gray color of her eyes gleamed in the light. Kathryn's own eyes were gray, but this woman's were so light and shining they were almost like silver.

"Oh!" the woman breathed, an elegant hand sweeping up to her throat in surprise. Then her eyes warmed and her breathtaking countenance became the very epitome of concern and sympathy. "You're awake, at last!"

The woman swept into the room farther, gliding down to Kathryn's level in a cloud of a divine lilac-scented perfume. She took up Kathryn's limp hands in her own.

"How are you feeling?" Then she was pressing her palm with gentle, fluttering concern all around Kathryn's forehead and still-damp face. "You're still a bit feverish, my dear. You really should not be out of bed!"

"I . . . I fell," Kathryn said dumbly. What on

earth was going on? What place was she in this time? Who was this woman?

"I can see that." The woman smiled radiantly at her and Kathryn felt a little calmer for it. Whatever was happening, this woman was a marked improvement from the beast she had encountered in that horrid chamber. "Come now, back to bed. You need a bit more rest before you should be getting up. But I must say," she went on as she helped Kathryn to her feet and back amongst the covers, "it is such a relief to see you conscious and lucid. You gave me and my brother a terrible fright."

"Your brother? Is he that awful creature I saw? With the hideous face?"

The woman laughed, looking down at her as a mother would look down at her fanciful child.

"I'm not sure my brother would take kindly to that particular description. He's rather vain, all ego, you see." Then the woman seemed to notice Kathryn's fearful and suspicious expression and frowned with sudden worry. She sighed with a look of understanding entering her eyes. "I can see you are still not well."

"I don't understand. What's happened to me?" Kathryn was very confused.

"Why, you've been ill. My brother was riding the estate when he came across you. You were acting quite out of your head, you poor thing, but it was obvious you were riddled with fever. Adrian scooped you up and rushed you to me as fast as he could. That was well on a week ago. You've been in bed with a raging fever ever since."

Ill? With fever? That could explain a lot, but . . .

but it had all seemed so real! She looked down at her hands.

"What happened to my hands?" She held them up defiantly. She wasn't going to be tricked by a soothing voice, a convenient explanation, and a lovely face.

"Well, you did that to yourself. You would become quite violent with delusion. You kept throwing yourself against the wall, demanding to be let out. I hated to see you hurting yourself, but there was nothing we could do to stop you. You've scratched yourself all over. But the doctor says he's seen that and worse with the fever you've had. It seems to be going 'round the entire county."

Kathryn stared in shock at the woman. Was it true? Was she supposed to believe that this had all been nothing but a delusion? But . . . didn't that make much more sense than what she had thought she'd seen? Kathryn looked piercingly into the other woman's eyes, but she saw not even a glimmer of deception.

"Are you all right? Really, you should lie back and rest." The stranger put warm hands on her shoulders and pushed her down into soft—not abnormally soft, but just plain soft—pillows. Kathryn let herself relax a little.

"What is this place?" Then she shot into an upright position again. "My family! How is my family?"

"Your family? Well, I hardly know who *you* are, never mind your family. But if you tell me, I'll send my brother out right away to find out. As for where you are, we call our home the Willows. Perhaps you have heard of it?"

Kathryn shook her head slowly, her blue eyes wide with confusion.

"Well, never mind. We're just an estate and horse ranch. We've bred some of the finest thoroughbreds on the continent. I'll show you some of our special beauties once you're well enough to walk about. Now, can I get you anything? Something to drink or eat?"

Kathryn was suddenly famished and, she realized, extremely thirsty. She nodded eagerly, hoping this was a good sign that she was getting better.

"Yes. I would love something to eat. But I'm sure I can come with you—"

A sharp staying hand had her sitting back in the bed and pulling covers up against her chest. There was a stern no-nonsense feel to the action that so reminded her of her mother. And even though she had been wife and mother for their household for three years now, she was surprised how readily she wanted to give over that power to someone else. If only for a little while.

"You're not to get up unless the doctor says you can. He should be here shortly to check on you. Do you promise me to listen to all that he tells you to do or not do? I am relieved to see you lucid at last and I would hate for us to lose hard-earned ground because we didn't follow the rules."

"I promise to do exactly what he says. Only . . . can I have a phone? I need to call my dad. I need to make sure they are all right."

"I tell you what. I'll send Adrian out to check on your family. You can call them in a day or two when you're stronger. I don't want you getting all upset or excited."

"But—"

"It's only a day or two more. And Adrian will check on them to make certain all is well. Tell me where they live."

Kathryn did so with haste, but she still didn't see why she couldn't just call for herself. Would anyone even answer? Were they even alive? She couldn't simply sit there waiting and resting while she didn't know if they were safe!

"You see? Just talking about it has you flushed and your heart racing. Imagine if the news weren't good, how you would react." Aerlyn tried to smile kindly at her, knowing very well that there would be no rest for this girl until she had spoken to her family or knew what had become of them. "You must behave yourself if you are to get well."

"I'm sorry," Kathryn said absently.

But in truth, Kathryn was ecstatic with relief that she was here, in this place, being a trouble to this kind woman, rather than being *in* trouble in a gilded hell with a monster who wanted to keep her there forever. A monster who wanted to relish the corruption of the beauty he saw in her.

"Don't worry yourself so much," the kindly woman urged when she saw the upsetting memories reflecting on Kathryn's face.

"It's okay. I"—she pressed fingers to her forehead—"I am just remembering some of the awful things I was . . . um . . . imagining while I was ill. It seemed so real that . . . all of this now seems like a dream."

"Nightmares are quite common with a fever. The

memory will pass," she promised, giving Kathryn's hand a comforting pat. "Now, for introductions. My name is Aerlyn Winston. My brother, Adrian, and I own this home and the land around it. As you can no doubt tell from my accent, we were not born here. But we like it here well enough. And you are?"

"Kathryn. Macdonough."

"Now then, Kathryn, I'm going to send my brother out to your family while I make you something to eat. You rest," she reiterated sternly.

Aerlyn then swept through the door with her perfectly elegant posture and Kathryn doubted she'd ever once seen the inside of a kitchen. She seemed too refined and far too wealthy to waste time and her beautiful skin on tuna fish sandwiches and dish soap.

But Kathryn did take note of one very important detail.

She'd left the door open.

Just a crack, but it was open. Not locked.

Kathryn couldn't help herself. She crept out of bed, wincing when her steps made the floor creak. She made it to the door and realized that she was utterly exhausted by the trip. It lent credence to the claims that she had, indeed, been ill. Just the same, though, she peeked out the door and into a hallway. She could see stairs nearby. There was no one about. No toady-looking little men, no huge frightening ones either. She was tempted to find the front door and walk out, just to prove she could, but her legs were beginning to shake. She hurried back to the bed, but before she climbed in she heard loud voices. A woman calling out.

"Adrian!"

Kathryn hurried to her window and quickly pulled it open. It was a brisk, cool day, but she didn't care. What she did care about was the huge amount of land she saw, the enormous paddocks and meadows all boasting the most beautiful horses with their brilliant gleaming coats. Not too far off there was a dust trail being kicked up, a horse and rider turned to race toward the house.

They were a magnificent thing to behold. The large man in the saddle leaning close to the horse's neck and the shining, rippling muscle of a well-made beast. Actually, she thought as he came close enough for her to see him in better detail, he was a well-made beast as well. A very big man, but not as big as the creature she had encountered. She shivered, glad to think it had just been a dream.

He reached the back of the house and dismounted to speak to his sister, holding the horse with one hand and using his hat to smack dust off himself with the other. He had long, black hair, settled into curls similar to his sister's, and it was caught in a rather full ponytail at the nape of his strong neck. He was taller than her by almost a full head, and he was roped with thick and powerful muscle. She couldn't hear what they were saying, but she could hear how deep his voice was. Then, suddenly, he looked up at her window and she gasped and ducked back without even understanding why. In that brief instant, though, she'd seen his handsome face and the very grimly serious expression on it. She had seen the chiseled definition of his features even from this vantage point. He was stunning and remarkably good-looking. Well, in a dark sort of fashion. But very striking just the same.

After a moment she dared to peek back around through the window. His attention was back on his conversation with his sister. She took advantage of the situation to slowly run her eyes over him. He had fine broad shoulders; his close-fitting clothes enhanced their shape and width as well as the defined curve of his very masculine chest. His waist and hips were quite lean, flowing into the strongest, sturdiest legs she had ever seen on a man. Damn, but he was far too striking for his own good. Or maybe for her own good, she amended her thoughts as she smiled.

She did notice that never once in the conversation did he smile. It looked as though he was more likely to frown than anything. She wondered why that was. Then, with remarkable speed, he was mounting the horse and reeling away from his sister. But before he went he looked back up at Kathryn. His expression was inscrutable, but it left her with the impression that he was not very happy she was there.

Of course she was just guessing, she thought as horse and rider raced off away from the house. Her heart went with him, for she knew that he was going to see her family . . . or at least find out what had become of them.

Please let it be good news, she thought. It was all she could think. The alternative was unacceptable, and her mind rejected the images that were stirred up by the negative thoughts. No, she thought, it was completely unacceptable.

Nervous and weary, she abandoned the window and returned to her bed.

Aerlyn sighed and looked over at her brother. Each had entered Kathryn's dreaming state from their own mirror portal and together they were orchestrating the world she had "awakened" to. It was difficult for Adrian because he was so tempted by his darker side and more used to conducting people's innermost nightmares, but at the same time it was giving him a break from all of that and his sister could see it was settling him. When Aerlyn had insisted they would need to return Kathryn to her life, he had been torn between his greed for this beautiful thing he wanted and his fear of it. When Adrian had explained what had happened, she had been just as puzzled as he was by his reactions of agonizing pain. Neither could explain it. Adrian's sister had often been kind to him—in fact, tried to keep him in balance with her goodness as best she could—and it had never caused Adrian harm.

"We need to discover what has become of her family," Aerlyn said to him. "Can you find out?"

"As soon as they sleep," Adrian said gruffly. They both knew he could not go out to look for them and ask after them because of his appearance, and Aerlyn didn't trust him to manage Kathryn's sleep and dreams for the length of time it would take for her to do the task.

"Then I'll leave you to it. Only take care not to frighten them, Adrian. They are ill enough without you adding to the stress of it," she warned him sternly.

"Do not fear, sister," he ground out darkly. "Despite what you think of me, I am not all evil yet."

He pulled away from her and went in search of Kathryn's family, walking through the dream walls of the large ranch house they had created for the benefit of their recovering guest. It was going to take constant work and surveillance to keep the deception going, but all they had to do was hold on to it until she went through her "healing" process in a normal manner and then they would deliver her back to her home and her bed. She would hopefully be none the wiser for it. She would put her experiences with Adrian down to the most vivid nightmare of her life and that would be the end of it. Aerlyn and Adrian's presence on the dream and nightmare planes would continue on uninterrupted and unexposed. The Ampliphi need never know how badly Adrian had behaved. Then, as soon as was possible, they would go before the Ampliphi and remove Adrian from his duties as a Guardian. The strain was too much and Aerlyn feared there would be nothing left of her brother if he continued on.

She feared that he might already be too far gone and that she had somehow let that crucial point pass right in front of her. They had been placed in the Barrens together, given the job of gathering much-needed energy, but she and Cronos were supposed to watch Adrian carefully. One being could not constantly take in the kind of dark emotions that Adrian must manage and remain sane or stable. *They* were supposed to have provided him with balance. A touchstone. But now she could see that Cronos had only been playing into Adrian's descent into darkness. The Companion had reveled in it. He had been too close to Adrian's side all of this time and been exposed to the same negativity he had. Cronos must be dealt with as well, but it would be a touchy matter because the Companion could blackmail Aerlyn and Adrian at any given moment by exposing what Adrian had done to the human woman. If this did not go well, if she wasn't safely returned to her life, Adrian would stand trial for his crime. Regardless of his service to his people and the extenuating circumstances, the court of the Ampliphi would be harsh. They had little tolerance for behaviors that might expose the presence of those who were sent to gather the energies they needed so badly, and even less for those behaviors that were, in general, reprehensible. Aerlyn might have stopped Adrian from doing something truly evil to Kathryn, but the intention had been there.

Aerlyn dreaded to think of what might have happened had she not recognized the trouble he was in. Would he have simply kept Kathryn like a pretty thing, leaving her untouched and precious to himself, or would he have taken her into a dark place, using her to sate the wicked desires his corrupted soul now craved?

Aerlyn shuddered to think of it. She wanted to believe that, at his very core, Adrian was still the good man he had once been. That some sense or sanity would have come through at the last minute and he would have controlled his urges. But her doubts were much too strong. Her fears too well founded.

She reached out through the miasma of the dream state she held innocent Kathryn in and gently touched the other woman's face. "You have to forgive him," she murmured softly. "He doesn't mean to be this way."

More importantly, though, she had to forget him. Forget what she had seen and done. All they had to do was get through two days. That would make it believable enough for her. Then she would be back on the Earth plane, back home with the loved ones she cared about and for.

"Just two days. Please, let him hold on for just two days," she prayed.

Chapter 5

After twenty-four hours confined to her room and her bed, Kathryn was beginning to feel like a prisoner again. Part of her frustration was that she had seen Adrian Winston return, yet no one came with news of her family. That did not bode well. She was afraid they were keeping the truth from her because it would upset her so much. So now she paced the floor until she grew tired or leaned out of the window looking out on the vast property. Very often the landscape was disrupted by the presence of the man of the house, he and his brutish stallion riding together. And it was always a seemingly violent ride, as if the man were being chased by demons that he would forever be only a hoofbeat ahead of. She might have frowned on his treatment of his animal but for the fact the wickedly powerful creature seemed to enjoy and thrill in every minute of its rampant flight.

Surely the man had a death wish. Even though

there was no doubt he was by far the most accomplished horseman she had ever seen, no one's luck could run as well as his had for too much longer. Just yesterday she had seen him jump the stallion over a hedge that, by any reasonable standard, should have been too high to clear. But in a flex and coiling of powerful muscle, horse and rider had sprung over the obstacle as if it were merely any other low fence.

It had been an impressive sight, regardless of the fact that it took an hour to get her frightened heart out of her throat and back to its calm home within her breast.

"Daydreaming?" a gentle voice at her back asked her.

She smiled and turned to face her hostess. Today Aerlyn was wearing a pretty violet-colored dress that made her silvery eyes leap out in relief. Kathryn felt a moment of true envy, wishing for a moment that she was an Amazon goddess like Aerlyn.

"I have a bit of cabin fever," she said with a sigh. "And I'd like to get dressed."

"I think that can be arranged." Aerlyn walked over to the wardrobe across from the foot of the bed and opened the doors. Inside there were clothes hanging at the ready. Not many, just a couple of dresses and some jeans. "I guessed at your size and had Adrian get them while he was seeking news of your family. You were asleep when we brought them up."

"My family. What have you found out? Please," she begged her, "I've been waiting so patiently and I just can't take not knowing."

"Easy, Kathryn," Aerlyn soothed, coming to her and giving her a hug.

"Why is she disturbed?"

The booming sternness of the male voice startled Kathryn. She looked past Aerlyn to see Adrian standing there, drawing hard for breath and looking like he'd rolled in a dustbin.

"She wants to know about her family. That's all, Adrian," Aerlyn said with a careful sort of firmness, almost as if she were scolding him. "I was about to tell her that they were both taken to the hospital, but beyond that we don't know."

"But help came for them," Kathryn said with relief. "They weren't left alone to die."

Adrian shifted, as if in discomfort, and he frowned. Up close he was like a wild storm, Kathryn thought. Cranky and thunderous, as if something inside him was driving him to belch lightning down on the earth.

"They would have lived or died whether you were there or not," he said gruffly.

"I could have helped them," she bit back at him suddenly. "If they had died, imagine how I would have felt for abandoning them. As sick as they were, they couldn't even lift a glass of water!"

Her flare of temper was met with soothing pats from Aerlyn to calm her, but Adrian took a deep, satisfied breath and for a moment she thought he might smile.

"You are right, of course," he said, carefully choosing his words when Aerlyn shot him a warning look. "I only meant to say you had become too ill to care for them yourself. That you could not lift a glass of water to save yourself, never mind for them. I only wished you were not so hard on yourself for things you couldn't control. Now, excuse me."

Adrian backed out of the room and with heavy strides he walked down the hall to the stairs. The wood creaked loudly beneath his every step and Kathryn wondered why she hadn't heard him approach before. Now she felt bad for her reprimanding tone. He and his sister had done nothing but help her. She shouldn't be so quick to judge his meaning.

"I think I'll get dressed," she told Aerlyn, pushing away from her to seek what was in the closet.

"Very well. I'll see you downstairs."

Aerlyn left the room and headed quickly into Adrian's wake. She caught up with him at the stairwell.

"Adrian," she scolded, "you must be careful."

"I am not a careful man," he snapped at her, his ferocity making her pull back in surprise. The moment he saw the reaction, though, he took off his hat and ran an agitated hand through his hair. It was so strange to him, to feel himself in his former face and body. It had been gone from him for so long; it was like putting on a lightweight mask. It was still the same man beneath it, but the mask made all the difference in fooling the eyes of others. Did he miss this shape and form, he wondered. Did he wish for what was now gone from him?

Unwilling to examine himself to find the answers to those fruitless questions, he turned his attention back to his sister. "I will try. But I cannot bear to feel her troubled emotions. I wish to take the feelings away and make her feel some kind of joy instead." He fidgeted with his hat. "So strange for me to want that, but it is the compulsion inside me and it is hard to deny."

Aerlyn couldn't help but be pleased to hear his confession. It was a positive thing. It was a good desire. Something so rarely seen in him any longer. For a moment she found herself wishing the other woman could stay with them a little while longer, especially if this was the influence she had on Adrian. But it was almost certainly a fluke, and it would be madness to delay her return to her normal world. The longer she stayed, the more chance the Ampliphi would find out.

"You must control yourself," she scolded Adrian. "For just a little while longer."

He nodded, and then went down the stairs in hard, heavy footfalls. He had just made it to the bottom when Kathryn appeared at the top. She caught his eye because she was wearing a brilliant robin's-egg blue, and he came to a halt so he could look at her. She was self-conscious in the pretty dress, as if she weren't used to wearing one. She picked up her skirt in both hands, nervously tugging the fabric taut as if she were going to give a curtsy. The soft fabric clung cleanly to her every last curve, especially the generousness of her breasts. Adrian's immediate impulse was to turn around and launch himself back up the stairs, where he could touch her and play with his beautiful toy, but he knew that was not the right thing to do. He wanted very badly to do the right things for a change. Besides, Aerlyn was standing between them, well in the way of his wishes.

But perhaps later, he thought, a wicked smile creasing his handsome face. Maybe later he would find her alone.

Kathryn was so preoccupied by the fact that she was wearing a dress for just about the first time she could remember that she almost missed seeing that devilish grin that suddenly came over Aerlyn's brother. When she did see it, she felt her entire body flush hot with unexpected feeling. At first she thought it was embarrassment, but quickly realized it was something very different. It was the first time she'd seen him smile, and to say it changed his whole face was truly understating things. There was mischief of some kind in that grin; you could see it in his sparkling dark green eyes.

She immediately decided to take it as a compliment.

It certainly felt like one.

He turned back to the stairs and quickly slung an arm around the banister, looking as though he were waiting for something special to happen. That smile stayed hooked into the corner of his lips all the while, his eyes watching her carefully as she started to come down the stairs one slow step at a time. The closer she got to the bottom, the harder her heart was racing. As soon as she was within reach, he put out a hand and cupped her elbow, helping her down the rest of the way.

Lord, he was a big man, she found herself thinking as he towered over her in height and bulk. It was enough to catch a little fear in a girl's heart. She found herself wondering what kind of temperament he must have. He seemed to be obliging enough just then, but she couldn't forget the volatile way he rode his horse.

But what is he really like? she wondered.

"I was wondering if you'd mind taking me for a short walk," she asked him, hoping her ploy for an opportunity to sketch his character wasn't too obvious.

He looked at her, seeming very skeptical. He glanced back at his sister, as if wondering if she would give him her permission. Then he gave her a short nod.

"But not too far," he said sternly. "You are still ill."

"I'll let you know the moment I grow tired," she assured him.

He led her to the back entrance to the house, showing her the expansive brick patio that led out onto acres of land. His boots were loud on the bricking, his stride heavy and powerful. He took her elbow in hand very gently when they took a few short steps down, as if he were afraid to break her by accident.

Or perhaps even afraid to touch her, she thought as he quickly let go of her. That struck her as odd because he didn't seem like the kind of man who would be afraid of much of anything. It was a hard life out where they lived, ranching being a tough way to earn a living. Especially during the wet season. There were any number of dangers at any given time, although growing up with them didn't seem to make them any more special than others. But with all of that to face, why would a man be afraid of one simple girl?

Kathryn laughed at herself for making mountains out of a simple withdrawal. She was being fanciful, she told herself. And was it any wonder? With the dreams she'd been having lately?

Silence grew heavy between her and her escort and she wondered what he was thinking as he absently toyed with his hat between his hands.

"I've seen you riding," she offered up awkwardly. When he narrowed his dark eyes on her she began to stutter. "I-I mean, you like horses."

Oh, what a dumb-ass thing to say, she thought with an inward groan.

"I do like them," he said to her carefully. "They are fast and violent animals, with the potential to do great harm if they wanted to. And yet, humans are able to make them tame." He shook his head as if the idea baffled him. "Yet, once tamed, there is something lost. They are no longer so wildly beautiful. No longer relentlessly powerful."

Kathryn gaped at him for a long moment, and then she smiled, bright and wide. Aerlyn's brother, she realized, was a poet at heart.

"But isn't it a trade-off?" she asked him. "You trade away the violence and earn the ability to be on the horse's back, where you can ride him as wildly as you dare."

The look he shot her was dark and full of intimacy as he let his gaze roam down over her body. "And how wildly would you dare?" he asked her.

"Me?" She flushed, laughing uneasily in a poor attempt to lighten the innuendo. "I just ride for work. I'm not much of a pleasure rider." It came out more like a confession than the off-putting remark she had intended.

"I don't believe that," Adrian said, his look all the more intense now. "I think you just need the right beast to ride and it will bring out the best in you." He turned, moving into her personal space, and just about came up against her. She held up her arms against her chest in automatic defense, and he looked on the gesture with disdain. "Of course, you must be brave enough to want to try. No coward will ever succeed at such a task."

"I'm no coward!" she burst out, her hands fisting and arms dropping down by her sides. "Bring me the wildest beast you have and I'll gladly ride him to exhaustion!"

"Oh, now there's a tempting thought," he growled low and hungry in her ear as he reached out for her. His fear of coming into contact with her seemed to evaporate as he caught her around the waist with both of his enormous hands and bluntly hauled her up into the bend of his body. For the first time in her life she felt small and fragile, as if he might be able to break her into bits if he wasn't careful. But he was careful, after a fashion. Rough at first, but then more gentle as he pressed her to his huge and hard-muscled body. He radiated an incredible heat, making her feel as if she might ignite at any moment. She reached to grip his shoulders, her hands so tiny and insignificant. The fear of knowing there was nothing she could do to stop him flushed through her, and it made her heart race with excitement.

"Oh, sweet agony," he said suddenly through his teeth. "Such a painful pleasure."

"W-what?" she stammered, trying to take in so much all at once. Like the way he smelled, of the stark outdoors and the aroma of a hardworking man. There was also a smoky underlay to it all, as though he'd stood too close to a burning fire.

"I mean you," he breathed against her neck. "So sweet and fresh. So infinitely innocent. And yet here"—he reached between their bodies to run a hand down her breastbone and on to her belly—"deep inside your soul, you crave the darkest of passions." Adrian slid a hand down her backside and drew her pelvis tightly to his with a confident yank. He ignored her squeak of protest and covered her mouth with his.

Adrian never knew what was driving him from one moment to the next, all of his thoughts and urges like a cloud of chaos in his mind. But the moment he pulled Kathryn close, he knew exactly what he was thinking and exactly what he was feeling. She burned him with the incredible heat of her human body, so ready to be devoured. He had no choice but to take a long, deep taste of her. It didn't matter that this was all a dream that he and Aerlyn were in control of. He didn't care that his sister was no doubt keeping a seriously watchful eye on them at that very moment. Kathryn was projecting herself as real as she thought she was, and with his own memories of the reality of her to sustain him, he might as well have his hands on the actual body of this bewitching creature.

Oh, she frightened him, he would admit that. When she touched him sometimes he could feel bright shadows of the pain she had caused him before. But that didn't matter to him. He knew that had they been in the real world, he would have disgusted her and terrified her with his beastly appearance. But now he looked like what he once had been and he knew she found him attractive as such. What he couldn't change was the darkness writhing around inside his soul. He was greedy as he kissed her, thrusting his tongue deep for the elusive taste of her. At first she was too stunned to react, so numb that she responded automatically, like a doll designed to do something on command. But this was only a frustration for Adrian. He wanted more from her. He would make her give him more. To that end he bit her lip, making her gasp, but not so hard as to make her bleed. He gnawed for a long, erotic second, until she was panting with surprise and her dove gray eyes were darkened with arousal. His hand had come up to cradle the back of her head, holding her very still as he licked the slightly abused lip and then went back for another kiss.

This time she was all there. He could tell because there was passion and awkwardness in her kisses, as if she were trying too hard to do the right things. As if she were afraid of disappointing him. But disappointment was impossible. She could do no wrong. Not as long as her body continued to lean eagerly into his and she continued to try to draw his taste onto her own tongue with enthusiastic desire.

But Adrian wasn't about necking in the fields with his sweetheart. That sunshine-and-roses image had nothing to do with who and what he was. So he ran his free hand up to her breast, embracing the lush weight of it and taking the nipple that tipped it tightly between his fingers. Kathryn reacted with a gasp of surprise and a reactive jolt of her entire body. She broke from his mouth and the hands at his shoulders gripped him all the harder.

"Wait!" she cried out.

He laughed at her. She didn't want him to wait. Not really. Not her honest, passionate self, anyway. He could feel the energy of her arousal ebbing into him. He'd felt how it had spiked the instant he'd tugged on her nipple. She very much did not want to wait. And neither did he.

"Don't you tell me to wait," he said tightly as he massaged her, the hard nipple rolling between his knuckles. "Not unless it's what you really want."

Kathryn was gasping for breath, and every time he manipulated her breast, liquid heat oozed down through the center of her body, wetting her between her legs. Embarrassed and overwhelmed, she tried to pull away from the man who was the cause of it all, but he wasn't budging. Her heart began to race madly as she struggled against him.

"I do mean it!" she insisted, trying to fight the impossible.

He laughed in her face. It was a rich, merry sound, something she might have enjoyed under other circumstances.

"What you mean is my touch arouses you, and your stunted perception of morality is telling you that you can't cope with it. But I think you can. I think you really could ride the wildest beast in the barn if you'd just let go of your fear."

He let go of her suddenly, but only long enough for her to suck in a sharp breath. Then he was spinning her around and yanking her back into his hold, her back to his chest, his hand now running up her leg as the opposite one reacquired her breast, only this time he dove beneath her clothing to find it. She wasn't wearing panties, not having found any amongst the clothes given to her, so it was easy for him to cup her sex, thrusting his fingers into a nest of wet warmth and intimacy. She should have been horrified as he held her like that, trapped against him, a prisoner between his deftly working hands, but all she was was stunned and aroused. One hand was molding her breast, tickling and tugging her nipple, while the other found her clitoris and toyed with it in bold, blatant circles. Together they formed a perfect line of heat, stimulating her vulnerable body until it was practically split down the middle with unexpected pleasure. All the while she could hear him breathing hotly against her ear, feel his incredible arousal against her backside as he pulled her tightly close to himself.

"Oh, so passionate," he whispered against her ear, almost in time with every purposeful swirl of his fingers. He burrowed his face against her hair even as his fingers burrowed into her warm, vulnerable folds. Kathryn was speechless, overwhelmed and paralyzed by his hold on her. She thought that she should be screaming, that she should be beating the hell out of him or something very much like that, but all she could do was gasp as warm slivers of excitement peppered her body from every point of contact he had achieved. "I bet you'd taste of a most exquisite arousal, Kat," he murmured. "Shall I see?"

Before she could answer one way or another, he pulled his hand free of her and she watched with fascination as he slowly drew his wet fingertips across his bottom lip. Then he licked it leisurely, obviously savoring the taste, his forest green eyes dark and hooded with pleasure. As Kathryn watched, he released a low, predatory growl, making her heart-beat quicken, as any creature's might when faced with an unpredictable and savage animal bigger and most certainly badder than itself. Who could have known that under all that brooding silence there was something so dangerously sexual?

It was enough to make a girl go very weak in the knees.

For that matter, so was the wall of muscle she was being held against. Frustratingly, she felt like she was facing in the wrong direction. She couldn't touch him in return while facing this way. Though she could never be as bold as he had been with her, she might at least like to run her hands over some of those tightly sculpted muscles across his huge chest or perhaps even his shoulders and arms. Maybe even get a handful of one of those rock-hard ass cheeks on his superior butt.

Kathryn scandalized herself with the sheer wantonness of her thoughts and her erotic permissiveness to his bold intrusion of her body. She had never allowed anyone to touch her so intimately. Not that there'd been a whole hell of a lot of choices for her living out in the back of beyond on the family ranch, but still . . .

She should be kicking up a storm, fighting his hold and protesting at the top of her lungs. Instead her insides were writhing with heated longing, wishing he'd touch her some more, craving it so badly she thought she might scream if he didn't.

As if he'd heard the desperation in her thoughts, Adrian burrowed his face against her ear and growled low in his throat. "Yes," he breathed against her, sending chills scooting down her skin, "you want more. I can feel it."

She did want more, she thought with a blush. He was right. But how was it he could be so utterly certain of it? What was more intimidating was that he immediately reached to cup both of her breasts in his big palms and began to mold them in strong, tight pulls. At the same time he was crushing her harder into his body, making sure she felt every inch of him. His thigh pressed between her legs, coaxing her to give him entrance, but she was too distracted by the thrills of sensation radiating through her body from the points of her nipples, which he was alternately abrading with his roughly callused hands and tugging and pinching gently with his fingers. It was strange, but she got the impression he was forcing himself to be gentle, as if he was not used to handling delicate things. The almost brutish way he'd handled her so far would certainly attest to that. But if she had to admit it to herself, she liked it. She liked understanding that he was barely in control of himself because of how she was making him feel. It was a powerful female feeling, one that every woman craved.

Then she felt his teeth on the back of her neck, opening wide just at the juncture of her shoulder, scraping the area again and again in erotic gnaws of attention. It was as though he wanted so badly to sink those teeth into her, but civilization was holding him back.

Barely.

The sounds erupting from deep in his chest were primal and rough.

"Mine."

The word ejected out of him as if he couldn't control it. Nor did he control the way he gripped her, his nails biting into her and making her gasp at the small pain. When had his nails grown so sharp? And what did he mean by "mine"? She wasn't his. She wasn't anybody's. Just her family's. Nobody else wanted her. And even if they did, she was trapped where she was, helping her father raise her younger sister and manage the ranch. There was no escape from her responsibilities. As much as she wanted to run with the fantasy of letting powerful arms sweep her away from all her troubles and the weight of what was expected of her, it wasn't going to happen.

Abruptly she wrenched herself out from under his secure grip. It took a few clever twists of her body, but she eventually ducked under the hands that reached to resecure her and backed several steps away. She readjusted her dress and smoothed a hand over her hair as she raised her chin and faced him down. She tried to pretend she wasn't embarrassed by the liberties she had allowed him to take with her body.

"I-I'm not yours," she stammered, scrubbing at the flush she knew was coursing over her cheeks. "I'm not anyone's."

"Untrue," he argued as he stepped up closer to her again, invading her personal space with his overwhelming presence and the deeply male scent of him. He reeked of the vast outdoors, horses, and just pure animal male. "Your family has possession of you in a way you cannot seem to break free of. And you are unhappy about it."

"Now see, how do you know that?" she demanded to know. "I didn't tell anyone that!"

"But it's true, is it not?"

"That's not the point!" she cried, flustered by his interest in this part of her life.

"Oh, but I think it is the point. Deny me rights to you if you will, but do not sit here and claim no one else holds your leash. Your family has you caged like a pretty little parrot, doing and saying everything they expect of you. You'd have more freedom with me."

"I don't even know you!" she exclaimed.

"Does that truly matter? Wouldn't anything be better than being somewhere that crushes your spirit so thoroughly?"

"No," she said through a suddenly tight throat. "I love my family and they love me. I have responsibilities—"

"You have taken over as your father's wife. The only thing he doesn't expect of you is to fuck him. All the rest, however, he demands you do perfectly and without complaint. And you do it well. You do it with sweet patience. But I know what lies in your heart. You cannot lie to me, Kat. You cannot hide. I see everything inside your heart and mind."

"How?" she uttered in complete and total shock. How could this stranger know the deepest secrets of her heart? Even her own family had no idea she wished for escape in the worst way. In her fevered delusions she had even made up the idea of a horrible beast granting her wishes. As if she would do anything to be free, even submitting to the whims of such a vile creature.

But that had just been a transfer of one prison for another. Perhaps it all had been an expression of her subconscious, a deep internal reflection of just how lashed down and trapped she felt day after day after day.

But that still didn't explain how Adrian knew so much about it.

"Adrian."

Aerlyn's voice was stern as she stood several feet behind them. They both turned to look at her, her long black hair whipping in the wind as it wound freely down her body. Adrian immediately tensed, as if he were a boy being called to task for doing something wrong, and his entire face darkened with a mix of irritability and resignation. He looked back at Kathryn as if he hated the idea of leaving her in any way, and Kathryn couldn't help the hot blush that raced over her in spite of her confused thoughts and emotions. She had a thousand questions and uncertainties, but it seemed her body was quite sure of itself and what it wanted. And it seriously craved the idea of being back in Adrian's hands.

Adrian gave a soft, short growl of frustration before he turned on his heel and marched off in Aerlyn's direction. Maybe her eyes were playing tricks on her, but she could swear the brother gnashed his teeth at the sister as he passed her. If he did, she made no sign she cared about it in the least. Instead, she beckoned softly to Kathryn.

"Come, it's time you were resting again," she said.

*   *   *

Adrian snarled fiercely at his sister, his fists clenching with the effort not to strike her again for keeping him from his precious treasure. She might be trying to force him to give her up, but he certainly didn't have to like it, and he wasn't going to waste his remaining time with her by pussyfooting around things. He was overwhelmed by the way she had responded to him. He had never expected she would . . . but then again, she hadn't realized she was being touched by a monster. He could never have attempted anything close to that in his real form without ensuring she'd scream the world down on them all.

The thought made him even angrier and he knew his sister could sense that because she took a cautious step back away from him.

"You cannot accost the girl in such ways!" she scolded him fiercely. "And you cannot tell her things that are in her mind that she has not spoken aloud. You are going to ruin the protection of the dream!"

"I don't give a damn," he bit out. "This dream was not my idea! I don't know why I ever agreed to go along with it!"

"Because you know that there would be consequences to your actions far harsher than me scolding you if we do not get her back to her home seamlessly, without her realizing just how real we are! How real *you* are."

"I like that I feel real to her. She is not afraid of me when I touch her." He rumbled with appreciation, the sound accenting the expression on his face and hands that reached out as if they were ready to grasp Kathryn once again.

"That is only because she doesn't know your true face, Adrian," she said as gently as she could, trying to remind him that this was all illusion no matter how they sliced it. "If she did, she would be repulsed and would run away as frightened as ever from you. You know that. Why are you making this so difficult?"

Adrian clenched his fists, wanting to scream at her what was so obvious to him. Why wasn't it obvious to her? Kathryn was his! Body and soul, she belonged to him, and the more he touched, the more painful it all became, the more certain he was of his choice. Just the way she had responded to him had convinced him of it. But nothing he said was going to make Aerlyn see that truth. His sister was determined to take Kathryn away from him. And as far as he was concerned, that made her the enemy. One that he had to defeat at all costs.

He worked up a tight-lipped smile.

"I will not make it difficult any longer," he said.

The capitulation made his sister wary. She loved her brother with all of her heart, but she didn't trust him as far as she could spit, and that wasn't very far at all. *Tomorrow*, she thought. *This all must end tomorrow.* For some reason Kathryn's presence alone was like tormenting a savage dog with a treat, dangling it in front of his nose, yet yanking it away every time he got close to it. Eventually, the dog would lose patience and get to the snack no matter what, even if it meant biting off its master's hand. But with the heart of a sister it was hard to suspect the worst of him all the time. She didn't trust him, but she wanted to so badly. She had once trusted him with everything and anything. He had been a valiant and powerful spirit of honor and goodness. She had to believe that those parts of Adrian still existed. That they would one day return.

She moved closer to him, reaching to wrap her arms around him. In an explosive rejection, he pushed her off and away.

"Keep your pity to yourself!" he roared at her. "I am sick to death of it! I have never asked for your simpering solace, nor have I any need for it!"

With that, Adrian stormed away from her before he was tempted to strike her again or before he lost all control of his temper. But instead of finding his horse and riding it until his temper cooled, he searched for Kathryn. Damn Aerlyn to hell and back. He was going to spend as much time with her as he could, whether his sister liked it or not. It was true that sometimes when this mental form of touching happened he could feel his real body flashing briskly with pain, but it was getting easier to bear and he was driven to find a way past the pain and into her graceful, trembling little hands.

He knew exactly where she was. He was aware of every detail of the world they held together with their skills and power. He had to be. Nothing could fail or be flawed, or their butterfly in this jar would see it for what it truly was—mere illusion.

What surprised him as he stood over her in the living area some time later was that she was asleep. No doubt having a dream within a dream. That was a nuance Aerlyn would be taking care of. He wanted to shake her awake and demand she interact with him, but he stayed himself as he stared at the sleeping softness of her perfect features. Her full lips had parted with the depths of her sleep, her breathing deep and rhythmic. For a moment he thought she might give off a delicate little snore. If she had, he would have marveled at Aerlyn's attention to the smallest details. As it was, she had a superfine blush on her exposed cheek and a strand of misplaced hair that kept trembling like a bowstring every time she exhaled.

Watching her now as though she'd cast a paralyzing enchantment on him, Adrian noted the fetal position she was curled up in, her arms crossed under her breasts and her knees folded tight to her chest as if she were freezing cold. There was, in fact, a large window open nearby, and a cool breeze blew in and out, lifting the curtain and carrying with it the sound of gently toned bells. His sister had created wind chimes along all points of the house, a way of covering up mistakes in noise should they forget some detail. Creating a dream from scratch to the point of convincing the dreamer it was absolute reality was like creating an epic film that would run for two days. But they were responsible for every part of it, from set dressing to sound design to special effects, and even continuity. All of it. It was exhausting, and after this he and his sister were going to need a lot of rest and a lot of energy to feed from.

How they were going to explain the gap in their delivery of dream energy to the Ampliphi was anybody's guess. He supposed his clever sister would think of something. He could come up with something too, if he gave a damn. But he didn't. The only thing he gave a damn about right now was himself and his beautiful little Kat.

Adrian couldn't help staring at her as she slept. Her long, graceful neck was exposed in such a way that her pulse could be seen. Suddenly his tongue itched to feel the thrum of it against his taste buds. Her hip was pronounced as she lay on her side, the curve of true womanliness that led into a juicy backside making his mouth water.

Initially he had planned to only keep his treasure, to literally place her on a pedestal and admire her again and again for the perfection he saw in her. He had not thought much past the urge to take her when it had fallen on him, but now he'd had time to contemplate this precious creature that his sister said he could not have, that he had to give back. Everything about that idea felt wrong to him. And he wasn't standing there in a haze of rage and stupidity, letting it cloud his thinking. In fact, he had not felt such true clarity in many, many years.

She was a fighter, and in her heart she yearned for great adventure. He could give that to her. More than she'd ever dreamed. Unfortunately, it would mean she could never see her family again. But she would get over that, he thought with a dismissive nod.

It was the alternative that could not be tolerated. Let her go? Let her fade away into obscurity in a world that didn't appreciate the first thing about her, a world full of people who could not see the wondrousness of who she was or relish the innocence inside her?

No.

Adrian couldn't stomach the way it made him feel just to think of it. So yes, the more he thought on it, the more clear his purpose of mind became. He was sorry for what must come and all the pain it would cause, but his soul screamed at the idea of leaving her behind, and he could not tolerate it. Even now he wanted to roar with fury at the feelings it garnered, but he didn't want to do anything that would draw attention to what he was about to do.

Aerlyn must not be made aware until the last possible second.

Adrian's consciousness transferred out of the dream and into his real body. He took a deep, silent breath at the change, then looked around. He was in the environs of his mirror just as his sister was in the environs of hers. They could not cross into each other's mirrors without causing themselves excruciating pain. Hers was a focus of all that was good and light; his—well, his was truly the stuff of nightmares. As good and clean as Aerlyn was, she couldn't mentally or physically cope with the heavy blackness of his mirror.

And the only way Kathryn could safely do so was through her own nightmares.

So while they manipulated the dream world, they stayed in their respective mirrors and Kathryn's physical body lay on a stone table directly between the two rooms they used. When he saw her there curled up in a fetal position and shivering, he cursed himself and his sister. The stone had leached all the warmth from her body and she must be freezing. Cronos had been refused permission to touch her or to even come near her. Otherwise he might have thought to throw a blanket on her. But there was no telling with Cronos. The little mongrel might have sat there enjoying every minute of Kat's suffering. The very idea broiled Adrian with flames of anger.

Wait . . . wait . . . softly, now. Do nothing to attract attention or you will lose her forever.

Telling himself this forced him to calm down and control himself, something he never would have done before, never even would have been capable of. But Adrian didn't mark the change in his control. He just used it as he planned to betray both of the women currently in his life. He walked up to the stone table and peered down at his deeply sleeping treasure. She would not awaken because of the sleeping spell she was under. It was part of his and Aerlyn's powers, the ability to draw people deeper and deeper into sleep. Now he checked her and felt the theta waves of her deepest sleep state rolling over him like a blanket. Then he reached out and ringed one clawed hand beneath her neck and shoulders and the other under her knees.

Then he carried her to his mirror, and without a moment's hesitation he stepped through.

The darkness of the portal lashed at his goodhearted burden with stinging, painful power. It wanted to suck the white and light out of her, wanted to destroy the innocence. Like trying to nibble on a food it was allergic to, it nibbled at Kathryn. The agony jolted her out of her sleep, as he'd expected. She gasped as the pain rode through her, but she screamed when she saw his face and realized he was holding her.

"It's just a dream. It's just a dream. *It's just a dream!*" she said hastily to herself, squeezing her eyes shut.

"This is no dream, Kat," he rumbled at her. "This is the beginning of a new life. For both of us."

Her eyes flew open and she gaped at him, staring into his eyes for the longest moment. Then, "*Adrian?*" she asked, her voice crossing between horror and fear.

Adrian was surprised she had identified him. He no longer carried any traits of his former self, of the man she had eagerly let touch her. And for a moment, Adrian was jealous of himself. She would never react so hotly for a monster like him. She might always want the handsome man who had once been but was now gone.

"How did you know?" he asked gruffly.

"Your voice. Your *eyes*." Kathryn was astounded she hadn't recognized it before. Or perhaps she had and her mind had dismissed it because she couldn't process the concept. If this was another nightmare, why was she demonizing Adrian? He had done nothing wrong. Not unless giving her those wild moments of pleasure was wrong. And she didn't think that at all. Didn't feel it in her heart. So why this nightmare version of the man?

"This is not a dream," he told her gravely. "This

is the reality. I am sorry to be the one to tell you this."

And as he said it, he stepped out of the mirror. But instead of stepping into her world, the earthly plane, he stepped into his.

The plane they called Beneath.

Chapter 6

The room they'd been in a moment ago had been more like being out of doors, Kat thought, when it was the dreariest of days. It was that combination of heavy grays and barely blue skies, only there had been no skyline. That color had surrounded them completely, like a rolling bank of dense fog. But then a moment later he was stepping free of it, not through an obvious doorway or anything she could see at first, just a step that took them from one room into the next.

This new room was like pitch all around them, except for . . .

No, Kathryn thought, she had to be seeing things. Or dreaming them. Yes. Definitely dreaming. Before her was an arced table, too high for her to see the surface, and seated at it were six beings, most of whom were made purely of light. Like ghosts. She could see through five of them as they all, one by one, lifted their eyes to stare at her.

"Adrian," one intoned deeply, "what is the meaning of this?"

"He has brought a human here," one of the females said with obvious surprise.

"Adrian, you had better explain yourself, and quickly. We've no patience for this kind of misbehavior. You have not been given leave to bring any human women across the planes."

The more they disdained his actions, the tighter his grip grew on her body. It reached a point where she squeaked out a sound of pain because his fingers were pinching at her so hard. Of course, there was also an element of fear included in it as she felt the pain. If this were a dream, would she feel pain so sharply?

"Wait," another said, but instead of being a ghost, this one was as real and solid as she was. He stood from his high seat and leaned forward to peer at her more thoroughly. "Can you not sense the energy aura on her? It's overwhelming."

Now they all seemed to take new interest in her, and as they narrowed their translucent eyes on her, she began to feel like a butterfly pinned to a board.

"Have you brought us a gift, then, Adrian?" one of them asked, almost proudly. As if his son had come home from a hunt with a mighty trophy. "Let us see your treasure more closely."

"No!" Adrian's voice was savage, barely human, just like the rest of him. "This is my treasure and mine alone!"

"Hey!" Kathryn shouted as his grip tightened to punishing levels of pain. "I'm no one's damn treasure!" She tried struggling against his hold on her, but she'd known even before she started that it wasn't likely she'd make any headway against his brutal strength.

"Explain yourself, Guardian," the same male as before boomed out in a terrible and now angry voice. "You do not dictate to the Ampliphi, Guardian, but you follow its rules and dictates. You were not given leave to seize a human female."

"She is mine. Mine."

It was as though he couldn't say anything else except to lay claim to her over and over. Kathryn didn't know who to be afraid of more, the ghosts or the beast who held her.

"Adrian." The solid male spoke up again, this time much more gently, as if he were coaxing a wild creature to come closer. "Why don't you explain to us why you are here and why you have brought this woman with you?"

"I have a better idea," Kathryn snapped. "Why don't you let go of me so I can march my ass back home!" She reached out and pressed both hands against his chest, struggling for her freedom like a fly in amber. But it was utterly useless.

"I am come to retire from my position so I may take my leisure with a mate." Kathryn heard the words with disbelief, but more amazing was that he cleared his throat as if he were unsure of something. Well, he should be unsure, damn it, because she was nobody's mate, especially not the mate of this monster who'd stolen her from her family and her life!

"Are you telling us this woman is *kindra* to you?"

Rennin demanded the answer with no lack of disbelief dripping from his words and expression.

Adrian's mentor was shocked by his audacity and the sheer unlikelihood that something as twisted and dark as he was would ever be deserving of something as precious as *kindra*.

But Adrian had not considered the question of *kindra* before the Ampliphi had mentioned it. He stood there blinking and trying to remember what he knew of the connection of *kindri* to *kindra*. It was supposed to be overwhelming, soul deep and irrepressible. The male was often driven to extremes to capture and cleave the female to his side. And wasn't that what he had done? From the very moment he had seen her? Her pull on him had been an overwhelming thing; it still was. Even as he stood there in front of the panel of his people's leaders and faced down their displeasure and disbelief, his body was raging with need and demand. All he could think of was taking her somewhere so he could be alone with her. He wanted to explain what was happening so she would not be frightened. He wanted to touch her and woo her in sweet and rough ways until she learned to ignore the filth of his outside appearance and saw only the image of the man he once had been. If that was what she truly desired, he would struggle to find a way to be that man once more. No matter what it took. No matter how long he had to try.

"Yes," he said, sealing his fate. "She is *kindra* to me." And he knew a sense of real and terrifying fear when he said it. He had just put his entire life on the line by saying so. Anyone who falsely claimed *kind* was punished with death.

He would have to make it the truth.

"Will you put me down!" Kathryn barked suddenly as she kicked her feet and twisted her body. Her contortions slipped her free of his hold and she slid down the length of his body as both his hands clamped down on her shoulders to hold her tightly to him. She was facing the Ampliphi, straining toward them. "Listen, I don't know what the hell is going on around here, but you can't just let this beast kidnap me and manhandle me! Do something! Make him let me go!"

She kicked back into his shin for good measure, disappointed when he didn't make a single sound of pain. He was so big she was probably no more significant to him than a mosquito. But she felt better for doing it, just the same. At least she felt like she was fighting to get free instead of falling for tricks or crying like an idiot. She might not be the strongest or bravest woman in the world, but she had her moments. And now that she had seen Adrian with a more human face, she found she wasn't as overwhelmingly frightened of him as she had been the first time she had seen him. Now he didn't even look half as scary as he had before, bulging body and claw-tipped fingers aside. What was scary, though, was that he was laying some kind of medieval claim on her ass as if she were a prime piece of livestock, and the six beings in front of her were just humming and nodding about it as if it made perfect sense to them!

"We are sorry," the one who looked like a normal man spoke up. He was actually pretty damn handsome if she thought about it, but she wasn't in the mood to admire the scenery. "Unfortunately, we cannot let you leave here. No human being who comes Beneath can be trusted to leave and never speak of what they have seen."

"B-but I haven't seen anything!" she exclaimed, trying to ignore the fact that glowing, see-through people qualified as anything. "I don't know anything about where I am! I wouldn't have even known what it was called if you hadn't said anything!"

"You came through a portal to this world, and that is enough," he said regretfully. "As I am sure Adrian intended, you are beholden to this plane for the rest of your life no matter what else may come afterward. Here you are and here you must stay. That is the law here and there is no changing it."

"But . . ." She said the word so softly, unable to help the sudden tears of shock and dismay that filled her eyes. "What about my family?"

"Are you wed, with children?" he demanded, flicking hard eyes up to Adrian.

She wanted to lie and say yes, grasping on to the hope that it would change their minds and let her go home. But Adrian knew the truth about her family, and she knew with a sinking sense of dread that he had no intention of letting her go back to them.

"No, she is not." Adrian answered for her when she couldn't bring herself to speak the words that would seal her fate. "She is innocent of men."

Kathryn gasped and her entire face and chest heated with embarrassment as they all leaned forward as though to check out the freakish little virgin. How the hell had he known that?

"You didn't have to tell them that!" she hissed at him, trying to hide her face under anything she could. "How did you know?"

"I've always known," he rumbled in her ear. "I know anything you dream of."

That only made her blush deepen so darkly it was a wonder her face didn't catch fire. She closed her eyes with a mortified moan.

"Then perhaps you cannot be trusted with something so delicate and precious." One of the females spoke up at last—finally, someone taking her side in this mess! Her eyes flew open and she fixated on the speaker. She was so beautiful that, had she been solid flesh and blood, it might have been painful to look at her. Next to the planes of her gorgeous face, the long snake of thick hair over statuesque shoulders, and the fullness of lips that would give Angelina Jolie a proper showdown, Kathryn suddenly felt very dumpy and small. "It is no secret that your work in the nightmare realm has corrupted you deeply, Adrian. You are more beast than the man you once were. Even if she is *kindra*, I am afraid you cannot be trusted not to hurt her."

As if on cue, Adrian's grip on her tightened to agonizing levels, mostly because his claws had punctured her clothes and were now pressing deeply into her skin.

"You cannot and will not take this away from me," he snarled at them. "I have the right to my *kindra* no matter what I am! I gave up the man I was in order to serve you and our people's needs. I sacrificed everything to give you what you needed!" His teeth gnashed above her head and she could sense his control slipping more and more. In the end, he would prove them right.

Kathryn didn't know why she did it, but she brought a hand up to cover one of his, trying to soothe him with her touch. It wasn't until she felt him stiffen sharply that she remembered her acts of pity and kindness caused him physical agony.

But this time he didn't react as strongly as before. In fact, whatever he felt must have been like a bracing slap in the face. He eased his painful hold on her. She exhaled with relief. She didn't want to be taken away from Adrian and thrust into an unknown future. At least she knew how to handle him if she needed to. It was much wiser to stick with the devil she knew than to risk facing these ethereal devils she didn't. Maybe it was the most insane idea she'd ever had, but she didn't want to leave him.

And besides, if this was some kind of governing body over him, if even one thing went wrong she could run screaming to them, couldn't she? She was half convinced this was all a dream anyway. Soon she'd wake up and . . .

Oh, who the hell knew where she'd be the next time she woke up.

"I want to stay with Adrian . . . f-for now," she said, her voice becoming less confident as she went. She could tell by the shock and surprise on their transparent features that it was the last thing they had expected her to say. Added to it was the way Adrian caught his breath in obvious disbelief.

She didn't blame them. She had to be out of her mind.

"Very well, Adrian. You may return her to your

home in the Barrens. We will assign Aerlyn to watch over you, to watch over every moment of your treatment of your *kindra*. If you slip in even the smallest way or come even close to harming her, we will take her from you where you can no longer do so and she will serve the needs of our people."

"Never," he spat. "I will never let that happen."

"Then see to it you treat her well." The female spoke again. "And remember, you have very little time before you must prove she is what you claim she is. Although I think in this instance we will extend your deadline due to the . . . circumstances." She shook her head and it was more than clear by her expression that she didn't think he would succeed at whatever this proof positive was. "You have a week. No more. We will not be this flexible in any other way."

"I understand," he gritted out between tight teeth, obviously working hard at containing the rage Kathryn could see was in his eyes.

"Then go. We will see you back here in a week."

There was a backhanded gesture of dismissal and Adrian bent to scoop her from her feet. He turned with her and she watched as he stepped up to and then through the creepiest-looking mirror she'd ever seen in her life.

Rennin turned and glared sulkily at his counterparts. Julian ignored him at present and instead confronted the female who had done all of the talking.

"Sydelle, what game are you playing?" he demanded to know. "You know as well as I do that the girl is much too fragile to withstand Adrian in his present state. You may as well have sacrificed her life on an altar!"

"What's done is done," Sydelle said with a careless shrug. "No use arguing over it."

"There is a use. I want to know what you are playing at!"

"None of us believes for a moment that Adrian has found his *kindra*," she scoffed. "*He* doesn't even believe it. But he came here with the claim all the same, knowing the consequences of his actions. If that is the case, why shouldn't we oblige him? Face facts, my fellow Ampliphi, Adrian has been becoming more and more volatile as time has passed. He is a monster we let loose in the nightmare plane and he is growing more reckless and more out of our control every passing day. If he wants to hand us the method of his own destruction, then why shouldn't we let him?"

"Because that monster used to be a man," Julian said. "A friend to many of us. He is what he is only because we asked him to make that sacrifice for us. Now you want to murder him for it?"

"Our wants and desires mean little," Sydelle remarked. "He came to us, remember? He came with this claim of *kindra*. I have even been so kind as to give him extra time in which to prove the claim. He—"

"Could rip that innocent girl to shreds!" Julian burst out.

"Are you saying he doesn't deserve the right to prove *kindra*? You had your chance and proved Asia was your *kindra*, why would you deny it to another man?" Rennin asked crankily. "Is it because he is *my* Guardian that you think he should be denied?"

This remark made all the heads of the Ampliphi turn in unison to face Julian. It was well known that Julian held Rennin in some measure of contempt for his coldhearted ways. But Rennin's sudden benevolence toward his Guardian didn't ring true. Julian put narrowed eyes on the other Ampliphi, trying to figure out what his game was.

"He is no longer your Guardian," Julian reminded him. "He has just retired his position. I no longer have to hold that against him," he added smugly.

The barb visibly rankled the more powerful Ampliphi.

"This is mere academics," Rennin volleyed tightly. "*Kindra* or no, Adrian cannot pull off a mating with that fragile little human. He will fail either way. That will open the way for me to train a new Guardian and rid us of this encumbrance once and for all."

"Rennin, he just retired! There's no need to obliterate him in order for you to train a new Guardian!" Julian protested. "You're free to do that now."

"And what, Julian?" Sydelle broke in. "Are we supposed to let Adrian run around freely the way he is? Let him come back to his village Beneath? He could never reintegrate with mainstream society. Even if this girl was his *kindra*, even if she somehow miraculously survived his monstrous attentions, it wouldn't change the facts. There is no place in *any* world for a creature like Adrian."

* * *

Adrian stepped through the mirror once more and brought them into his dank workshop. He suddenly wished it was lighter and drier, something worthy of his fine treasure. Instead it was the same dark hole it had always been; in truth, the way he'd always preferred it before now. He'd held no love for his work from the beginning, and then, as it had taken him over, it had reflected in every other corner of his existence. With one exception. His treasures. Even his treatment of his beloved sister had fallen to the wayside under the darkness of what he must do every night, but the one true beauty and one pristine thing he'd held pure in his life had been that room full of baubles and one-of-a-kind items that no one saw but him.

And Cronos.

He thought of the little toady instantly because he was standing in the circle of torchlight awaiting them. The minute she saw him, Kathryn gasped and flung her arms around Adrian's neck, clenching him tightly. He might have enjoyed her hold on him, but it was tainted by his knowledge that she did it out of fear. She remembered that Cronos had brutally struck her . . . and that *he* had allowed it to happen.

"Cronos, what are you doing here?" he demanded of the underling.

"Awaiting your pleasure, Master." He bowed so low he scraped against the floor, head and shoulders tucked down in total submission.

"I have no need of you! Never come unless you are called. And you are never to come within sight of Kathryn again. If she ever reports to me she has seen you, that will be the end of you!"

Cronos never stopped kowtowing to his Master as he moved back and away, the shadows swallowing him up. Adrian could feel the fine, continuous tremors running through Kathryn and instinctively he squeezed her tightly to himself. But he was as gentle as he could possibly manage, unwilling to hurt her as he already knew he had done in Justice Hall while the Ampliphi had challenged his claim to her. He didn't know how to keep himself under control from one moment to the next, his volatile nature taking the reins much too often. In the past he would have indulged in that gladly, but now there was Kat's safety to be considered. He had to stop hurting her.

To the end of caring for her, Adrian left the morbid little room he worked from and carried her upstairs, just as he had when he had first captured her. Only this time she was wide awake and alert and he felt her looking around with interest as they went. But he barely made it to the first floor before Aerlyn confronted him, stepping in his path, her eyes snapping with anger and her face etched with betrayal.

He heard Kat gasp with surprise as she saw Aerlyn in her true form and not the watered-down version they had provided for her in the dream they had tried to trick her with. His sister was stunningly beautiful in any form, but more so in this true rendition. Plus, the black curtain of her hair was peppered with stars that winked and glimmered with her every movement. It was something about the dream dimension she worked in and the goodness of the dreams she manufactured that made it so. It didn't happen to him, only to her, and that was what told him the nature of her work made all the difference. It was a unique effect that only added to her beauty.

And even in her anger with him she was breathtaking. Gorgeous and good, from top to bottom. And normally, in the past, that thought would have been enough to enrage and frustrate him. She was ever a reflection of what he *wasn't* anymore, and it infuriated him no end. And while he still felt that frustration, perhaps even more so now that he wanted so badly to be worthy of the creature he held in his arms, he was able to grit his teeth together and resist the urge to rage at his sister.

"Adrian! What have you done?" she demanded, her hands clamping onto her hips, her chest rising and falling with the fury of her breaths.

"I have taken her to the Ampliphi and made claim of *kindra*," he said flatly.

Aerlyn gasped, her hand flying to her mouth in shock and dismay. "But she isn't your *kindra,* Adrian! Why would you say that? If you lay false claim to a woman, you will—"

"Who says she isn't *kindra* to me?" he interrupted her sharply. "You? What do you know of what I feel?"

"I know you are no longer capable of feeling the way you should with a *kindra!* You wouldn't know your mate if she came up and bit you on your ass! And I don't think fate would ever be so cruel to any woman as to saddle her with someone so irreversibly damaged, so deep down to the soul tainted as you are!"

"Put me down," Kathryn whispered.

"No," he said. "Do not listen to my sister's ranting. She does not believe I can be better. I will prove to you that I can be." He turned his head so he could look down into her soft gray eyes. He felt her trembling in fear, the look of doubt in her eyes stinging him. He had given her so much cause to be afraid of him. How was he ever going to fix that if his own sister wouldn't even believe him capable of it?

He looked back to Aerlyn and was surprised to see shock written across her expression. "You . . . you *want* to be better?" she asked with obvious disbelief. "Adrian, you never want to be better. You haven't wanted it for years. You gave up long ago. . . ."

"I am different now," he said with a low growl of irritation. He pushed past her and continued on up the stairs. Aerlyn was like any dog with a bone, though, and she raced up behind him, keeping to his heels the entire time.

"How are you different? The wanting isn't enough, Adrian. You and I both know you will hurt any innocent that crosses your path in the wrong way. You cannot control the rage inside you. After decades of darkness and negative emotion soaking into you, you cannot just say you are going to be different and make it so!"

"Just watch me," he said, taking the next flight.

"Don't I get any say in any of this?" Kathryn asked with a squeak.

"You had your say when we faced the Ampliphi. You chose me."

"But that doesn't mean I'm going to sit here and do everything you want me to do!" She kicked her feet out and tried to get down, but this time he was ready for her wriggling moves and he kept hold of her as he continued to march up the stairs.

"You see! You're no different!" Aerlyn accused him at his back. "You won't even listen to her wishes!"

"Shut up!" he roared at his sister, dropping Kathryn suddenly on her backside on the landing so he could backhand his annoying sibling. She ducked just in the nick of time and his knuckles punched through the plaster on the near wall with his momentum. He freed himself with a yank and a roar, facing off against his sister and her now-smug expression. Blood and anger were rushing through his head and he could hardly hear, but he had heard Kat gasp at his actions. Realizing what he had done, he whirled around to look at her.

As his hulking height and hostility flowed in her direction, Kathryn hastily scooted back away from him on her hands and heels until her back bumped into the next set of stairs. He reached out beseechingly for her, wanting to wipe away the expression of utter terror on her face, but he so hated it when she looked at him like that and he couldn't control the rush of fury that bled through him.

"Stop looking at me like that!" he roared at her. "Why must you both push me to my limits?"

"W-why are you always so angry?" Kathryn countered in a shout. "Why can't you hold your temper together for two seconds at a time here in th-the r-real world!" He could tell by her stumbling speech that she hadn't reconciled what was real and what was fantasy yet to her own satisfaction, and frankly he didn't blame her for being confused. They had done that to her. Him and his sister. "You kept your temper in the dream," she whispered.

She was right. He had managed to keep his temper in the dream. Perhaps he had been subdued by the power it had taken to maintain the world they'd created for her, or perhaps it had been his ability to ride hell-bent for leather on the horses he'd conjured for their power and magnificent speed. Adrian didn't know what the answer was. But he realized he had to find it, whatever it was, and use it to temper himself or he would never keep his sweet little treasure. She would run from him in terror anytime he turned to her and he would never have the chance to enjoy anything about her. That wasn't what he wanted.

He took a deep, drawing breath, squaring his beastly shoulders as he drew for composure. Then he exhaled steadily and held out a hand to her. She greeted the hand with an expression that asked him if he thought she was stupid or something and that she'd just as soon swim with sharks.

"Please," he said in a gentled, gravelly tone. "I promise I will not hurt you."

He heard his sister's indrawn breath of disbelief but ignored her, instead focusing solely on the wary gray eyes that were running over him in measured calculation. It was as if she was sizing up the level of threat he might pose, deciding if she should reach her hand in through the cage bars to pet the great beast within.

Slowly she reached out with shaking fingers and settled her palm against his. Adrian stifled a moan at the softly sweet sensation of her touch. He could immediately smell the jasmine scent of her as he carefully pulled her up to her feet, bringing her body up close to his own. She didn't come into voluntary contact with him and, knowing how he looked outside of the dream, he didn't blame her. But neither did she step away and yank her hand free of his hold. He would have thought she would immediately do so, expected her to withdraw in revulsion. Why wouldn't she? He was revolting in every way.

"Adrian," she said instead, her beautiful eyes glimmering and soft, "where are we?"

"We are home," he began simply. "There are many planes of existence, many worlds residing above and beneath the Earth plane that you come from. The plane we just visited is where my people are from. We call it Beneath. This place"—he lifted his free hand to encompass the fortress he and his sister shared—"is in another plane we call the Barrens. Once, very long ago, a powerful race of beings lived in magnificent cities and homes all throughout this plane. Then, one day, they were eradicated as if they'd never lived at all, and all that was left of them were those cities and homes."

"Eradicated? How?"

"No one from Beneath really knows what happened to them. Most avoid it like humans would avoid a dank graveyard. This is why it has made a good home for us."

"You mean because no one is around . . . you?" she asked carefully.

"Correct," he said honestly. "Aerlyn is my sister and also my keeper, but even she cannot contain me on occasion. It is not my choice, but it is the way that it is."

"And you expect me to not be afraid of you?" she asked with no little incredulity.

"No," he said. "I know what I am. I only hope that I will become better. There is . . . I need to become better. I feel it. For you."

She looked up at him, utterly astounded. "You can't put that on me," she protested. "I don't want to be responsible for that!"

"Wait."

It was Aerlyn who spoke up, her voice careful and thoughtful. She came around his exposed side, walking up onto the landing and behind Kathryn's back. She gently touched Kathryn's shoulder in a gesture of support as she raised her gaze to his face and searched it slowly.

"Oh my God. Adrian," she breathed, "you've changed." She had been so furious with him, so wild with emotions that she hadn't even realized it. But no one knew him the way she did. She had made herself become familiar with every grotesque feature of his face and mangled body because she had felt that she needed to know him and remind herself, every night and every day, of what his sacrifice had been. The change was nothing anyone else might have marked, but the sunken placement of his eyes had smoothed away, making the vibrancy of the green of them stand out with emotional expression that had, for once, nothing to do with rage or venom. He was merely puzzled by her declaration, just as she was baffled by the physical change. And yet, she realized, it went beyond physical. Not two days ago, if Adrian had been confronted by a problem he would have raged his way through it. Like a monstrous child throwing a tantrum, he would have destroyed half the household, but today he was expressing wants and needs in a way she hadn't heard in ever so long. He *desired* to do better. Her brother, who couldn't care less about anything other than his own gratification, cared if this girl was afraid of him or that she might or might not trust him.

Aerlyn wanted to reach out and touch his changed face, but Kathryn stood between them. Kathryn. Was this girl the reason for these changes? She had to be. What else could have accounted for it? Was she, perhaps, bringing back small pieces of the brother she loved?

Tears sprang up along with her hope. She tried to wrestle to control it, fearing she was setting herself up for disappointment, knowing there was so much trouble and danger brewing if she let Adrian take this innocent girl somewhere and let him have his head. Who knew what he might do?

But he had *changed*. She couldn't deny that. The proof was right before her eyes.

"She's right." Kathryn spoke up, reaching a touch up to the corner of Adrian's eye, exactly where Aerlyn had wanted to touch him herself. "There's something different in your eyes. Why would that be?" She turned to Aerlyn for an answer, but Adrian's sister mutely shook her head. She didn't dare voice her suppositions aloud; wouldn't dare give it voice, as if saying it would make the magic of it vanish into thin air, leaving her brother without hope once more.

Instead she reached to stroke a hand of comfort down Kathryn's hair and said, "I'm sorry we tricked you with the dream. I wasn't trying to hurt you or toy with you."

"Y-you were responsible for my dream?" she asked, bewildered and yet having seen enough things in the past hours to make a believer out of her.

"It's what Adrian and I do. Our special gifts. Our mirrors are our portals to the dream planes. Once there we can guide and manipulate the dreams within. I focus on what's good and energetic, happy dreams and dreams of fulfillment. Adrian—"

"I focus on the rest. The dark of nightmares or forbidden fantasy, the guilt of things done or the malice of things to come," Adrian explained, cutting off his sister. He had wanted to explain all of this to Kathryn at a place and time of his choosing, not one his sister had chosen.

"So . . . you both made the dream? Every part of it?"

Adrian saw a flush creep up over her neck and onto her face. He knew exactly what she was thinking of, and his body flashed hot in response to the memory. But he was hasty to add, "We merely shaped the aesthetics of it and guided it. You provided all your own free will to it and all your own . . . responses."

That final word growled out of him like a purr. Kathryn's blush deepened dramatically and Aerlyn suddenly cleared her throat.

"Well, I'm just going to go . . ." She pointed a finger downward. "If you need me for anything, Kathryn, simply call out my name and I will hear you."

Adrian watched his sister beat a hasty retreat down the stairs and one side of his mouth perked up in what could almost be considered a smile. Now that they were alone, he turned his full focus back onto Kat. Her little hand was trembling in his big paw, so delicate and nervous. She was so pink with embarrassment that it was a wonder her knuckles weren't glowing red as well. He decided to put an end to it right there.

"Do not be ashamed of your responses to me," he said. "It was what I would have done had I been the man you met in that dream. It was honestly meant and your responses were honestly come by. There is no shame in that."

"Shame?" she said through her clenched teeth. "Try *anger*, you moron!" She lashed out suddenly with her free hand, punching him hard in the chest. Hmm. He really must be changing as his sister and she claimed. He shouldn't have felt it through the thickness of his hide, and yet he did. Oh, it was rather like a butterfly landing on his nose, certainly nothing painful, but still . . . "You're a jerk! A total user and a manipulating . . . jerk!" She punched him again, but only managed to hurt herself in the process as she pulled her fisted hand back and shook it out as if in pain, muttering "ow" under her breath.

"As I said, it was honestly meant. That was the man before you now who was in that dream, and I did exactly what I would have done had it been real. The only difference between them was the look of me. You'd have never let this beast touch you like that, and that is what has you so angry."

"I—" Her mouth shut closed with a snap. What could she say? That he was wrong? They both knew it would be a lie. That he was right? She didn't want to admit to herself that she could be so shallow.

"Come, I will show you to your room."

He stepped forward but she yanked back against his hand. "You're not going to put me back in that—that *cage,* are you?"

He looked back at her, puzzled. "You'll be free to come and go as you like now. Before, I was trying to keep you secret from Aerlyn. Now she clearly knows you're here and it no longer matters."

"Please," she implored him, her big gray eyes going wide, "don't put me back in there!"

"But . . . that room holds the most exquisite treasures any of the planes have to offer. Why would you not want to sleep among them?"

"Because I don't want to be one of those treasures!"

"Well, that is unfortunate," he hissed through his teeth, "because you already are one of those treasures. That is my bed and my room and you will sleep by my side, where I can enjoy you!"

"Enjoy me?" Her already wide eyes were huge. "Do you m-mean . . . you expect me to . . ."

"No, damn you! I am no fool! I know what I am! I don't need your looks of horror to know what a monster I am. I would never force you to take me.

I may be a brute, but I am not a total fiend. You would never survive me by even the largest stretch of the imagination, and I take much better care of my treasures than that!"

He turned to the next flight of stairs, yanking her up behind him.

Chapter 7

Kathryn stumbled in his wake as she was pulled cruelly along, but she didn't make the smallest sound of complaint. She was too busy being relieved that he didn't expect her to have sex with him. Just with her imagination alone she couldn't even grasp the concept of how something like that would work. She was so relieved that she didn't even complain when he dragged her into that hateful room and flung her onto the bed. Everything was kept in such supreme order, she found it hard to believe someone so big and so full of volatile emotions had managed to never go off on any of these priceless trinkets. As she looked around at some of the fragile sculptures and fine-worked glass touched in hand-painted gold, she again wondered at how he had managed to avoid doing any damage. How was it that in some part of himself he could exercise enough control to spare his precious ornaments, and yet just now he'd nearly yanked her arm out of her socket?

She got to her hands and knees and crawled up to the head of the bed. There were a dozen plush pillows up against the headboard, each one unique in fabric or stitching or some kind of design. Kathryn had to admit that they were each lovely on their own, but as a collection it seemed a shame to even touch them, never mind sleep on them. But now she climbed on top of them, clinging to the finely etched stone of the bed, the coldness of it seeping into her fingers as she watched with wary eyes the beast who had captured her.

She couldn't believe she was there again. What had she been thinking, asking to stay with him? Oh. Right. The other choice was to stay with a bunch of ghosts. The Ampliphi, he'd called them. Creatures from another plane. Perhaps even another dimension. Alternate realities that were similar to one another in some ways and vastly differing in others. For instance, this fortress Adrian and his sister lived in. It reminded her of one of those old castles in Europe. Everything lined in marble and elegant plaster, vast spaces and curving staircases, all of a grand design. Yet nowhere in this room was there a window. The basements had been lit by torches like something out of old Dracula's castle, but here there were gas lamps smoking softly from every wall, sending flickering but steady light against every precious surface in the room.

And Adrian. A man yet not a man. Clearly he was a being with all the lustful desires of a man, but it was obvious to anyone who saw him that there was no human woman alive who could bear the brunt of his desires. They would most likely be very dark, almost, if not completely, violent. If he couldn't contain his rage from one moment to the next, how did he expect to control something as volatile as passion?

He didn't expect to. He'd said it himself. He could not and would not touch her, for fear of breaking her. Kathryn shivered, tucking her knees up tighter to her chest as she watched him prowl and pace at the foot of the bed. He ran darkly clawed hands through his hair as he chuffed and growled in short, punctuated bursts. He turned suddenly, making her gasp as those vivid green eyes pinned her in place. After a moment he went to a small lacquered sideboard, inserted a single claw in a polished ring, and pulled open the drawer in the center. He reached in and pulled out a long sheaf of liquid fabric, the length of it snaking and fluttering in his wake as he rounded the bed and came up to her.

"Put this on," he commanded gruffly.

He dropped the thing at and over her feet, the pale peach color of it almost blending with the skin on her ankles. Unable to help herself, she reached down to touch it, feeling the liquid-soft silkiness and stifling a little moan at the pleasure of how it felt. She pulled it up into her hands so she could see what it was, and it only took her an instant to realize the thin spaghetti straps and the finely worked lace bodice belonged to a night-gown. One that would cling to every curve and leave her very, very exposed. The fabric was so tissue thin and pale in color it was most certainly see-through.

"I can't wear this," she whispered, not sure if it was the immodesty of it or the tiny hand-painted leaves on the lace that made her say it. Such painstaking work surely was never meant to be worn by a simple girl from a ranch in Australia. It was meant for someone much more refined, someone who breathed rarified air and drank wine from precious bottles of reserve.

"You will wear it and any others I give you," he barked at her.

This time *she* growled, huffing out an angry breath of frustration. "So am I supposed to dress in front of you, or is it too much to ask that I get a little privacy?"

"It's too much to ask," he said flatly.

He stood at the foot of the bed watching her every action and reaction, so he couldn't have missed the lethal daggers she shot him from her eyes. Oh, if only looks could kill! Her glare right then would be poison tipped to boot!

Pressing the nightgown to her breasts for cover, she tried to keep concealed as she wriggled free of her clothing. She felt a hot blush burning up over her face as he watched her intently through every second of her struggle. She tried to gauge what he was getting out of watching her like this, but his expression was as inscrutable as everything else about him seemed to be. To cover for her shame and embarrassment, she began to talk.

"S-so you control people's nightmares?" she asked

him. "Does that mean everyone's nightmares everywhere? All at once? Or can you only do it one at a time?"

His lips twitched as she asked questions too fast to allow for answers. He fought the urge to smile because he knew it would flash her a mouthful of fangs and she hadn't proven to be very accepting of such things.

"I do not control anything. I guide what an individual person's mental energy is seeking for. I create the images and environs that will provoke the greatest response."

"You mean what will frighten them the most," she said with a frown.

"Often," he agreed. "But nightmares are not just about fear. They can be about our darkest desires as well. They express unresolved issues from the waking world. They are cathartic fantasies that generate huge amounts of energy."

"That's the second time you've talked about energy," she noted. She was struggling to figure out how to put the gown on while remaining fully covered at the same time. She had worked her blouse free, treating Adrian to flashes of a smooth midriff.

"Energy is everything," he said. "It is powerful and all encompassing. It fuels everything in the world in one way or another. Energy is the reason I do what I do. I was not born to conduct the nightmares of others, but like Aerlyn, I was born with the talent to guide dreams. Some time ago, at a time when I used to truly be the man you met in your dreams, I made the choice to work with nightmare energy and all the power of the emotions it

created. Years of indulging in this task has warped
and contorted me into the beast you see before
you."

She blinked liquid gray eyes of surprise at him,
forgetting to keep her chest covered as her hands
dropped into her lap with her shock. Her lush little
lips parted as she made a sound of disbelief and
Adrian swallowed back a groan at the tempting
sight of them. More and more he was noticing
these sweet little details about her, and more and
more he felt his desire for her growing. It didn't
seem to matter to the rest of his body that his head
was well aware she wouldn't let him anywhere near
her if she could at all avoid it.

Well, she couldn't avoid it, he thought hotly. He
would see to that. He might not be able to do anything else, but he *would* touch her.

"You mean you did this to yourself on purpose?"
she asked with disbelieving awe. "Why? Why would
you do something like that?"

"I had little choice in the end. I am a Guardian
for my people. They are starving more and more
with every day that passes, and the only way to feed
them—"

"Is with energy," she filled in for him, her tone
absent and thoughtful. "Those beings whom I met
were pure energy."

"The Ampliphi." He nodded. "Our governing
body."

"But one was solid . . . like us."

"Julian. He has not yet evolved to the point of
being able to exist as pure energy. That faded state
takes much less energy to maintain than a corpo-
real state does, so those who can prefer to remain

the way you saw them to be. Each Ampliphi has a Guardian, who is like a reaper who goes out into your emotionally energetic world and harvests energy to bring back to the Ampliphi, who then doles it out to the villages of Beneath and its peoples. We do our best, and yet our people still want."

"Because they can't exist in the energy state like the Ampliphi can?"

His mouth curled at the corner as he appreciated her quick and bright mind. He had taken her for many reasons, but he had not realized just how intelligent she was.

"Correct," he replied. "We are very sensitive to emotions of any kind. Anything will feed our hunger, but the type of energy received heavily influences us."

"Like before. When I was able to hurt you," she said in a small voice.

"Yes. Although . . ." He frowned. Should he tell her that normal people from his world suffered the opposite of what he did? Should he tell her that he now thrived on negative emotions, the darker the better, and apparently, thanks to what she had shown him, he now knew that positive emotions and kindnesses were shockingly painful? It had taken him completely off guard when it had happened. Aerlyn was everything he wasn't, light and positive and good, and she often tried to touch him—didn't she? Adrian tried to think back to the last time Aerlyn had made actual physical contact with him.

"So, this nightmare energy has clearly poisoned you," she said, her eyes running down over him like a rapid physical touch that made him tense responsively. "Wouldn't it poison your people as well?"

"The Ampliphi filter and buffer what I bring them. They dole it out evenly along with the more positive energies like what Aerlyn brings them. So by the time it gets to my people, it is a blend of many energies and not the pure knot of tainted emotions that I deal with every single night."

"Why didn't you simply get energy from good dreams like your sister does and bring back only good energies to your people? Why bother with the negative at all?"

"Because there must be balance in everything. There must be negative energy in order to enrich the positive. Only that way can my people live full lives."

Adrian reached out to grasp the footboard of the bed, needing to feel its solidness beneath his fingers, for some reason. It bothered him to speak of his people and the safe, normal lives they lived. It never had before, but now as he stared at Kathryn sitting curled up in his bed, her arms and shoulders exposed almost all the way to her breasts, he suddenly found himself craving the normalcy he could never have. He found himself craving her.

"Stand up," he commanded throatily.

Surprised by the sudden demand, she moved her hands back to the silk that was clinging to her breasts.

"B-but . . ."

"And leave the gown on the bed."

Kathryn felt heat crawl all over her skin as she realized what he wanted. She also realized she wasn't in the position to deny him anything. The last thing she wanted to do was provoke him in any way, having seen what he was capable of.

She angrily got to her feet on the bed and threw down the peachy silk creation he'd given her, exposing her bare breasts. "Just when I am starting to feel sorry for you, you have to go and act like a monstrous pig!"

"I do not ask for, nor do I want, your pity!" he snarled from the foot of the bed. But even as he tried to act the beast, she saw his eyes rivet onto her breasts with something that didn't feel so much like exploitation of her vulnerabilities. The heat creeping around her skin turned into a whole new kind of blush and she raised her arms to cover herself in her resulting confusion. "Keep your hands to your sides—unless you plan to touch yourself, Kathryn. That would please me very much."

Kathryn dropped her hands instantly, her face coloring so deeply at his suggestion that he was tempted to smile. She truly was as innocent as she had appeared. Not just in the physical state of her body, but in all things sexual. He thought about how he had touched her in the dream and immediately grew aroused and hard for her. It was a state that he could keep concealed behind the height of the footboard, so he let it rush through him as he looked his fill of her. She was still clothed from the waist down, but he was more than happy to spend his time roaming the creamy skin he could see. Her full, womanly breasts were tipped the fairest pink he'd ever seen, and he imagined they would darken considerably at a lover's touch or bite.

"Take off the rest," he ordered throatily. Oh,

Adrian knew this was a bad idea, but he couldn't seem to help himself. Maybe he wanted to torture himself, or maybe he just needed to see her, but whatever the motivation, he wanted her naked in his bed as soon as possible.

"Forget it," she snapped at him. "I'm not here to give you a free peep show! In fact, I don't know what the hell I am here for—except to be one of your precious treasures!"

"And I like to look at my treasures. I like to admire their beauty. Sometimes for hours. You are breathtaking, Kat. Let me admire you."

"I . . . I'm not breathtaking," she protested, reaching to rub her fingers over one blushing cheek. "I'm overweight and . . . and dumpy."

Was it possible she didn't realize just how stunning she was? Adrian could hardly conceive of it. How could something so beautiful have made it so long without learning of the admiration of others?

"There is nothing the slightest bit dumpy about you," he huffed, irritated by the people of the Earth plane who would let such a treasure go so unappreciated. "You are a round and curvaceous woman, proportioned perfectly to fit in a man's hands. Your lush little body would tremble and shimmy with every thrust your lover made inside you."

God, how he wanted to be that lover. He knew it was impossible, but that didn't keep him from craving it wildly. He wanted more than anything to come around the bed and reach to touch her, but he knew she would be braver if she felt there was an obstacle between them. As it was, if she blushed any deeper her cheeks were going to catch fire.

"Let me admire you, Kathryn," he repeated huskily, his forest green eyes almost imploring her to give in to his wishes.

Kathryn had never stripped in front of a man before. There simply had been nothing for her except her family and the ranch. There had been no time or opportunity for things like boys and boyfriends. Certainly nothing as intimate as a lover. Adrian and her dreams had been the only erotic experiences in her life. This one was fast entering her top three. She could see the hunger in his eyes, the tightening of his whole body as he struggled to hold himself in check. She would have to be out of her mind to give in to his wishes. It would be like dangling Brie in front of a rat. A very dangerous rat.

"Do it, Kat, or I'll come around and do it for you."

Alarm raced through every nerve ending. Allowing him that close under these circumstances—while she was naked—would be asking for all kinds of trouble. And she knew she wouldn't have a chance against him because she was so insignificant compared to his power and brute strength.

With shaking fingers she reached for the button at the waistband of her pants. Then, suddenly, she realized she was wearing something different than she had been before. It wasn't the diamond-dusted creation she'd first woken up in. These were her clothes. Clothes she'd been wearing when he'd kidnapped her.

"You've already seen everything," she realized irritably. "Why do you have to see it again?"

"Because I want to. Because it's worth seeing

over and over again. I'll never grow tired of your beauty, sweet Kathryn. And I will gladly dress you up in beautiful things and drape you with beautiful jewels and trinkets, but always there will be nothing to compare to you, naked, perfect just as you are."

Kathryn felt liquid heat swirling through the center of her body, his compliments warming her in ways she'd never felt before. How could a creature so harsh and so innately malevolent say such beautiful things? Unless . . . maybe it was because his malevolence was not innate at all. He had once been a normal man. A man who had done what he must in order to feed his starving people. He'd sacrificed all that he had once been for their sake. Now he was this warped creature who clung to unique and beautiful things in a bid to . . . to keep himself sane. To keep grounded. Perhaps to keep from going over into darkness completely in a way that would unleash an unstoppable monster on some unsuspecting population.

Realizing this had the power to change the dynamic between them almost instantly. It wasn't pity she was feeling now, but she wasn't ready to understand what it was. She couldn't put a finger on it. So, instead, she bolstered her courage and reminded herself that he'd already seen everything there was to see, and whatever his saving graces, he was still a volatile entity that could be unpredictable when provoked. She knew she had to do this or risk his temper, and she simply wasn't brave enough to take that risk.

It took less courage to strip for him.

With shaking fingers she unzipped her pants.

Then, hooking her thumbs around the waistband, she slowly eased them down over her hips. She refused to look at him as she did this, but she could feel the intensity of his gaze on her. It touched her like wild caresses and she felt her nipples tightening in response. She wished she could blame it on the chill of the room, but it was warm and comfortable and the only thing giving her chills was the unrelenting regard of the beast at the foot of the bed.

She slowly stepped out of her pants, dropping them over the side of the bed as she stayed crouched by her ankles. Then she reached for the gown.

"Not yet. Stand up first."

She had been afraid he would say that. Her temper flared and she straightened up sharply, her hands going to her hips. "Fine! There you go. Get your jollies and see if I care!"

"You do care or you would not be so angry," he mused as he looked her over. "You forgot something."

She followed his gaze to the simple pair of cotton panties she wore.

"No way. Forget it!" she snapped, stomping her foot for emphasis.

"Take them off, Kathryn. I want to see every part of you. You'll hide none of your beauty from me."

"Why?" she demanded to know. "Because you own me? Just like all your other little treasures?"

"Yes. Exactly for that reason. And because I find myself drawn to your beauty like nothing else has ever drawn me before. I must have all of you, Kat. Every bit of you I can safely take."

That sounded almost ominous, and Kathryn swallowed against a new wash of fear. What did he mean by that? Maybe she should just shut up and be grateful that he wasn't asking her to touch him or to let him touch her. At least not yet, anyway. She didn't want to strip down and tempt him into taking it further and further. But then again, she didn't see that she had much of a choice in the matter. She was helpless. She supposed she could scream for Aerlyn, but what good would that do her? It would only piss him off and make things worse all around.

So she pressed her lips together and snared her panties with her thumbs. Trying not to think about what she was doing, she shucked them free of her body and then stood up, trying to resist all the urges she had to cover herself with her hands and arms. She looked up to see him watching her, could see the tight grip he had on the footboard of the bed, and saw that his thick claws were gouging into the stone. There was something so primal about his reactions, something so purely male, that it called to the innate female inside her. Hadn't she always wished a man would look at her in that way? As though she was the only woman in the universe that mattered? There was no mistaking the devout zeal in his dark eyes. She felt, for the first time in her life, as though it wouldn't matter to him if there were a hundred supermodels stripped naked before him just then, he would still only have eyes for her.

Why, oh why, did he have to be this thing that he was?

Adrian took several deep breaths in through his

nose, but instead of calming him, it brought the jasmine-sweet scent of her into his senses, and something else as well. He could smell her distinct arousal. She might protest and deny all she wanted to, but his keen senses had found her out.

Unable to stand still any longer, he rounded the foot of the bed and walked up to face her from the side. She was nearly in the center of the bed, always trying to put as much distance between them as possible. Well, that was going to stop. As of right now.

He reached forward and snagged the silken gown, drawing it over to him, and then he reached out a single clawed finger and beckoned to her. She hesitated, and just the thought of coming closer to him made her cross a protective arm over her chest. He let her get away with it. He could still see every sweet slope of her shoulders, the warm curve of her lower spine, the gentle rounding of her belly, and the wide flare of her juicy hips. Her ass was a thing of beauty and the dark brown curls protecting her womanhood were like a mysterious lock waiting to be breached. Oh, what he wouldn't give right then to be the man he once was. He would trade away every single treasure he'd ever acquired just to be man enough to be her lover.

She came over to him in slow, careful steps, not realizing that it put sensuality in her movements, making her body curve and sway as if in seduction. When she was finally standing before him, her ripe breasts level with his mouth, he forced himself to clear his throat of its sudden tightness and said, "Kneel."

She obeyed him, kneeling like a supplicant,

making his entire body scream with savage need. But he kept tight rein on it.

"Raise your arms above your head," he said gruffly.

She did so slowly, her eyes always wary as she watched him. He gathered up the silky peach creation and then reached to drop it over her arms and head. He hated to cover her up, but he appeased himself by remembering that she would have to change again and again in the days to come, and he would see to it he was there every time. It might be a form of self-torture, but he really didn't give a damn.

The silk settled over her, sliding over her breasts the way he wanted his mouth to slide over her. But he knew she didn't want him to touch her. Not sexually, anyway. The thought pissed him off and he reached for her, his big hands encircling her waist as he drew her up against his chest. He found her ear beneath her hair and growled, "Tonight and every night you sleep with me. I will fall asleep with the smell of you in my nostrils and the feel of you alongside my body."

"B-but you said you wouldn't—"

"There are other ways I can have your affections, Kathryn," he said ominously. "But do not be afraid. I will never hurt you."

"You have before," she argued on a whisper, her hands going to his shoulders and knotting into the fabric there.

She had a point and he couldn't possibly deny it. And he really shouldn't make the promise since he was just as volatile to himself as he was to her and everyone else, but it was important to him that she trust him, and he would fight himself into the ground to keep his promise. He never wanted to harm his precious treasure.

"It will be different now," he swore to her, almost believing it himself with his newfound control lacing through him. "I will make you a bargain. If I ever hurt you again, you will be free to go from me."

"F-free? You really mean that?"

"In return," he continued, "you give me everything I ask for."

"I can't do that," she protested. "If you ask me to kill someone or . . . or something like that, I can't make that kind of blanket promise!"

"I wouldn't ask you to do that. All my requests will be reasonable, things you are capable of."

"But not necessarily things I will like," she quantified for him. "Like stripping down in front of you."

He nodded for his reply. He watched her lips thin as she suppressed her anger with him. Those gorgeous gray eyes were snapping with irritation and aggravation and her fists were clutching his shirt so tightly he thought she might rip the fabric. He wanted to smile at her, a feeling he wasn't used to having anymore, and he wondered over it. Was it possible that this lovely little creature was making him . . . *happy*?

He shook the query off. That didn't matter right now. What mattered was the feel of her against his body, the weight of her breasts against his chest, and the warmth of her that bled into him everywhere. This he wanted to feel. This was safe to feel. For now, anyway.

He reached for the first button on his shirt.

Kathryn gasped when she realized he intended to strip off his clothes as well. She backed off away from him but he grabbed her arm and made her stay where she was, only a few inches away from him as he pulled off his shirt. He knew he was exposing her to his ugliness and he could tell by the widening of her eyes what she was thinking of him, but that didn't stop him.

"Are you going to get n-n-n—"

"Naked?" he supplied when she couldn't seem to force the word out. "Yes, I am. I am sorry to expose you to the sight of me, but that is how I sleep, and that is how I want to feel you beside me. Of course, if you wish to level the playing field, feel free to remove the gown at any time."

The suggestion so flustered her that this time he did smile, from his fangs all the way to his eyes.

She caught him in the act.

"You're just saying and doing these things to upset me! You take perverse pleasure in my embarrassment."

"On the contrary. I find it charming and delightful. Your innocence is one of the most precious things about you."

"And testing that innocence delights you! You said it yourself, you would take great joy in corrupting me!"

Adrian frowned at that. "I was angry when I said that. I did not mean it. I was just lashing out at you for the pain you had caused me."

She tilted her head, regarding him through narrowed, thoughtful eyes. "Does it still?" she asked even as she reached to touch his bare skin with warm, open palms and slightly trembling fingers. "Does it still hurt you when I touch you?"

Yes. It was like being on fire from two different sources. Her tenderness sent bracing pain down his spine and all throughout his nervous system, and the touch itself was heavenly and arousing. He hadn't been touched like this in decades. He couldn't even remember the last time a woman had touched his bare skin. He would have thought he'd remember that, but he didn't. All he could think about was his clever Kat and the way it felt when her fingers rubbed warmly over him.

"In many exciting ways," he informed her with a low rumble of honesty.

The information took her by surprise, but despite that she didn't jerk her hands away. Instead, she shaped the line of tendons between his shoulder and his neck, stroking gently as she made her way to his throat. When her finger touched him there he swallowed hard, making his Adam's apple travel beneath her curious touch. He groaned softly at her kind and curious stroke as waves of pain flew through him, nauseating him even as she continued to thrill him with the contact.

"I thought you'd be all shaggy and . . . deformed. But mostly you're just bigger and bulkier than a human male." Yet even as she said it she ran her hand back over the shoulder that was deformed, the one that threw off his gait and made it almost impossible to find proper-fitting shirts. And

it ached whenever there was bad weather. But she
didn't seem to mind it much at all as she moved
her touch down to the enormous bulges of his bi-
ceps.

He hadn't expected her to explore him. It was
something he thought only to dream about. And
though he knew she didn't mean it in a sexual
manner, he could not help becoming aroused as
she went. Especially when she went back to his
chest and brushed against the dark nipples beneath his crisp hairs. She shaped the huge expanse of his rib cage, tracing the lowermost ribs
on each side. Then her fingers began to travel
down over his sectioned abdomen.

Kathryn was aware she was playing with fire, but
she couldn't seem to help herself. He had seemed
somehow so much more monstrous when she had
first set eyes on him, but with every passing moment she became less afraid of his looks. Oh, she
kept a healthy fear of his temperament, and at any
time his disposition could grow out of control, but
the ugliness that had so scared her was now reduced
to a brilliant pair of eyes the color of a mighty
jungle teeming with life and danger, and this magnificent chest that was full of awesome power and
incredible muscle.

She stole a look up at his face, the cruelty of his
lips and the pronouncement of his features not so
scary anymore. She could see his fangs beneath his
lips, their monstrous size still very intimidating.
Had he ever bitten anyone with those vicious
fangs?

Before she realized she was doing it, she touched
his lips where she saw the lump she knew was a

hidden fang. "Can I see?" she asked softly, unsure if her curiosity would enrage him.

"You can have anything you want," he breathed in a whisper softer than anything she'd ever heard from him to date. His words bolstered her courage even more and her next touch on his lip encouraged him to draw it back and expose the awesomeness of his teeth. It reminded her of looking into a lion's mouth, that was how tremendous they were. And she didn't doubt for a second that he shared the same jaw power as that mighty predator as well. She touched the pointed tip of one fang, feeling its strength.

"Is it uncomfortable for you? You didn't always have them, right?"

"Not always, no," he agreed, careful not to accidentally bite her fingers. "But I am used to them now."

And like water coursing naturally from one place to another in a stream, she flowed to his ears and their odd triangular shape. But she didn't seem to mind that oddness as she explored them carefully. He felt chills of erotic delight chasing down his body as she did so, the sensitivity of them almost too much to bear on top of the racking pain she was causing with her good intentions. He didn't understand how it could be both wonderful and agonizing all at once, but he didn't want to question it. He simply wanted to feel. It was so overwhelming and so free of anger and rage, the only things he had known for so long now.

Kathryn started when he reached up suddenly for her hand, wrapping it up in his big paw, making certain his claws didn't touch her delicate wrist as he lifted it to his mouth. He brushed his lips over her pulse there, a warm, slow movement that exposed a fang, allowing it to scrape over the skin until she was racked with shivers of sensation. They chased up her arm and into her body, making her nipples prominent beneath the silk she wore and raising a flush to her skin that had nothing to do with embarrassment. But how could that be? How could she be feeling this way toward someone . . . like him? He wasn't even human!

But there was something about the way he was struggling with himself now, the way he was fighting his own nature to treat her gently. His demands were still crude and coarse, but he really did intend to keep her safe from harm. Especially from himself.

After a long minute, Kathryn pulled her wrist away and sat back on her heels away from him. She put her hands in her lap and gave the impression that she was waiting for something.

It took all of a minute for the haze in Adrian's head to clear enough for him to realize she was waiting for him to continue undressing. He reached for his belt with great hesitation. He had been goading her before about sleeping naked with her, trying to provoke her blushes and ire. But after feeling what her touch was like on his bare skin, he couldn't conceive of what it would be like to lie next to her completely exposed . . . and *not* being touched because of her fear.

His hands worked his belt free nonetheless. Perhaps he had grown sadistic as well as vengeful in his years inside his blackened mirror, but whatever the reason, he found himself stripping off his pants almost eagerly. He was a fool. Setting himself up for—

She gasped, a hand going to her succulent mouth, hiding her vibrantly colored lips. Her stare was riveted below his belt, more specifically at his cock, and like magic it began to rise and grow all the more for her. He knew why she was so shocked. Like everything else about him, his cock was monstrous. Oh, it looked normal enough, he supposed; it was just that the size was well beyond expectation.

Adrian had been a big man before he had begun to change into what he was now; the changes had only made it worse. This was why he wouldn't dare even think of touching her with it. He'd easily rip her in two.

But it was easy to forget about things like that when he stood there under her transfixed gaze. Then, for a moment, he wondered if she had ever seen a naked man before. Not on television or in magazines, but real live and up close. When her stare continued, he was willing to think not. By then he was heavy with arousal and standing at perfect attention for her.

"Are you going to let me into bed?" he asked her hoarsely.

Kathryn didn't realize she was staring until that very moment. Now color raced to flood her features, heat quickly following, and she backed up across the fine bedspread to let him enter his bed. He lifted a corner of it and slid all that muscle and frighteningly huge male flesh between the silken sheets. Then, once he was settled, he lifted the other corner of the spread and beckoned her to join him.

Whatever nerves had been keeping her going until then quickly abandoned her. She knew she had to go or he would come and fetch her, but she was truly afraid.

He promised not to hurt me, she thought to herself, over and over, as she forced herself to crawl to his side and slide beneath the covers. She pulled the sheets up over her breasts and lay stiffly beside him, keeping a good foot of distance between them.

He made an angry sound and suddenly his arm lashed around her middle and he yanked her up against himself. She squeaked in protest as he pressed her back to his chest, her bottom snuggling up against that enormous male member and his heavy leg insinuating itself in between hers.

"Fear not," he hissed in her ear. "This monster is exhausted from the dream of normalcy he tried to give you for days. I'm too tired to be the bastard I know you think I am." He pushed her head onto the pillow. "Sleep. I won't be in your dreams today."

Chapter 8

Kathryn didn't think she would be tired since, in essence, she'd been asleep for days. That proved to be wrong eventually, but for at least an hour or two she lay there spooned up against him and was left with her own thoughts. The first was the same as always. How had she gotten into this mess? Why her? Of all the millions of women in the world, why had he chosen her? Was she just cursed, or was she somehow lucky? She had to admit, this had been quite an adventure so far. How many times had she longingly wished for the freedom to go off on some kind of adventure? Of course, she had always thought it would take the shape of going to the States or something. She could never have imagined this in even her wildest . . .

Dreams. He was some kind of sandman, only he'd been cursed to experience only the worst of the worst that the human subconscious could create. It had fed him pure evil for year after year as he held on to provide the energy his people desperately needed. It wasn't his fault he was the way he was. He was a byproduct of something he couldn't control.

Why was he holding on to her so tightly, though? It was obvious she caused him great pain whenever they touched, as long as she wasn't angry with him, that is. Why would he want to subject himself to that over and over again? Was he some kind of sadist? She thought back to the enormous erection she'd been mesmerized by, the one she now felt nestled against her backside. What had given him that kind of pleasure, her presence or the pain she caused? Did it really matter which one it was? Either way she was the cause of it, and that deadly thing wanted *her*. She made no bones about that. She might be inexperienced in the ways of men, but that much she could figure out for herself.

Eventually Kathryn's racing thoughts ran down and she grew sleepy. She comforted herself that he was sleeping there beside her and that meant he couldn't invade her dreams, dark or otherwise. She didn't like the idea of him having access to her most intimate thoughts and desires. Even she didn't fully understand what those were; she certainly didn't want to be sharing them with Adrian!

Adrian was aware of the moment she fell asleep because that was the moment that pain stopped coursing through him. Bearing up under the brunt of it was exhausting, but he believed it was getting to be more tolerable and not nearly as strong as time went on. With any luck it might go away altogether and he would be able to touch her free of pain. At the same time, the thought scared him. If there was nothing left to intimidate him about touching her, how was he going to keep himself under control? What leash would he use to control his wild nature?

He fell asleep worrying on that thought, but woke up to other thoughts completely. During their sleep she had tossed and turned, rolling over the width of the bed, and every time he'd dragged her back to his side. By the time he woke up she had tangled herself up against him, facing him front to front now with one long leg thrown up high over his hip and an arm wrapped around his neck. Her nightgown had ridden all the way up her thighs to her hips, and because she was asleep and feeling nothing for or against him, he was completely free of pain and left with only the delightful possibilities.

The first thing he did was take a deep breath. The sweetness of her scent wrapped up with his was almost unbearably wondrous. He amazed himself that at the moment he had first taken her he had thought to keep her in a cage, safe and protected, not even subject to his touch. This way was infinitely better. The pain was incidental compared to the joy of touching her and smelling her like this, feeling her wrapped around him as if she were his lover. Oh, that he could make that so! He closed his hand into a fist and fought back the wave of rage the thought provoked. He wished he was the man he had once been, someone worthy of her, a true match for her. Not this beastly thing who frightened her to death. He knew exactly how he would approach her, how he would use her own sensual body against her. She might be innocent in the ways of sex, but she carried desire in her deeply and naturally.

Adrian reached out with a single claw and ran it over her shoulder and down her arm until she squirmed in her sleep at the tactile sensation. She made a soft, provocative sound and he was lost instantly. Throwing all caution to the wind, he reached between their bodies and cupped her sleep-warmed breast in his hand, taking great care not to scratch her by accident. Silk and skin shifted against one another and he exhaled harshly when her rigid little nipple thrust out against the peach-colored material. It was such a beautiful sight to behold, the material thin enough for him to distinguish the color of even her fair nipples. He remembered the soft color of them, the way they barely stood out against the warmth of her skin. Her arms were darker than the rest of her, the tan no doubt coming from working out of doors. He wondered what it was she did on the family ranch to keep so darkly tanned even in the winter months.

The inane question flew out of his thoughts when she arched against him in her sleep, clearly thrusting her breast against his palm. Her leg squeezed restlessly against his hip and he began to grow hard for her. In for a penny, he left her breast to smooth his hand down her ribs and side, coasting up over the generous swell of her hip. He remembered how he had touched her in that dream, remembered how wet and hot her roused flesh had gotten. He longed to touch her like that again, but he feared hurting her. Still . . . if he was to be very, very careful . . .

He lightly scraped his claws down the back of her bare thigh, tickling against the back of her knee at the end. Then he shifted around to the front and traveled back up, this time with the pads of his fingers only, his rigid palm refusing to allow a single claw to come into contact with her.

Yes, he thought hotly, he could control this. He could be careful enough not to hurt her. He could enjoy the textures of her body like any lover might enjoy the body of his woman.

Oh, but it had been so long since he had touched another person. And now for it to be this exquisite creature—it was making his hand tremble in fine movements as he stressed about his potential to hurt her. He wanted so badly to taste as well as touch that his mouth went dry with the desire. The only thing that would make his contact with her better was if she were awake and welcoming it. But he doubted she would let him be so intimate if she were awake.

He pushed his hand up over her naked hip, moving her gown farther up and out of his way. He could smell her instantly, the aroma of a deliciously aroused woman. His touches had affected her even in her sleep, her mind open even to him in that state. But he wanted her to be open only to him. In her dreams, did she think of another man? Or worse, did she think of the man he had been and could never be again? He'd never have thought he could be jealous of himself, and it was a ridiculous thing to spend his energy on, but he couldn't seem to help himself.

"Wake," he rumbled into her ear as he nuzzled against it. "See who makes you feel this way."

He drew back and watched her eyelids flutter briefly, but she did not wake. He dipped his head and caught her mouth against his. He had meant to kiss her gently, but the moment he tasted her lips against his he was lost to his craving for her. He licked at her softly parted lips, his tongue flicking against her closed teeth. Then he kissed her again and again, soft noninvasive kisses, until he felt her respond with equal pressure and lifted his gaze to hers. Her eyes were still closed, but her hand drew up to weave fingers into his hair.

"Open your eyes, Kat," he commanded her. "See who it is that makes you feel this way."

She did. Her lashes swept up and her dilated pupils shrank to accommodate the light in the room. He pressed his mouth to hers once more and willed her to respond now that she could see whom she was really kissing.

But instead, she gasped and drew back, the action sending pain lancing through his chest that had nothing to do with her touch against him and everything to do with the removal of it. He knew the very moment she realized how she was wrapped around him, and only the strong clamp of his hand on her thigh kept her from rolling away from him. She was breathing hard, a mix of fear and residual arousal. How did she explain it to herself? he wondered angrily. How did she excuse the responses of her body? She felt these things for him. He knew it. And he could use it against her to get what he wanted from her.

"Do not pull away from me," he said sharply.

She settled instantly, but it was fear that motivated her, not any desire to actually stay close to him.

"Don't hurt me," she whispered. "You promised you wouldn't hurt me."

"Does this hurt?" he asked, reaching to press a gentle kiss to her lips.

"N-no," she answered honestly, licking her lips, taking his flavor onto her tongue. He groaned at the sight of her doing that and this time moved in for a kiss that was not so gentle. He kept his lips closed, protecting her from his fangs, but kissed her with as much deep passion as he was feeling.

The moment she responded to him was a moment of joy and excruciating agony all at once. But he welcomed the pain. It meant she was feeling warmly toward him, feeling positive emotions instead of negativity and fear alone. That was exactly what he wanted.

Adrian let his hand slide down the length of her thigh, and caught a gasp in his mouth when she reacted. It was so sweet, so perfect, to feel her respond to him while she was awake and aware. Maybe it would not matter to her that he was a beastly-looking thing. Maybe he could find ways to make her forget that he was so evil inside.

Kathryn was trembling beneath his touch and kiss, proving to him just how aware she was in that moment. He drew back from her lips and found her wide, beautiful eyes.

"Is it so horrible?" he asked her. "Am I really so horrible that you cannot even bear to have me touch you?"

"No," she breathed against him. "I . . . didn't think it was horrible at all."

The surprise and delight that rushed through him had him tightening his hand on her hip, and the wildest urge to smile came over him. But he suppressed it, not wanting to break the tenuous moment between them by flashing fangs at her when she was so close to him.

"You didn't?" he asked. "Then why do you quiver like a flower in a rough wind?"

"Because I'm confused and I don't understand this. I don't understand why you're changing, and I'm always afraid you're going to lose your temper suddenly if I do something wrong and displease you."

"You could never really displease me," he said to her honestly. "When I feel anger it is at myself, not at you. Though I know it seems otherwise to you in the moment. I swear to you that I will try not to do that."

"I see you trying," she agreed, reaching to touch two tentative fingers to his lip where a fang hid beneath. "And the changes?"

"What changes? In my temperament?"

"Among other things," she said. "I meant the changes in your face and features, though. Last night I studied you, remember? And this morning you are different. Much different."

This was news to him. He glanced over his shoulder at the large ornate mirror hanging in the room, but it was too far for him to see and angled in the wrong way. He would have to change that. He wanted to see what they looked like in bed together. But for the moment he ignored it, not wanting to separate himself from her warmth and closeness. His touch had lightened up on her and she had not made any movements to withdraw from him in spite of their provocative positioning and the intimacy of his hand on her bare hip.

Adrian did a double take and looked back at his hand. He lifted his fingers up and studied the curve of his claws. Last night they had been dark and long with a wicked curve; this morning they were lighter and distinctively shorter. Was this what she meant by changes? Why did he not feel them for himself? And why was this happening to him? Why now?

He looked back into the curious gray of her beautiful eyes and began to swiftly posit a theory that it was all because of her. Was this why he was in so much pain when she touched him? Was she changing him with every touch of her gentle hands?

Adrian reached for one of her hands and laid it against his chest over his heart. He closed his eyes and absorbed the shock of pain, but beneath that was the pleasure of the touch itself. Her skin was warmer than he expected from one moment to the next. Even though she was wrapped around him in many ways, it was still new and different every time she came into contact with him.

"Sweet Kat," he said softly. "Are you changing me? Are you going to be my salvation?" He reached up and drew a single nail down the side of her face, shaping the contour of her gorgeous cheekbone and the hollow above her jaw. He traced along her chin, over her dimple at the corner of her lips and then up the slope of her nose. He tracked over each of her eyebrows and then, magically, she smiled at him. Her smile brightened her entire face, lighting her eyes so magnificently it took his breath away. There was so much he owed her in explanations, so much she didn't know and would probably be angry with him for, but for right now she was smiling and that was all he cared about.

"Your fangs are smaller today," she noted, making him realize he had smiled back at her. He quickly pressed his lips together but she reached to touch the corner of his mouth. "No," she said, "don't do that. Don't hide yourself because of me."

"But I frighten you," he said.

She bit her lower lip, worrying it for a long moment. "Only because I don't know anything about you. I don't understand why I am here. I miss my family and I am worried about them. Was it true? What you and your sister told me about my family in the dream? Are they recovering in the hospital?"

"Yes, it's true. We were able to enter their dreams and cull the information from their subconscious minds. It would have made no sense to lie to you about that when we had planned to return you to your home."

"And . . . now that has changed? You won't let me go home?" The question was full of potential pain and he didn't want to answer it, but he knew he must and bear the consequences for his actions. He had hoped to somehow make it softer, to woo her into at least liking him a little before he told her the truth.

"The moment you met the Ampliphi it sealed

your fate," he said in a low voice, keeping her eyes the entire time. "The law is, no one who enters our plane can ever return to theirs. This plane, known as the Barrens, is an example of the harm that can happen when one world invades another. There isn't a soul alive on this plane except for me, Aerlyn, Cronos, and now you. We must protect Beneath from a similar fate at all costs. It happened once before to us . . . we allowed a woman from another plane to return home and she told a scientist about us. Together they found a way back into our world, bringing diseases with them, and as a result our female population was decimated. There is one woman to every two hundred males in my world. Our population dwindles because they cannot give birth fast enough to replenish it."

"But . . . that's so unfair! I swear I wouldn't tell a single soul!" Tears welled up into her eyes and she moved to withdraw from him. But he held her fast where she was, unwilling to give up her warmth and nearness. He had been cold and alone for far too long to let her slip away that easily. "Why couldn't you have just followed the dream and let me go back home? I would have never known the difference! I would have been free to go back! You did this on purpose!"

"Yes. And now this is your fate. You must accept that."

"I don't want to accept it! Let me go!" She tried to move free again and tears tracked over her face as she moved. Adrian felt a tremendous pang of regret, an emotion so foreign to him he barely recognized it.

"Listen to me," he insisted as she gripped his wrist and tried to force his hand from her hip. "I had to have you. I had no other choice."

She made a sound of disbelief and gaped at him.

"Are you kidding me? *You* had to have me? *You* had no choice? *You* had the choice of letting me go! But you didn't care what I might have wanted! You didn't even ask me!"

"Because you would have said no! You would have screamed it at the top of your lungs! Who would volunteer to stay with one such as me? I've done nothing but horrify you from the moment you first laid eyes on me!"

"You stole me out of my life!" She finally squirmed free of him because if he held her any harder his claws might have punctured her skin, and he couldn't bear the idea of breaking his promise not to hurt her.

He sat up as she flew from his bed, running her hands through her hair and pacing wildly back and forth on her side of the bed.

"Tell them you made a mistake. Let me go home! Please! I'll do anything if you'll just let me go home." Her eyes were beseeching him, filled with pain and fear.

"It's too late," he said with soft regret, although he knew he would do the same thing again and again. She wasn't ever getting away from him. "You may as well give up the idea. You'll not see your home again. This is your home. For now, anyway."

She whirled at that, facing him down. "What the hell does that mean?" she demanded to know.

"What do you care? You despise me, and there's an end to it." He jerked back the covers and got to his feet. He moved to a dresser close by, ignoring her gasp at his bold nudity.

"I-I don't despise you," she stammered, clearly flustered as he pulled clothes free of the drawers.

"You're just saying that so I'll explain what I meant. Suffice it to say, you'll partly have your way in a week's time. You'll never see me again. But even so, you still won't be allowed to go home."

He marched away from her, trying for all he was worth not to fly into the rage that was seething inside him. But why should he resist? She hated him anyway. There was no changing that.

He burst into the bathing chamber just off the main room. Not one to usually care about his grooming, he was suddenly desperate to shower and brush his teeth. It was as though all the desires for the trappings of the normal world were somehow seeping back into him. Rather like her touch seeped pain into him. But if she touched him now it wouldn't hurt, he would wager. She was furious with him and held him in clear contempt. All because of a family who had held her prisoner to their needs, a father who had enslaved her for years and made certain she never had the chance to break away from them. He had denied her college and more, even though they had the money for it. But her father had lied to her and told her otherwise. Anything to keep her close. She might as well trade that prison for another. She should be glad for the change of scene. And he wouldn't make her work her body until it was bone tired and then expect her to be mother and teacher to her younger sister as well. He wouldn't expect her to care for an entire ailing household and maintain the abandoned chores too.

He started the shower and let it grow hot while he put his toothbrush to good use. Unwilling to end their argument, Kathryn bearded him in his new den.

"Tell me what you mean," she demanded. "What happens in a week?"

"Get out." He turned and faced her with a low, predatory sound. "Get out or you'll find yourself sharing my shower."

He said it on purpose, knowing she'd blush and quail. But though she did blush she braced herself up and faced him down.

"Is that what it will take for me to get an answer out of you?"

He smiled at her, and this time it was a feral thing that made her swallow visibly. "If you share my bath, little Kat, you'll get more than answers from me."

"You're just saying that to embarrass me! You're just trying to make me go away, and I won't!"

He took a hard step up to her, towering over her as he growled in her face. "I don't make empty threats," he snapped.

"Tell me what happens in a week," she said, shaking mightily but still holding her ground.

"Take off the gown."

Kathryn wished she could stop shaking so hard. She would be much more convincing if she did.

"Take off the gown," he growled at her, looking

more and more the beast as he very successfully tried to intimidate her.

Just the same, she wasn't going to let him back away from this. She was going to shame him into telling her what she wanted to know, and she didn't care what it took.

"Will you tell me if I do?"

That offer seemed to take him by surprise, but only for a moment. A darkly sly look came over his face as he took a moment to contemplate his answer.

"It will take much more than showing me what I've already seen to get you your answer."

Kathryn felt every blood vessel she owned heating up and opening wide. She knew she was blushing bright red all over, but damn it, she just couldn't help it! He was constantly speaking in crude and suggestive ways she'd never heard before. She'd grown up so sheltered from men other than her father. Were they all like this?

"L-like what?" she asked in a squeak.

"You'll touch me. No," he corrected himself, taking full advantage of the moment. "You'll bathe me. Everywhere. No shyness. No fear. Like a woman would bathe her lover. Do that and you'll earn your answer."

"You would do that to me?" she cried. "You know I can't do that! I-I've never done—"

"Then go away and leave me be!" he roared in her face, forcing her to step back and bump into the door frame. Finally he touched the right place inside her and pissed her off. She exploded back at him.

"No! Fine, you freakin' pervert! If that's what it

will take to find out what future you've sentenced me to, then I'll do it!"

She grabbed the gown and yanked it over her head, throwing it at him. She took huge satisfaction in the shock that registered on his features, but it was only momentary. The next expression was all male and all about him recognizing he had dominance over the situation.

Her fleeting courage evaporated just like that.

"How do I know you'll keep your word?" she asked him in a suddenly small voice, unable to meet his penetrating gaze.

"Nothing I can say will reassure you. You'll just have to trust me." He held out his hand for her, palm up, open and waiting. The cynicism she saw in his eyes told her he didn't believe she was going to go through with it, and frankly, she wasn't all that sure either. She looked over her shoulder and out at the vast chamber beyond the bath, as if someone there might rescue her from this insane situation. But there was no one. It was just her. She had to make the choice all by herself and face the consequences, again, all by herself.

She lifted her hand and set her trembling fingers against his palm. Like a Venus flytrap waiting for its feast, he quickly closed his fingers around hers and drew her closer to him. She took a breath in through her mouth, the faint sound not so much reflecting fear as awkwardness. She didn't know how to do what he wanted. Maybe she could fake her way through parts of it, but she feared she didn't have the guts to do everything he would demand of her.

"Don't fret," he said gently, as if reading her mind. "You're a natural at sensuality, Kat. You enjoy all things visual and tactile, and that's all you need for this."

His entire demeanor had changed on a dime. He went from raging and furiously mean to gentle and bolstering. But of course he would. Anything to coax her into doing these acts for him. He was determined to get his jollies at her hands, damn him. She tried to hold on to that thought of anger as he drew her closer to the shower, hoping it would help fuel the courage she needed to do this.

He let her step in ahead of him.

"Too hot?" he asked.

She shook her head. She liked super-hot water when she bathed. Right then it was a bracing sting of heat, just one more too real sensation that reminded her this wasn't a dream anymore. It was all too real, and so was Adrian.

The moment he stepped into the confined space, she felt overshadowed and small. Not an easy trick considering she was as tall as some kind of demented Amazon and had a bum the size of Sydney. He, on the other hand, had an amazing ass, she thought as he turned his back to her for a moment. She pushed her wet hair out of her face so she could get a better view of those rock-hard glutes and the enormously solid and undeniably powerful thighs they flowed into.

Oh my God! I'm ogling his ass! She realized this just in time to rip her gaze away before he turned back and caught her at it. Why was it that with every passing minute he became less and less grotesque to her and more and more irresistible to look at? What the hell was going on around here? Maybe she *was* in another dream.

She hoped that wasn't the case, she thought as he held out a bar of soap and a washcloth to her, because if it was, she was some kind of pervert in her subconscious brain. But in the light of day he wasn't so intimidating in size as he had seemed the night before. Her eyes riveted to the flesh hanging below his waist, the relaxed state of his penis making it seem somehow harmless. Not totally harmless, though, she thought as it seemed to twitch right before her eyes. Like its master, it could become a volatile monster at the drop of a hat.

"Generally it helps if you rub the soap onto the washcloth."

His voice startled her and she blushed hot as she met his knowing eyes. She'd been staring at his *privates* and he *knew* it! Kathryn lowered her face and began to furiously scrub the soap into the cloth. God, how was she ever going to pull this off?

When she had a lather well worked up, he reached out to stop her frantic scrubbing. She looked up into his eyes, expecting to see some kind of smug satisfaction there, but was surprised to see tenderness instead. He laid the soap aside and, taking her by the same wrist she held the washcloth in, he drew her closer and settled her soapy hand against his chest.

"I'm not going to bite you," he teased her softly.

"With you I can never be sure," she quipped back before she thought of what she was saying. To her relief he laughed. The sound seemed to surprise them both. Rich and rolling and inherently male, it was also a tad bit rusty, as if he didn't use it often at all.

Feeling suddenly more at ease, she began to move her hand in slow, widening circles on his chest. She took her time studying what she was washing, finding him so much closer to normal when she broke him down into parts instead of seeing him as a whole. He was incredibly muscular, as if he lifted weights maniacally, each muscle sculpted hard and definitively. His nipples stood out starkly before she washed over them, two disks of russet in amongst the paleness of his skin. It was obvious to her that he didn't go outside much. He had nothing resembling a tan on any part of him. Why would that be, she wondered. From what he had told her, they were alone in this particular plane. There would be no one to see him, no one he had to hide from. In the dream he had seemed to relish being out of doors, riding the mounts he had fabricated with zeal and, perhaps, fervor.

"Are there no horses here?" she asked him, obviously surprising him with the question.

"I don't know. Even if there were, it would be hard to care for them. It's easier to manipulate a dream and ride that way."

"Easier, but not as real. I know you're good at what you do—I've experienced it for myself—but no dream can beat out the real magnificence of riding a horse."

"I'll have to take your word for that."

She looked at him in surprise. "You mean you've never ridden a horse for real? Never at all?"

"Never," he assured her.

"Then how do you know what it's like? How can

you possibly make it up when you have never done it for yourself?"

"Because someone dreamed of the experience and I felt it as if it were real. Just as anyone can feel the experience when a great writer puts it down on paper, only I truly get to see and feel everything. Like a three-dimensional movie. It's no different from any fantasy you may have." He slowly reached out and fastened his hands onto her waist. He leaned in and sniffed against her wet hair. "Have I told you how amazing you smell?"

"*Smell?*" She laughed uncomfortably. "I don't think so. I haven't even showered in a couple of days, I don't think."

"Then let's fix that." Before she could stop him, he took the soap from where he'd left it and spun it rapidly between his hands until he'd worked up a fierce lather. Then he reached for her, wrapping soap, hands, and the tips of deadly claws around her neck and shoulders. The erotic danger of having them against her skin sent a shot of pure heat down the center of her body, causing her nipples to tighten almost painfully and wet warmth to gather between her legs. She caught her breath at both the sensations and her body's reaction to it. Then he used his grip on her shoulders to turn her away from him, his hands running down the long length of her back as the hot water pelted her sensitive skin in front. He went slowly over her, again and again, leaving no contour unexplored, no nerve ending untouched. She gasped when he slid below her waist and shaped each cheek of her bum with care and focus, those ever-present nails of his running over her again and again until she was flushed with a heat to outshine the shower itself.

Then his hands came around her waist and onto her belly. He wasted no time at all before he was reaching to palm both of her breasts in his hands, washing over them again and again in excruciatingly slow swirls until her nipples were screaming from the sensation and her whole body was flushed hot and teetering on pinpoints.

"This wasn't part of our deal," she murmured inanely.

"Do you want me to stop?"

And just to prove he would, he stopped still on her breasts, not moving an inch.

Adrian prayed she would say no. He had never felt anything so glorious as her wet, slippery flesh in his hands. Because there were so few women in his plane, he had never had the opportunity to touch a woman for real before. Oh, he had been a dark and sometimes violent lover to many in their nightmares and darkest fantasies, but never in the real world. Never had he experienced anything so richly arousing as having his hands on her body. He had thought having her bathe him would be the most exciting thing ever, but right now it was paling in his mind compared to how it felt to touch the warm globes of her breasts with the slickness of soap to heighten the sensation all the more.

He wanted more. So much more. But he wouldn't continue without her permission. He was determined to prove to her that he could be trusted, determined to prove it to himself as well.

"No," she said in a very small voice, "I don't want you to stop. I . . . I like what you're doing. It feels good."

The air decompressed from his lungs in a sudden gush of shock. He had known she was aroused, his sensitive sense of smell telling him that loud and clear, but he hadn't expected her to admit to it in any way. His own aroused state skyrocketed at the admission, his mild erection suddenly becoming anything but mild. As close up against her back as he was, he knew she'd feel the change if she pressed back against him in any way.

And as if she read the thought right out of his mind, she did exactly that. Her soap-washed buttocks backed right into his heavy cock, the weight of it sliding up along the crease between her cheeks, the head bumping into the small of her back. She made a sound of surprise at the sensation and she whipped around, her belly now becoming his resting place. She gaped down at him for a moment, and then she reached out quite boldly and ran her fingers down the length of his shaft. Instantly it leapt up into her touch, like a dog bumping an owner's hand for affection, and he heard her giggle. He couldn't be as amused right then. He was hyperfocused on what her touch felt like, and the rivers of shocking need it sent straight to the seat of his testicles. Just when he thought he'd never felt anything quite so stimulating in his life, she carefully closed her hand around him. Well, almost around him. He was far too thick for her to make it. Still, it didn't matter. He closed his eyes briefly as it overwhelmed him to feel her, to understand she was doing this of her own free will and not because he had suckered her into some kind of unfair bargain. If she had meant it to be a part of that, she would have used the hand with the washcloth in it.

Instead she fixed herself with blatant curiosity around him and blushed deeply as she kept her eyes lowered and trained on what she was doing. He wanted to watch it too, but he couldn't take his eyes off her beautiful face and the expression of wonder it held.

"Am I...? Does it hurt?" she asked him in barely a whisper.

"Not in the way you mean," he said gruffly.

That earned him the swift lift of her gaze to his. "What do you mean?" she asked.

"Remember, whenever you touch me with good intentions it causes me a measure of pain." She gasped and went to pull away, but he anticipated her and closed his hand over hers to hold her right where she was. "It isn't like it was when it first happened. It becomes more and more bearable each time. And even if it wasn't, I wouldn't want you to stop for anything in the world."

"Oh," she breathed, her thumb flicking absently beneath the head of his cock and sending pleasure rocketing through him and straight to his heels. "Don't think I'm... It's just that... I've never touched one before."

"Never?" he echoed, the words helping him to focus.

"Never. Until last night I'd never seen a real one. And this isn't hurting you?" she double-checked, pinning him with stern eyes as if she might catch him in a lie about it.

"Kathryn, it's the most incredible feeling I've ever known. You forget, there aren't many women where I come from. This . . . this is the first time a real woman has ever touched me like this."

Oh, she liked that. He could tell by the expression of satisfaction that bled over her, not to mention the smile that curled the corners of her lips.

"So you're just as innocent of women as I am of men," she realized as her closed hand rode down his entire length.

"I have been with many women in the realms of their dreams."

"And I've been with Gerard Butler in the realms of my dreams. That doesn't make it real. *This* is real."

Adrian groaned when she rushed her slick hand back up to the sensitive head of his cock and then cradled it against her palm as she rubbed around and around the knob of flesh. He reached out to steady himself against the shower wall, trying to take deep breaths as his heartbeat kicked into overdrive. She was right. This was nothing like any dream he'd ever been a part of. Firstly, it was so much . . . *gentler*. Secondly, the sensations were far keener than he'd ever imagined. The difference between his own hand and hers was like night and day. So much so that he quickly realized he was in real danger of reaching climax just from her simple and extraordinary touches.

"Do you want to make me come?" he growled into her face, his mouth feinting for hers and then catching her in a kiss. Without thinking, he opened his mouth and thrust his tongue in search of hers.

She made a little surrendering sound as she opened wider and took the sudden, heated onslaught. It wasn't until their teeth accidentally clashed that he remembered this was reality, not a dream where he could change himself into a real man. But to his surprise, she didn't balk from thrusting her tongue into a mouth full of sharpened fangs. That she was kissing him at all should have baffled him completely, but he was too afraid of ruining it with thoughts and stuck to only actions. The taste of her was utter divinity, and he couldn't keep from plastering a hand to the small of her back and jerking her up tight and close to his body. The feel of her breasts against him was amazing and he began to feel a little light-headed from all the conflicting and harmonious sensations buffeting through him.

He broke from her mouth, panting hard for breath and awash with more pleasure than he had ever known. But there was a sour note to it that had nothing to do with the shock of discomfort that accompanied her touch.

"Kat," he breathed harshly, "in a week, when I cannot prove you are my *kindra*, they will take you away from me and send you to live Beneath. Because I have lied and claimed you as *kindra*, as my soul mate, I will be put to death when I cannot prove it true. Because of their rarity, it is a high crime among my people to falsely claim a woman in this way."

"Why are you telling me this now?" she asked.

"Because I don't want you to do anything you feel forced to do. I want you to touch me because that's what you want, not because I blackmailed you into it. You can leave now and not look back, and I would understand. I wouldn't blame you at all. It was wrong of me to force you here."

"Why? Adrian, why would you make that kind of claim knowing it was a lie? And just how are they going to know one way or another?"

"Because when *kind* come together, *kindra* and *kindri*, an explosive force of energy is released, one that all the Ampliphi would feel."

"C-come together? You mean . . . make love?"

"Yes. And I think they know I've lied. They know I am too monstrous for any woman to take. I am baffled as to why they did not try to take you from me immediately. Perhaps it was your eagerness to stay." He shook his head. "I don't know."

"Maybe because they felt you deserved a chance," she said softly, both her hands coming up to brush his wet hair back from his face.

"Or maybe because when I fail it will finally give them the right to demolish a monster they have been afraid of for years now."

"Adrian, why would you do that? Why would you lie like that knowing what would happen?"

"Because Aerlyn was going to send you away from me, and I couldn't bear the idea of it. I had to do something to keep you as long as I could. And anyway," he looked hard into her ash-colored eyes, "I am done living like this. I wasn't always this thing that reviles. I was once a better man. That's gone from me now. All I do now is thrive on the pain and struggle of others, manipulating it to my ends at any and all costs. Maybe once I did it to feed my people, to do something good, but now I do it purely for the pleasure it gives me to watch others suffer or help them indulge in their unspoken and inhuman fantasies. I don't deserve life any more than I deserve you."

"Adrian, that's not true!" she insisted heatedly. "If you have regret for what you've done, then there is hope for you!"

"I felt no regret. No shame. Not until—" He looked at her with no little surprise. "Not until you were brought here. Ever since you first touched me, I've been changing."

He abruptly stepped out of the shower and walked up to the large mirror over the sink. He had ignored it earlier, like he always ignored his reflection in all glass save his special mirror. He couldn't stand the sight of himself most of the time. But now he set his large palm against the foggy wetness and with huge swipes cleared the way to his reflection.

This morning you are different. Much different.

Adrian stared at himself in the glass, not believing what he was seeing. It had to be some kind of trick, either of his own mind or of the universe. It had been years—*decades*—since he had seen any hint of the man he could now see in the mirror. It was the smooth curve of his shoulders that especially fascinated him as he turned to see the huge deformity that had been there was now nearly gone. He still scowled too easily, was nearly twice the thickness of a normal male in mass and muscle, and still sported the claws and fangs that marked him for the beast he was. But there were definite hints of the Adrian of old in his features and in his eyes. Yes. He was different.

She was different.

Now that he wasn't so overwhelmed by her presence and touch, he realized that wasn't all that was different. His size had altered in other ways. Taking his straining penis in hand, he saw everything was different about it. Normally he'd have been three times as thick as he was just then. Last night that was exactly what he had been. Still, he was too big to think any differently about having sex, but it made him question where these changes were going to go. Where would they stop? Was this temporary? Or was it all that pain he was suffering every time she pressed her good intentions onto him?

Now he knew he could never let her go. Not just now, but a week from now. It was the only explanation for this.

She really was his *kindra*.

Chapter 9

How was he ever going to prove it to anyone else? He couldn't subject Kat to the normal methods of proof. God, how could he subject her to him at all? He had no idea how she had survived him this far. He was far from rehabilitated, still losing his temper savagely and doing things to her like making her bathe him. He was a nightmare . . . a real-life nightmare.

And still he couldn't bear to let her go. The struggle inside himself was massive, pulling him in two opposing directions. He grunted in pain, bending forward and grabbing on to the marble vanity for balance.

"Adrian!" she cried out from the shower. She moved as if she would help him, but he knew he wouldn't be able to bear her touch on him just then, so he threw out a halting hand.

"Finish your shower," he instructed her through his teeth.

Then he stumbled out of the bath and headed for his clothes.

The door slammed open without warning, Adrian's usual style of entrance, but this time it startled Aerlyn terribly because she hadn't sensed him coming as she usually did. Such a raging wall of negativity was hard to miss. As she turned to face her brother, she wondered why she had missed it this time.

Aerlyn gasped and dropped her teacup from nerveless fingers, the crash punctuating her reaction.

"*Adrian!*" She walked through shattered shards without care and raced to take her brother's face in her hands in a way she had not done for years. But then again, it had been years since she had seen her beloved brother. And it wasn't because his normal face was suddenly so easy to see in the bloated features of the monster he'd been for so long now, but because she could see conscience in his eyes. Worry and guilt and all the things he had abandoned long ago as the poisonous mirror he'd used had taken him over. He had become less her brother and more a scion of that cursed thing in the basement. "Adrian, how can this be?" she asked as she ran shaking fingers over his straightened shoulders.

"Kathryn," was all he said, and really all he needed to say. She should have realized it herself.

"Oh my God," she breathed as she stared into his eyes. "The pain you've been feeling. She's been undoing all the damage that's been done! Oh, it must be agony!"

"Never mind that," he said gruffly, brushing her concerns aside. "You have to tell me . . . do you think it's possible this is happening because . . . because she is my *kindra*?"

Immediate doubt and disbelief crowded Aerlyn's mind, but she realized then that doing so left her without any rational explanation for what was happening. But who had ever thought that a *kindra* could effect a change like this? True, one's mate lent balance and emotional stability, but to such a degree? Was this plausible or was this wishful thinking? Would Adrian continue to change or would good and evil level out before he reached the goal of becoming who he had once been?

And looks were only the surface of it. In other ways her brother as she had once known him was forever lost. These years of suffering would make him a changed and unpredictable man. His softness and innocence were long since traded away, all for the need of energy.

"Adrian, only you can say for certain if she is your *kindra*," she answered him at last, taking care to move out of his reach lest he lose his temper when she didn't say exactly what he wanted to hear. The movement made him frown at her as he recognized it for what it was. "It's something a mate feels . . . something he knows from deep inside himself."

"What I feel is need. Bone-deep need for her, Aerlyn. Is that what you mean? This out-of-control craving? It must be," he muttered, more to himself than to her. "Otherwise why would I look like this? Why would this be happening to me now if it wasn't that?"

Aerlyn could only shake her head. "I don't know. It's said that the moment you see your mate for the first time you'll know without a doubt. I have no idea what that really means. But . . . Julian would know. He has recently been through this."

"No! I can't go up to one of the Ampliphi and tell him that I'm not sure about this—that I lied to them about it. The moment I admit to that I'll be as good as dead!"

"Well, you should have thought about that before you recklessly went behind my back and claimed her as your *kindra!* And truth won't matter if you don't bed her and prove it to be true. How are you supposed to do that?" Then it struck Aerlyn. "Oh my God, that's what you wanted, isn't it? You walked right into it because you wanted a death sentence! You want them to kill you!"

"Obviously not any longer," he said tightly, his hands clenching and unclenching. "Not if this is a permanent change. If it continues, if I continue to get better in form and temperament, Aerlyn, then life might just be willing to have me, and I it."

"But none of that will matter if you don't claim her one way or the other, and frankly I'll be shocked if she lets you anywhere near her after the way you've been treating her."

He looked belligerent, as though he wanted to argue the point with her, but to her continuing amazement, he kept his temper under wraps.

"She likes me," he said softly. "Despite her own common sense and despite what I've done to her.

I-I don't think she even minds how I look that much."

That surprised Aerlyn a great deal. Had she been in Kathryn's position, she didn't think she'd ever come close to liking her captor. But then again, wasn't there a syndrome that humans suffered from when they were taken captive? Maybe that was what was happening to her brother's prisoner. Regardless, if Kathryn was disposed to give her brother any latitude, then Aerlyn would help to nurture that in her. She would do anything to save her brother's life, both from the Ampliphi, and from himself. And if all she ever got was this moment, this moment where she was looking into her brother's beautiful, *aware* eyes once more, that would all be worth it.

"Adrian," she said softly, leaning in to kiss his cheek because she knew, at long last, that he would let her do so. As she did so, he reached up and engulfed the back of her head in his hand. Not to hurt her or hurl her away from himself, but to express return affection. Aerlyn's eyes filled with unexpected tears, but she was all smiles when she moved back away from him. "Tell me what you need from me to help. Shall I give her sweet dreams about you? I can—"

"No!" He shot the word out hard and fast. "I'll not have her manipulated any more than we've already done. If I am going to come by this, I want to come by it honestly. No deceptions or tricks and no more hurting her. I'll do this myself and with full truth between us."

"Does that include telling her everything about the dreams you've caused over the years? All the potential violence you may have been a party to in the waking world because of your influence in the sleeping minds of others?"

"No. Or yes." He shook his head and ran his claws through his hair. "She already knows what I am capable of. She's thought the worst of me from the outset. Now it's time for me to show her I can be more than what I was. Better. If you want to help me, then help me with that."

"All right. Then I think your first step should be to get rid of that nasty little man you call your Companion."

"You're right," Adrian agreed. "He frightens Kat and has a hunger for the vileness in what I do . . . er . . . did. Being close to me and the mirror over the years has only made him worse. I'll find him now and send him back to the Ampliphi."

"Good. I will see about getting us some proper servants. Then you can focus purely on Kathryn."

"Thank you. Have you seen Cronos?"

"He just served me tea, so he should be around here somewhere. He might be avoiding you after your temper of last night."

"I'll find him. And thanks, sis."

As he left Aerlyn fanned her face. She wasn't about to start crying just because he'd called her sis.

She wasn't!

Cronos breathed harshly as he hobbled and ran from the dining hall breezeway. Oh! This was terrible! Everything was terrible! They wished to banish Cronos from the house! *Bad treasure! Bad treasure!*

He knew it was all her fault. That meant if he got rid of the bad treasure, then everything would return to what it had once been. She was responsible for the changes in the Master. She was responsible for getting Cronos into trouble! She was responsible for everything bad that was happening!

He had no time. He had to get to her fast. He had to do it before the Master found him!

He had to hurry!

Kathryn had showered and then, because she didn't want to wear her same dirty clothes from yesterday, she started to poke around in some of those magical little drawers Adrian seemed to have things stored in. She had already gone through the rest of the sideboard, finding other nightgowns even finer than what she'd seen and worn so far. She could swear one of them was made with actual gold rings to support the straps and golden thread in the weave of the lace.

It was much too rich to be worn and she didn't feel worthy of it, so she went to the bureau she'd seen him take his clothes from. There everything was for a man of his tremendous size. But unlike the almost threadbare things she'd seen him in yesterday, these were made of fine cloth and were well tailored. Silk shirts and rich, dark slacks . . . She wondered why he hadn't worn these before. Then she realized it was because he hadn't cared about what he looked like. This morning, however, she had seen him pull out a midnight blue silk shirt and dark pants, lying them on the bed before they'd started their row in the shower.

She flushed as she thought of how boldly she'd just started touching him. It had been such an insane thing to do! But she'd been so curious for so long, and she'd never felt a man like that before. Now she wished he hadn't stopped her. Oh, she appreciated what he'd been trying to do, and was glad for it really. But if only she'd had the chance to go further. She'd wanted to see. . . . She'd wanted to feel.

Sighing, she closed the last drawer in the bureau and turned to her next victim several long paces away. A wardrobe so huge she could have stepped inside and paced circuits within. She pulled open the doors and was greeted with the heavy scent of cedar. Then she began to make out that these were all dresses in here. Gowns, actually. *So beautiful!* There had to be a hundred of them! Fur and silk, sequined and embroidered, daring and conservative, and everything in between. She couldn't have dreamed anything so exotic and spoiling in all of her life. These were red-carpet gowns, not Kathryn Macdonough gowns.

But hadn't he let her wear that diamond-dusted creation? And she didn't want to wear one around the house, where it'd get ruined; she just wanted to try some of them on. She glanced over at the beveled glass mirror not too far away and stopped to bite her nail for a moment.

"They probably won't fit my fat bum anyway," she said as she inched closer to them. Why would he have all these here? Were they part of his one-of-a-kind collection? Were they perhaps his sister's? She was a one-of-a-kind beauty. She was the type who deserved dresses like these.

Slowly she began to look at them, sliding each hanger past her so she could gasp and admire the next in line. Some of them were outrageously indecent. No backs, barely any fronts, see-through and short or slit so high you couldn't possibly wear underwear with them!

She brushed past all of those and then, suddenly, she found one that she didn't think she'd blush just at the thought of putting it on. She'd never had dresses, really. No use for anything but jeans and tees on a ranch. But if she had had one, this fire engine red minidress might have been exactly what she'd have picked. The empire waist would hide a world of sins, and the way it flowed it might actually fit over her backside.

Sneaking a peek around the room first, she carefully eased the dress off its hanger and dropped her towel to the floor. Very carefully, so as not to rip anything by accident in case it didn't fit over her butt, she dropped the dress over her head.

It fell over her like water and perfection, as if it had been made to fit her. If this was a dream, then she was going to hate waking up. She smoothed her hands over the satiny fabric, watching it shine all around her body. Then she remembered the mirror and practically ran over to it. She tilted it so it was just right and then gasped at what she saw.

Long, wet hair aside, she looked *awesome!* Not just okay or passing or like she was trying on someone else's clothes, but perfectly tailored to her body sexy and *awesome!* Oh, her sister would just die—

She cut the thought off before she could finish it. Of all the things real and imagined she'd been through these past days, she had a rock-solid understanding that she was never going to see her family again. Whatever the future brought her, seeing her family wasn't going to happen.

Kathryn lifted her chin and trying to leap back into the joy of the dress. As she pivoted, she wanted to enjoy it so much, but she just couldn't stop worrying about her dad and sister. How would they get on without her? Dad was getting older now and her sister was still school age. Who would do her lessons with her? Who'd help her dad feed the stock and do the hundreds of never-ending chores the ranch always demanded?

When the door across the room creaked, she looked up and saw that awful little man scurrying her way. He came right up to her, and she immediately backed away. "What do you want?" she demanded. "I thought you weren't supposed to come near me!"

"Cronos will not hurt you. Not ever again," he promised in a high-pitched plea, his hands held out in supplication. "I apologized to my Master and now apologize to you. Cronos will never hit you again. I know better now."

"W-well, good," she said carefully. "Apology accepted. But you shouldn't come in here without knocking! I could have been dressing!"

"Apologies again. I will remember to knock next time. But now, we must go. The Master wants you to come." He curled his bony hands forward as if he wished to pull her along by a rope, leading her like a horse. Kathryn shivered and knew she was never going to like this horrid little man, but

Adrian had apparently sent for her and she had a few things she wanted to talk to him about.

She followed Cronos out of the room.

He led her down what appeared to be back stairwells. The enormous house seemed to go on forever as they went down and down. Before long they were in the basements, and she had a feeling she knew exactly where she was going to end up.

Sure enough, Cronos took her to the workroom, with its single torch and the black-fingered mirror standing large and ominous in its special spot. Cronos walked up in front of it and gestured with both his hands toward the mirror.

"My Master awaits you," he said.

"In there?" She knew she sounded as disbelieving as she must look. "You want me to step inside that thing?"

"Yes. He's just inside. You won't get lost or be alone. My Master would care for you above all other things."

"Then he should have stayed out here," she muttered under her breath.

She wasn't certain about this at all. There were very few things that made sense to her these days, but one thing she had a certain understanding of was that this mirror was nothing to fool around with. Still, Adrian had promised he wouldn't cause her any harm. He wouldn't ask her to come to him if he thought she could be hurt—would he?

Kathryn decided he wouldn't. She couldn't explain it, but she trusted his statements to that effect. At least she did now. He had exhibited a great deal of control lately and had made great efforts to be sensitive to her. This made it highly unlikely that he'd ask her to do something he didn't think she could handle.

Taking in a shaky breath, she reached to touch the mirror. To her surprise, blue electricity jumped out and struck her wrist. It didn't hurt her, but it did tingle strangely up her arm. And it wasn't a good tingle at all.

"Faster is better. It hurts less," Cronos advised, bending to look behind her for a second. She looked too, but no one was there.

"Faster is better," she echoed, shaking out her hands and trying to gather her courage. She had seen Adrian do it twice. All it took was a step. Just a single step. She held her breath and jumped in.

Cronos watched as blue lightning shocked her from all sides, just as it did the Master when he went through. The difference was the Master was bigger, as well as ten to fifteen times stronger than the girl. He could tolerate and survive such a shock. With luck, she would be dead by the time she crossed planes. If she did survive, she would be immediately lost in the nightmare plane. Only his Master had the power to find the mirror and only he could step out of it. Everything else was bespelled away from the mirror, so no dreams could cross into their plane. *Yes! She is gone now! Gone for good!*

But the longer she was lost the better, so Cronos raced away from the scene of his crime and went to continue eluding his Master. All he had to do was wait until he realized she was gone for good. Then all would return to what it had once been.

All would be well.

* * *

Kathryn lay on her face in the strange gray world she'd been thrust into. She'd been shocked pretty savagely by Adrian's mirror as she'd passed through, making a lie out of the theory that she would feel it less if she'd just gone through faster. She felt numbed all over and sore at the same time, like someone had shoved her from behind and sent her sprawling head over heels. Her heart raced erratically and her chest hurt.

She became immediately put out. Why in hell would Adrian beckon her to come through that awful thing if he'd known it was going to hurt so badly? He had promised . . .

She tried to get to her hands and knees, failing miserably. She had an awful taste in her mouth, like limes gone rotten, and this place smelled of the smoke that seemed to be everywhere. She was covered in the stuff, as it clung close to the ground for the most part, and she was most definitely a part of the ground in that moment. She worried about her pretty new dress and made another effort to get her face out of the floor. Her limbs were all wobbly from the shock and didn't seem to want to coordinate themselves under her command, but eventually she got the unruly buggers to pay attention and go to work all at once.

On her hands and knees, she rose above the better part of the smoky flooring. She looked around the endlessness of the dismal gray world she was in. She didn't see Adrian anywhere. Her heart skipped a beat, her stomach sinking cold and wet within her. She whipped around to look

for the mirror, but couldn't see the portal anywhere.

It has to be somewhere nearby, she told herself.

There was no need to panic. Adrian was around
there . . . somewhere.

"Adrian!" Her voice was rough and squeaky at
first, but rose strong by the second time she
shouted, "Adrian!"

Where is he? she wondered after five minutes of
calling for him proved fruitless. He wouldn't just
leave her alone like this! He regarded her as a precious thing, a treasure to be carefully cared for
and guarded. He wouldn't just . . .

Suddenly the cold idea that Cronos had not
been acting on his master's orders entered her
head, leaving behind a soul-deep chill unlike anything she had remembered feeling before. *No*, she
tried to convince herself, *he wouldn't dare!*

"Adrian!" she cried out.

And then, like sudden magic, he was there,
striding through the dullness of their surroundings,
lending it vibrancy and life. Her breath caught as
he came closer to her. He looked even more like
the dream Adrian than ever. It must be a progres-
sive change, happening more and more every single
moment. She could see his handsomeness shining
through now, his eyes full of emotion and, quite
frankly, a distinctive lust for her. She saw it there
before he even reached for her to pull her sharply
forward and into his braw body. Kathryn gasped as
his grip on her wrist held her almost painfully. She
tried not to balk, remembering he had promised
not to hurt her.

"Oh, but is that really what you want?" he asked in a rough whisper against her ear.

"Ex-excuse me?"

"Gentleness. To be treated like porcelain." He bent to smell her hair.

"How did you know—"

"What you were thinking?" he finished for her. "I know everything about you. Including what you really want." He spun her hard and fast so suddenly that she nearly tripped over her own feet. Then she was being slammed face-first into a solid wall that hadn't been there a moment ago. Was he manipulating the things on this plane just as he was trying to manipulate her?

She felt his hand splay flat and wide against her spine right between her shoulder blades. That was how he held her prisoner against the wall as he came up close behind her. He moved his hips forward until she felt the thrust of him against her backside. She gasped and tried to move, but he was having none of that.

"No, no," he whispered in her ear just before he reached out and licked it all along the rim. "Prisoners must please the king or be punished for their wrongdoings."

"Prisoner? I thought I was a treasure," she gasped as his free hand suddenly stroked her down her flank, taking a great deal of time to shape the cheek of her ass as he went. She caught a chill and shivered hard. He'd been bold with her in the past, and she'd been bold with him, but something about this didn't feel right to her. And not just because he was suddenly calling her his prisoner. Of course, that was exactly what she was, but he had never said so before in so many words, content to fool himself that it would sit better for her if he simply called her treasure.

"You are mine to do with as I please," he growled into her ear as his body pressed flush up against hers. The press of his weight now trapped her, freeing both his hands. They immediately dove for the hem of her dress, jerked it up over her hips.

"No! Wait!" It didn't feel right! Why didn't it feel right? Until this moment she'd felt inexplicably drawn to his intense sexuality and even the toying foreplay he had wanted to engage in, but now it was like a stranger had hold of her. She felt nothing of what she'd felt before. It was all wrong!

"Do not tell me to wait!" he barked in her ear. "Didn't I warn you about that?"

"You said not unless I mean it, and I do mean it!"

"I don't care!" He rumbled savagely against her ear, shoving himself hard against her, crushing the breath out of her as she was flattened between him and the wall. "You are under my power now, little trinket. Mine to play with. Mine to toy with. There is nothing you can do about that."

Tears sprang up into her eyes as his cruel words sank into her, the very attitude she'd feared from him and accused him of before. But it wasn't until that moment that she saw the difference between the way he had tried to treat her with kindnesses versus this cruel disregard for her every need or desire. The Adrian on her back had no interest in her free will. This Adrian would do just as he said—

he would take from her and he wouldn't give a damn what she thought about it.

Adrian picked up the damp towel Kathryn had left behind and sniffed it with a frown growing over his lips. It smelled heavenly, fresh with vanilla and lilacs, one of the many scents he'd had lined up on the inner shower shelf, simply waiting in anticipation of her. Her favorite was there as well. Night jasmine. But she hadn't used it. He wondered why.

But all of that flitted quickly out of his mind as he wondered where she'd disappeared to. Of course, he'd given her free run of the citadel. She could go anywhere she liked as long as it was within the safety of these walls. But he hadn't clearly explained to her the dangers of the outdoors. When the humanoid population of this plane had been destroyed, nature had come to take back what should have been hers all along. That included the wild beasts that sometimes trotted through the backyard. Yet another reason why it would not be a great idea to keep horses in this realm. They would be like sitting ducks. A free buffet.

The thought disturbed Adrian deeply and he lifted his nose to the air. He realized immediately that with his change in appearance, some of the keener senses he had were fading. But they didn't fade too far. His people were naturally born with sharp senses. Certainly sharp enough that he could pick out the scent of lilacs and vanilla drifting through the air. He began to follow the trail, curious at the circuitous route it took through the

house. He was unhurried as he tracked her . . .
until he realized she hadn't stopped descending
the stairs at the main floor. She'd continued downward. There was only one thing of interest down in
the basements and suddenly Adrian was running.
He took the stairs five and six at a time, not realizing he was growling dangerously as he went.

Little fool! Didn't she have the sense to know
that mirror was not to be trifled with? Common
sense alone should keep her away! Why would she
seek it out?

He didn't know the answers to his questions,
but he would find out soon enough. He burst into
the mirror antechamber with a roar, fully expecting
to see her there peering at the thing and examin-
ing it. But she wasn't there. She was nowhere in
sight. He sniffed the air, confirming to himself
that her scent was in the room. He went to the mirror and stared at his own reflection in it. Was it
possible she had gone through? The thought filled
him with dread and terror. Without a guide she
could get severely lost! And not knowing how to
control her own thoughts and desires in the nightmare plane could be all too dangerous. Adrian felt
horror creeping across his soul. Surely she would
have felt the warning electrical charge and backed
off.

She must have. She must have doubled back
onto her own scent and he had missed it in his
haste. She had to be somewhere else in the house.

But even as he moved to leave the room, he
couldn't help but look at the mirror one last time.

* * *

Fingers tipped with much smaller claws reached around her front and grabbed hold of her breast. By this point, Kathryn had tears running down her cheeks. She didn't want this! She didn't want him to do this to her. What was wrong with him? He ground against her again, sweeping up the dress where it settled over her hips and baring her backside to the chill air. She felt exposed and helpless and, for the first time, a bone-deep victimization at his hands that made her stomach lurch. She thought that if she'd eaten she surely would have hurled all over herself.

"Stop," she whimpered as she felt him stripping off his shirt. "Please, stop."

"Kat!"

The shout of his voice was distant and savage, but for some reason she found it perfect and beautiful. Her heart leapt in beat, her entire spirit lifting, her soul reaching out to that call with everything in her.

"Adrian!" she screamed.

Adrian thundered onto the scene in a rush of violence and muscle, slamming into his doppelganger as he ringed an arm around his neck. Adrian peeled the beastly version of himself off her and she immediately collapsed to the floor, her weak, shaking knees unable to hold her upright. The massive men began to wrestle with each other, and for a moment she couldn't tell which was which. But in the end it was the savagery with which he fought that marked her Adrian. He fought to protect her, while the other fought for the right to own her. She could tell the difference so very clearly, and now she wondered how she could have ever mistaken one for the other.

But Adrian was fighting himself, his equal in power and strength. Only his passion gave him the upper hand, allowing him to pin the beastly image of himself to the smoky ground.

"Kat! You created him, you must destroy him!" he shouted at her.

She didn't know how. She didn't understand. Her traumatized mind wouldn't absorb anything, so the fight went on. She numbly watched as Adrian began to batter his doppelganger with brutalizing punches and openhanded swipes of his claws. It was when the antithesis managed to rake vicious claws down Adrian's chest that Kathryn was jolted out of her shocky state.

"How?" she cried. "How do I get rid of him?"

"Change your desire. You called him to you, now shed him from you."

"But I already don't want him here. I already want him gone!"

"Change your desire," he gritted out as he grappled with his fiendish self. "Change what brought him to you in the first place."

What had brought him to her in the first place?

Of course! She had wanted Adrian to find her. She had wanted him there whatever it took, to save her from her rocky situation. The nightmarish world around them was what had corrupted him into this hateful version, this true beast. Well, she didn't need him any longer; didn't want him to come to her rescue. She was going to rescue herself.

The minute she thought the independent

thought, the doppelganger faded away. She sobbed hard, almost like a laugh of relief, as she tried to get her feet under herself. But before she could move she saw Adrian charging toward her, looking as mad as a bull with a bee in his butt. He reached down and scooped her off the floor in a single effortless motion, dragging her to his chest and squeezing her so hard she almost popped.

"You stupid little fool!" he hissed in her ear, the words gritting out through his clenched teeth. "Why would you do such a thing? The dangers you could have faced in here!"

"I know! I know!" she said in harsh exhales against him as she wrapped her arms around his neck and squeezed him back. "It was awful. It was you . . . but it wasn't you. It felt all wrong. And he almost . . . he was trying to . . . to . . ."

Adrian didn't need her to finish. He shuddered with repressed rage as he tried not to rip her head off for being so blatantly stupid. He had thought her much smarter than this. To at least have some common sense!

"Why did you do this?" he demanded of her. "Why would you do something so foolhardy and dangerous? Didn't it once occur to you that this wasn't safe?"

"Of course it did!" She jerked back to look into his face. The same face she had woken up to this morning, only it was full of anger . . . and something else. Fear. He had been terrified for her. "Do you think I would have come in here on my own? You were supposed to be waiting here for me. This was your idea!"

"My idea? To bring you into this brackish hell? I

want you pure and good, just the way I found you. This place will corrupt and destroy you. Stay here long enough and even your beauty would turn monstrous. I wouldn't wish that for you in a million years!"

"Then why would you tell Cronos to bring me downstairs to the mirror? Why did he seem to think you were waiting inside for me?"

"*Cronos?*" The word started out normal enough, but by the time it reached the second syllable it was a radiating roar of rage. She felt Adrian shuddering with his anger, the quickness and the power of it no doubt exacerbated by the mirror they were in. "Cronos did this to you? He sent you in here?"

She could only nod.

He grabbed hold of her hand and dragged her to his side, marching through the thickened smoke. It was almost like a physical thing now, with weight and substance, as though Adrian's presence gave it power. It wasn't long before he stopped, waved a hand to clear the heavy smoke, and revealed the back side of the mirror. Standing there she could see the torchlit room beyond. Who could have thought that such a dank little place could suddenly feel so much like home? Adrian tightened his grip on her hand and drew her up hard against his body. Then with a single broad step, he took them through.

Once through, Kathryn felt as though an astounding weight had been lifted off her, as though she could breathe again after being held down underwater. She hadn't been aware of it before, but there had been an allover sensation like pins and needles pricking against her skin. Also, the numbness that had persisted from her electrical shock immediately disappeared. Maybe it hadn't been from the electrical shock at all. Maybe it had been from that awful place.

Whatever the reason, it was all over now. But there was something she didn't understand.

"Why did I see you? When it wasn't you? You came and were rough, and mean, but it wasn't like before. The touch of your hands was all wrong. I knew it wasn't right."

That seemed to bring him up very short. He frowned as he stared down at her for a long moment, but as the seconds ticked by his frown smoothed out and then she could swear he was trying not to smile.

"You created a phantom," he explained. "You wanted and expected to see me, so you made me appear with just the power of your thoughts. The phantom usually behaves how you expect it to behave. It feeds on your deep-seated desires and thoughts. If not controlled, it preys on your deepest fears. It takes much practice and much strength of the mind to be able to control a phantom."

"So what's so funny, then?" she asked defensively.

"Not funny," he corrected her. "I am just pleased."

"About what?"

"That you weren't excited by the actions of the phantom."

"Well, he was pawing me like a beast!"

"And don't you like to be pawed?" he asked her, his voice dropping several octaves and his eyes firing with deep intent. He snared her around the waist and yanked her into the bend of his body.

"Seeing you wearing a dress like that makes me want to do some pawing of my own."

And there was the difference. Instantly it came. That rush of instant excitement and overwhelming heat. Despite what had just happened to her, she suddenly wanted him to do some pawing as well. He must have read that in her eyes because he growled low in his throat and she could feel him growing hard against her.

"I saw the dress and I didn't think you'd mind," she said lamely. Why was it she always turned into a blithering idiot when he got like this with her?

"You can try on any dress you like. They're yours. And believe me when I say I don't mind in the least." He reached out with one hand to shape the swell of her backside very suggestively and she felt the caress all the way down to her toes. It was as if he had magic in his hands. Nothing about the way he touched her felt bad or wrong. *Shouldn't it, though?* she asked herself. Shouldn't she be just as repulsed by him as she had been by the phantom? After all, look at all he had done to her!

But despite that reminder, she couldn't make herself turn away from his compelling touches and adamant attentions. When he reached out to flick a playful claw against her nipple through the fabric of her dress, she gasped and almost shot off the floor like a rocket. But just when she was going to tell him to do his best to her, he drew back and away, leaving her standing there aching and feeling more than a little lost. Oh! She had to be out of her mind! Nothing could ever come of all this toying and teasing. All she was doing was tormenting him and torturing herself. And still she yearned for him when he put distance between them. It was so stupid. So utterly insane.

"As much as I would love to continue this, there is something that must be done first," he said roughly, the sound of his voice telling her he was just as affected as she was by this wild, unreasonable chemistry between them.

"You mean Cronos?" she guessed, clearing her throat when she thought she sounded like Demi Moore.

"Yes. He tried to hurt you. Again. For that there is no forgiveness. I will not allow another hour to pass by with him in reach of you. I protect what is mine."

"But why would he do something like this?" she wondered.

"Why does not matter. He is a vile little man in need of correction, and I am going to see that he gets it."

"Adrian, be careful," she said, snagging his arm when he went to leave her. "Don't underestimate him. Whatever is motivating him is making him desperate. He had to know if he got caught he'd risk your wrath. He didn't intend to get caught. He didn't intend for me to ever be found again."

And he'd almost succeeded, she thought with a shiver.

"If you had moved any farther from the portal," Adrian rasped, "he would have succeeded. It was pure luck that you hadn't moved out of shouting range. Even so, the nightmare plane could have toyed with my shouts, keeping them away from you." She heard his teeth grind together as his anger at the possibilities grew. Then Adrian went to leave once more, and yet again she pulled him back.

"Don't leave me alone here," she begged him.

He seemed to stop and think about it for a moment. He sniffed the air carefully. He could smell Cronos's recent travels through the room and scented Aerlyn's perfume, but there was nothing to indicate Cronos was anywhere close by.

"This is the one place I can be assured Cronos is not present," he told her. "That makes it the safest place for you to be."

Kathryn glanced over her shoulder at the dark and ominously deadly mirror, and a flood of willies skipped down her spine.

"Are you sure?" she asked. It sounded good in theory, but she'd much rather be with him.

"I'm sure. I'll work my way out from here until I find him and then he will be gone for good."

"Okay then. I'll stay." She tried to sound firm but knew she didn't as she backed up against a wall where she could see anything coming at her. She wasn't particularly strong, so she didn't know what she could possibly do against Cronos if he came, but at least it would give her time for some hearty screaming for help.

Chapter 10

Adrian could see she didn't trust him to be right about leaving her alone, but that was to be expected. He hadn't protected her well enough and that was the price he had to pay. He would find a way to regain her trust later. Right now it was more important to remove this threat once and for all.

He left her slowly, feeling his own reluctance strangely. He didn't want to leave her any more than she wanted him to leave. On the one hand, he felt an overwhelming sense of satisfaction that she saw him as a source of refuge; on the other hand, he hated the idea that she had needed him and he had let her down. He sniffed the air, seeking Cronos's trail, and he began to climb the stairs out of the antechamber. The only thing he could smell, though, was his sister's cloying perfume.

That drew him to a sharp halt.

Why would his sister have been in his work-room? She despised coming anywhere near the dark influence of his mirror, claimed it made her ill just to look at the thing. And his sister did not wear her perfume in cloying ways. She used it lightly, enhancing her own scent and not destroying everything around her with it.

Adrian couldn't change direction fast enough. He bolted down the stairs and ran into his workroom. He skidded to a sudden halt when Cronos suddenly jerked around to face him, his arm locked tightly around Kathryn's neck and the tip of a wickedly sharp dagger pushed under the point of her chin. She had a look of utter terror painted across her features, her vulnerable gray eyes pleading with him to help her. Adrian felt terror and rage roll through him and forced himself to get the volatile emotions under his control lest he make a mistake that might cost Kathryn dearly.

"Cronos!" He barked the name roughly, making the little man jerk in fear.

"No," he whined. "I have to get rid of her! Everything was so beautiful and perfect before. Cronos served Master with all his heart and did good at it! If I don't get rid of her, you'll send me away!"

"No, Cronos. I'll send you away if you let her go; I'll kill you if you hurt a hair on her head."

This made the underling hesitate, and he seemed to be thinking of the alternatives for a long moment. Then he seemed to make up his mind.

"She is ruining you, Master. Ruined. Remember how things used to be so clear? So pure? Now it's all confusion and doubt. I can fix that! I will fix it!"

The point of the dagger pierced Kathryn's skin,

and a dark red trail of blood ran down her throat from her tipped-back chin. Adrian saw tears of pain and fear in her eyes and something very feral roared in his head. He could hear his own pulse against his ears, felt his blood running high and hot; every muscle and tendon in his body was straining to jump on his enemy, pounce him into the ground.

And just like that, he snapped. None of his more human thoughts could spare his actions as he leapt across the room with a deafening roar. He landed on Cronos, ripping Kathryn away and shoving her down and away from his enemy. Savagely he bit down on the shoulder of the hand that wielded the dagger. He instantly tasted blood, and all it did was remind him that Cronos had spilled the blood of his mate. Powerful jaws clamped down, he shook his head, sending Cronos flopping and jerking in all kinds of directions, as if he were a rag doll in the mouth of a dog. The claws on his hands sank into Cronos's hips. He was prepared to rip the man into two pieces.

"No! Adrian, don't kill him!"

The frantic plea of his mate sank into his head, making him realize that she shouldn't be exposed to such violent behavior if he ever expected her to warm to him. With an angry growl he dragged his victim to his mirror and leapt through.

The Ampliphi were just gathering when the electrical light show of Adrian's mirror went off, exposing the monster as he leapt through with the limp form of his Companion in his mouth. Settling on all fours, he spat his victim out so he could speak to their shocked expressions.

"He tried to destroy my mate. Twice."

That was all he said before he reached to snare Cronos by the back of his neck, taking him between his powerful jaws. Then all it took was a single violent shake before his Companion's neck snapped cleanly in two. Again, Adrian spat him out. Then he left the body there, like a cat bringing home a prize hunt for its masters, and disappeared into the mirror once more.

The stunned Ampliphi watched the growing pool of blood around the body, the random twitches of nerve impulses that were now going nowhere, with a morbid sense of fascination. They simply couldn't believe what they were seeing. Then Rennin turned to Julian with satisfaction.

"Still don't see why he needs to be destroyed?" he asked smugly.

Adrian returned only a minute after leaving her, finding her curled up on the floor. He immediately leapt to her side, his huge hands awkward as he tried to pet her with care and comfort. She laughed, her eyes dry and distant as she looked up into his.

"Whatever did I do to deserve all of this?" she asked of him.

Instantly the forested color of his eyes reflected guilt. *As well they should,* she thought petulantly. All of this was his doing. His fault. There was no

way around that knowledge for either of them. Just
the same, she didn't have the heart to leave him
feeling the way he was about it. She reached out
and hugged him around his neck, unwittingly
smearing her blood all over his clothing, sharpen-
ing the scent of it in his nostrils. It only served to
make him feel even guiltier, she realized, as he
hung his head against her shoulder.

"I'm sorry. Truly sorry. I never wanted to see
you hurt. He will never bother you again," he
promised her.

"You didn't leave him in there, did you?" she
asked him, her hands shaking against the back of
his neck at just the thought of the voracious mirror swallowing him up.

"No, I delivered him to the Ampliphi. Facing
their justice is all the future he has now."

She didn't know why, but she relaxed considerably at the information. She should still be stressed
out about being taken from her home and her
family, but for the first time she realized that she
wasn't. She was satisfied that they were safe and
healing and she was even beginning to think that
they would find some way to make it on their own
without her. Had she been able to go to college as
she had dreamed, she would have had to leave
them alone. How was this any different from that?
Well, except for the part where she *wasn't* in college and had actually been kidnapped by a raging
beast.

But maybe, one day when he trusted her, she
would be allowed to somehow contact her family
and let them know that she was alive and well; that

she hadn't just abandoned them recklessly at the worst possible moment. She didn't want her family thinking the worst of her. But as far as reasons for leaving them were concerned, this one definitely had to take the cake. In fact, she had to bet that if she told them the truth of the matter, they would think she was cracked. Surely she could make up something plausible. Adrian could help her.

Oh, but would he? Would he ever let her out of his sight long enough to do anything? He was still treating her like a prized possession. Although, in the instance of Cronos, that had been a very good thing. He hadn't given a single damn about the peril to himself, only that he wanted to get her out of danger. It had been reckless and ridiculously brave. She would bet precious money she wouldn't have ever found a man like that on the Earth plane. Certainly none who would have gone through the trouble for *her*.

She pulled back to look at him, seeing how changed he was in her eyes as well as in the actuality of physicality. She was beginning to care about what happened to him. Even to the point of fretting about his false claim on her and what that would mean at the end of a week's time. Less than a week, she realized. Six days, provided they counted a week the same way Earth did.

Wow. That thought was almost surreal. She wanted to indulge in the utter weirdness of it, but felt she didn't have the time or circumstance for such a luxury.

"Are you all right?" she asked him, looking him over for any obvious signs of wounds. She was well aware of just how sharp that dagger had been. She didn't need to guess how badly it could have potentially hurt Adrian if Cronos had gotten half a chance. Once she was satisfied he was all in one piece, she sat back with a sigh.

"This whole situation is like being in the wildest dream. Like something the mind dreams up after you've had a spicy dinner or taken cold medicine."

"You mean it's like a nightmare," he said tightly.

"No. I mean dream," she returned firmly. "Yes, some parts have nightmare qualities, but they speed by and are quickly forgotten. Just as it should be in any dream. This will be forgotten as well."

"How can you ever forget or forgive me for endangering you like that? For letting him trick me? He doused himself in my sister's perfume so I wouldn't catch his scent. He did it to trick me and it worked."

"Lo and behold, the mighty Adrian fell for a trick that was intended to deceive him," she said grandly. Then she drew herself in. "Stop worrying about what you can't control, Adrian. I don't blame you for this, I blame Cronos."

And as soon as she said it she realized it was true. She really was becoming less inclined to blame Adrian for every little thing that happened to her. The truth was, life had never been so exciting, so daring and adventurous. Every hour that ticked by held something else new and unexpected for her. It was something she had always wanted, granted to her by a most unexpected source. She wouldn't go so far as to say she was grateful to him for turning her life upside down, but she would say she was feeling differently toward him about it.

"Come on, let's get you cleaned up," she urged.

"You as well," he said, touching her under her chin. "Would you like Aerlyn to look at that? She has an amazing ability to heal."

"No, this is fine. It's a nick." She played it down when she saw the concern and anger warring in his eyes. She saw him struggling so hard to keep his more volatile emotions under wraps for her sake, and she didn't want him to fail.

"You're lying," he said, regarding her carefully. He studied her, as if trying to posit the reasons why she would do that. It only took a moment for his eyes to light with pleasure. "You're lying for my sake. So I won't be upset about it."

She flushed under the direct confrontation and swatted the air in front of his face with her hand, trying to push him off topic. "Whatever," she said. "Let's just get out of this room."

Aerlyn found her brother later that night just before she was going to begin work for the evening. To her surprise, his little prize was nowhere in sight. She thought for certain he would keep her on a very short leash after what had happened with Cronos. Their laws were very clear about what happened to a man who tried to kill a woman. Cronos would be sentenced to death. Because women were such precious commodities on their plane, it was absolutely intolerable to let anyone consider harming the only thing standing between them and utter extinction. This entire barren plane was an example of what happened to a people when they didn't execute stringent enough laws to protect themselves. The Ampliphi passed laws that were harsh and perhaps unfair in some instances, but it was enabling their people to recover from the terrible plagues that had decimated their female population not once, but twice. Now women were the most precious thing they owned, the key to creating powerful emotions needed to feed their starving young and elderly; needed to keep their men strong so they could protect them from the natural dangers to their world as well as the unnatural ones.

One day Aerlyn would have to do her part to increase their population, but for the moment it was her gift for dwelling in dreams and retrieving strong positive emotions from them that made her most valuable. Every night she gleaned a tremendous amount of energy to bring to the Ampliphi. Every night she fed hundreds of people, and that was worth far more than giving them one baby at a time.

"Where is Kathryn?" she asked, coming up behind him so she could enjoy the privilege of touching her brother once more. This time she ran a hand through his hair, as if he were a little boy in need of tidying up. He was a bit unkempt, after all. He had grown out of practice with keeping himself perfectly groomed, seeing no point in grooming a monster, as he had put it.

"In bed," he informed her, thumbing over the next page in the book he was reading. Adrian had once been a great reader, but over time the beast had robbed him of the patience for it. She was so delighted with him it was all she could do not to fall on him with hugs and kisses. Old or new temperament, that would fluster her brother no end, so she restrained herself. "She had an exhausting day and I thought I would leave her to some time by herself."

That couldn't be an easy trick, Aerlyn mused. Keeping *kindri* away from *kindra* before he had staked his proper claim on her was painfully hard on both parties. More so, she imagined, on her brother, who was genetically predisposed to do everything in his power to claim his mate as soon as possible after finding her. Being human, Kathryn might not feel as strong a drive. Aerlyn hoped the little Earth girl could appreciate the sacrifices her brother was making on her behalf. Especially as she watched time tick away and the week grow shorter, along with his life span. She had just gotten large pieces of her beloved brother back. She was not inclined to lose him again after they'd been through so much together.

"Shouldn't you be wooing her instead of reading?" Aerlyn suggested, reaching over to flip some pages over, making him lose his place. She giggled when he gave her a dirty look. Oh, how she enjoyed teasing with him again!

"I cannot think to woo her," he said darkly, a frown marring his handsome lips.

She straightened in surprise, all the fun bleeding out of her. "What do you mean?" she asked him.

"I mean I am not suitable for her as I am."

"You are more than suitable," she argued. "You are my brother. A good man at heart. Why do you say these things?"

"I mean *physically*," he said roughly. "Look at my hands. Look at my teeth." He flashed her his claws and fangs. "Would you make love to one such as me? And do not say yes, because you are speaking as a sister who loves me if you do. And that consideration aside, I . . . I cannot touch her, for fear of scratching her badly. I cannot put my mouth to her, for fear of puncturing her or biting her by accident. And that's to say nothing of the rest of me. My weight, my size. She might be of good size by human standards, but to me she is small and fragile and I *will* break her if I'm not careful!"

"Oh, Adrian, I'm so sorry," she crooned softly to him as she leaned forward and hugged his head to her breast. "I know these changes are only half measures in your eyes, but I see much more than you do. I think you might be surprised what you can do, and what she can take, if you both had a mind to."

"And that's the other thing," he grumbled. "She doesn't have a mind to sleep with a beast, and I don't blame her."

"Adrian, stop it," she scolded him. "With that kind of thinking you'll never claim your *kindra,* and if you think I'm going to let you die at the end of a week's time you are sorely mistaken. I'll have a talk with her and—"

"You will not!" He surged to his feet, the book dropping forgotten to the floor as he whirled to face her. "I will handle this on my own or not at all,

Aerlyn. I will not have her coerced into my arms or talked into it or bartered or anything like it! She will come to me because it is what she wants. No other reason!"

"Well, I wasn't going to bribe her! I was just going to talk to her. Girl to girl. See what she's thinking. She's been through a lot, and sometimes talking to someone can help you process better. But if you want to do this all by yourself and not accept my help, then that's your prerogative!"

She turned away with a significant flounce, marched away from her brother and toward the stairs. He caught up to her just as she took hold of the railing.

"Aerlyn," he said.

She hesitated, frowned, and turned to face him, crossing her arms tightly beneath her breasts. "Yes?"

"I am sorry. Your help is always welcome, of course. Just know its limitations. Know . . . know how I would feel if I didn't win her on my own merit."

"I understand," she said, immediately softening toward him. "Adrian, I wouldn't do anything to hurt you. Do you know that? Do you remember what our relationship once was?"

"Yes, I remember. Now I do. We were born twins, born with this cursed power to be able to manipulate the dreams of others. We are rare creatures in our world."

"We were more than that, my love," she whispered gently to him, wrapping him up in a strong hug. "We were inseparable. We loved each other in the way twins do. It's why I stayed devoted to you even when you were at your worst. Because you were, and will be again, a wonderful man." Tears came to her eyes and she blinked them away. She had endured so much at his hands, but it was instantly forgiven. And it was possible all because of one human girl who had begun to change him back to what he once had been. All they needed now was for that human girl to save his life.

Kathryn woke slowly the next morning, finding herself a prisoner of powerful, almost desperate arms. He had both his arms wrapped round her midriff, pinning her back to his chest in a very adamant spooning. She was wearing another of the outstandingly unique and delicate nightgowns he seemed to have in such abundance, this one a fiery red threaded through with silver filament to shape the bodice around her breasts and trails of hand-painted silver stars to play over all of her curves. She had been afraid to wear it at first, afraid her overpopulated bosom would damage the silver. She eventually gave in and tried it on, once again amazed that everything seemed to fit her so very well. She wasn't exactly a mainstream figure, so she wondered about it. Eventually exhaustion had won out above curiosity and she had crawled into the huge, beautiful bed that no longer seemed so awful. The next day, she had thought, she would take the time to explore some of these treasures of his.

She had fallen asleep before he had come into

the bed and hadn't stirred an inch when he had. He had pulled her this tight and close and apparently all she had done was snuggle against him as if she had done so for all of her life. She supposed that should disturb her on some level. After all, she was still essentially his captive.

Slowly she tried to turn around so she could observe him in his resting state. He was such a vital creature with an unequaled presence; it would be interesting to see him while he slept. But it was hard to move even a little bit, that was how tightly he was holding her to him. Using a little ingenuity, she began to pet him along his forearm. Only lightly; she didn't want to wake him, after all. There were thick, crisp hairs all along his arm, not beastly but more than manly. He stirred when she ran the pads of her fingers over the backs of his. His grip loosened as his hand tried to follow her gentle touch and she had to stifle a giggle. Biting her lip hard so she wouldn't make any noises, she slowly pivoted around in his embrace. She did it as gently as she could, but the moment she shifted her weight against him, his subconscious mind took that as a cue to lock his arms around her once more.

Now front to front, her breasts were smushed into his bare chest and their hips were in healthy contact. Healthy enough for her to recognize he was getting an erection even in his sleep. Just from her small movements against him. My, she thought, he really was a lusty creature. Or maybe that was true of all men. She was hardly the person to ask.

She studied his face and realized it was even

smoother than it had been yesterday. Was that because he was asleep? Or was it because he continued to change? She wriggled an arm free of his
imprisoning grasp and touched him on his forehead. Yes, she thought, he was definitely different.
It wasn't his skin that had smoothed out, but his
bone structure. What amazed her was that now she
could see he had remarkable cheekbones, like his
sister. His lashes were long and beautiful, his mouth
like something carved perfectly out of stone. His
jaw was long and strong, with much more character than his avatar in the dream he had created for
her. In fact, she didn't think he had done himself
much justice at all in that dream. But people always saw themselves differently than they actually
were, so it made sense in a way.

Tempted by their shape, she reached to touch
his lips with soft, barely there touches. They didn't
seem to be so altered by his fangs this morning.
She wanted so badly to take a peek, but didn't
have the nerve to do it.

That was exactly when he smiled, flashing those
fangs at her. And though they were smaller now,
they were most certainly there, and likely just as
deadly as they had been yesterday when they had
sunk into Cronos's shoulder. Still, the smile startled her, telling her he'd probably been awake for
quite some time. She reached out and pinched
him hard on the shoulder before she could think
about whether that was a good idea or not, given
his volatile temperament. In response he gnashed
his teeth at her, making her squeal, which made
him laugh.

"Oh! You're mean!" she scolded him, beating a fist against his chest.

"I'm a beast," he said, helping her with her description.

But she didn't entirely agree with that any longer, so she shook her head. "No. You're just mean. How long have you been awake?"

"How long have I had a hard-on?" he countered.

She gasped and blushed fiery hot, almost red enough to match the gown she wore. "Maybe you are a beast!" she retaliated when he chuckled at her discomfort. "You like to shock me. It's terrible of you."

"It's fun is what it is," he said, catching her hand when she would have pinched him again. "Now, stop. All your thrashing around only serves to turn me on more."

She went still in a heartbeat, her reddened cheeks giving off heat as he bent to kiss one. Then her lashes lifted and her gorgeous gray eyes turned silvery and sly. "And you don't want me to turn you on?" she asked.

He opened his mouth, but no reply was forthcoming. She couldn't help the mischievous smile that spread across her mouth. Then, without knowing where she got the courage for it, she stretched her neck forward and slowly kissed his lips.

His response was instantaneous. He was rock hard in an instant and pressing heavily against her lower belly, and his breath hitched sharply. Then the next thing she knew, she was under his big body, his hand cradling the back of her head and his mouth pressing hotly against hers. His tongue dipped against her lips, coaxing them apart for him, and then plunged deep into her mouth when she finally did. Kathryn was instantly overwhelmed, her heart racing beneath her breast and her whole body suddenly creeping with heat from head to toe. The hand at the back of her head burrowed deep in her hair, massaging her scalp in slow, firm circles until she went utterly boneless beneath the ministration. She moaned into his mouth, and he captured the sound with relish as he rolled her fully beneath him, using his elbows to keep from crushing her.

It changed everything. Suddenly their position became everything erotic and titillating. Her knees instinctively rose up so her thighs were cradling his hips. His strong belly lay against her softer one, and trapped between them and a thin layer of silk was the heaviness of his adamant erection. She had never been so exposed before. She'd never felt such a delicious weight lying over her. As if it were some kind of trigger for her, her body went wet and hot almost instantly.

She saw Adrian take a deep breath in through his nose, the masculine flare of his nostrils somehow so very primal in her eyes. She realized almost instantly that it was her excitement he was sniffing for, and she knew the exact moment he found it. The hunger that fell over his dark eyes was powerful and lustful. Suddenly his mouth was voracious against hers, as if he couldn't possibly get enough of her, and she gasped for her breath beneath the onslaught. He was just about wild as he devoured her lips again and again, exposing the erotic danger of his fangs against her lips without any sign of fear or regulation. His hands dove beneath her back, cupping her shoulders tightly, his claws curving against her collarbone. The sensation turned her liquid beneath him.

Part of her wanted to let her arms drop down helplessly on the bed; the other part of her couldn't resist the opportunity to run her hands freely over the exposed skin of his back and shoulders. Her touch acted like a catalyst, making him grab hold of her even tighter and loosing a deep growl from the depths of his chest. It was a purely possessive sound, warning others to back off, that she was his prize to have and he wasn't ever going to share.

Suddenly he broke away from her mouth, panting hard for breath in unison with her. Then with a slow downward slide of his body, his head lowered toward her breasts.

"Oh! I don't think that's a very good idea!" She squeaked out the protest and was completely ignored. Especially when she followed up with, "I'm really not at all sensitive."

Her preconceptions clearly meant nothing to him. He closed his mouth on her nipple directly through the silk of the nightgown she wore. He used teeth to do so and she nearly leapt off the bed using her butt muscles alone as sensation rocketed through her. He chuckled, low and wicked, and curled his claws into the strap of her gown and dragged it down her arm until she was covered in a rash of goose bumps and her stiff nipple was prodding against his confident mouth. He captured her instantly and easily, and she almost squealed at the power of his sucking mouth. The insensitivity

theory flew right out the window as her entire
body melted and twisted like fine wires he pulled
with masterful ease. He cupped her opposite breast,
the heavy weight of it like nothing in his big hand.
He scraped his claws against her and she shivered
so hard that he immediately did it again. He ran
the sharp points directly across her nipple, coursing over it again and again until she was likely to
scream from hypersensitivity. All the while his
mouth sucked greedily at her other breast, making
her squirm beneath him in ways she'd never imagined herself doing.

Adrian made a passionate tribute out of his play
against her breasts, but all the while he was working his way deeper and deeper against her widening thighs. Then, with a final press, he was seated
firmly against her truest heat. He wanted to shout
in triumph, to roar out his victory to all the world,
but he managed to control himself. Barely. He remembered she was an innocent and tried to appreciate what she must be experiencing. In a way,
he was experiencing it too. He hadn't known the
real touch of a woman. Now here was an astound-
ingly sensual woman beneath him, her seeking
hands running all up and down his back, shoulders, and sides, and it was as clear as day that she
wanted him. *Him.* Beastly flaws and all, she was accepting him. More than accepting. She was passionate and hungry for him to the point that she
forgot herself, forgot her shyness, and lifted seeking hips up against his, rubbing his shaft right
down the center of her core. The only thing that
could have made it better was if the silk of her
nightgown hadn't been in the way. But he was far

from complaining. The connection was pure heaven, a true sign of how much she wanted him.

And he wanted her, with a passion so savage he could hardly keep it under his control. But he must. He must be careful or he would risk frightening her or, worse yet, hurting her. If she was going to be so generous as to save his life, then he could see to it that everything she experienced was well worth the pain she might suffer.

The thought almost made him stop. He feared for her, didn't want to hurt her. But just the same, he couldn't make himself quit her. In fact, he wanted to lose himself even deeper against her. To that end, he planted his hands firmly against the mattress and slid farther down her amazing body, the presence of her gown alleviating all friction and making it an easy and sensual slide. But once he was able to kiss her against her inner thighs, he no longer had use or patience for the red silk covering her precious flesh. He pushed it away, baring her secret heart to him, a sound of painful delight escaping him at the sight of her. That was to say nothing of the exotic smell of her. Her arousal was flushed wet, dampening the soft, dark curls protecting her pussy and releasing a heavenly aroma that was purely aroused and waiting woman.

And she had never been kissed. Never been touched. By none, he thought, but her own hand. This was his treasure and his alone. Unique and precious and just waiting for him to touch her. He bent his head and kissed her at the very crest of her mons, unable to resist the flickering touch of his tongue. Kathryn gasped and gasped again when he repeated the action only half an inch farther down. Half an inch more and he'd be toying close to her sensitive clit, and the idea of it thrilled him no end. He brought his hand to her, touching her between her nether lips in a long, seeking stroke. The exploration wet his finger and made her flesh swell like a waiting flower about to bloom. He wanted to taste her so badly, and it was all he could do to keep from falling on her voraciously. *Careful*, he kept telling himself, *it's only her first time!*

He opened her up to him with the slide of two fingers, parting her folds wide and welcoming to him. She was already drenched and needed no help from him there. All she needed was a fine tonguing. Something to make her scream. Yes, that would be perfect. And with that thought, he fastened his mouth to her.

Kathryn nearly leapt out of her skin when he did it. She had, of course, heard all about oral sex and had fantasized about what it would feel like, but never once had she come close to imagining the feeling accurately. She hadn't realized that a man's tongue could move so quickly, or that when it did it would make her tumble back into herself again and again. Her feet climbed his back, pressing in counterpoint to his actions, and her hands found a home deep in his hair, holding him to her with a wantonness that would have made her blush had she had even a moment to think about it. But that moment never came. Not when she felt him wrap his lips around her clit, framing it for the fast flick of his tongue. She gasped and moaned, her hips lifted for more . . . anything . . . anything she had to do to keep his glorious mouth working against her. And swiftly, swiftly now she began to burn inside, began to climb up to a very high point as if preparing to leap down with nothing but the wind and Adrian to catch her.

Now his hands curled around her thigh on one side and her hip and buttock on the other. As he attacked her voraciously he forgot himself, forgot the tips of those deadly claws, which pinched into her skin painfully. But she welcomed that bracing pain, for it kept her from flying away too swiftly. It made her build up all over again, back up and up to that point, her whole body shaking, determined to leap off this time.

She came with an explosive shout. It might have just been noise, it might have been his name, she didn't know which and she didn't care. She was pulsing in powerful rhythms, her whole body stretched out tighter than a drum. Then, with a drawing gasp for breath, it all stopped. It all came down to delicious little spasms of pleasure slithering through her, and a clit far too sensitive to bear the attentions of his tongue any longer. Still, she didn't have it in her to push him away. And she didn't have to. All it took was one suck of air between her teeth and he knew she'd reached her tolerance for him. He backed away from her, using everything in his power to keep from giving her one last, hearty lick. He buried his face against her soft belly instead, rubbing his nose against her and relishing licking the incredible flavor of her off his lips. It sent him over the delicate edge he'd been walking between the man being in control and the beast.

He surged up her body to capture her mouth,

drinking her in long, ravaging kisses until she was dizzy and distracted with it. Then he settled himself against her, his cock resting directly along the exposed heart of her. Once he was there, once he was coating himself in her wetness and bathing in her heat, he couldn't control the thrust of his hips that brought him directly across her sensitive clit. She cried out against his mouth, her nails biting into his shoulders with sudden, glorious ferocity.

Yes, he thought, *yes! Be savage for me! Lose yourself deep inside me, the way I will lose myself deep inside you!*

He groaned at his own thoughts, his cock feeling enormous and heavy as it sought a home inside her. He notched up against her opening, seating himself true and hard, feeling the resistance of her untried body. So tight. So very brilliantly tight! Just one thrust and he'd take her. One thrust and she'd be his forever. His. No one could ever take her away from him. She would be his one true and finest treasure that no one could have but him.

"Mine, Kat. All mine. Say you'll be that. Tell me you'll be mine."

Kathryn was panting hard, her body writhing for what it wanted, the movements mindless and seeking. He groaned, wanting her so badly, but this was important, his mind told him. This was utterly crucial.

"Kat!" he shouted, tested to his limits.

"Yours," she coughed out at last. "I'll be yours."

The affirmation made him want to howl with joy. The pleasure he felt would only be outstripped by the grasp of her body when it came. But he tried to focus for a fraction of a second more and he looked down into her trusting gray eyes and found the strength to say, "This might hurt you, love. Know that I don't want it to, but . . ."

"It's supposed to hurt the first time," she acknowledged, her gentle hands in his hair absolving him of responsibility for that. But he would not be absolved. He would take responsibility for it every second of the way.

Making certain he was thoroughly wetted by her body, he came back to that breaching point. He so wanted to have the wherewithal to take this slowly, to do his best by her, but the savage inside him was clawing at the door and demanding everything all at once. *One thrust. One shot deep inside her will bring us home.*

He let loose with a rumbling sound, a savage sound, just before he thrust powerfully into her precious body. The resistance he met was utterly extraordinary. He'd never felt anything so strong and so tight before. He barely made it half the way inside her. He was throbbing hard with need of her, everything wildly angry at his failure to take her all in an instant. He rammed forward suddenly and hard, lifting her hips off the bed with the movement. She cried out, a sound of real and bracing pain, and it was enough to give him the presence of mind to wait her out. Oh, but it was so hard to do! She was so blessedly tight around him! So blindingly perfect. He wanted to fuck her within an inch of her life, make her come again and again, until she couldn't think about anything else.

To that end, he reached down between their joined bodies and dragged a claw across her twitchy little clit. She tightened around him so strongly that it took his breath away. She was hardier than she thought she was, he realized. Braver too. Well, he would make it worth her while.

Starting now.

Chapter 11

Kathryn hardly knew which way was up at the moment. All she felt was this invading force in her body. He was so big, too big, she thought with momentary panic, remembering what he had said about their fitting together being impossible. But somehow, it worked. The pain, however, was frighteningly bracing and she pressed her hands against his shoulders as if to push him away. But he was far too big for her small hands to have any effect on him. She was overwhelmed, wondered why she had thought this was a good idea, and felt like she was stretched to the breaking point. Then he reached down between them and tickled her with that deadly claw of his, making her gasp in shock and confusion. How could she hurt and feel pleasure all at the same time? It made absolutely no sense at all.

He looked up then, finding her eyes and seeing something he didn't like, because he frowned.

"Relax, sweet," he said tightly. "I'm not going to hurt you."

"Too late," she gasped.

"I mean besides that." He chuckled. "There's nothing I can do about that." The frown deepened. "Do you want me to stop?" But even as he asked that devious claw flicked over her once again, and there was nothing in his expression or his body language that said he had any interest in stopping. And just to prove the point, he added, "I don't think I could, sweet Kat. You're an instant addiction. One taste of you and now I must have more."

She knew the feeling. She didn't want to stop either. She was too curious and too ready to stop now. She felt as though she'd waited all of her life for this moment, for the instant when she had finally broken free of her life at her father's house and moved on to her own life and her own experiences instead of the ones her father hand-fed to her. Oh, she loved her dad dearly, but he was always controlling every instant of who and what she was. And while Adrian was proving to be just as controlling in his way, there was still a freedom in his embrace that she hadn't felt before.

While she was thinking, he slowly slid free of her body, almost removing himself completely. She could have claimed a feeling of relief once the pressure of his girth was removed, but that was far from what she felt. She understood his claim of an instant addiction in that moment, because now that he was gone she wanted him back. More than anything. Her hands slid down his powerful back, clutching at his tight buttocks as if she could pull him back where he belonged. But the fact was she didn't have to try so hard at all to make him return. He did so readily and with a fair amount of gusto. She sucked in her breath, anticipating pain, and then exhaled with surprise when it didn't come.

"I told you," he rumbled against her ear, "I'm not going to hurt you."

She believed him now. In fact, she was experiencing something very opposite to pain. It was queer the way it felt, and yet her heart was racing in her chest.

"I don't know what I'm doing," she confessed all in a rush just as he dipped for her mouth and kissed her within an inch of suffocating her. When he lifted away she was gasping for her breath, her thighs clenched tight against his hips and holding him still while she tried to process all of the information rushing through her. He had no intention of helping her, though. He made that very clear when he dropped his head to capture her nipple between his teeth. He let her go just as quickly and raised vibrant green eyes up to hers.

"You don't need to know anything. You're perfect just the way you are. I like that you're untried. I like being the only man you'll ever know."

Well, she wouldn't go that far, but she wasn't going to pop his delusional bubble right in the middle of everything. Even someone as green as she was knew that would be a mean thing to do.

"Okay," she said idly, her focus disintegrating as he cupped her knee in one hand and pushed her leg away from its grip on him, opening her wide for him. As soon as he was certain she had relaxed a little, he moved inside her once again, a long, slow thrust that belied the savage need she could see in his eyes. He wanted to be doing something far wilder to her. She could see it and feel it in the vibrating energy of his body as he held himself back for her sake. His consideration made her smile, made her relax considerably. She reached for his now handsome face, cupping it between her hands and then pulling him down for an almost chaste kiss.

Adrian wasn't interested in chaste. His desires ran deeper and hotter than she could possibly have imagined. She didn't know what it was like to be a beast on fire for a beauty, but he was determined to show her. He pumped himself into her in a long, earth-shattering undulation of his hips, making Kathryn gasp in significant surprise. She'd had no idea that such simple movements could hold so much power over a body. And if the look of utter bliss on his face was anything to judge by, Adrian was feeling exactly the same way.

"Oh, you feel so fine, my pretty Kat," he said, his voice so low and sexy and sending a thrill straight down the center of her belly. "I'm going to make you scream for me, sweetheart," he promised her. "You'll scream the name of the man who makes you feel pleasure like no other ever will."

She didn't even have the presence of mind to protest his second possessive remark in as many minutes. The fact of the matter was that she felt like screaming. But it was more likely because he was moving so damn slowly and her body was craving something much more than slowness.

"I want to feel you," she heard herself panting

baldly, her nails once again burrowing into his butt in an effort to make him do what she wanted. "I need to feel you, Adrian."

Her words seemed to fire something in him because suddenly he reared up and out of her grasping body and hands. With the grip of a single strong hand on her shoulder he flipped her over in the bed, a grunt leaving her as she landed on her face in the pillows. Then she felt his hands bracketing her hips and hauling her ass high in the air, his knees coming between hers and spreading her legs far apart. She scrambled to get her hands under her, wanting to push up and look back at him, but he planted a powerful hand right between her shoulder blades and held her face and chest down against the pillows.

"Feel this," he ground out as he abruptly thrust deep into her channel. She gasped at the sudden and swollen intrusion, the sheer size of him once again overwhelming her as she took him from a completely different perspective. "And this . . ." He drew back and slammed forward so hard it took her knees off the bed. She had to scramble to clutch the sheets, to keep herself from sliding into the headboard as his thrusts went deeper and harder as they increased in speed.

Kathryn longed to be able to see him and touch him. Both were impossible as he knelt over her like a conquering hero, keeping her from moving in the slightest way. She felt stunted by the position and frustrated, but he seemed to thrive on it, his breaths leaving him in rising growls of pleasure as he moved into her again and again. Needing to do something to gain his attention, she clenched every muscle in her body, wrapping tight feet around his calves and resisting the pressure between her shoulders. She also locked around his working cock like a fist and she knew the very instant it caught his attention because he gasped out loud and then groaned as he worked past the resistance she was putting up.

"Ah, God, yes! Kat. Oh, my beautiful Kat . . ." His hands raked down the length of her spine, claws streaking downward, bumping over each of her vertebrae until she was racked with shivers of stimulation and excitement.

What was more, she was aware she could push up on her hands now and even look over her shoulder to see him. What she saw made her blush from head to toe. Not only was he magnificently naked, gleaming with sweat and concentration as he used her body for his pleasure, but he was studying her bare backside as if he'd never seen anything quite like it, his hand shaping over her in slow, affectionate rubs. Then, just to startle her, he ran a claw down the cleft between her cheeks all the way to the spot where they were joined. The intimacy made fire explode along the entire length of her body, even as it made her face heat in a blush. She could tell he liked doing it, too, because he shifted into faster thrusts, punching into her until she was awash with the strangest sensation of pleasure she'd ever known. In a way it was similar to the orgasms she'd given to herself over the years and the one he'd more recently triggered, but it was very different at the same time. Deeper. She felt threads in her chest and belly tugging downward, as if she were a marionette and he was gathering the strings to manipulate her with each thrust inside her.

"Adrian," she cried out helplessly, shaking her head and not knowing what she should do. Her hair flew around her head as he stroked into her harder and faster, the rhythm impossible for her to keep up with. All she could do was push back against him while he held her in place with strong, needful hands. "Adrian, something's wrong!" she said, her breath as panicked as her words.

"Nothing's wrong. Nothing has ever been more right, Kat. Don't be afraid. Just relax and don't be afraid. God, you feel so amazing. Do I feel even half as good to you?"

He did. And then some. She just couldn't seem to bear all of that wild sensation all at once. He was asking way too much of her, she thought. Maybe she just wasn't like other women. Maybe she didn't work right like they did. Would he be disappointed in her? Would he regret the day he'd chosen her above all others?

As if he knew she doubted herself he suddenly turned her on her side, pulling her leg way up so her knee was hooked around his shoulder. This forced him to slow down just a little and he reached forward to grab her chin and made her look at him.

"You'll not hide from me," he said. "You'll look at me and know who and what it is that makes you feel this way. And you will feel it. I'll not stop until you do."

And she knew he'd make good on that threat. He didn't let go of her until she looked directly into his eyes. She'd never seen so much lust and passion in the eyes of another before, and she wondered if she looked anything like that. Did she have that expression of borderline desperation in the depths of her eyes like he did? She could almost believe that she did as the tension in her body wound up to an incredible tightness. The hand that had held her face now fell to embrace her breast, the flicking of a claw back and forth and back and forth over her sensitive nipple making her want to scream.

"That's it," he coaxed her softly. "There you go."

She was going somewhere, all right. She was spinning in her own head, twisting inside and all around. She panted madly for every breath as everything dragged her around inside. Then, suddenly, all the threads seemed to snap at once, and like a released balloon she went soaring. Rich spasms of pleasure rocketed around inside her, clamping her down tight on him, milking him for equal measure. He started to growl in bursts of succession, his hips jerking as he tried to fight her body for depth. Then, with a deafening roar, he came apart inside her. She felt the hot rush of his ejaculate, felt the wild way he couldn't control himself as he gripped her leg and pushed against their mutual spasms.

Sleeping soundly after a long night of gathering energy to give to the Ampliphi, Aerlyn was completely unprepared for the brutal onslaught of energy that struck her out of nowhere. The power of it physically flung her from her bed, forcing her to

awaken and take it all in. She felt the pure pleasure of it, felt the resonance of her brother's release as he abandoned himself to it. That was when
she realized what was happening. This was the
power of *kind* coming together, the energy of
kindri and *kindra* reaching a point of passion together. Powerful enough to feed an entire village.
There was no place for all of that energy to go except into her; the other option was to let it waste-
fully dissipate into this dead plane where no one
had use for it, and she would rather drop dead
than let that happen.

She sat on her knees, her head bowed and her
hands gripping at the floor as it continued to ride
her like a bucking bronc. She needed to get to her
feet. Needed to move. She could only take so
much before she burnt herself out or her head exploded. It took several tries, but she was finally
able to grab one of the curtains to her bed. She
used it to drag herself over to the bed and with a remarkable show of strength she pulled herself up to
the tips of her toes with just a single pull. And still
the energy kept coming, rolling into her now like
breaking swells in the surf. She wasn't built to take
in so much energy. No one was. If she didn't find a
way to stop it she was going to do herself serious
harm, and Adrian would blame himself for it. Her
brother was taking the weight for a great many
wrongs of late, whether he was responsible for
them or not. She would not add this to his pay-
load.

Aerlyn staggered into the hallway and straight to
the stairs. She almost broke her neck as she stum-

bled down them at a hazardous speed. Next were the narrow stairwells leading down to her and Adrian's workrooms.

Her workroom was everything her brother's wasn't. She had decorated it warmly with a desk and footstool, a comfortable chair to rest in after a hard night's work, and pretty little china bits she'd taken a fancy to over the years. Her own version of a treasure room, she supposed. Sage and potpourri were scattered everywhere, so the room smelled fresh and not of the dank basement location it was in. If she'd had her choice, she would have worked out of one of the upstairs rooms, but Adrian had demanded a low, dismal place in which to work, reflective of his hateful duties, no doubt. She couldn't bear the idea of him working alone down here, so she had moved herself in across from him. Her love for her brother had never wavered. Not even when it had gotten to its very worst.

Now she knew she had to do something crucial for him. She walked like a drunkard toward her mirror. Oval in shape and framed in white, ivy-like fronds of worked metal, it was twice her height and equally large around. The bottom of the glass touched directly to the cold stone floor. She looked inside the glass, gasping at her own reflection. The stars in her hair looked as though they were going supernova, tiny bursts of light that had they been to scale would have blinded the cosmos. Her silver eyes glowed with depth and energy. So much so that she knew she had gone well beyond her tolerances. The only way to stop it now was to leave the house . . . hell, the surrounding area, for that matter. So she took the quickest route she knew. With a charge of green electricity, she stepped into her mirror.

The Ampliphi were arguing, as they did quite often, when Aerlyn staggered through her mirror portal and into Justice Hall.

"Aerlyn, what is the meaning of your intrusion?" Rennin demanded irritably because he had been the one losing the argument at hand. He didn't like to lose. What was more, he despised being thwarted.

Instead of explaining herself, Aerlyn did what she was designed to do. She unleashed all of the energy she had absorbed on the Ampliphi. Like her, half of them were knocked out of their seats. Their ethereal forms slowly but surely turned to solid flesh and blood, a state they so rarely indulged in, in order to conserve energy. But there was no need for conservation today. What Aerlyn had brought them was a treasure trove. The Ampliphi picked themselves up and reordered themselves. Flushed with the nature of the passionate energy they had received, they all changed in demeanor from belligerent and stubborn to easy and sated.

They turned to Aerlyn, whose eyes were still aglow as she tipped her chin and took them all in with the sweep of her arms.

"My brother has found his *kindra*, and I have brought you the proof of it. His life is no longer on the line and you must accept that now."

There was so much silence for so long that Aerlyn began to doubt that they had heard her. What she didn't know was that their recent argument had been about the best methods to destroy her brother when the opportunity finally presented itself. Now that opportunity had vanished before their eyes and they were astounded by the impossibility of it. Yet there was no questioning what Aerlyn had brought to them for proof. The last time they had been so solid had been when Julian had first taken his mate. That had been such an explosive coming together that no one had starved that week. The same would likely have been true had Adrian taken his mate here on their plane.

"Aerlyn." Sydelle had to stop to clear the huskiness from her throat. "We thank you for this generous gift."

Christophe, the leader of the Ampliphi and Aerlyn's mentor, sat forward in his seat. His steady eyes were apologetic and Aerlyn felt a frisson of worry wend its way down her spine.

"Aerlyn, you must go to your brother right away and tell him we will not tolerate his absence Beneath for another day. He and his mate will relocate to your former village, where the energy from their bond together can feed thousands."

"But you can't do that!" The stern folding of his handsome face told her she had overstepped herself with the outrageous shout, but she really didn't care. She was always the first to respect the wise Ampliphi, but in this she would argue for her brother's sake. "I understand your reasons for wanting this, I do, but he has barely won his mate's trust, and now you want to thrust them into a world that is so alien to her own? At least the Barrens closely resembles the world she knew!"

"And what will you do, Aerlyn? Take onslaught after onslaught of this energy they create? Look at what it has done to you already. You can barely stand and your eyes are bloodshot beneath their glow. You are lucky you didn't have a stroke trying to manage that all on your own! This setup is a danger to you and wasteful besides. It was not a suggestion, Guardian, it was a command."

Fury rolled through her as she faced down the man who had taught her how to rein in energy from the world of dreams. She had known nothing when she had come to him, only sporting a raw talent she'd been born with. He had taught her so much, more than anyone there might realize, and now he was passing down dictates on her as if she were a dog expected to obey.

"What is wrong with you?" she demanded directly from him. "Is it that you wish for Adrian to fail at this? Are you angry to have your opportunity to kill the monster taken out of your hands?" The moment Christophe cast a look at the other Ampliphi she knew, with horror, that she had hit the nail on the head. "Oh my God. You were hoping he would fail!"

"Untrue. We did not think he would succeed. There is a difference," Christophe said.

"And now you want to throw their relationship into trial before they are ready. It sounds to me that you are still thinking," she accused.

"If Adrian fails to please his *kindra*, it is not because of his location. And this is no longer about your brother but about the thousands he and his mate will feed every time they come together. This is not open to discussion, Aerlyn. He will be here by night's fall or he will suffer consequences. Am I making myself clear to you?"

"Perfectly," she bit out.

She turned on her heel and with a wild green electrical show, she and her anger stepped into her mirror. Once they were sure she had left, Rennin turned to the others.

"So now how do you propose we get rid of the bastard?" he demanded.

It took all of Adrian's remaining strength not to collapse on top of Kathryn and crush her beneath his considerable bulk. Just the same he lay on her heavily, drawing for each breath as though it might be his last. He was stunned, to say the least. His entire body was humming with the power rushing through it. How could he possibly feel so weak and so energized all at once? He brushed both of his hands through Kat's hair, cupping her head and making her look at him while he tried to comprehend his own thoughts.

"Your eyes are glowing!" she exclaimed. "How do they do that? Is that because of . . . That's so freakishly cool!"

"I am glad my freakishness fascinates you," he said with amusement.

"You're lucky it does, because you've shown me quite a lot of it so far."

"Oh?" He frowned. "Then why would you let me anywhere near you?" he wondered.

"I've been wondering that myself. Wait!" She grabbed his shoulders when he moved as if to

leave her. "Adrian, I'm only teasing you. Stop this."
She brushed at his turned-down mouth. "I don't
care about the fangs and the claws or the eyes.
Well," she paused, "I do care, actually. But only in
the sense that you do that wicked cool thing with
the claws to me and I would hate to lose that. It
gives me goose bumps."

Finally, he smiled down at her, flashing her considerably less fang than the day before. "Liked that,
did you?"

"Mm-hmm." She nodded healthily.

"My eyes glow only when I am loaded up with
energy, enough to deliver to the Ampliphi for feeding to others. But . . . it's never felt like this before.
Always it was like something vile crawling beneath
my skin. I used to hate it . . . and then I began to
crave it."

"It changed you a lot, didn't it? All that negative
energy?"

"And now it's all the good things about you that
are changing me back." He held up a hand between them, indicating the long nails and their
only slight curve. They were lighter in color, more
like natural nails now. He looked into her eyes, so
deeply she gave a self-conscious giggle. "You've
saved me," he said.

"Oh! No, I didn't!" She laughed, the sound
catching in her throat as she tried to wave the idea
off.

"Yes. You did." His mouth curled into another of
his newly ready smiles. "In so many ways. And I feel
as though I owe you something for it."

"I think you just gave me something," she joked.

"Kat, I'm serious. Let me give you something. Anything." He lifted his head and looked around the room. "I know!"

He moved from her, finally disconnecting their bodies and making her pout in consternation. But he ignored the moue, knowing it was about to change. He went over to a jewelry chest and began to pull open drawers and doors. He passed by dozens of stunning pieces that might have made any woman on any plane die of happiness, but he was looking for something much more specific.

He found it with a triumphant "Aha!" and then hurried back to the bed.

"Good, you're back. I'm cold," she fretted, giving him a theatrical shiver to back up her claim. He chuckled at her and slid beneath the covers with her as he dangled the pretty piece of jewelry from two of his fingers.

"Ooh, it's so pretty," she said as she reached for it. But he jerked it up out of her reach and teased her with it. "Oh, you're so mean! And after I saved you and everything!"

He sobered. "True. Very true." He lowered his arm and pooled the diamond and sapphire chain at the very base of her throat, filling the little hollow full of precious gems. Once he finally let go of the chain she reached for it and wound it around her fingers. She'd never seen anything so exquisite and so expensive in all of her life. And true to his nature, it was also quite unique. Each sapphire was in a setting of diamonds, like an eye shaped around a pupil. The links between were either silver or white gold, she couldn't tell the difference because she'd never had jewelry before.

"It's called the Eyes of Irina. It was the necklace of a queen, generations of them to be exact, made to commemorate the great sacrifice a queen once made for her lover that cost her her sight. The lover commissioned the necklace in gratitude to her."

"And why isn't a queen wearing it now?" she wondered.

"She will be," he said with a smile of pure mischief.

"That's the charming thing to say," she scolded him. "I'm serious. Did you steal this from someone?" *Like you stole me?* It was the unspoken thought to follow and they both knew it. He frowned down at her.

"I am not a thief. That line of queens is from the Barrens and is long extinct now. Their things were left behind, useless to them. On your plane that would make me an archaeologist. There is no crime in appreciating things from other cultures, and the stories to go with them."

"No. There isn't," she agreed softly, reaching to pet his face warmly. "Will you tell me something?"

"If I can," he agreed.

"Tell me why you have so many clothes here for a woman. All these pretty things. Jewelry for a woman. Were you always planning on giving them to someone?"

"Not someone. You."

She blinked at him. "Well, not me specifically. You mean someone like me. Someone you wanted to woo with pretty things one day?"

"Not someone," he reiterated. "*You*. You specifically, Kathryn. I have been in your dreams for a long while now," he confessed to her. "I left you alone because I knew you were too good for me, but I guess I dreamed of you being here one day and started to collect things based on that idea. All the clothing is in your size and is something I longed to see on you. All the jewels are meant to complement your gorgeous eyes. Every delicate thing here is meant to caress your sweet skin. Please, don't look at me as if I have committed a crime. I felt that since I couldn't have you, I would pretend that I could. And one day . . . one day pretending was no longer enough for me. I had to have you here. I had to be able to touch you and kiss you." He leaned forward and kissed her still lips, willing her to accept the things he was telling her.

"And keep me and hold me like every other thing you acquired. God, what the hell was I thinking?" She pushed away from him, wriggling back into her nightgown as fast as she could. Panicked now, Adrian sat up and reached for her. She yanked herself away before he could get hold of her. "Don't touch me!"

"Kat, please . . . I was different when I took you. Selfish and brutal and, yes, uncaring of how it would affect you. I wanted a treasure to complete my collection. You want me to admit that? I will. It's the truth. But I'm not that thing that took you anymore!"

"How do I know that? You know where everything is, what everything is for. You've gotten your way. You've taken everything precious left to me. Wasn't that your plan all along?"

He could hear the tears in her voice, though she struggled valiantly to keep them at bay. She got out of the bed and broke into a run, but since he was on the side near the doors, she had to get past him first and he wasn't about to let that happen. He got to his feet and caught her arms in his hands, holding tight when she struggled against him.

"No! You're not running away from me, Kat! You stand here and you yell at me or tell me off or any number of things you might want to do, but you will not run away from me! That's the trick you pull with your father, isn't it? Never argue. Never confront. Never demand what you want or what you deserve. Isn't that right?"

"What do you know about it? Leave me alone!"

"I know everything about it, sweetheart. Everything you can't resolve in your waking world comes with you into your dreams. Every single frustration you felt at your father's hands I felt too. You don't remember half of it, but you always came and talked to me. You railed and fought like you could never do when you were awake. You have a hell of a lot of fire wrapped up inside you, but the only thing it burns is your delicate insides because you never let it out!"

"Shut up! Stop talking like you know me! Oh my God, I can't believe I let you . . . Oh!" She hauled back and slugged him hard in the shoulder, immediately feeling the impact in her wrist when his much stronger body wouldn't give way.

"Wouldn't you rather your first time have been with someone who knows you, Kathryn? And knows you not from secondhand sources but your own lips and mind? Do you want me to tell you what else I know? Do you really want to talk about deception?" His temper was getting the best of him because of his fear that she would leave him. The statement was out before he could check it and he regretted it instantly. Her head perked up and her eyes narrowed warily on him.

"What do you mean?"

"Nothing. Forget I said anything. It was a mistake." He turned, running both hands through his hair in agitation. But she was hot on his heels.

"No. It's not nothing. You know something that has to do with me. Tell me what it is."

"Kat." He shook his head vehemently. "You don't want to know. Believe me."

"Tell me or I'm walking out of here!"

"And where are you going to go?" he railed back at her. "This plane is dead. There's no one here to take care of you or help you or anything. It's just you, me, and my sister. I'm sorry to say it, sweetheart, but we're all you've got."

"Oh! You . . . you monster! You plot my kidnapping for months, possibly even years," she corrected herself as she took in the scope of the things he had collected. "And now when you have a chance to do one honest thing for me, you won't do it!"

"Because I don't want to hurt you!"

"*Too late!*"

She tried to push past him, but he wasn't going to let her get away with that.

"Are you telling me you are going to hold against me the things I did when I was half mad with rage and lust and every evil emotion you can possibly imagine? Are you really going to treat me like that is who I am?"

"If you aren't that same monster still, then just

what the hell are you? You're still keeping me a captive here. You're still treating me like a freakin' doll you get to dress up and make pretty." She threw the necklace at him and he let it fall to the ground. It wasn't important to him. Not if it wasn't important to her. "The only thing that's changed is I bought into it for a little while. Long enough for you to finally get your rocks off. I hope you had fun, because it won't be happening again anytime soon!"

"Hey! I seem to recall us both getting our rocks off, sweetheart," he snapped at her, grabbing her hard and giving her a shake. "Do not conjure up reasons to be mad at me because you're having second thoughts about what you did with me!"

"I'm . . . I'm just mad! I feel like I never have any control! Everything is always about what everyone else wants out of me! When is it going to be my turn to do what I want?"

"Honey . . . honey, listen to me," he said, making her look at him squarely. "This is all about you doing what you want. If I had kept my head about it I would have preferred to wait before taking you. I would have preferred to have more honesty and more trust between us. More understanding. Thing is, I didn't think we were going to be able to make love at all, remember? I was terrified I was going to hurt you. That we wouldn't fit right. Remember I said that?"

"Yes," she sniffed, not looking at him. "That just means you got lucky you didn't hurt me."

"No, it doesn't. If I'd thought for a moment during our lovemaking that I was going to cause you any real harm, I would have stopped. Look at me, Kat." He gave her a shake and she turned her angry eyes up to him. He was terrified she was going to leave him, destroy what little trust they'd earned with each other, but he still had to take delight in that anger. She repressed so much, let people push her around all the time, and it was good to see her finally fighting. She would need that fight in her if she was going to survive outside of the Earth plane. "I make no excuses for myself for the way I brought you here. I did it for all of the most selfish reasons you can accuse me of. But surely you can see how different I am?"

"I can see it," she agreed sullenly.

"Then why are you holding against me things I cannot change?"

"Who else am I supposed to hold it against? Changed or not, the fact of the matter is *you* brought me here. *You* trapped me here. And *you* planned it for a long, long time. There is no one else to blame."

"You could put a little of that blame on yourself," he said smartly. "Let me remind you of how many times you cried about getting away from home. 'Take me away. Take me far away.' Over and over again, crying on my shoulder about how miserable you were. If I could take you back right this second, Kat, would you really want to go? Would you want to go home to a father who was suffocating every single dream you ever had right out of you? He was beating you down with your responsibilities, using your sister to make you stay as long as he could keep you. In the end, he would have broken your spirit and you would have spent the rest of your life on that ranch."

"That's not true!"

"Oh, really? Then why didn't you go to college, Kat?"

"We didn't have the money," she said by rote. It stung, though, to hear him talk about it like he knew her so damn well.

"Are you sure about that? Connor had you doing every damn thing on that ranch you could, but the one thing he kept from you was what?"

"I don't—"

"You do know. What's the one thing he wouldn't let you do, Kat?"

"Th-the books," she stammered, shaking her head to negate the understanding she'd always known on some level.

"The books. Because he didn't want you to see just how flush the ranch was. That he could have easily hired a hand to replace you. That he could afford college not just for you, but for Jillian too. And he was such a damn tightwad he'd rather squeeze all the life out of you than ever spend so much as a dime helping you."

"No, that's not true." But the huge tears dripping down her face told him she knew exactly how true it was.

"Hate me for telling you the truth if you must, Kathryn, but it is the truth. And you know it is."

She sobbed into her hand, trying to find a way to turn so she wouldn't have to face her pain. But there was nowhere for her to go. It would follow her everywhere. Anywhere. Even across planes of existence.

"Oh my God. Why? Why would he do that to me?" she wanted to know.

"He needed a mother for his youngest daughter. He needed a wife to keep his house. He never once considered whether or not he needed a happy daughter."

"How do you know all of this?" she asked him as she leaned into him for support, crying her pretty eyes out and breaking his heart.

"Because his guilt ate him up at night when he slept, sweetheart. He did love you on some level, just not enough to let you go. He had horrible nightmares about you getting fed up and leaving him to manage on his own."

"Nightmares you gave him?"

"No. I didn't need to create those. And he knew right and wrong when it came to you, he just actively chose wrong every time. This is what I didn't want to tell you before. I didn't want to hurt you like this. Your ignorance was protecting you. But I won't let you think you weren't already in a prison long before I brought you to this one, because you were. And that doesn't make me right for taking you, either. It just is what it is. And I am what I am. A different man. One who still wants you with every fiber of his being. One who will do just about anything to keep you. Anything but hurt you. I promise I won't ever hurt you on purpose ever again. I'll be possessive, I'll be a little crazy now and then, and I know I'll lose my temper, but I won't have nightmares at night about the way I'm treating you." He tipped up her chin and made her look into his eyes. "I swear, I'll never hurt you."

"You can't promise me that." She hiccupped. "People always hurt each other."

"But I won't hurt you. And I can make that

promise because I know if I do, you will have every right to walk away from me. For good. And because you are my *kindra* that would be a fate worse than death for me."

"Oh, don't say that." She wept, striking her hands over her tear-streaked cheeks again and again. "I don't want to be responsible for that."

"But you are. The glowing in my eyes proves it just as much as the perfection of our joining does. We're meant to be together, Kat."

"But it's just another prison. Someone else telling me what to do."

"No, not this time." He lifted her face in his hands. "This time you'll be the one to tell me what to do. My job is to take good care of you, your job is to take us wherever you want to go. Anywhere in the Barrens or Beneath, it's all open to you. I reserve only the right to protect you from something too dangerous . . . and even then it will be a discussion, not a dictate. Agreed?"

"B-but . . ."

"But what? Tell me what you want. Let me give it to you."

And the moment he said it, he knew exactly what she would ask for,

"I want to see my family."

Chapter 12

Kathryn couldn't believe she was standing in front of that awful mirror again, contemplating what she was contemplating. *Whose idea was this, anyway?*

Oh. That's right. It had been her idea to begin with. And true to his word, Adrian had found a way to make it happen.

"Come with me," he said gently, taking up her hands and leading her toward the mirror. This time they were both completely naked.

"Why do I have to be naked again?" she asked uneasily.

"It helps you to walk seamlessly through dreams. If you wear a set style, then it might look out of place if someone is having a medieval fantasy or thinks they're a caveman from the past. This way when you enter the dream you will end up wearing exactly what they expect you to be wearing."

"All right," she said, shyly uncrossing her arms

from in front of her breasts as he drew her toward the huge mirror. "I hate this thing. It gives me electrical shocks."

"Only when I'm not here with you," he corrected her. "I'll absorb the worst of the shock. At most you'll feel an energizing tingle. Although you may not like the sensation since the mirror is polarized so negatively."

"Great," she muttered as the glass loomed closer.

"Hey." He stopped and tipped up her chin, making her meet his eyes. "I'm here and I am going to protect you. Nothing will hurt you."

Maybe she was crazy, but she actually believed him. After all, wasn't this dream thing his area of expertise? He'd done this thousands and thousands of times. Of course, it had also warped him into a demented monster that had kidnapped her ass and . . . *Whoa. Time to jump off the thought train.*

He let go of one of her hands and reached out to touch the mirror. Or *caress* it was a better descriptor. He ran his hand over it to awaken the magical energy within and it woke with a vengeance. Blue arcs of electricity shot out to connect to his wrist, following it everywhere it went as it traveled broad strokes across the mirror. Once his wrist was ringed with the reaching arcs, his hand slipped through the portal. She gripped his opposite hand fiercely with both of hers, imagining just how much the surge was going to hurt him once they crossed through. And then, with a swift yank on their hands to bring her close to his body, he swept them into the mirror.

The thick rolling smoke and fog consumed

them almost immediately. But Adrian kept her hand in his and pulled her through it with confidence in where he was going. She couldn't see how he could tell one part of the plane from another, never mind how he was going to locate the dreams of a specific person.

"You're not going to suddenly appear again out of nowhere and start groping me, are you?" she asked him.

"Do you want me to grope you?" he asked.

"Um . . ." That was definitely a trick question. He laughed at her hesitation.

"Well, that's good to know," he said with a grin. "Just keep your mind focused on what you really want. If you let it stray to things like passing desires, you might find them coming true."

"So that's what happened last time? It was one of my desires coming to life?"

"You had a strong expectation of finding me here, so you found me. Then you had expectations of how I would behave, so I behaved that way. I'm sorry I gave you the impression I was a . . . a . . ."

"Groper?"

He laughed. "Yeah, a groper. But perhaps I'd say more of an opportunist. If the chance presents itself, I'm going to be more than happy to grope you."

"I'll bet," she said, making sure her bare body didn't come into contact with his. Just the thought of him putting hands on her was distracting her thoughts and she knew just how dangerous that was in this place.

"This way," he urged her, pulling her along.

She had expected to be cold, but she wasn't in the least. She could just as easily be fully dressed. And no sooner had she thought that when a simple blue and white gingham dress appeared on her body. On her feet was a pair of brilliant ruby stilettos.

"Whoa." She stopped to look at herself a moment. There was no way Dorothy ever wore a dress this short or this tight. She felt like something out of a bad porno movie. She touched her hair and found it very neatly plaited on both sides. "What the hell?"

"Sorry about that," Adrian said as he pulled her along. "You nicked someone's fantasy."

"Eww," she said. She shivered theatrically, making her bosom display prominently in the low-cut dress. "This is just so wrong."

"People dream up all manner of things," he told her. "That's nothing. You ought to see what the really perverted ones dream up. Kids and stuff like that."

"Eww! I don't want to see that!"

"Then don't think about it. Control your mind. Control your desires. Focus solely on seeing your family. And remember what I said before you agreed to this. You'll be in their dreams. You'll be seeing some of their darkest thoughts and emotions. You might not like what you see." He frowned. "Maybe I should just have Aerlyn take you through from her side. She deals with a much happier plane than I do."

"No. I want you with me, and you said you can't go through her mirror."

"I haven't been able to for a while now," he agreed absently. "Just like she is too good to come through mine."

"Does that make me bad? Because I can come through?"

"No, sweetheart. We all have good and bad parts inside of us. The mirror is made to corrupt. It wants to corrupt. It welcomes those it thinks it can spoil. Aerlyn is too strong for it. She would never succumb to its powers."

"And I'm weak?" she asked. "I could succumb?"

"You are simply not as strong as she is. Not many are, sweetheart. Don't try to compare yourself to Aerlyn. Everyone would come up wanting against her."

"Oh." She followed him closely as he led the way. She didn't know how he knew his way, but it seemed as though he did. "How do you know where to go?" she asked at last.

"Well, it depends on where the dreamers are. All creatures in all planes come here or to Aerlyn's plane in order to dream. First you have to choose the plane the dreamer is on. Earth plane is in the center of everything, so we go to the center here first. Here." He came to a stop, drawing her up close against his still-nude body. "Now you have to select the part of the Earth plane you want to focus on."

"You mean Australia?"

Smoke suddenly whirled away from around their feet, exposing a map beneath them that rotated sharply to indicate Australia. With a gesture of his hand, Adrian focused on a specific part of the continent and then magnified it time and time again until, like a shot from a satellite, she could see her home.

"You see the red dots on the house? Those are the ports to access the dreams of the people sleeping under that roof. I wasn't sure they'd be back from the hospital yet."

"Are you kidding? My father would want to be out as soon as possible. But there're three dots there."

"Hmm. It looks like someone is sleeping in the house with Jillian and Connor." He gestured again, plugging in to the port and suddenly a whole new world erupted around them. They were in a small kitchen with a table set for at least eleven people and there was rapid Spanish flying across the room between several people. In an instant she could understand the good-natured arguments between family members. The dream seemed to center around a woman named Rosa, and Kathryn quickly understood that it was Rosa doing the dreaming.

"But this is a good dream," she noted.

"It might seem so to you, but all this teasing is a sore point for her. Her mother makes fun of her cooking, her brothers make fun of her weight, her sisters tease about her not having a man in her life. Listen to them and you'll begin to feel her pain. They undermine her in every possible way and all the while cloak it in this so-called good-natured ribbing."

"But who is she? Is she . . . is she sleeping with my father?" She flushed at the very thought. She didn't want to be walking around in the mind of her father's mistress.

"No. Look at how far apart the ports are. She must be a maid he hired to help with Jillian and the house." He gestured out of the port and instantly the dream disappeared. "Who do you want first? Connor or Jillian?" He looked up and met her eyes, remaining neutral for her sake and letting her make all of her own choices in this situation . . . just like he'd promised to do.

"Connor," she said quickly, before she lost her nerve altogether.

Adrian plugged them into the port in a heartbeat and Kathryn found herself at ground zero in her father's nightmare. He was in their house, running from room to room frantically.

"Kathryn! Kathryn, where are you?" He was drenched in sweat, throwing open door after door over and over again. Even in rooms he had just searched. "Kathryn!"

"Can he see me?" she asked, her hands wringing together.

"Not yet. You have to step into the dream. Not physically, but mentally. Make yourself appear to him. And don't worry, your clothes will change to suit. He'll see you exactly as he expects you to look."

Kathryn nodded and closed her eyes, willing herself to appear in front of her father. She had no idea what she was going to say to him, but she knew she couldn't bear listening to him shouting for a daughter he simply couldn't find.

Suddenly he threw open a door and looked straight at her.

"Oh, thank God! Kathryn, where have you been?" He rushed up to her, catching her up close to him in a hug so tight she could hardly breathe.

She'd never known her father to be overtly affectionate, so the hug took her by surprise. The sheer desperation in it made her eyes tear.

"I'm here, Papa," she said soothingly. "I'm safe. I'm sorry I had to leave you."

"You have to stay," he commanded her. "Your sister needs you."

Her heart fell. How many times had she heard that same phrase over and over again? That same entrapment, keeping her perfectly caged.

"I can't stay, Papa. I have to go."

"No. No, Kathryn, don't go." He moved back away from her a little, searching her face and touching her hair gently. "Whenever I look in your face, I see your mother perfectly. How will I see her without you?"

She swallowed hard, anger welling up even as her heart went out to him. What about her? Didn't he want her to stay because of anything he missed about her as a person? Didn't he miss her laugh or the way she burned his toast nearly every morning or when they played gin rummy for hours before bedtime? Didn't he miss her for *her*?

"Papa, don't you miss me?" she asked.

"Of course I do. This place is going to hell without you. I had to hire some Hispanic gal just to keep up with the housework."

"Oh, Papa," she said sadly. "I . . . have to go now."

She turned toward Adrian, reaching out to take his hand.

"Wait," he father said. "Where will you be?"

"Somewhere safe," she said, and stepped out of his dream and against Adrian's side.

He hugged her close and pressed an apologetic kiss to her brow. But he didn't have anything to be sorry for just then. This pain was squarely on her father's shoulders—and on her own for letting things go on so long.

"Let's go see Jilly," he coaxed her, pulling the third port forward over them. The dream blossomed into Jillian's room. She was sick in bed, looking miserable, and she had Kathryn sitting beside her tending to her, just as she had been doing before Adrian had swept her away. "This time, just step into yourself. You'll take over the role like a possession."

She only hesitated a moment, afraid just then to have her image of Jilly shattered as well. But she longed for her sister too much to pass up the chance to speak to her and touch her again. She moved forward and quickly sat down in the chair she was occupying. Her body fused to the dream image and she found herself leaning over Jillian and pressing a cool cloth to her forehead.

"Rest, honey. You'll feel better soon," she said to her ailing sister, just as she would have done were it not a dream.

"Kat, I missed you," she said plaintively.

She laughed tearfully, relieved to hear Jillian say those very simple words.

"I'm right here. I'll always be here when you need me, love."

"No. You'll be gone. I need you. Who is going to look after me when I'm sick? Who is going to teach me my lessons? Who is going to let me cheat them at cribbage?"

"Jilly, I can't come back. I want to do all of those things with you again and again, but I-I need to find my own life right now. And part of that means I can't come back." She bit her lip. "But I'll come to you just like this whenever I can, okay? When you're dreaming."

"Careful," Adrian warned her. She knew he meant that she couldn't expose her sister to the truth of what they could do. If she knew too much then she'd be taken to Beneath as well. Kathryn didn't want that. She wanted her sister to have a normal life. A normal life that would occasionally include dreams of a big sister who had vanished from her life without explanation.

"Okay," Jillian said. "I'm glad you got a life. You needed one badly. Is there a boy?"

Jilly was perpetually telling her to get a boyfriend, that she needed a good man in her life. Kathryn heard Adrian chuckle and she resisted the urge to stick her tongue out at him.

"Yes," she said with a flush creeping up her neck, "there's a boy. But he's a bit of a jerk," she added.

"Aren't they all?" Jillian questioned.

"That's very true," she agreed smugly. She felt him step up behind her even before he put his hand on her shoulder. "I have to go now."

Jillian sat up and threw her arms around her neck, squeezing tightly.

"Don't," she said painfully. "Not yet."

So she stayed a while longer, just hugging her sister and hearing soft words that made her feel so loved. It more than made up for what she had lacked from her father. But it also made it harder for her to leave. This was her sister's nightmare, though, and the bad part had to happen sometime. Slowly she worked free of her arms and stepped away.

Then she turned to Adrian and hugged him hard. He knew she was thanking him and despising him all at once. It radiated into him through her very thorough and expressive hug. He regretted her sense of loss. He really did. But at the same time he could never make himself regret having taken her. She belonged with him. It was written down deep inside her genetic code, just as it was written in his. Because she was human, she didn't feel the connection the way his people did, but that didn't mean she couldn't come close to an approximation of it. He knew she had to be feeling something already; otherwise she never would have given herself to him so quickly. He didn't fool himself into thinking it had been because of any charm he had shown her. He knew well enough what a bastard he had been to her. But for now they had chemistry on their side, and that would have to be enough—enough to make a start, at least. And, he thought, perhaps they were starting to have understanding as well. He certainly understood her emotions of the moment. He didn't have to lose his sister to know how much it would hurt him.

Now he did, anyway. Mere days ago he probably could not have cared less. But in his present state of clarity he knew it would tear him up. He had been responsible for doing that to Kathryn. He had a long way to go to earn her forgiveness for that, if that kind of forgiveness was even remotely possible. And at the moment, he was hoping it was starting with a heartfelt hug.

"Where have you been?"

Aerlyn was breathless as she asked the question, everything about her looking tense and anxious. That immediately worried Adrian because his sister was ever the calm and patient one between them. To see her standing there twisting her hands together meant that something was very wrong.

They had just stepped back into his workroom to find her waiting there for them. Adrian knew Kathryn was already in emotional turmoil from her mixed results with her family visit, so he didn't want to include her in whatever was upsetting Aerlyn. He reached for the cloak she had worn down to his workroom and swept it around her shoulders. He didn't care about being naked in front of his sister, but he knew Kathryn did.

"Kat, why don't you go upstairs for a bit? I'll be right behind you."

"No," his sister said, holding out a hand to stay his *kindra*. "This concerns both of you."

Immediately Adrian felt like a lead weight had been sunk into his stomach. Whatever this was, it couldn't be good. Everything about Aerlyn was broadcasting it.

"Speak," he said sharply, more sharply than he'd intended. He reached out and curled a protective hand around Kathryn's elbow.

"Earlier when you . . . when you made love," she said quickly, "you released a tremendous amount of energy. I had no choice but to deliver it to the Ampliphi. I thought I was doing the right thing, showing them proof that she was who you had claimed her to be."

"And?" he pressed, ignoring the blush of embarrassment he could see creeping over Kathryn. He couldn't put her at ease. Not until he knew what was so distressing to his sister.

"They accepted the proof. Your life is no longer in danger."

"Oh! That's wonderful!" Kathryn exclaimed suddenly, reaching to lean her entire body against his side in an enthusiastic hug. "I was so worried about that."

"I wasn't," he said flatly. "I knew you were my *kindra*. I had no doubts once I saw the effect you were having on my outside appearance. Not to mention the inside."

"Well, you could have told me that," she huffed in consternation. "I've been afraid for you ever since you told me your life was on the line."

Adrian looked at her, wanting so badly to pursue this obvious line of concern for him that she was showing. Was it possible she was already coming to care for him? He wanted so badly to know the answer to that. But his sister's anxiety was pressing against him and he knew there was more to come.

"Aerlyn, what is the trouble?"

She took a breath and exhaled slowly through her pursed lips, her eyes alight with the fire of anger, and Adrian realized it was for his sake.

"The Ampliphi have ordered you to relocate back to our village, where you and your *kindra* will live from now on. It's for the sake of the people who need the energy you will deliver. You'll be feeding thousands with pure, unadulterated and positive energy. It could eradicate starvation and illness in the village once and for all."

Adrian knew she was explaining that for Kathryn's benefit, not for his. He knew full well why the Ampliphi were laying down this dictate. He also knew that it could be just the thing to push Kat over the edge. She had been through so much these past few days, their relationship was tenuous at best, and she had just learned about the betrayals of her father. Forcing her into an alien plane and making her adapt to it could very easily destroy what little sanity she might have left. Aerlyn knew this, and that was why she was so anxious and upset.

"We won't go." He said it flat and hard. A dictate, not a discussion.

"You have no choice, Adrian. You cannot defy the Ampliphi. They will come for you and force you to obey. Or it will give them another excuse to threaten your life. Do not balk at this, Adrian, I beg you," Aerlyn said, her voice bordering on panic.

"I won't put Kathryn through such a dramatic change in circumstances! It is asking too much of her!"

"And you can't selfishly starve the masses of our people who need the two of you so very badly!"

"You can carry the energy back and forth just as you did today," Adrian said shortly.

"No. I can't. It was too much for me, Adrian. I thought I was going to explode if I didn't get out of here fast enough. I almost didn't escape in time. I am not equipped to handle all of that. And that would leave tons of energy to waste. No. There's no way around this. Believe me, I have been trying to think of one for the past couple of hours. It's the right thing to do for our people."

"And what about doing the right thing for Kathryn? Doesn't anyone but me give a damn about her feelings and her well-being?"

"Um . . . I think I qualify for that." Kathryn spoke up softly, raising her hand. "And I think you ought to ask me how I feel about all of this instead of assuming you know better."

Perhaps it was because she didn't yell at him for the mistake that it made such a tremendous impact on him. He felt immediately sheepish and it showed in his expression. But it didn't change facts.

"You don't understand. Life Beneath is dramatically different from life here or on the Earth plane. There are dangers and rules, and there are things you've never seen before. I'm not certain you could handle just how different it is, Kat."

"I see. Well, thank you for your concern. And thank you for explaining it to me. I'm sure I have very little idea of what I'd be getting myself into. What I do know is that I can count on you to protect me. If nothing else, I know that much. I also know that I can't let anyone starve, no matter who they are or where they live, if I can in any way help change it." She hesitated for half a second. "Um . . . does that mean they want us to—to do it, and everyone will know every time it happens?"

Adrian tried very hard not to smile. She couldn't

possibly know how red she was right then as the truth of the situation occurred to her.

"Lovemaking is one of the most powerful and beneficial energies there is," he said, reaching out to rub the back of a claw over her burning cheek. "Lovemaking between *kind* is something far off the charts. Immeasurable. Yes, everyone will know every time it happens. They'll know because they won't be weak from lack of energy any longer. They'll know because children who are too sick to move will suddenly jump up from their beds and play. They'll know because the elderly will finally be able to relax and live without pain and discomfort."

"Oh my God. Performance anxiety much?" she said, waving her hand in front of her face.

"No one expects it of you, Kat. They only are grateful when and if it does happen," Aerlyn said gently. "Don't be worried. Our people are fed in other ways as well, but this is just the strongest and purest of ways. You don't have to do anything you don't want to do. No one would ever make that expectation of you."

"Good," she breathed. "I'm glad. That could be really stressful for a gal." She gave Adrian a sidelong look. "Or for a guy."

Adrian chuckled at that. "Believe me, sweetheart," he said, "as long as you're anywhere near me, lack of performance will not be an issue."

He had meant to make her blush and it worked famously. She also knew what he was up to, so she elbowed him hard in the ribs.

"You big jerk."

"Are you sure about this?" Aerlyn fretted over

them. She was twisting her hands together again. "You've been through so much, Kathryn. And I don't think you understand just how different our home plane is."

"Well," she said with a nervous little chuckle, "I guess I'm about to find out."

Chapter 13

Kathryn stood on the walkway and gaped openly at what she was seeing. Apparently the people of Beneath did not believe in living on solid ground. Instead the entire village was strung up—suspended, even—between two sides of opposing cliffs. The village was level after level of pointy little buildings and hundreds of walkways *without railings*. This was particularly insane because they were suspended in midair *above* the line of fluffy clouds she could see scudding between the cliffs about a half a mile or so beneath her feet.

"Oh yeah," she gulped, "this is different, all right."

Adrian had hold of her arm as they walked toward the first level of the village, keeping her steady on the unrailed walkway. The path was just wide enough for two people to walk side by side comfortably, but there was certainly no room for horseplay or running around.

"I lived on this level. The house is still mine and

Aerlyn's. It's nothing as grand as the castle we just left, but I think you'll be comfortable there."

She was barely listening to him, though she knew she should be. She was busy watching everyone on the walkways. Men. Bunches and bunches of men. Not a single woman to be seen anywhere. Except for her. And people were beginning to notice her presence. Heads turned and curious eyes followed as she went, and some of those looks were much more than curious. They were covetous.

And she wasn't the only one noticing. Adrian was growing very tense beside her, a low sound of warning rumbling out of him now and again when someone's eyes lingered too long on her. She reached out and covered his hand with hers, squeezing with reassurance. What she wanted right now was to get to this house of his and sit in peace for a little while. She'd barely had time to process her encounter with her family, or how she was feeling about Adrian. Now she was in this vastly different world with all its unspoken dangers and she was starting to get a headache from it all.

"Come on, let's get you inside."

Kathryn didn't know if he was reading her mind or trying to get her away from the eyes of other men. A little bit of both, perhaps. Regardless of his motivations, he had them standing in front of a heavy metal door within minutes. It looked like the kind of door you saw on a bank vault. Adrian reached out and turned the center wheel hard and she could hear bolts retracting. For a frightening minute she was left to consider if the door was meant to keep someone in or what the hell they were trying to keep out.

"Don't go outside during the hours of sunrise or sunset," Adrian warned her, again uncannily divining her thoughts, it seemed. "The *okriti* are on the move during those times and they sometimes come into the village."

"*Okriti?*" she asked with a swallow.

"A wild beast that roams the land. They are in great abundance and travel in packs. It's the main reason why we don't build on the land. They aren't afraid of us, and they can do a great deal of damage."

"Why do they come here?" she asked dumbly.

He shut the door behind them and latched it tightly in the closed position. "Why do you think, Kat? They are looking for food. And the competition for resources is fierce. But that's okay," he said with a wolfish smile. "*Okriti* make good eating for us too. The village is designed to thwart them and as long as you know what to do to avoid trouble, you'll be safe and sound."

"So . . . you eat food too?" she asked. "I thought you fed on energy."

"We feed on both." He moved to her side, taking her shoulders warmly in the cupping strength of his hands. "But food only feeds our bodily energy. We need to feed our souls as well. And what happens to the soul inevitably reflects on the body."

"It sounds terrible . . . to starve like that."

"It is terrible. If not for Guardians like me and Aerlyn venturing onto other planes to seek sources of energy, we would long be extinct. Earth plane is by far the richest resource there is. Your people throw away emotions, both good and bad, and think absolutely nothing of it. The sexual energy you expend alone is a crop well worth harvesting."

"I see. Well, this might sound simplistic, but why don't you come and live in the Earth plane? You look just like us. I mean, the rest of your people look just like us," she corrected hastily. "No one would know the difference."

He held up a finger and then, using a claw from the opposite hand, he cut it across the tip. Instantly a bubble of pink fluorescent blood welled up.

"All it would take was one cut, one accident, and humans would know we were among them. Knowing humans as you do, do you see them accepting us then?"

Kathryn shut her mouth with a snap, only just then realizing she was gaping at him. She slowly shook her head, knowing as well as he did that humans would see them as a threat just because they were different. History had proved time and again that visual differences had always been the cause of terrible and inhuman crimes against others. She would like to think the human race had risen above that, but she wasn't willing to test that theory any more than Adrian's people were.

"So, the Guardians . . . how many are there?"

"Six. Just like there are six Ampliphi. One for each of the major villages we have here. Each Guardian reaps as much energy as they can in their specialty; then they bring it to the Ampliphi, who make it more than what it was and spread it out among the people. But there is a hierarchy of who gets what," he told her. "Women are among the first. They are the key to our future, and there are so few left. We must take care of them. Next are the leaders of the villages, the men who guard them and keep them safe, and then, lastly, the others—the children and the elders. And often there's not enough to make it worth their while. This is why the connection of *kind* is so treasured. The emotional energy put out between *kindri* and *kindra* can save a village like this one."

"Wow. Pressure. A lot of pressure," she said, laying a hand over her suddenly racing heart.

"No pressure, Kat. You're doing enough just standing here talking to me. Even the panic you are feeling now will feed souls here. You can really do no wrong. Except for violence." He frowned and looked down at his own hands. "Violence is like a plague here, and it spreads like wildfire. You have to be careful of that. *I* have to be careful of that."

"Thank you for warning me. Luckily, I am more likely to scream and run than I am likely to commit an act of violence. I'm sure I've proved that to you by now." She placed both her hands in his and firmly squeezed. "And don't worry. I'll help you keep your temper under control."

He looked up at her quickly, surprised he had been so easy to read. His mouth turned down into a grim line. "Kat, I am going to tell you something because I think you have a right to know." He cleared his throat. "I think part of the reason they called us here so quickly is because they want me to . . . to . . ."

"Fuck up?" she prompted, lifting one brow.

"Yes. To them I am the monster you first met. The Ampliphi haven't seen how much I've changed.

But I'm not sure the exterior changes are enough. The laws about violence or taking a life are very clear here. Because we are a society made up mostly of men, an aggressive sex, they've had to be really strict. I could do something that will earn me the death penalty. I may already have."

Kathryn felt the bottom drop out of her stomach. "What do you mean?"

He suddenly shook his head and turned away from her. "It doesn't matter. What's done is done."

"But I thought your life was spared now. Because you proved I really was your *kindra*."

"This has nothing to do with that. It's something else. And please don't ask me to elaborate. You think me enough of a monster as it is."

"That's not true!"

"Isn't it? Just this morning you called me a monster."

"No! I-I mean, yes, I did, but I didn't mean in the physical sense. Oh, I don't know what I meant!" she burst out in frustration. "I was angry and hurt. This has been a lot for me to take. You have to cut me a little slack here, Adrian."

"Let's drop this discussion," he said softly, his tone sounding so alone and forlorn. It broke her heart to hear it and she cursed herself for the things she had said to him.

"Adrian . . ." She came up behind him and ran her hands over his big back and broad shoulders, laid her cheek against his spine. "Adrian, a monster doesn't take a girl to see her family one last time. A monster wouldn't care about her feelings. He wouldn't even think twice about it. You were a monster when you first took me, it's true, but ever since then you've come farther and farther away from that and you've done nothing but try to make it up to me ever since."

"Trying to make up to you doesn't make the original sin right." He turned beneath her hands and cheek, presenting her with his chest. "I fear that you'll never forgive me for taking you from Earth. I fear that every new thing you experience here is only going to remind you more and more of what you have lost at my hands."

"Adrian, no . . . that's not entirely true." She looked up at him and could see in his eyes that he thought it was very true. "Yes, I'll miss my home. But I will forgive you one day. I can't possibly hold a grudge against someone forever. It's just not in my nature. I learn and I adapt to things and make do with what I've been given. If I learned anything in my father's house, I learned that."

Adrian reached to brush at her hair and face with a massive palm, making her feel small and delicate. The gentler he was, the more it belied his potential for violence. She wondered then if he would one day return to his full normal self or if this transformation might stop at some point. It didn't matter to her either way, but thinking about what he said about energy feeding their souls made her think he would return to normal eventually. He had been feeding his soul with the corrupting energy of the mirror and the dark emotions of the people within the nightmare plane, and that had corrupted him violently. Now he was no longer using the mirror and was feeding strictly from her energy—his *kindra*'s energy—and he was changing to reflect that.

She was happy for him. He had made huge sacrifices in the name of feeding his people. He deserved to retire peacefully. And if this village was where it must be done, she would see to it that he made the transition flawlessly.

"Come," he said softly. "Let me show you your new home."

Everything was woven. The floors, the roofs, the walls—all of it was woven out of this incredibly hard material that also gave off an ambient light. She imagined the entire village must glow at night. She wondered if that would make it more attractive to the *okriti* or if it was like building a campfire to keep wolves and wildlife away. Regardless, she felt very safe inside these woven walls with Adrian. He took her up to the next level, a process rather like when you were a kid and walked up a slide in the playground the wrong way. There were no stairs and only the weaving provided traction.

"In the unlikely event the *okriti* ever made it indoors, they couldn't climb to the second story, leaving you a haven until help could come," Adrian explained.

"Good to know," she said with a loud swallow.

"Don't worry," he reassured her. "They only move this way during dawn and dusk, and even then they will be more likely to keep away. And even if they do attack, the entire village is designed to ward them off. First, there are no rails on the walkways for them to hold on to, and the *okriti* are not known for their excellent balance."

"So they'll fall." She frowned. "So what are the nets for beneath the village? Is it like hunting?"

"The nets are meant to catch children who accidentally fall. Anything heavier than that or anything that struggles hard and it will break away, sending the contents down into the crevasse."

"Oh my God." She blanched. "And here I was thinking I would be saved if I fell."

"I won't let you fall," he assured her, bringing her close so he could hug her tightly in reassurance.

"I'll hold you to that," she said vehemently.

"The roofs are all cones, the houses are all round, making a steep, slick surface the *okriti* can't cling to," he continued. "And these doors can only be opened by someone strong with the ability to use opposable thumbs. That being said, if all else fails, this village is packed full of warriors who would defend it with their lives. The *okriti* are easy pickings to them, I assure you."

"And good eating," she added in a lame attempt to act comforted by all of this. Still, it sounded as though they had planned for everything. It was well thought out, and with the exception of those frightening walkways, it seemed very safe.

"Come here," he said, pulling her into a room.

There was no mistaking it for a bedroom. The central piece of furniture was a rope-supported bed, a very big one that stretched from wall to wall. Although, technically, because they were round, it was all the same wall. Just the same, the bed was made by a form of the same woven material as the house was, although this was flexible whereas the other was not.

"What is this stuff?" she asked, running her fingers over the bed ropes.

"*Shanshi*. It's a plant that grows wild all over. It has phosphorescent properties, as you can see, and a mixture of water and salt makes it as hard as steel. The weavers in the village are always busy gathering and weaving and salting the *shanshi*. The village is always growing so we always have a use for it."

"You know something, this is a really fascinating place you've got here."

"Thank you," he said, his eyes roaming slowly down the length of her body. "I think you make it fascinating."

"Do I?"

Adrian was delighted when she suddenly turned coy, pretending she didn't notice his regard for her. She was fishing for compliments, desiring them from him, and he desired to give them to her. He knew she had not had the opportunity for appreciation from others. Her father had never acknowledged her as anything but a workhorse, and she dismissed the things her sister said as being the bias of sisterly love.

But the fact was she was beautiful. In every way. He had always thought this room to be plain and utilitarian, but her presence there changed all of that. She was wearing another of the dresses he had gotten her, this one a basic black made of a satin that was anything but basic. The snug bodice and the straps over her arms and shoulders, coupled with the demure business-length skirt, just made him want to take it all off her. It was like a wrapped gift with bow and frills. The outside was nice and all, but it was only the inside that mattered.

Adrian took the step needed to bring him closer to her, reaching out to run his slightly curved nails over her pretty bare skin. When he ran into one of the straps, he hooked it and began to pull it down.

She finally looked up at him, her gray eyes liquid soft like smelted nickel.

"What are you doing?" she asked, her voice tremulous.

"I'm telling you how beautiful and irresistible you are," he said deeply.

"But you didn't say anything until just now."

"I know. I like to play show-and-tell." He bent his head and kissed the side of her neck, taking a moment to nip at her delicate skin with the tips of his fangs. She tasted so fine, and smelled even better. She had showered with yet another scent, this time roses and sage. He would have to see to it that all of her things were brought here for her. He wanted her to always smell this good, always be a changing surprise to him and yet the same gorgeous Kat.

"A-are we alone?" she asked him unsteadily, her hands pushing at his shoulders a little.

"Yes. No one else will come here. It's just you and me." He reached for another strap on the same side and tugged it down as well. "And I would really like it if I could make love with you, sweetheart."

"Because people are hungry?" she asked.

That gave him pause and he looked up into her eyes, seeing she meant the frank question exactly as it had sounded. How could she think that thought had even entered his mind? Did she think she was always only going to be a means to an end?

"Because I am hungry, Kat," he growled softly. "For you. I want you for you, not for any other reason. I'm crazy for the way you smell, the way you taste," he bent and licked the soft hollow of her shoulder, "for the way you feel," he reached up to boldly cradle her breast in his hand, "and most of all, for how damn beautiful you are."

"I'm not beautiful," she whispered weakly.

"Oh yes, you are." He pulled her bodice away from her breast, exposing her nipple. He bent his head and sucked it firmly into his mouth, just as quickly releasing it with a little pop. The nipple was now stiff and flushed, her breast full in his hand. "Now look at yourself," he said reaching his hand up to the side of her head to make sure she did so. "Tell me that isn't beautiful."

She didn't have a response for that and he took it as a good sign. He swept aside the straps of her dress, baring her shoulders and drawing the bodice down completely. The whole time he didn't take his eyes off her. He couldn't. With her perfect skin and her fair-colored nipples, she was an amazing sight. And she was all his. He still couldn't get over that understanding. His. His *kindra*. His mate. Oh, he knew he owed her a lot, owed her time to come to grips with everything, but for right now, she was letting him look his fill and touch her at will. It was more than he could have asked for. Hoped for.

That part of him that was still savage wanted her with a fierceness he could hardly control. It growled

and hissed in his mind, furious with him for not
seizing her and making her his right away. And oh,
how he wanted to do that. Make her his. Again and
again. To that end he pushed the dress down off
her hips and looked his fill of her.

"Perfect," he said as he shaped her soft, rounded
hips in his hands. He knew she thought she was
fat, could feel the emotional insecurity radiating
off her. Did she know how easily he could hear her?
Did she know how wrong he thought she was?

He knew words meant little to her, so he would
show her his proof. He went down on his knees before her, his hands never once leaving her body,
and leaned forward to kiss her belly just below her
navel. Her hands came forward to grasp his wrists,
as though she wanted to stop him from touching
her. Well, she wasn't going to get her way. It would
take a damn herd of *okriti* attacking him to get
him to stop.

He drew his fingers softly forward, from the
point of her hip down to the nest of curls protecting her. He ran his claws through the tight curls,
making her gasp at the sensation. It was as erotic
to give the touch as it must be to receive it. He
raked through again and again, until finally she released her hold on his wrists and buried her fingers in his hair instead. He could smell her. The
sweet scent of an aroused woman. His woman.
Then he planted both hands firmly on her hips
again and jerked her forward onto his mouth.

He had meant to be gentler, but the beast in his
brain had wanted her on his tongue *right now*. So
he opened his mouth against her and delved deep
for her most exotic of flavors. Her legs parted nat-

urally, a gasp erupting from her lips. His hands curved down to grasp her thighs right beneath her buttocks, dragging her deeper onto his mouth.

Oh heavenly sweet. She was soaking wet and hot, the musky flavor of her like ambrosia on his tongue. He devoured her, wanting more and more of her, pulling her leg up over his shoulder so she was spread wide for him. A feast for his taking. Her fingers were growing frantic in his hair, clutching and reclutching it by the very roots. He waited for it, teasing his tongue lightly over her clit, giving her nothing she truly wanted. He teased and teased until she made a sound of ultimate frustration and grabbed the back of his head, pulling him forward, deepening his presence in her pussy. He would have chuckled had he the presence of mind to do so. Right then, however, he was too busy taking her up on her adamant invitation. He sucked that juicy little bud between his teeth again and again until he felt her trembling on the one leg that supported her weight.

With a single surge of strength he hauled her off the floor and dumped her onto the bed. Once she was flat on her back he pulled her to the edge of the bed and tossed both of her legs over his shoulders. Now he was ready for her. Ready to play with her. He slid his tongue deep between her labia, rimming the entrance to her body several times before giving in to the command of her straining hips and burrowing his tongue deep into her channel. As soon as he did that, he brought a thumb up to her clit to circle it in slow, tight revolutions. He could hear her gasping for every breath, felt her legs tightening around him, those hands in his hair ready to snatch him bald.

And then she ignited. Like a firestorm, she surrounded him with the strength of her orgasm. Her clutching hands, her heels digging into his back, her come rolling sweet and hot against his tongue. It was pure bliss and he wanted to do it again. He didn't even give her a chance to come down from her explosive peak. Instead he kept her there, pushing her for more, tonguing her until she screamed.

She tried to push him away then, and this time he listened. He listened because hearing her cries had him just about wild, tasting her just pushing him over the edge. He stood up between her legs, fumbling at the button to his jeans. They were too tight, these wretched human clothes, strangling his desire for her, keeping him away from her.

And then he felt her soft touch on his hands, pushing them out of her way. He groaned when she cupped him in her palm straight through the unforgiving denim. Then she slid the confounding button through its hole and carefully drew down the zipper.

He fell right into her hand. He had to reach out to grab her by her shoulder, needing a steady as she used that inconceivably light touch on his cock, almost as if she weren't there at all. He couldn't help thrusting against her palm.

"Hold me tight," he ground out.

And like magic, she did exactly that. Almost too tight. But at that point he was hard enough to ram through steel. Her strength was nothing compared to that. He had to teach her the right way to touch him. She was so inexperienced. . . .

Adrian gasped when out of nowhere her lips touched wet and warm to the head of his cock. The instant she kissed him he went wet at the very tip, threatening to drip on her. She saw that threat, and with only a moment of awkward hesitation, she stuck out her tongue and swiped it over his slit. He felt the act straight to his tightening balls, his vision blurring for a second as he tried to reconcile what he was seeing and what he was feeling.

"My God," he croaked. "Take me in your mouth, sweetheart. Please . . . please . . ." He continued to beg her, soft, coaxing pleas when he felt her fear and doubt. Not fear of the act itself, but that she would somehow fuck it up and hurt him. "You won't hurt me," he told her. "I swear, you won't hurt me. Just . . . don't be afraid."

"How do you do that?" she asked him. "How do you always know what I'm thinking?"

"I'll explain later," he growled at her.

She giggled at him. He didn't mind because it eased her fear to laugh at him. Then she opened her lips and closed her mouth around him. It was all he could do not to react as wildly as he wanted to. But he knew he'd scare the crap out of her if he did that, so he held it all back, except for a long, low groan of pleasure.

"Perfect," he uttered. "Just . . . per—"

He was a liar. Perfect came an instant later when she suddenly sucked him into her mouth. This time he couldn't keep the rough cry from bursting out of him. To countermand the potentially startling sound, he grabbed hold of the back of her head and kept her right where she was, not letting her pull away.

"It's good," he rasped. "It's so good, Kat."

Apparently that was all she needed to hear. She repeated the act with relish, taking him as far into her mouth as she dared, which was pretty damn far, actually. He had thought himself too big for much, too overwhelming for her, but she didn't seem to care about that.

He only let her suck him a couple more times before he stopped her. He couldn't hold it together anymore. He couldn't even wait to get completely undressed. He just shoved his pants down to his knees and pushed her back onto the bed. Her legs were hanging over the side and for him that was perfect. He hooked her knees into his elbows, hoisting her bottom off the bed until she was right up against him. He slid against her, wetting himself with her juices, making sure his desperation wouldn't cause her pain. Then, with just an artful slide of his hips, he found her entrance and shoved himself in.

She was still so tight that he barely made it halfway into her. It was frustrating and exciting all at once. He liked that she was still so new, liked that she wasn't experienced enough to know she should have relaxed instead of tensing up. It made it all so much better. And besides, it only took one more thrust to seat him fully inside her. Then he just stayed there, basking in her heat and wetness, letting her stay hugged tight around him.

But then it quickly became unbearable to stay still. He tested himself, seeing how long he could tolerate not moving. But even she worked against him, tightening her legs and pussy around him to urge him on. It was so gorgeous. So painfully wonderful. He started to thrust and thrust and thrust, each one harder and faster than the one before. He wasn't happy until she started to pant and cry out.

"Oh God! Adrian! That feels so good!"

Her words only spurred him on to deeper penetration, making him burrow hard into her until the sound of wet, excited flesh sliding into wet, excited flesh was filling the air around them. The arousing smell of her was all around him, soaking deep into his pores, taunting him with the need to come and mix his own scent directly with hers. But not before her. Not before.

He didn't have long to wait before she let loose with increasingly loud cries of pleasure, warning him she was building to an explosive release, much more powerful than the ones she'd had so far. His testicles were on fire, building for a hard release of their own, and suddenly . . . she stopped.

Tension writhing through her, the need to come keen on her, she suddenly drew back and he couldn't stop to figure out why. He was too far gone. He roared with release and frustration, his orgasm ripping wildly out of him. His fingers were gripping hard into her thighs, unthinking of the claws at their tips. He shot inside her with deep, unending pulsations. But it infuriated him that she had not come with him. He let go of her legs and pounced on her in the bed, yanking her hard into the center of it.

"Where did you go?" he demanded roughly.

"G-go?" she asked weakly, but he could tell she knew exactly what he was talking about.

"Damn it, Kat, *where did you go?*"

"I just . . . I just couldn't . . . I felt like everybody would know."

"They'll know anyway because of my orgasm, honey. You may as well have yours too," he scolded her.

"I'm sorry. I'm just new at this and it's a lot of pressure!"

He saw her eyes fill with tears and had the immediate epiphany that he was an ass. Putting more pressure on her was certainly not the way to deal with the situation. "Kat, you already had two orgasms. Why not go for the hat trick?" He said it lightly, teasing her.

"I know. I'm silly, I guess." She sniffled and rubbed angrily at her eyes. "I wish I wasn't. I wish I wasn't such a coward."

"That's too harsh," he said sharply. "You've experienced very little in your own world and then are thrust blindly into another. Frankly, I think you're taking it all pretty damn well."

"Do you?"

"Yes. I do. And to prove my point, I'm going to give you another chance."

"Another chance at what?"

He grabbed hold of her hand and wrapped her fingers around his stiffening cock.

"At this."

"Oh! Hey, wow . . . That's some recovery time you got there, mister. I thought normal men couldn't do that."

"I'm not normal," he reminded her.

"I'll say!"

He shut her up with a kiss, not minding her giggles against his mouth.

Adrian was determined to help her over this, but more importantly, he wanted her again. She had been able to let go during their oral play earlier, and he was going to figure out how to get her to relax. He didn't want to put too much pressure on her, knowing that would only make it worse, but he was willing to pull out everything in his arsenal.

He started simply, with a kiss on her mouth that was, in comparison, fairly chaste. Just the same, it made her smile. That made him realize just how important it was to him that she was happy. Seeing her smile sent such satisfied pleasure through him, it was actually overwhelming. What was most overwhelming about it, though, was that it didn't hurt in the slightest to feel it. He realized then that it didn't hurt when she touched him anymore, either. He had grown so used to bracing himself against the pain, so how was it that he didn't notice when it was gone?

Adrian reached out to stroke his thumb over her cheek. That gorgeous face was so precious to him, he realized. She had gotten under his skin from the very moment he had first stumbled into her dreams. Turned out, he liked having her there.

He was just about to kiss her again when there was a resounding banging coming from the main part of the house.

"Ignore it," she tempted him, reaching to nip playfully at the point of his chin.

"Now that's a fine idea," he said, kissing his temptation, "but in a dangerous world, it's a little more than just being rude if you don't answer the door. It could cost someone their life."

With that he launched himself out of her arms, immediately regretting the act as he saw her lying there all bare and beautiful. Grumbling at the sound of the repeated knocking, he reached for his pants and then hurried out of the room. As he rounded the door he saw her crawling across the bed to find her clothes. That provocative position had his mind reeling, and he was determined to get rid of whoever the hell it was who had disturbed him.

He turned the wheel to the door and yanked it open.

"Holy hell. They weren't lying," was the greeting he received.

"Kine," Adrian said in return. Then he looked at the second man standing there. "Daedalus. Long time no see."

"I could say the same," the other man said, his low voice as rough as his appearance. Daedalus had once been as big and robust as Adrian now was, but like Adrian, he trafficked in energy that was on the harsher end of the spectrum. Daedalus dealt strictly in grief and in all the energy released because of death, and it showed. He had grown gaunt and pale, his cheeks sunken; long fingers gave him the appearance of a wraith. His eyes were immeasurably weary, as though he had seen far too much. Adrian only needed to look into his eyes for a moment for the two men to realize they were kindred spirits. Both had sacrificed who they were for the sake of their people, rewriting everything about themselves and paying a very heavy price.

Kine broke the momentary silence. "My God, Adrian, you look—you look great!" Kine was one of the few people who had seen Adrian in his full monstrous state.

"Thanks," Adrian said dismissively. "So what brings you both here?" he asked them.

"Can't a couple of fellow Guardians come say hello to an old friend?" Kine asked as he pushed past Adrian and entered the hut-styled home.

"They can also come to ogle my *kindra*," Adrian mused under his breath.

Daedalus chuckled, having overheard him. "Let's call it meeting, not ogling. We're happy for you, Adrian. We've missed you a great deal while you've been hidden away in the Barrens."

"Have you?" Adrian scratched the back of his neck uncomfortably. He hadn't thought much about his former friends the way they had clearly been thinking of him. Part and parcel of his mentality and self-involved fury at life, he thought.

"Don't worry," Daedalus reassured him with a hearty clap on the shoulder, "Aerlyn spoke with me many times about what was going on with you. I understand the situation and what it must have been like."

By the look of his friend, Adrian didn't have a hard time at all believing he understood.

"Adrian?"

Kathryn's voice brought his head up with a snap. It jolted him out of his feelings of being an inadequate friend like nothing else could. She was at the top of the slideway, trying to figure out the safest way to come down.

"Allow me," Kine said quickly, dashing up the slideway in a few easy strides. Then he took Kathryn's hand by her fingers and helped her to walk down, assuring her the entire way. "I know it looks treacherous and steep when you're standing at the top," he said to her, "but the weave of the flooring provides a natural traction for bare feet, making it really quite safe."

"I can feel that," she marveled as she came down the slide. Then, as soon as she was on the main level, Kine walked her up to Adrian and handed her over to him with a gentlemanly bow at the waist and a wicked gleam of mischief in his eyes.

"Your *kindri*, madam," he offered as he released her hand. "Adrian, she's luscious. First Julian and now you. A fellow can get jealous if his friends flaunt their good fortune too much."

"I have only just begun to flaunt," Adrian informed them. "She's mine and she's beautiful and she's new in our village. Everyone is going to know her."

"In a way they already do." Kine smirked.

Adrian realized what the inference meant only half a second before Kathryn did. Then she flushed a brilliant shade of red. Adrian reached out and smacked the other Guardian on the back of the head.

"Ow! Hey, what was that for?"

"Because you're an insensitive ass," Daedalus said helpfully.

Adrian stifled a growl of frustration. Kathryn

was already self-conscious enough. She didn't need strangers making commentary on their sex life. She was far too inexperienced to cope with it.

"Oh." Kine looked sheepishly at Kathryn. "I'm sorry. I forgot that you are human and probably don't speak comfortably about these things as we do. We're a pretty frank people."

"It's okay," Kathryn excused him graciously. "If I'm going to be living here from now on, I guess it's something I'll just have to get used to." She cleared her throat and smoothed a hand over her hair, not realizing just how sensuously tousled she still was from their lovemaking earlier. It made Adrian smile, but he was very careful not to let his feelings emanate too hard and far. Now that she was living among his race, a race of inherently empathic and telepathic people, she would start to become just as attuned to those things as they were and begin to use parts of her brain she had never used before.

"You think that's tough, wait until you have to learn how to navigate the town. It takes some doing to learn which paths lead where, which go up and which go down. It's just like any roadways, I suppose, only you have to keep your balance at the same time."

"Kine, are you trying to scare the shit out of my *kindra* on purpose?" Adrian demanded angrily when Kathryn put a nervous hand to her throat. She was a very strong woman in her way, but her major weakness was trying new things. She feared what she didn't understand. But he knew her. He knew that she would adapt to all of the challenges his world would offer her and be strong and confident in her abilities in no time at all.

"No! Adrian, I was just—"

"Shutting up," Adrian said sharply.

"Right. Shutting up," he agreed quickly, knowing that making Adrian angry was not a good idea no matter what form or shape he was in.

"Now that I have a moment to speak," Daedalus said, stepping forward and reaching to clasp Kathryn's hand warmly, "welcome to our world. I hope you find it as beautiful and fascinating as we do."

"Oh, I already do," Kathryn said breathily. "I want to see so much more of it."

"Then let us take you and Adrian out for dinner," he offered with enthusiasm.

"I don't think—"

"Yes! I would love that!" she responded over Adrian. Then she realized what he was saying. "You don't want to go?"

"I just think you might want to take things a little slower. You just got here. You should adjust."

A mischievous smile curled over her lips and she gave him a sizzling look. "I think we've adjusted enough for the time being."

Kine snorted out a laugh and Adrian gaped at her in shock. Where had that come from? She was so shy about sex except when she was in the middle of it, but now she was tossing around flirtatious innuendo in front of others?

"Very well," he said, unable to help smiling at her when she looked at him with such dancing amusement in her eyes. "We'll go. What time is it now?" he asked the other men. "Just about sunset, we'll go out right after."

"Well, meanwhile, why don't you boys sit down and tell me everything you know about Adrian."

That was an invitation for potential disaster, Adrian realized with an inward groan. Daedalus was circumspect, but he could never tell what was going to come out of Kine's mouth from one moment to the next. But he couldn't tell them to go off into the sunset with the *okriti* running around, so he sat with them with Kathryn tucked up tightly against him and his arm secured around her shoulders. Everything about his positioning and body language claimed her as his, and every last one of them was well aware of it.

Chapter 14

Kathryn liked both men immensely. They were distinctly different in their personalities, and very different from Adrian as well. Kine was a cutup, often faking ignorance as to the effect the things he said would have on others. Daedalus was more serious, almost to a fault. There was something very sad about the thin stoic. She would have to ask later why he looked the way he did, like death warmed over. But despite his looks, he was very sweet to her and that was really all that mattered to her. If she had learned anything these past few days, it was not to choose a book by its cover. Even now it was hard to believe the handsome and passionate man she was curled up against had been trapped inside a monster for so very long.

"It makes sense that finding your *kindra* would reverse the effects of the mirror," Daedalus was saying. "You see, Kathryn, our species is very sensitive to energy. Especially emotional energy. If one of us grows angry, he can infect others of us with his rage if we are close enough and the emotions are strong enough."

"I didn't know that," she murmured.

"The mirror had corrupted Adrian. To the point where it would no longer hurt him to enter the thing or to take in the energy he reaped. But still, every night he was reinforcing that negativity. When you came, you were a source of good energy that he was predestined to draw into himself and hold close, whatever the cost. You were the most important treasure of all."

"All of the Guardians reflect the energy they collect in their duties. Each to a varying degree and each according to the type of energy they are required to harvest. Take old Daedalus here, for example. He deals in all the stages of death and grief. We call him Reaper for a reason. And all of that heavy emotional energy has affected the way he looks, just like it affected Adrian," said Kine.

"So . . . you're like an angel of death? You kill people?" Kathryn was aghast.

"No. I only reap from those who are already dying, and from the family who survives them. I reap from natural disasters. But death isn't always about grief," Daedalus reminded them. "People take great joy in sharing their memories of the deceased person. There is great love when a family says final farewells to each other."

"But mostly grief is a heavy and draining process," Adrian spoke up grimly. "It drains you as if you were in a perpetual state of dying and mourning."

So that was why he looked the way he did, Kathryn thought. And that was probably why Adrian felt such kinship with this man. But it was Kine who had come to visit Adrian, apparently, despite his corrupted and cantankerous state.

"And what about you, Kine? What kind of energy do you reap?" she asked him.

"Well, I deal in two energies. Two that always seem to go hand in hand with one another. War and faith. The two mesh constantly when you might think they shouldn't. But you see, they both breed the powerful emotions of belief. There is so much power in the escalation of both altercation and rapture. For instance, fervent soldiers and jihad fighters put more heart and energy into a war against their enemies than anyone else. Ignorance and intolerance breed feverish faith, even if it is blind. Unmitigated faith is a soaring and powerful energy that you cannot believe the power of."

"Wow," Kathryn uttered. "I never would have thought—that's just amazing. Tell me, what are the other Guardians focused on? Who are they? Where are they?" She sat forward eagerly.

"You don't want to hear about all of this, do you?" Adrian hedged, not wanting her to be overwhelmed with too much, knowing that some of the Guardians might shock her with the power they retrieved. But then again, she'd barely batted an eyelash when she'd heard about Daedalus, and next to Adrian he was the worst there was, really.

"Of course I do! I want to hear about everything. You brought me to this world. And I'm going to learn how to navigate it in all ways. That way I can best learn how to enjoy it."

Every time she spoke like that, Adrian felt his

heart clench with joy. She was becoming more and more accepting of her fate, accepting of her future with him. Perhaps . . . perhaps one day she might even come to care about him. Might crave him in ways other than a sexual appetite.

"Let's see . . ." Kine mused a moment. "You already know about Aerlyn, I take it. She reaps good dream energy. Ah, Shade. She doesn't know Shade. You think I'm bad? He's literally the clown among us. He reaps humor. Laughter. It's something humans gather together to do. To laugh. Comedians and such. Unfortunately he's also precognitive. That means he literally knows everything. He gets very bored very easily because of it. Nothing surprises him."

"Oh. Well, that's kind of a shame, don't you think?" she asked.

"It's a pain in the ass is what it is, and so is he." Daedalus frowned. "And they let him get away with far too much. Irreverence with the Ampliphi is bad enough, but he plays fast and loose with a lot of the rules as well."

Kathryn couldn't help but smile. "It sounds like I would like him a great deal."

"Yeah, you would, unfortunately. Everyone likes the little bastard."

"Adrian," she scolded.

"Well, it's true."

"Okay then . . . that makes five Guardians, if we still include Adrian. Aerlyn told me there is one Guardian for each Ampliphi. I counted six Ampliphi."

"Julian is only just become an Ampliphi. That's why he is always in a solid state. He just found his *kindra* too, a few months back. But before he was Ampliphi he was Guardian. Care to guess?" Kine asked with a twinkle of pure mischief in his eyes. "It's the most powerful burst of energy humans can create in a single moment."

"Well, I don't know. . . ." Suddenly she realized what he meant and pinked up instantly.

"I love how she changes color like that. A little pink chameleon."

"Don't make me come over there and break your neck," Adrian warned him.

"Stop. He's just making fun." Kathryn poked him in the ribs. "Don't treat me like I'm made of spun sugar. I won't fly apart over a little teasing. Besides, it makes me feel welcome."

"Well, you are welcome," Daedalus assured her. "And the sun ought to be down by now. Shall we go?"

"Great idea. I am starving!"

"Good. Then you'll want to try all of our best foods," Kine said. "Though I'm warning you now, keep away from the purple stuff."

"P-purple?"

"Not to be confused with the blue stuff, which is divine."

"He's going to make me break his neck before the night is over, I just know it," Adrian sighed.

The truth was, they had a wonderful time. A very normal time, with the exception of the strange foods, purple or otherwise. Kathryn liked to laugh, and Kine's antics and teasing did the trick. She'd never been very social, mostly for lack of company or occasion, but she discovered she liked this. Adrian was quiet most of the time, and she realized that he was out of practice socializing as well. They made quite a pair, she thought, as he closed the door to the house tightly.

"No locks?" she asked.

"No need. Crime is severely punished in this world. With an overpopulation of men, it has to be. The men who dare are swiftly executed." He didn't look at her as he said it, perhaps showing that he was ashamed of his society's extreme tactics.

"And women?" she asked.

He looked up quickly. "You really don't want to know this," he said firmly. "Can we discuss something else?"

"Such as?"

"Such as, why were you flirting with my friends all night?" She could see he was very tense as he asked the question. Had he been so rigidly on edge all night? Was that why he was so quiet?

"I wasn't flirting," she said, her tone aghast at the accusation. "I don't even know how to flirt!"

"Maybe," he said flatly. "Maybe not."

She laughed, a short burst of shock. "Are you . . . Are you *jealous*?" she demanded.

"Not jealous," he said shortly, "just trying to protect what's—"

He broke off before he said it, but he might as well not have.

"Go on, say it. *Mine*. After all of this I'm still just your pretty little treasure you want to lock in a room where no one else can see!"

"No. Not like that," he said sharply. "Not anymore. In fact, quite the opposite. I want to show you off. And not as a treasure, but as my mate. I am proud to have such an exquisite *kindra*, Kathryn. And yes, at times I do want to keep you to myself. That makes me possessive, I know, but I cannot help what nature forces me to feel for you. You are the one special thing in my life, Kat. I won't lose you to another and I won't let harm come to you."

"Lose me to—are you kidding? Do you really think I would do that to you? After all the craziness we've been through, you think I'm going to suddenly hop off with someone else?"

"I don't think it, I fear it. Irrational or not, it is what I feel." He looked down at the floor, not meeting her eyes as he spoke. That was when she realized just how afraid he was. She had never meant so much to anyone before. Oh, her family had needed her terribly, but more as a warm body than who that body was. Adrian had gotten to know her pretty damn well over the months he'd been tracking her in her dreams. She wondered exactly how long that had been. She imagined him being obsessive about her in his former state. It was going to be hard for him to let go of that obsession now, despite his changes.

But in a way that was okay with her. She kind of liked that she was so important to him. The thing she was insecure about was the sex thing.

"Is this just a sex thing? This thing between you and me."

That got his attention fast. He raised his eyes to hers, and the ferocity she saw told her the answer before he even spoke.

"This is not just about sex. I cannot give you a

definition to satisfy me, but it is much more than sex to me. Sex I could find anywhere, Kathryn. You . . . you are one of a kind. And I will always treat you that way."

She swallowed as a warm melty feeling spread all throughout her midsection. She smiled at him, cocking her hip and swinging it just a little as her body went into full flirt. Yep. She had definitely figured out how to flirt. And what was more, it was working. All she had to do was watch his eyes. They swam over her fast and hot, the air between them heating up rapidly.

"I think I like the way you treat me," she said as she tugged down one of the black dress's straps and exposed her shoulder a little bit more to him. She moved her hand to her waist, tugging on the ties that cinched the waist of the dress. "I think you've treated me very well since you've become more . . . yourself."

"Have I?" He sounded thirsty. He looked it too.

"You don't think so?" She unraveled the bodice laces until the dress hung loose on her body. Then she went to tug on the remaining straps holding the dress on her body.

"I've tried," he said passionately. "I know I've failed on many occasions, but know that I've tried my best to please you."

"I think you're doing fine," she said as she dropped her arms, did a little shimmy, and let the dress fall on the floor around her ankles.

"Suddenly I want a lock on the damn door," he growled as he closed the distance between them in a single hard step. He grabbed her by her bare waist, jerking her up against his body. "Do you feel? Do you feel how hard you make me just by undressing for me?"

She did, and it was amazing. She reached down between their bodies and stroked his length right through the firm denim he wore. Or maybe it just seemed firm because he was so very, very hard. Now that he had fully reverted to his normal self, she knew that this huge and beautiful cock was going to remain this size forever. She wasn't complaining one bit. She loved the way he felt under her hand. She loved even more the intense sounds he made as she slowly stroked over him. She realized there would always be a little monster in him, but she would always be able to tame him with her touch just as she had from the first time they had met.

She worked open his fly quickly and carefully, then sank her hand in to grab hold of him. She smiled up at him as he filled her hand and burned her palm with his incredible heat.

"What you do to me," he murmured, pressing kisses along her hairline. "I've done things in dreams that I once thought were the best in sexual extremes, but I was wrong. Nothing compares to the reality of you. Nothing." He cupped the back of her neck in his large hand, pulling her up on tiptoe so she could meet his kiss. She felt as though she was swallowing the most voracious of hungers, and then she was meeting it with a hunger of her own. She thrust her tongue deep into his mouth, teasing him and tasting him again and again and feeling his hands grow tighter and tighter around her naked flesh.

Their kisses became long and drugging, making

her body go limp against his, making her go soft and wet for him. She suddenly wanted him inside her. She didn't care how, she just wanted it. She pulled from his mouth with gasping breaths, then reached for his pants and pushed them down off his hips. She dropped to her knees before he could even formulate an idea to stop her, and in the next instant he was past her teeth and against her tongue. Oh, she could so grow to love this, she thought. She licked him clean of the sweetly salty fluid that her touch on his cock had milked from him, moaning softly at the taste and at the understanding that it was because she excited him so much. She felt powerful as she swallowed it down, felt like she was taking in a magical elixir that strengthened her desire for him. Made her hotter. Made her better at pleasing him.

Adrian sucked in his breath through his teeth. He wanted nothing more in that moment than to sink his hands into her hair and hold her head to him, but he resisted mastering her like that, choosing instead to let her do whatever she wished to do.

"Ah, sweetheart, I can't tell you how good that feels." He closed his eyes briefly, tipping his head back with his pleasure, but he preferred to watch her work her magic. "I love your mouth," he breathed.

She loved how frantic he sounded so quickly. She licked him all around the head of his cock, then sucked him in hard and deep. She repeated the steps over and over again until he couldn't help himself and he put his shaking hands deep into her hair. He crushed the strands in his fists and between his fingers, but still made no physical move to guide her. She was doing just fine all on her own as far as he was concerned. But that didn't preclude him from giving her verbal instructions.

"Touch my balls while you're doing that," he instructed. "Even if it's just the lightest scrape of your nails . . . Oh God, yes!" he cried when she followed his instruction well. Too well. Now she was sucking and manipulating him with zeal, making it impossible to focus on anything but her and the buildup of sensation going on in his body.

Satisfied she was getting to him in all the best ways, she was relentless. She could tell by the sounds ejecting out of him that he was fast losing control, that he was swept up in what he was feeling to the point that he had very little to no power over what was happening to him. This was exactly what she had wanted. She reached out with both hands and crawled her fingers up his thighs, making sure to tickle through all the sensitive hairs she found there. He drew his fingers through her hair, clutching and reclutching it at different lengths and intervals. Then his hands moved to her face, his thumbs stroking over her concave cheeks as she drew on him again and again, sliding his length as far into her mouth as she could manage.

"Enough, Kat," he rasped, holding her head still between his hands. "I won't come until I'm inside you."

But she could tell by his breathing and the shaking of his hands that he was very close. He was trying to exhibit control where there was none to be had. To prove the point, she tongued him within her mouth, making him suck in his breath in shock and sensitivity.

"God . . . I'm warning you, Kathryn, don't."

But his gruff warnings and behaviors didn't frighten her any longer. He had lost that power over her long ago, perhaps even before his looks had fully reverted from those of his monstrous counterpart. Reaching up to take him hard in her hand, she slid her fist up his length until it kissed against her lips. She repeated the action until he moaned. She looked up and saw his head shaking, as if he could ward off what was coming with the power of his will alone.

When he realized how determined she was, that his warnings and wishes otherwise were being completely ignored, he gave himself over to the inevitable. Until now she had always been so caught up in her own pleasure at his hands that she hadn't really gotten a chance to see what he looked like when he came. She saw it up close and personal now, the way it built in him, the way he couldn't be still, had to thrust into what he was feeling. His teeth were clenched tight; she could tell because the sounds he released were shot out between them in harsh bursts. Every muscle in his body stood out in relief, the veins beneath his skin drawn clearly in contrast.

"Kathryn . . . Kathryn, you'd better be good and wet for me," he ground out, "because right after this I'm going to fuck you within an inch of your life."

She laughed, the vibration of it clearly passing

along his cock because he cried out and abruptly became more frantic before her.

"Kat! My God!" He tried to pull free of her mouth, but she wasn't having that. She'd always wanted to know. She wasn't going to let him cheat her out of knowing.

His orgasm was ferocious, from the sounds he made to the burning heat shooting into her mouth. She was surprised by the salty, tart taste of him, swallowing him down before she could even register it fully. But there it was again, over and over in hard spurts against her tongue. And she watched him as he gripped her face fiercely between his palms, clearly forcing himself not to give in to the wild thrusts his body was demanding of him.

She finally allowed him the freedom to escape her mouth. He did so with haste, nearly falling flat on his back as his knees gave out. He sat down hard, gasping for breath and, by the look of him, trying to uncross his eyes. Kathryn giggled at the thought and was surprised to hear him laugh as well.

"No doubt, love. My eyes are well and truly crossed."

"Hey!" she gasped. "How did you know I was thinking that?"

He gave her a look. "You mean you haven't realized that we're a pathic species?"

"Pathic? Like telepathic? Like you know everything I'm thinking?" Her voice grew higher pitched until she was squeaking by the end of the question.

"There isn't an English term for what we do. It's more like—the louder the thought and the feeling behind it, the more clearly the impression and words come through. It has to be projected to be received. And you have to be receptive to hear what's being projected. You can do it too, you know."

She snorted. "I can not!"

"You can and you will. It just takes practice. Other human women have come to this world and adjusted to the way we speak. So will you."

"Hmm. Well, this explains how you always knew everything all the time. That's poor sporting, not letting me know before now."

"It simply didn't occur to me until just recently. I was going to say something, but I think I got distracted."

"Well, next time when it's something that important, don't get distracted," she huffed.

"Not even if it's by you and that fascinating mouth of yours?" he asked her.

"Not—fascinating?" she asked, hearing the compliment on a delay because she was still flustered to realize he could read her thoughts all this time.

"Beyond fascinating," he said, moving forward on his hands and knees until he crowded her flat onto her back. "I would be remiss if I didn't also add 'extraordinary' to the list."

"I think you're trying to charm me," she accused him, "so I'll forget about your little lapse."

"And if I am?" he asked, running a finger up the center of her belly.

"Well, it might not work," she warned him.

"Won't it, though?" He grinned at her as his finger changed direction and headed directly south of her navel. He kept going until he was traveling deeply between her labia and probing teasingly at the portal to her body.

"You think you can use sex to get your way?" she breathed.

"I do. Mainly because from the very start you have struck me as a sexual creature, Kat. I know you don't think of yourself that way, but I have never seen you as anything but. Your sensuality is stunning. From the scent you wear to the clothes you choose." He dipped his head and tongued her belly button, making her giggle an instant before he thrust his finger inside her. "Mmm, it's a wonder how you can still be so tight when you've had me inside you already today. It's as if I was never here. I'm not sure whether to be fascinated or put out."

"I'm sure it's not a commentary on your performance," she assured him with a smile.

"Let's hope not. But just to be safe, I'm going to test the theory."

"Already?" She laughed as he whipped his tongue around her navel once more, then drew a line straight down to her pubic curls. "I must say, that's, like, porno impressive."

"Have you seen many of those?" He glanced up in time to see her blush. He chuckled.

"Well! I was curious," she defended herself.

"And more power to you," he assured her. "I was laughing at your penchant for blushing. You're an easy book to read sometimes."

"All the time, according to Jillian. She says I wear my heart on my sleeve. Oh! Don't," she begged him when he went to kiss her very intimately.

"Why not?"

"Because I haven't showered since the last time. Please . . ."

"Nonsense. That only means you'll smell and taste like both of us. Which makes you more provocative, in my book."

To prove his point, he flicked his tongue against her saturated folds, tasting her deeply. He made an appreciative sound, but all she had needed was the look in his darkening eyes to know he was telling her the truth. He found everything about her compelling, she realized. And realizing that was a powerful feeling. A strong and feminine feeling. It was enough to power her courage so she could brazenly kick up her legs and sling them over his shoulders. He took the hint and lowered himself to the task of taking an even deeper taste. He also worked a second finger inside her, making her squirm at the combined sensations.

He played over her for a good long while, stroking her like a fine instrument tuning up to play in the orchestra. He waited until she was writhing hard on the floor, her legs clutching him in such a grip she could have bruised a lesser man's back. Instead it just excited him more and more, every time her heels dug in. But he didn't let her climax, much to her audible frustration.

"Oh no," he said as he freed himself from her legs and climbed up her body. "No shortcuts for you, Miss Kat. We're going to save it for the best part, and this time, you're not going to hold out on me."

"But . . . what if I can't help it?" she asked with a

swallow of anxiety. "Just the thought of everyone knowing every time I . . . I . . ."

"Come?" he supplied.

"God. I can't even say it. You must think me such a child," she said, her voice falling to a whisper.

"No. Never that. I think you're young, inexperienced, and very, very innocent."

"Not so innocent anymore," she noted, her color deepening.

"And are you ashamed of that?" he asked as he kissed the side of her neck.

"No," she said, and he knew immediately that she spoke the truth. "Never."

"Good. There is no reason for shame. Not for either of us, Kathryn." He opened his mouth on her, biting her gently on the crest of her shoulder. It gave her chills and she shivered because of them.

"I'm not ashamed," she promised him. "Just . . . painfully shy."

"So strong and so delicate. A beautiful conundrum," he said. "But there will be no shyness this time, love. This time you'll give me everything and not give a damn about anyone else but us."

He punctuated the order with a deep, wild kiss, one where she could taste herself on his lips and felt heightened excitement wash through her because of it. The scent and flavor was unique and intoxicating. It was them. Together. It was the most amazing thing she had ever experienced in her life. No wonder he enjoyed it so much.

"Okay," she said breathlessly. "I'll try not to be shy."

"Don't try," he countered against her lips. "There should be no effort at all when it comes to this. Just relax. It comes so naturally to you. There will be little effort necessary."

"All right," she said, a promise to herself as much as it was meant to be a promise to him. He worried that she was putting even more undue pressure on herself as she mentally chanted to herself to relax. That was when he realized it was going to be up to him to get her through this. He just had to push her past the point of being able to think about anything. Only then would she be able to let go.

Distraction was going to be his first technique.

He moved back and grabbed her legs, crossing them before reaching for her hips and flipping her over. He prevented her from going up on her knees when she naturally would and instead straddled her backside. She twisted around, trying to see him. He forced her to face the floor and then began to rub her back in long, relaxing strokes. Then, just as she started to moan in pleasure, he bent forward and swept her hair aside so he could bite her on the back of her neck. She yelped at the minimal but startling pain. Then he went to her midspine and did it again. He moved back off her and after shaping her buttocks with his hands for a long moment, he bent to nip her on each one there as well.

This startled her and made her laugh. Adrian was willing to bet it made her blush as well. But at this point, he wasn't going to let her get away with any shyness. Even if he had to shock it out of her. He wanted her to be so comfortable with his uses for her body that nothing he did would shock her anymore.

To that end, Adrian molded her backside, one cheek in each hand, massaging for a moment before pushing them apart, exposing the crevice between them, then bent his head and licked her from her perineum back. He thought she might have exploded from the floor if he'd not been holding her down. He could see the back of her neck coloring and it made him smile.

"Adrian!" she gasped.

He turned her over, facing her furious blush.

"There is no part of you that is off limits to me and anything I want to do," he told her when she tried to sputter out a protest. "There is nothing to be shy of or ashamed of." He came up to her and kissed her mouth. "Everything about you is precious to me. Every inch of you is utterly delicious. Never forget that."

He reached for her hand and wrapped it around his thick and heavy cock, reminding her how aroused she made him.

"Nothing bothers you," she murmured. "I wish I could be like that."

"You can be. Just let go and feel. Feel everything. *Want* to feel everything."

To punctuate the point he bent her legs at the knees, pushing them up and apart.

"Hold on to your legs. That's a good girl." She grabbed her knees, pulling them up toward her chest, exposing the very core of her sex to him. He wanted to bend his mouth to her again, to taste how lush and warm she was, but he honestly couldn't bear being outside her any longer. He came up to her until his penis was touching all that wet and wonderful flesh, then took a moment to bathe himself in her, rocking back and forth against her, his cock taunting her clit with every stroke until she was shuddering with ripples of pleasure.

Once he was good and wet with her juices, he made no pretense of hesitation or teasing. He notched himself at her entrance and, putting a thumb against her clit, he thrust deeply into her. Normally he would take time to let her adjust to his girth, but he had no patience for that and wanted no more delays. The longer she took to reach climax, the more time she'd have to think and fret about it.

Working from both the inside and the wet little clit on the outside, he thrust into her in steady, rocking movements. Her hips came up with each rolling impact, and she moaned out soft little sounds of pleasure almost immediately. And why wouldn't she? He was engaged in a two-pronged attack, and he was determined she was going to win this battle.

Kathryn quickly lost track of which way was up. She couldn't figure out if she wanted her eyes closed so she could focus on the feelings she was experiencing, or open so she could see her magnificent lover in all his dominating glory. She loved to watch him, the expanse of his chest, the tight taper of defined muscles down along his belly that stood out in stark definition each time he thrust forward into her, and that magnificent cock of his moving in and out of her body. The sight of that was enough to spin her brain, to coax her on a ride up toward the peak he wanted so badly for her to jump from. She tried so hard not to think about all those people in the village who would know every time they made love like this. She tried not to feel like they were being monitored.

The sudden smack on her backside startled her right out of her thoughts. She looked up at his darkened eyes in shock.

"That's what I'm going to do every time I catch you obsessing like that," he promised her.

The smack hadn't hurt. In fact, quite the opposite. A warm, devastating tingle ran right through her sex. And the moment she realized she liked it, he gave a little chuckle.

"I'll have to remember that," he mused, making her flush to realize he had read from her. Then she thought she didn't care if he had. What was the big deal? He was her lover. He was supposed to find out what turned her on. "That's right, honey. Just let go," he coaxed her, doubling his rhythm inside her to make it hard not to do exactly that. He bent to snare a nipple between his teeth, tugging at it just hard enough to make her gasp and moan as he drew a line with the action from breast to clit and from clit to deep inside her pussy.

She began to pant frantically, the power of his skill overwhelming her. She was coming up on a crest blindingly fast, almost before she could even anticipate it. She didn't realize that was exactly Adrian's plan. He continued to overwhelm her until she was highly wet with stimulation and swirling madly in her own mind. Her body was humming, singing hard for him, fast reaching the point of a scream.

"That's it. Now you let go, love. Fly for me, Kat."

She wanted to. More than anything. But she feared she wouldn't be able to.

"None of that," he scolded her with a deep growl. "I'm ready for you and I want you ready for me. Just feel. Only feel."

She had no choice but to feel. He was everywhere all at once, from bite to thrust to that maddening swirl of a thumb against her. She couldn't bear it another second. She cried out, long low sounds of pleasure as her body whipped up tight with need.

"Adrian!" she cried, fear in her voice. She wasn't afraid to let go per se, but she was afraid of the power of what was waiting for her. She knew it was going to be like nothing she had felt to date.

"It's all right. I'm with you," he breathed.

It was all she needed, to know he was there for her no matter what. She didn't know that was what she needed, but she did. She threw her head back and launched into a stunning orgasm, her whole body locking up around him. She felt like she was riding horseback, racing madly, jumping the highest obstacles. She cried out long and loud, her body squeezing him tightly until he was forced to come over with her. She felt him coming, felt him lose all sense of control, just blindly thrusting into her and following every feeling he had.

They collapsed together in a pile of panting breaths and tangled arms and legs. Adrian scooped her up against him and rolled with her, taking her off the floor and using his body to cushion her from it. He grinned as he caught sight of her flushed and sated expression.

"Better?" he asked.

She laughed.

"Much."

Chapter 15

In all of the drama about the Ampliphi wanting Adrian to move back to their home village, they had never taken the time to consider how damn lonely it would be for Aerlyn when her brother left her. Granted, he hadn't been much in the way of company in the past few years, but that hadn't really mattered to a sister who had loved him no matter what. But it only took a day of wandering around the fortress by herself for her to feel it.

She wondered if they were going to replace Adrian. Not in her heart, obviously, but in his mirror. There were better ways of gathering energy, but Adrian had been very effective at what he did. The problem was that anyone who had seen Adrian had seen what the nightmare plane had done to him. On top of that, it took a very specific talent to be able to manipulate dreams. But she supposed they would stick with what they knew, and eventually someone would take the mirror. They didn't

have to be there with her in order for it to work,
but the Barrens had been the best place to be in
order to protect themselves from others and others from them. At least with their setup, she had
been able to regulate Adrian, to keep him from
running wild. And that had proved to be very necessary. Even in a world without people, Adrian had
more than proven he was still a danger to others.
Stealing Kathryn was his final act of proof, although it was a poor example because she had
turned out to be his *kindra*. She was amazed
Adrian had had the presence of mind to even distinguish the difference, but instinct very often
won out over everything, so she shouldn't really be
surprised.

She was at her dressing table, preparing to go to
work, when she heard the distinctive sound of a
vortex opening. She and Adrian used the mirrors
to travel between planes, but other Guardians
used all kinds of different methods according to
their talents. Wondering who would be visiting
her, she went in search of her guests. She found
them on the main floor. In the marbled foyer, sitting wrapped up around one another, were a man
and a woman. The female sat in the male's lap at a
provocative closeness, her dress riding up her
thighs as her legs remained locked around his
waist. She was heavily flushed and they were both
breathing hard, as if they'd just had sex. And considering who the male was, she was inclined to believe it had been a close approximation.

Julian. Julian had been Guardian before he had
been Ampliphi. His specialty had been reaping the
dynamic energy released during sexual peak. It

was also the power he had used to travel from plane to plane. Aerlyn had never met the woman before, but she was willing to assume that the female was his *kindra*, Asia. About three years earlier, Julian had stumbled upon her in the human world and had taken her home. Now it was clear the couple had used one another to travel from Beneath to the Barrens.

But that seemed peculiar to Aerlyn. Now that he was Ampliphi, Julian no longer needed to use climactic energy to travel between the worlds. He should be powerful enough to do it purely by way of thought. Why would he revert to his Guardian ways and methods?

The couple seemed to regroup. They separated and got to their feet, both looking like children who had done something very naughty—yet were entirely unrepentant because of how much fun it had been. Aerlyn covered up a smile and greeted them.

"Julian, Asia, welcome to my home. I am honored."

Julian turned serious eyes on her, the expression incongruent with the healthy erection she could see he still sported from whatever play he had used to bring them there. The frown etching his lips was enough to give her a sinking feeling in her stomach. Something was wrong. Very wrong. And she wasn't going to like what she was about to hear.

"Hello, Aerlyn. I hope you are well."

"Well enough. I haven't seen much of you since you became Ampliphi," she noted, bringing her hands together to turn nervously in one another as she often did when she was agitated. She knew it was a terrible tell, but she simply couldn't help herself. "What brings you here, Julian? And in this method?"

He nodded, acknowledging that she had taken note of the way they had traveled from one plane to the next.

"Forgive us," he said carefully, "but this was the only way we could come here without being detected by the other Ampliphi. They have been watching me very closely, monitoring my movements through planes."

"Why would they do that?" she asked him through a tight throat.

"Because I have been a steady and vocal voice of dissent these past days."

"Dissent?" she echoed weakly.

"Aerlyn, listen to me. Your brother's life is in great jeopardy."

"What do you mean?" Her nervousness vanished as fiery indignation rushed up protectively instead.

He sighed heavily. "For some time now the Ampliphi have been watching him closely, waiting for him to go over the edge, waiting for an opportunity to put him out of his misery, as it were. They have felt that he is a danger to himself and others, an out-of-control monster that needed to be put down. To be frank, as long as you were able to control him they were satisfied, but once he started attacking you we knew something would have to be done."

"You knew he was attacking me?" she asked. "How would you know that?"

"Through occasional monitoring. The Ampliphi feel it is their right to monitor the duties of their Guardians, as you know. We were witness to him losing his temper with you not too long ago."

"If it is the incident I think it is, you have to understand that he felt threatened. He was afraid I was going to take his *kindra* from him. He didn't know or understand even for himself why it upset him so, but surely you can see how that would be upsetting, being that you and Asia are *kind*."

"I do understand. In fact, I am the only one who understands all of this. I have tried very hard to be Adrian's advocate in all of this. He has had a pretty raw deal from the outset. He volunteered for a terrible duty for the sake of his people, and now his leaders are trying to find a way to get rid of him? I find that unconscionable. Unfortunately, I agreed that he was becoming too dangerous to you and others when I saw him attack you and, frankly, your brother has only made matters worse since then."

"What do you mean?"

"When he came to claim *kindra*, the Ampliphi were positive he was demented and wouldn't know his own *kindra* if she bit him on the ass. They were certain that this was the opportunity they had been waiting for. Your brother would have made a false claim, allowing them to punish him to the max of the law and giving them a way out of the whole mess."

"But the claim was true," Aerlyn argued.

"Exactly. Much to the dismay of your leaders. Unfortunately, Adrian did something else that will allow them to pass capital punishment on him." He paused to run a hand through his hair in agitation. "He murdered his Companion in front of the Ampliphi."

"He *what?*" All of the color drained from her face and she stumbled backward to sit hard on the steps. Murder carried an immediate and unwavering death sentence. There was no way around it. There was no helping him. "But . . . he couldn't . . . if he did it was because Cronos was threatening his *kindra!* Cronos almost killed her!"

"They know that. But they aren't thinking of justifications and exceptions. All they are thinking of is how to destroy your brother and free themselves of an albatross. That's why I am here talking to you, Aerlyn. They feel that Adrian's entire village, including his *kindra,* is in danger from him. They are going to send guards to confront him and imprison him. You have to warn him not to fight them or hurt anyone in the process. If he does, I won't be able to help him."

"He's changed. He's different," she argued. "If they could just see how he's changed, they wouldn't be so afraid of him!"

"Changed or not, I feel that any member of a *kind* relationship must be given special consideration when there is a threat to his or her mate. The feelings we feel for our mates are so overwhelming, so out of our control that we would do anything to protect them. The rest of the Ampliphi do not understand this as I do. I have my mate, and I know I would kill for her, were she threatened the way Cronos threatened Adrian's mate."

"Kathryn," Aerlyn supplied for him. "Her name is Kathryn."

Julian nodded in acknowledgment.

"Warn your brother. He mustn't hurt anyone else. If he does, I can't help him. And then trust me to do the rest. To sentence a Guardian to death, the Ampliphi must be in total agreement. As you see, there will be at least one dissenter. But it will only work if he can keep his head."

"I'll warn him right away. Do you know when they are coming for him?"

"Possibly even now. You have to hurry."

"Thank you. I will."

Aerlyn abandoned her guests and ran for her mirror.

Adrian woke slowly, not wanting to disturb the heavy sensation of contentment that pervaded his every limb and cell. He was lying in bed with the body of his mate sprawled over him in exactly the last position they had made love in. Her knees still straddled his hips, and her breasts were bare and soft against his chest. Her head was nestled on his shoulder; her beautiful dark hair spilled this way and that over his shoulders and chest. He recalled how beautiful she had been as she had thrown her head back in her pleasure, exposing her throat and the curve of her breastbone to his hungry hand. He still couldn't believe that something this beautiful was *his*. He had no idea what he had done to deserve her. God knew he had done some terrible things over these past few years. Most especially to his sister, who had shown him nothing but patience in return. He owed her much for staying with him so long and putting up with so much. He would have to find a way to repay her.

For the time being, he wanted to focus a little more immediately on home. He reached out to pet her hair, but stopped in midair when he saw his hands. Or, more specifically, his fingertips. Gone were the claws he had grown so used to. Now there was nothing but strong and long nails, as if he hadn't had a manicure in a long while. But there was no mistaking the difference between nail and claw. The flexibility of them more than proved what they were. He took tremendous pleasure in the change. It brought him one step closer to normalcy, one step closer to being worthy of the woman who slept with him.

Curious now to see what other changes the night had wrought, he stuck out his tongue and searched for the tips of his fangs. His teeth were all nice and neatly rowed, none sticking out more prominently than the others, although he could still feel sharp tips to his canines. He smiled, unable to hold back his pleasure any longer. He grabbed Kathryn by her shoulders, preparing to shake her awake.

"Don't you dare," she mumbled into his chest.

"What?" he asked, trying not to grin like such a damn fool.

"Don't wake me up," she warned. "I've felt you tensing and twitching for a good five minutes now. I'm asleep and staying that way. Wake up someone else."

"Having good dreams?" he asked. But then he was struck with a sudden sense of jealousy. Was there someone in her dreams she didn't want to leave?

"I'm not having any dreams," she said with a contented sigh.

"That's because you're awake," he had to tell her.

"Shut up. Am not."

He grinned at her. He reached over and plucked up one of her eyelids, exposing the gray iris to the light, making her pupil contract sharply.

"Oh!" she growled, smacking him hard on his chest. "Quit it!"

He let go of her lid and she squeezed her eyes shut tight. Adrian could see he was going to have to try a completely different tactic. He reached down to run a slow, suggestive hand up over the curve of her exposed backside, his fingertips toying very close to the lips of her pussy. Her head suddenly shot up, hair flying all across her face, and she shoved it all back with a frustrated sound.

"That's just dirty pool!" she accused him. But his grin was relentless and unrepentant. He was in too good a mood to let anything sway him, not even her crankiness.

"You were already awake. You were just in denial," he pointed out.

"Well, I want to be asleep! I'm exhausted." She dramatically flopped back down on his chest. "You make me tired."

"You mean our lovemaking makes you tired?"

"Yes. That. We did it like twenty billion times last night. I am too worn out to move. I have achy places everywhere."

"Oh? I'm sorry, sweetheart," he crooned softly to her. "Tell me where it hurts." He took her shoulders under his hands and slowly began to massage away the tiny knots of tension he found there. It wasn't very impressive as far as tension went, but she had just woken up. Besides, there was a method to his actions.

"Mmm. Feels good," she murmured, relaxing under his touch. He didn't take long before he was running his kneading hands all up and down her back. She was moaning with pleasure and he felt his cock twitch with interest. It was going to give him away soon, so he had to make a bolder move.

He moved down to her buttocks, massaging the cheeks with strong and eager pulls. She was utterly limp across his body, but the strength of what he was doing to her was moving her against him. Then, without any shame at all, he worked his way between her legs and dipped his fingers in.

She squealed, leaping up so awkwardly she almost kneed him in the balls.

"Whoa! Careful!" he warned her.

"You snake! You . . . you are a wolf in wolf's clothing!" she sputtered. She picked up a pillow and smacked him in the face with it.

"I'm sorry?" he chuckled, trying to dodge a repeat swat. "A wolf in what?"

"Oh, never mind! It's just mean to play all sweet and caring boyfriend and then grope me in the middle of it. I thought you meant the sweet part."

"I did mean it. I mean everything you think I mean when I touch you. Can I help it if you're too irresistible for words?"

That made her hesitate long enough for him to ease the pillow out of her raised hands. Once she was disarmed she made a noise of consternation and put her hands on her hips. She tilted her head and looked at him carefully. Adrian held his breath as he waited for her input.

"Holy smokes," she whispered. "You are a full-on hottie!"

"I'm a what?" he choked out, trying not to laugh.

"You look like you again! Like the you in the dream. Only—damn, you didn't do yourself any justice. Your eyes are so beautiful." She bent forward and touched his face. "You have great cheekbones. Lashes I could only hope to get out of a bottle. And really delicious-looking lips." Her complete focus fell to his mouth and she wet her lips absently as she did so.

"They really taste delicious too," he told her, cocking half a smile at her.

"Oh really?" she asked. "And how would you know that?"

"I am just guessing. See, this little brunette I know can never seem to get enough of kissing me, so I assume it's something worthwhile to experience. I can tell you, however, that her mouth is the sweetest thing invented since candy."

"Really?" Her entire gaze softened, her whole face gone dreamy. "Do you really think that?"

"And much more," he assured her softly as he put a hand to the side of her face. "Kat, sweetheart, don't you know how mad I am for you?"

"Well, I'm starting to get the picture," she replied with a smile. "Although the whole kidnapping thing was a dead giveaway. Not to mention the treasure trove of clothes and jewels. It's just . . . sometimes I think you've made this huge mistake."

She bit her lip, her eyes a little sad. "I think now that you're all gorgeous and normal again, you aren't going to want a chubby, inexperienced girl from the back-ass end of Australia."

"Kat," he scolded her sharply. "The only reason I am normal is because of you. I owe you everything that I am. I was on the brink of falling down an evil hole I could never have come back from, and you saved me from that."

"So you're grateful?" she fished carefully.

"Hell yes, I'm grateful. But that isn't what has me lying here in bed with you, if that's what you want to know. Kat," he said, closing both his hands around her face, his thumbs trailing over her lips, "I'm crazy about you."

She gave him a little smile. "You're just plain crazy," she quantified. "And you can't possibly be crazy about me in just a few days' time."

"Hey." He gave her a little shake. "I don't need you to tell me what I do and do not feel for you. And for me it's been months, not days. Or have you forgotten that? Even as a beast with an obsession, I knew you were the one. Now that I'm myself again and have experienced everything about you firsthand, I am a man in love. Yes, love," he reiterated when she gave a little gasp. "And I think I knew that the very first time I touched you. No matter what I was at the time. You have to trust me, here. You mean everything to me now and will do so in the future. I'm not going to change my mind or suddenly wake up from it all and think, 'Oh shit! I made a huge mistake!' I do not work like that, Kat. I won't feel like that. And you have to stop thinking that you aren't worth my attentions. Because you are."

"But it's okay for you to think you aren't worthy of my attentions?" she lobbed back to him. "You say that to me all of the time. That you don't deserve me."

Adrian frowned and looked away from her. "Don't you think that's true?" he asked her. "After all I've put you through?"

"First of all, don't tell me what to think. I think I've had more than my fill of that for this lifetime. Second of all, I think I've quite forgiven you for taking me from my home. In fact, I think I kinda owe you one for that. Yes," she said, holding up her hand to stop him, "I will miss my sister terribly. But Aerlyn said I could visit her in her dreams any time I wanted. And on the good dream plane she won't be sad that I'm gone. I think, actually, it will make her happy to think I am well and happy somewhere. Whether she thinks it's only a dream or not. But all my life I've longed for adventures of my own, for a real life and existence of my own. You've provided that for me. And I wasn't going to ever break out and do it on my own. I can see that now. I was just going to let myself be swamped in responsibility and let my fear of the unknown get the best of me. But now look at me." She spread out her arms to indicate him and all their surroundings. "How cool is this? And I have a lover and everything. Pretty daring, I'd say."

He grinned. "Yes, very daring. Are you going to . . . miss the beastly side of me?" he asked abruptly.

"That all depends," she said as she bent playfully

for his mouth. "Are there any parts of him left behind?"

"Maybe one or two," he growled as he grabbed her and flipped her over in their bed, putting her squarely beneath him. He dove for her neck, making snarling and growling noises as he nipped at her. She squealed and laughed, pounding useless fists against him and kicking the bed.

It was probably the reason why neither of them heard the guards enter their bedroom. But suddenly Kathryn opened her eyes and saw them, screaming a very different scream than what she'd just been doing. Adrian noted the difference instantly and turned sharply to see what was behind him. Realizing who they were, he jerked a sheet over Kat to hide her from their amused eyes and he let loose with a warning growl that sent chills down more than one spine. Then the captain of the squad stepped forward.

"It is our duty, Guardian, to bring you before the Ampliphi to answer for your crimes."

"Crimes! What crimes?" Kathryn burst out in panic, her arm wrapping around Adrian's as if she wouldn't ever let him go. Adrian had to forgo the pleasure of that experience as he focused on the threat in his home. He had been anticipating something like this. He knew the Ampliphi far too well to have thought they would let him slide for killing Cronos.

"It's okay," he said softly to her as he laid a gentle hand on the arm clinging to him. "I did the thing they are likely accusing me of and I have to answer for it."

"You—what? Adrian, what did you do?" she asked him numbly.

"I killed Cronos."

Kathryn couldn't believe what she was hearing. She had thought that he had taken Cronos to the Ampliphi to answer for his crimes, not that he would take the matter into his own hands. But it was clear that the beast who had still been such a large part of his psyche then had gotten the better of him, and like any animal who saw his mate in peril, he had done what was necessary to eliminate the threat. The fact was, Cronos might never have quit trying to kill her. He had fixated on her being the cause of all his problems. She could easily see why he had felt he had no other recourse when it came to letting the horrid little man leave with his life.

But what scared her the most was that she didn't know the laws in this world. Did they believe in justifiable homicide? Would they see this murder as justified? Was it justified?

It had been in Adrian's mind. She could sense it from him and see it in his dark, pleading eyes. He was seeking her forgiveness, even as he pried her hands free of his arm and got up off the bed. He retrieved his jeans and stepped into them, then moved forward toward the guards.

"No!" she cried, flying off the bed and catching hold of him. "You can't leave me! It's not fair!" She wrapped her arms around his waist, uncaring of the sheet that snaked free of her bare body. "You can't leave me!"

"I'll try to come back," he swore to her, taking her arms and trying to push her free. "I have to go. I cannot disobey this command to be seen; it will only make matters worse. Please put something on and go sit on the bed, where you won't get hurt."

Just then, one of the guards stepped up. "Release him. We're taking him now."

Then he reached out to pull her forcibly away from Adrian.

Adrian exploded the instant the guard's hand touched her waist. With a primal roar he leapt between the guard and Kathryn, picked the man up and hurled him over the bed and into a wall.

"Don't touch her!" He whirled to snarl at the other guards. "No one touches her!"

For good measure he pushed Kathryn back into an unoccupied part of the room. That was just about the moment the guards pounced on him, dragging him down to the floor, holding him down painfully and brutally.

"Stop! Don't hurt him! He was only protecting me! He can't help it! Stop hurting him!" she cried.

"We know what a vicious monster he is. We're not taking any chances," the captain said.

Finally they had him bound tightly by his hands behind his back. They hauled him to his feet and she could see that he had cut his lip. She fought off the usual instinct for tears, getting angry instead. With fierce movements she recovered her black dress from the floor and yanked it on. When they marched him out of the bedroom she was hot on their trail.

"Stay here," Adrian commanded. "You don't

know how to walk the walkways yet. You don't know your way around!"

"Like hell I'm staying here," she shot back. "I'm not letting you face this firing squad alone!"

"Someone escort her, then," he begged the guards, twisting his body to keep his eyes on her as they exited the hut. "Someone walk beside her or behind her." *Just don't touch her.* The warning was silent and implied. Everyone knew it. The guards all looked at one another, waiting for someone to volunteer to get close enough to this volatile creature's mate.

"I'll walk with her."

Adrian and Kathryn both looked up in surprise when they heard Aerlyn's voice. She was flushed and breathless, as if she had run all the way to get to them.

"Just don't fight them, Adrian," Aerlyn said firmly. "I won't let anyone touch her. Just please go quietly." Aerlyn firmly linked her hand through Kathryn's, showing him that his *kindra* was literally in safe hands.

Satisfied, Adrian turned forward and let them take him to Justice Hall.

Chapter 16

Kathryn was a wreck by the time they reached
Justice Hall. She remembered the place well, with
its dark interior and its vastly stretched-out spaces.
She remembered the Ampliphi as well, the lot of
them looking so holy in their attitudes and car-
riages. But something was different. Instead of
them being all glowy and ghostly, they were all
flesh and blood, as solid as Kathryn was, and all of
them painfully beautiful to look at.

"Why are they all real?" she asked Aerlyn sotto
voce.

"I suspect that has something to do with you
and Adrian," she replied just as softly. "When they
have an overabundance of energy, they can become as solid as you or I."

"Oh." Then she blushed and exclaimed, "Oh!"
when she finally understood that this was the visual proof of what had made her so anxious the
night before in bed with Adrian. But that was the

least of her worries right now, she thought as they dragged Adrian roughly to the center of the floor, squarely in front of the Ampliphi, and forced him harshly to his knees.

"Hey! Is that really necessary?" she demanded, her voice echoing off the high ceilings.

"All who seek judgment from the Ampliphi must kneel. We make no exceptions."

"I don't mean the kneeling," she shot back to the man who had spoken. "I mean being so mean about it. All you have to do is ask him and he'll do it."

"That has not proven to be the case in the past," one of the Ampliphi said grimly.

"That was the past," she bit back. "Can't you just look at him and see how different he is?"

They all turned their heads to finally take a good look at the monster they had called to task. There were audible and surprised sounds from among the Ampliphi. Soft and swift whispers began to fly between them and she could feel their surprise and confusion like a wall hitting her. She squeezed Aerlyn's hand, hoping this was a good sign. But Aerlyn still looked very grim and worried. Kathryn could almost feel her heart racing in fear.

Then the leader addressed her.

"He may be different in appearance, but we have no proof he is anything different in attitude. Now be silent or we will remove you from these proceedings."

She wanted to tell them where they could go, but Aerlyn's warning squeeze of her hand helped her keep her tongue. For the time being.

"Adrian," Christophe said deeply, "you are brought before this council so that you may answer to the charges of murder. The punishment for this crime will be your death. Have you anything to say?"

"I told you, he tried to hurt my mate," Adrian said through his teeth. "First he tried to trap her in my mirror, tried to get her lost in the nightmare plane. While she was there, she was almost raped by a doppelganger of me. Then he held her at knifepoint, threatening her life while drawing blood. What would you have me do? Let him live so he could attack her again and again? And had he gone through this very court I am standing before now, you would have sentenced him to death for his crimes anyway. He was as much a monster as you accuse me of, and with much less reason."

"It is not your right to carry out sentence and mete out justice. You should have left that to us," Rennin said with disdain for his prodigy. "You have been my Guardian for decades, and in that time the evil of your mirror has consumed you beyond all reclamation. Your murder of your Companion proves it."

"I am not beyond reclamation," Adrian insisted, his deep voice so strong and beautiful as it echoed up to the ceilings. "Look there," he said, nodding toward Kathryn. "There you will see my salvation. You all have seen me again and again in my monstrous form. Now, because of her, I am the man I once was."

"Again, on the outside. But if you were so changed, you would not have attacked the guards just now when they came to fetch you," said Sydelle.

"He put his hands on my mate," Adrian said tightly. "While she was unclothed."

"Then it is an understandable reaction." Julian spoke up at last. "I can say from experience that anyone who touched Asia, especially if she were to be in a naked state, would very likely lose an arm. It is the nature of *kind.* Just as it was the nature of *kind* for him to want to destroy the threat to his mate's life."

"Nature or not," Christophe said, "the man beneath must have the wherewithal to control those urges."

"But there was so much beast within me at the time," Adrian confessed. "Which is not the case now."

"That is irrelevant," said Greison.

"I think it is quite relevant," argued Gisella. "It is clear that Adrian has gone though massive and traumatic changes. Surely we can account him a little latitude."

"A very little," Rennin said begrudgingly. "But the charge remains and this body will vote. Majority rules. If you fail to achieve—"

"Wait! Majority rules?" Aerlyn burst out, letting go of Kathryn and stepping forward. "How can that be? When judging a Guardian of a crime, unanimity rules. You must all agree or he is acquitted of the crime."

"Ah, but you see," Greison said with a smile Kathryn immediately wanted to slap off his smug face, "he is no longer a Guardian. He retired from his post before the incident in question."

Kathryn felt panic fly through Aerlyn as she met Julian's eyes across the room. He stood up immediately.

"Are you telling me that after sacrificing himself for us for decades of his life, after serving his people relentlessly, you are going to turn your back on his status as a Guardian and deny him a Guardian's justice?"

"It was his choice to retire," Rennin said, sounding bored.

"It was two days ago!" Julian railed. "Two days, and that gives you the right to miscarry what he deserves? What he is owed after years of loyal service?"

"I'm sorry, Julian," Christophe spoke up, "but Rennin is right. Whether it was two days or two minutes, he gave up all his rights as a Guardian the instant he retired. Now he falls under majority discretion. A tie or higher and he is a free man, but if majority rules, he will be executed."

"No!" Kathryn couldn't help herself. She ran across the room and fell to her knees beside Adrian, throwing her arms around his neck under the disdainful eyes of those unmovable leaders. Didn't they understand? It was all different now! He was all different! "You can't. Please," she begged them as she kissed Adrian's cheek. "Please, if I can forgive him for the things he did to me, then why can't you forgive him for doing what you would have done anyway? If I can see how much he has changed, why can't you see it? Do you think if he was still a monster I would be defending him? He took me from my family. I couldn't even say good-bye, but he found a way to give that to me again, just to give me peace. He gathered a trove of the most beautiful things in all the worlds he knows, and did it all for me. Just to make me happy." Tears ran down her face, the most important tears of her life. "Please don't take him away from me. We just found each other. We're *kind*. We could feed his entire village and keep them from starving for the rest of our lives. Please . . . oh please, you have to let him live."

She sobbed hard, her face pressing against his neck and wetting him with her tears.

"Shh," he soothed her in a whisper no one could hear but them. "I love you, sweetheart. It's okay. I'll be okay." He bent his head and kissed her neck. "Go back over to Aerlyn," he told her.

"No. I'm staying here with you. If they are going to do this to you, I want them to see me here. I want them to know what they are doing to me. I want them to see how goddamn unfair they are!"

"All right," he hushed her softly. "It's all right."

"No, it's not all right." She wept, hugging him with all of her might. "You did everything for them, sacrificed everything you were for them, and now they just want to throw you away or swat you like a pesky fly. I won't let them!"

She turned to face the Ampliphi.

"Let me take him home with me. Let me take him to the Earth plane. You never have to see him again. He'll be safe with me and I swear I won't tell anyone about this place."

"That is impossible," Gisella said. "We will never let a human return to Earth with knowledge of the planes. We certainly won't let someone from Be-

neath go to the Earth plane after he has proven to
be volatile."

"This wastes our time," Rennin said dismissively.
"We need to vote."

"Wastes your time?" Kathryn echoed in horror.
"This is a man's life you're talking about! If you are
going to send him to his death, you'd better damn
well take some time doing it!"

"Guards, remove her," Greison ordered.

"You touch me or my *kindri* and I will rip your
balls off."

The snarled warning might have been coming
from an unexpected source, but not one of the
guards took the chance of moving to obey Greison's orders.

"Did you hear me?" he demanded of them.

One of the guards spoke up. "I'm not getting in
between these two again."

"Finally," Julian said, "someone who is wise
enough to realize what it means to get in between
a couple who is *kind*."

"Cast your fucking vote," Kathryn spat. "And
look us both in the eye while you do it. And for
that matter, look into the eyes of the thousands
you will starve by this careless act."

"Very well. All in favor of punishing Adrian for
the crime of murder of another citizen of Beneath, cast your vote."

Greison, Rennin, and Sydelle lifted their hands.
Kathryn held her breath, waiting for another hand
to come up.

"All those for acquittal?"

Julian and Giselle raised their hands.

"I am abstaining," Christophe spoke up.

"What does that mean? What does it mean?" Kathryn demanded to know.

"It means we lose," Adrian whispered.

"No! No, you can't abstain!" she shouted at Christophe. "You can't be a coward about this. You have to pick a side! There's no such thing as washing your hands of this, because the act of abstaining is signing his death warrant. You either vote to kill him or you vote to save him. Choose!"

"The vote is done," Rennin said dismissively.

"Choose!" she yelled at Christophe. "You choose!"

"Very well," Christophe said.

"The vote is done," Rennin snapped.

"It's done when I say it is done," Christophe said sharply. He looked down at the man and woman kneeling before him. "What is your name?"

"Kathryn," she said hoarsely.

"Kathryn, you would so passionately defend your kidnapper?"

"To my last breath. He's not my kidnapper. He's my savior. I just didn't know it at first. But I know it now. Please, I'm begging you. He's no longer the beast you think he is."

"You say that because you love him," Christophe said dismissively. "It radiates off you so powerfully it's hard to look at you. That certainly counts as bias."

"You . . . love me?"

The soft query came from a hung head, his eyes suddenly lifting with his surprise.

"Oh, come on." She sniffled. "With all the stuff

you know before I even say anything, and you couldn't see that one coming?"

"It is hard to see the things we crave the most," said the Ampliphi leader.

"Yes," she said, "I love you. Very much. So much that you can't die." She turned to Christophe. "I don't know how else to beg you. Please. Vote."

"Very well. I vote for . . . acquittal."

"A tie!" Aerlyn squeaked. Losing all her elegant composure she ran for her brother and tackled both him and Kathryn to the floor. "A tie!"

"Correct. A tie," Christophe said. "But there will be a probationary period. Any incidents in that time, this vote will come again."

The jubilation on the floor didn't diminish. Both women had faith that Adrian would do just fine.

"Untie him," Aerlyn demanded of the guards. This time the captain stepped forward and gladly untied his prisoner. The first thing Adrian did was wrap his arms around his mate and hug her within an inch of her life.

"You saved my life," he whispered against her ear. "You saved me."

"You saved me first," she said. "It seemed only fair." She didn't cry a single tear, not even a happy one. She had no use for them just then. She had fought a huge fight and won. The fight of her life.

"Do you still love me even now when I'm alive to pay you consequences for it?" he demanded.

"Yes," she laughed. "I still love you."

"Then say so. A dozen times a day. And never stop saying so."

"Yes, sir. Whatever you say."

He stood up, dragging his women with him. Then he looked at the council before him. "You won't be sorry for this," he swore to them.

"Prove it," Christophe said back.

"I will. Thank you."

He herded his girls out the door and they headed for home.

"This was a mistake, Christophe," Greison said darkly.

"If so, it will be a great surprise to me," Christophe said dismissively.

"You were swayed by the sentimentality of a woman," Rennin said.

"I always planned to acquit," Christophe corrected him. "I was just wondering how strong his mate was. She has proved herself quite resilient and remarkable. She'll be a fine addition to our people."

"She would have been better if she could have had multiple partners and multiple children from them," Sydelle mused.

"Better than the relationship of *kind* feeding a whole village?" Gisella was aghast.

"You all speak so easily dismissive," Julian spoke up quietly, "judging the relationship of *kind* without really having the first clue of how powerful and how beautiful it really is." He looked down the length of the dais at all of them. "I think you are cursed, and it is a terrible shame. All of you who know not what *kind* means are living half lives and pale existences. Your faded states pale in comparison to your faded hearts and souls. Hear me now, it is the *kind* that will save this world. And not just the powerful energy it generates, although that is a part of it. Mark my words, only *kind* will see us through to the next generation of our people. And maybe, this time, *kind* will help us to resist the plague if it ever comes again."

"It will come again," Christophe said grimly. "It always comes."

"Let us hope not," Gisella said with a shudder.

"I can't believe it. Kathryn, you were wonderful!" Aerlyn said, reaching to hug Kathryn for the hundredth time. "I never would have thought you had it in you! You were so brave!"

"I was, wasn't I?" She preened proudly and Adrian laughed at her. He knew how important it was to her that she had stood up for herself. He slung an arm over her shoulders and drew her tight to him, giving her a soul-searching kiss until she had to pinch him to beg him for some air.

"Aerlyn, I love you, but we have some celebrating to do," Adrian said.

He felt the wave of emotion that suddenly came off his stock-still sister.

"Oh, Adrian . . . I haven't heard you say that to me in so long," she said, her eyes suddenly rimmed with tears. She covered her mouth to catch a startled sob. Adrian instantly left his mate and went to her, folding her up in his arms and kissing the rise of her cheekbone warmly.

"I love you, sis," he said softly. "I always have. Even at my worst I was aware that you were there for me. Had it not been for you, I would never have made it as long as I did. Certainly not long enough to hold out for Kathryn."

"You are really back, aren't you? The brother I once knew—you're back again at last."

"Back and better than before. Believe you me, I will never take a single thing for granted ever again. Not my looks or my emotions, not dreams or nightmares, not the simplest beauty of the simplest thing. I won't take you for granted again, Aerlyn. I just hope you can forgive me for the things I did to you."

"I forgave you instants after they happened," she said. "You couldn't help yourself, Adrian, and I knew that."

"Hardly a good excuse. But I am glad to hear that you don't hold it against me."

"No. And now that I have my brother's love, I am going to go back to the Barrens. Won't you come have dinner with me there tonight?" she asked.

"We have no way of traveling through the planes without my mirror," Adrian reminded her. "And I doubt they'll just let me walk in and use it."

"I wouldn't want you to anyway. The farther away from that vile thing you are, the better it will be for you," Aerlyn said. "Very well, then, I'll come here."

"We'd love to have you," Adrian said.

"We would? But I don't know anything about anything! I don't know your foods or how to cook them. I don't even know where the kitchen is!" Kathryn said in a rush of panic.

"Not to worry," Adrian soothed her. "We'll go

out to eat. We do have restaurants here, you know."

"Oh, right." She exhaled a huge body-sagging sigh of relief. "I'm so glad."

"You'll learn everything soon enough," he reassured her. "Meanwhile, Aerlyn, we'll see you tonight," he said, moving to rush his sister to the door.

She giggled and waved to Kathryn with a waggle of her fingers. "Have fun celebrating!"

Then she was through the steel door and Adrian was spinning the latch into place. He abruptly turned to face Kathryn. She snickered as he stalked over to her very purposefully.

"A man with a new lease on life," she noted as he approached.

"And the first thing he wants to do is make love with his beautiful mate," he told her.

"Charmer," she said as she opened her arms to him.

"Vixen. Wolf in sheep's clothing," he teased. "You tore into Christophe like you had no fear."

"Oh, I had tremendous amounts of fear," she told him. "Fear for you and for your life." She reached up and kissed his mouth warmly. A little too warmly. She almost forgot what she was saying. "I was so scared I was going to lose you. I had just found you, just found a new life and way of enjoying it, and they were going to take it all away."

"I am so sorry I put you through all of that," he apologized softly. "I didn't mean to kill Cronos. Something just . . . snapped inside me. I had him there, in front of the Ampliphi, and I just knew he wouldn't quit coming after you. I knew he'd find ways to get to you. It wasn't safe to leave him alive. I just couldn't do it."

"I know. I understand," she soothed him.

"You do? You don't think I'm a murderer?"

"Honey, I was the one with the knife stuck in her chin. I still have the boo-boo." She pointed to the scab on the underside of her chin.

"I see that." He bent his head and kissed her gently on her boo-boo. Then he began to kiss a gentle line of kisses down the side of her neck. He no longer had fangs to torment her with, but that didn't keep him from using his teeth against her skin, back and forth and back and forth until he ended with a nip on her earlobe. Kathryn gave a theatrical little shiver and he chuckled. "You are so easy," he remarked. "Just a nibble on your neck and you're ready to throw open your legs for me."

"Oh! That's so not true!"

"It is too," he said, wedging a leg between hers and drawing his knee up tight against her. "You're like an inferno already."

"It's just warm in here," she breathed.

"Really?" He slid his hand under her skirt and dipped his fingers past the furring of her pubis. "Is it raining in here too?" he asked. "Because you're all wet."

"Do you have to be such a smart-ass?" she asked breathlessly as his fingers toyed with her sensitive flesh.

"Today I can be whatever I want. Today I am invincible. All thanks to you."

"Careful," she warned with a little moan. "Don't

let all of that go to your head. You can't get in any trouble for the next six months."

"Not a long time at all. It just shows you how convinced they are I'm going to fuck up quickly."

"I know," she said as she ran her hands over his broad shoulders. "And we're going to prove them wrong, aren't we?"

"Monstrously wrong," he promised.

Did you miss HUNTING JULIAN, the first in the Gatherers series?

As a Gatherer for his colony, Julian Sawyer travels to Earth to bring back the Chosen—women who possess energy potent enough to help revitalize his people. The stunning, silver-clad beauty who strides into his club one night radiates a sensual magnetism unlike any he's encountered, and Julian realizes that Asia Callahan is not just Chosen, she is his *kindra*: his one true mate.

For months, Asia has tracked the beautiful and mysterious Julian across the country, convinced that he's behind the disappearance of her sister and a dozen other women. She's prepared to believe he's a ruthless killer, but when she presents herself as bait, she discovers that the truth is far more shocking. Taken to a strange, hazardous realm she never knew existed, Asia will face the ultimate choice—between abandoning the life she's always known, and forsaking a passion as dangerous as it is powerful.

In all the time she had been stalking him, the one thing she had noted above all else was that Julian Sawyer was a man of very few emotions. He was always calm and always steady. Perfectly controlled at all times. Except for tonight. Tonight he was different. Different for *her*.

"Asia," she offered at last, the firmness of her tone warning him that was as far as she was willing to go. "My name is Asia."

He digested that for a moment, and she wondered how long it would take before he considered his condition satisfied and subjected her to the slightly chill air-conditioned atmosphere of the apartment.

"Asia," he echoed, his large hands sliding smooth and warm up over her shoulders until, she realized, he had resettled the straps of her dress into a less precarious positioning. The unpredictability of his actions disturbed her a little. This wasn't how he had been with the others before her; he had shown no interest in speaking to them. Asia tried to remind herself yet again that a difference was a good thing. Something had set each pair of women of the past seven months apart from all the others. She needed to be set apart if she was going to be among that select class of victims.

In keeping with her character of the night, however, she dropped her hands onto her hips and cocked her head as she bent a knee forward enough to rub her leg between his thighs where it settled against them.

"I thought you were out for a fuck," she noted bluntly. "You can skip the Mr. Romance routine. I don't need it."

He studied her carefully a moment, reaching to trail his fingertips up along her throat. "I think you do need it," he observed. "I think you have a great many needs you'd rather not share with me. You want this to be uncomplicated and straightforward, where it cannot be."

"Sure it can," she forced herself to say even as his uncanny words made her heart race beneath her breast. "You are a man. I am a woman. As long as we have all the interlocking parts required—and I admit, a fair amount of skill would be nice as well—we can get straight to where we both want to be. You haven't had a hard-on for me for this long because you want to talk to me," she pointed out.

That earned her a wry smile, the expression a bit sheepish and fearfully endearing as he ran a hand back through one side of his dark hair. She had thought it was black, but up close she could see it was the darkest of browns possible. It bothered her suddenly that there was so much about him that was appealing. It was like roses. Something so fragrant and beautiful that you couldn't help burrowing your nose into it shouldn't have things like thorns and bees to hurt you. She appreciated how naïve and unlike her such a thought truly was, but just because she rarely indulged them didn't mean she didn't have them.

"My needs go well beyond those of my physical body," he said to her, those green eyes flicking up from their low position in his bent head. She felt snared by that look, her throat tightening with a strange sense of having gotten in way over her head. She wanted to laugh aloud at the ludicrous idea as soon as she had it.

"Well, mine don't," she countered, realizing she didn't sound as convincing as she should have. She reached out to cover that up with her touch, having already realized how easily it distracted him. She snaked her arms around his neck, drawing herself in tight and snug to his body. "Your physical body will suit me fine," she whispered softly as her lips brushed against his ear.

Julian groaned softly as she wriggled against him, his hands tightening reflexively against her shoulders. Before she knew it, he had turned his face against her neck and was . . .

Sniffing her?

Asia's brows lowered in a perplexed expression of disbelief as she felt him breathe deeply and sigh out an extraordinary exhalation against her pulse. Even more unusual was the fine tremor she felt run through him.

"Such a sweet invitation," he breathed against

her softly, his nose nuzzling against her pulse. "Too bad it is a lie."

He had her by her throat in an instant, his hand locking hard and fast around her as he kicked her feet out from under her and sent her slamming down to the floor on her back. He controlled the entire action, however, keeping the impact minimal, if not shockingly violent, as he ended up with his grip shy of throttling her and his face mere millimeters from hers. He had thrown a leg over hers, pinning her to the hardwood floor firmly as she instinctively reached to grasp the wrist of the hand at her throat.

"For a woman who wants to fuck so badly, you smell decidedly clean of sexual arousal," he growled harshly. "What game is it you are playing? Why are you here?"

"I don't . . . are you out of your mind?" she rasped, the pressure of his hand just enough to warn her of his strength and the possible consequences if she ticked him off enough. "What the hell are you talking about?" Indignation seemed the way to go. Maybe a little fear. The more she was threatened, in actuality, the calmer and more in control Asia got. His kindnesses had rattled her much more than this would. *This* she understood.

This was what she had wanted.

She thumbed the catch on her ring, then grabbed his wrist again so the micro-fine needle injected into his skin. He would mistake the sensation for the cut of her diamond. In a sense it was exactly that. The heavy narcotic serum flooding into him would make him hers in instants.

"I am talking about this."

To her shock she felt his hand sweep up under her dress. His fingertips dipped into her panties below the top elastic and it was all she could do to keep from freaking out as thick male fingers skimmed over her denuded mound and dove with intimacy between her nether lips.

"Warm. Damp, to be certain," he observed, "but in no way bearing the heat or wetness of a woman longing for sex."

"You're blaming me because you haven't done anything to turn me on?" she demanded incredulously.

"Your scent is fear-scent, and yet not. You smell of a hunter. The predator. The *ziniprano*. Tell me, *zini*," he said in a heated, fierce whisper of threat as he wedged himself in between her legs, "if it is a fucking you so desire, will it matter to you how it comes about?"

The intent behind his devious invitation and the hard actions of his heavy body over hers triggered a hell of a lot more than fear in Asia. She knew she needed to wait, if only to see the narcotic hit him like a ton of bricks, making all of this infinitely easier, but she couldn't. His intimate touch grew deeper as he spread her legs wide around his hips and Asia learned that there were just some things even she couldn't do.

"I don't know," she countered in a rasp of pent-up fury and hurt. "Why don't you tell me how you did it to my sister, first?"

He went still in surprise, just as she had hoped for, leaving himself wide open for her free hands to make their mark.

Asia was a jujitsu master. She had achieved black

belt status at a very young age, and had only increased in degrees until the time she had become the sensei of her own dojo. The art of self-defense, the art of power in small movements. This was what she used to drive rigid fingers into his throat and eyes simultaneously. She took satisfaction in his roar of agony as she used the ripple of her fit body to buck him off of herself at the first available opportunity. She spilled his significant weight onto the wooden floor and pounced on him in fisted, violent strikes.

She hadn't expected him to be an easy target, and he did not disappoint her. She didn't even know how he had grabbed her and thrown her, but the next thing she knew she was getting floor burns on her bare legs as she skidded and tumbled away. She rolled up to her feet in smooth continuity, her hair whipping back as it spilled free of its twist. She ignored it, even though it was now a liability, and focused on her giant adversary as he growled with ferocious anger and crouched as if preparing to charge her. His following hesitation was a godsend. The more time he took, the more time for the drug in his system to take effect.

"What is this?" he confronted her with a roar of fury. "Why do you play this brutal game with me?"

"Because you are nothing but violent, evil filth, and this is what you deserve! You stole the single most precious thing from my life, as well as those most precious to the lives of countless others, and it's time you paid the price for that!"

"And you are going to make me pay, *zini*?" His laughter irked her as it rolled in irritating waves of derision over her. "Little warrior. So coldhearted, no? To play such a game as the bait just to lure me in close. For what? What is this imagined slight I have done to you?"

"My sister, you prick!" she screamed, months of pain and fear suddenly overriding all of her cold control. Hot fury and unwanted agony burned in her throat and clenching fists. "You stole her! I want her back! You will give her back to me, or so help me I will kill you!"

Why wasn't the drug working? Damn it, Justin had guaranteed it would! She'd watched him test it on a gorilla, the injection taking under sixty seconds to drop the beast completely.

"I doubt that is how this will end," he said flatly. He seemed confident of that as he straightened and strolled directly for her across the room.

She fought. With everything she had and everything she knew, she beat him off of herself again and again. But every time she made a strike that should have taken him down, he would simply shake it off and keep coming at her. It was as if he didn't feel any pain at all, except she knew that he did when he grunted or bellowed out from her critical hits. Fighting in heels lent advantages and disadvantages. Not the least of which was when she drove a stiletto deep into the back of his thigh, shedding first blood as she yanked free.

That was when everything changed.

She had pulled free with a spin, so by the time she came full around, her fists raised in a pose of defensive aggression, blood began to pour down the back of his leg as he stumbled to a knee briefly.

At least she thought it was blood.

It was *pink*.

Not a thin or light red, not red of any variety or shade, but a brilliant carnation pink bordering on fluorescence.

The sight made her do a double take, the shock of it taking a moment to sink in as she stood frozen at the ready. Julian stood up slowly and turned around, his malachite green eyes glittering with a dangerous resignation. Asia had never known true and utter fear before, she realized. She knew that because she was feeling it right then when she finally understood just why the drug had not and never would work on Julian Sawyer.

He wasn't human.

And here's a peek at Jacquelyn's new novel,
coming in November 2010!

What in hell was wrong with him? He'd been sitting there, furious at the prospect that she'd been torn up inside by those miserable Jakal bastards, and here he was thinking about touching her himself! He might be Sánge, but contrary to popular outlander belief, *he was no beast!*

In the heat of his upset, Reule forgot that there was a huge difference between thinking and acting. For a telepath, it was the hardest and most important lesson to learn. A mind could concoct great fantasies; majestic schemes of both sinister evil and beauteous good. However, actually acting on those fantasies was quite another thing entirely. It was unfair to hold someone responsible for every stray thought. Reule neglected to forgive himself for basic inclinations of the mind.

Reule also forgot how hard his emotions could strike out at others when they emanated out of his control. He was harshly reminded of it when the woman in his arms awoke with a traumatized gasp and a forceful jerking of her body. It sent him off balance as he tried to hold her slippery body and keep her head above water simultaneously. Her bottom settled in his lap again, giving him some leverage as he verbally and mentally tried to calm her frantic flailing.

"Shh. Be easy, *kébé*. You're safe," he assured her, emanating a feeling of security to her, hoping to replace his hostile emotional disturbance of a minute ago. The rush of sorrow he'd come to associate with her assailed him once again, but he found it was fueled with fear as well this time. "Hush, *kébé*," he soothed. "Hush, I will keep you safe."

Then, all at once, she seemed to hear him. To comprehend. She went abruptly still, reached up and shoved the wet mass of hair off of her face so roughly that he heard strands tear and snap. Then she looked directly at him, allowing him to see her face for the very first time. For a long minute, where every muscle in his body seemed locked in a mystical paralysis, all Reule could do was stare at her.

It was her eyes that had the heaviest impact. They were so unreal, so brilliantly unusual, that he couldn't quite grasp the concept for a moment. He doubted he'd ever see anything like them ever again in his lifetime, and that was quite a monumental concept considering how long-lived his breed tended to be.

How to begin to even describe them? he wondered.

They were colorless.

No. That was inaccurate. They were far too en-thralling to be a null. They were as clear as crystal, yet white and silver all at once. They looked exactly like, and *sparkled* like, diamonds. Faceted, beauti-fully cut, clear and precious gemstones, with a plat-inum setting behind them to enhance every movement they caught in the light. She blinked thick, black, curved lashes over them, and that's when he broke away from her eyes and saw the rest of her face. It was shaped in the delicate curves of a heart, soft bow lips chapped from thirst and ne-glect were tucked into a permanent but enticing lit-tle pout, and she had a slim nose that ended in the slightest uptilt. She had bruises across both cheeks, some old and yellowed, others fresher, but they did nothing to hide the sweet structure of her bones beneath skin that promised to be flawless when free of battering. Youthful, but clearly a woman; unbelievably pretty, but sorely misused; and dia-mond eyes that looked at him in bald confusion for several heartbeats.

Then, like electricity flooding a dark room, recognition of some kind lit up her features and she smiled so wide her delicate lips split and began to bleed a little. Wet hands lifted out of the water and framed his face and he started in surprise as her palms rubbed over his three-day beard and her fingers curled over his ears.

"Sánge," she breathed, the single word full of excitement like he'd never heard before from any-one who knew he was Sánge. Not unless they were also Sánge. It stole his breath even as he tried to convince himself that it was a mistake, that she was just in some sort of shock.

"Yes, Sánge," he agreed, pausing to clear the hoarse catch from his throat. "What, and more importantly, *who* are you, little *kébé*?"